BLUEPRINT

A Novel

JAY PRASAD

ISBN: 1542679427
ISBN 13: 9781542679428
Library of Congress Control Number: 2017901203
CreateSpace Independent Publishing Platform
North Charleston, South Carolina

TABLE OF CONTENTS

PART 1

BERLIN TRAUMA

In these streets, which now consisted almost entirely of ruins and rubble, a few civilians might be busy trying to dig out the bodies of the dead who were buried under the buildings. They were placed on handcarts and taken to some place where there was earth—a garden or a park.

Then, suddenly, there would be the Russian...He held a submachine gun cocked in one hand and moved cautiously down the street...

—Curt Reiss, *The Berlin Story*

ONE

BOMBS AND WERWOLVES

The last bomb tore the facade off her house. Where there once was a boundary between her bedroom and the street, a curtain of dust now wavered and shimmered in the moonlight. The air-raid alarm had sounded, but she had slept through it even as she heard the wail of the siren as though in a dream. The shattering explosion threw her out of her bed and landed her on the uncarpeted floor. Her mind was jolted from stupor, and she wondered which was worse—a broken hipbone or being under a collapsed roof. She got up on all fours and whimpered, a scared animal. She then rose up, quickly changed from her nightgown to her work clothes, an old sweater and denim overalls, put on her walking shoes, and scuttled down two flights of stairs to the basement. There was an ear-shattering explosion as she was going down the rickety stairs. The steps shook, and there was a loud crash as the three floors of the building imploded and collapsed.

As she stumbled to the floor of the basement, she thought she had gone blind but quickly realized that the darkness was caused by the overhead light on the stairway going out.

"You crashed into me," said a voice she recognized as that of the landlord who lived in the basement. "Are you hurt?"

"I am fine, Herr Stumpfegger," she said.

"Damn these Yanks," said Ludwig Stumpfegger. "They've demolished my building. They want to wipe out Berlin, turn it to dust. Look at what they did to the Brandenburg Gate. You know they've already dropped thirty thousand tons of explosives on Berlin."

Hannah Müller paid no attention to him.

"My studio." She gasped. "It will all be destroyed, my work and the work of others."

She was thinking not so much of her own paintings but the ones given to her by Wasilly Kandinsky and Paul Klee and the works of her peers at Bauhaus. She had kept them in a steel trunk inside a closet in her second-floor studio.

"Just like a woman." She heard Stumpfegger's voice in the dark. "There are lives at stake, and all she can think of is degenerate art."

She knew now what she had suspected all along, and fear seized her. Stumpfegger must have been in her studio without her permission and examined the artwork, deemed degenerate by the Führer. The question why the Gestapo didn't make their visit to her studio to seize the paintings danced before her with an elusive, elf-like quality.

She heard the sound of a match being struck and saw Stumpfegger lighting two candles.

"I've to check on my other two tenants," he said, putting on a red-and-black swastika-patterned dressing gown over his brown shirt and pants.

"I'll come with you," she said.

"Only if you put on a helmet," he said grumpily as he put on his boots.

He had kept a spare helmet from his days in the army, during the First World War. It was too big for her, but she wound up her long braids around her head to make it fit.

Stumpfegger took a shovel and a pickaxe and strapped on a belt from which hung two flashlights, a spanner, and a screwdriver. He opened the small door that revealed steps to their garden, and as she went up, she saw the crushed tulips and crocuses and then the huge mound of wreckage to her right.

My studio must be at the bottom of this pile, she thought.

Stumpfegger took a ladder that was lying on the grass and leaned it against the mound. Slowly he climbed up the steps until he reached the top. Using quick thrusts with his shovel, he cleared a path all the way down and started shouting, "Frau Rudel, Fraulein Ritter!" at regular intervals. A sparrow cheeped and flew away from a nearby bush. Stumpfegger repeated his operation on the other side and suddenly stopped.

"Frau Müller!" he shouted.

Hannah moved over to his side and saw a woman's fat, varicose-veined leg sticking out of the mound. It looked like the leg of Else Rudel, wife of Hauptfeldwebel Heinz Rudel, a corpulent sergeant fighting the Russians out there in the East.

"Help me pull her out," said Stumpfegger.

It wasn't easy to pull her out, but they did it with a lot of grunting and panting. She was stone dead, with a frozen, insipid smile on her face as though she had been dreaming of sweet and pleasant things.

"She took those sleeping pills of hers," panted Stumpfegger. "I had warned her not to do that, but she didn't listen to me."

He picked her up and carried her to the garden. Hannah saw him kiss her on the lips. She had seen them together, drinking schnapps and eating sausages, but it had never occurred to her they were lovers. Morality goes overboard during the time of war, she thought. But who was she to judge others? She too had been no different—after the end of the First World War, she had been a hostess in a night club and had hung around with personable American soldiers to earn a few bucks until she discovered she was pregnant—but she was only nineteen then, and all Berlin girls did that to survive.

"I have to bury Frau Rudel," said Stumpfegger. "But first we have to see if Fraulein Ritter is alive."

They went back to the mound, and he started digging again. Occasionally he would stop to straighten out his back but would get to work again after wiping off the plaster dust covering his face. Suddenly he gave an exclamation and pointed to her what looked like a man's hairy arm with a tattoo of a skull on it. Stumpfegger grabbed the arm and pulled out a naked young man and along with him, with her arms entwined over his torso, the blond, beautiful Marta Ritter, who lived on the floor above Hannah.

"He must be a deserter from the SS," said Stumpfegger, scorn dripping from his voice. "The two of them had probably too much to drink last night and didn't hear the sirens."

Hannah looked at the two young lovers, arms around each other and a look of bliss on their faces. She thought it was a perfect death, quite unlike what she was used to seeing on the streets after bombing raids, the corpses showing terror and shock on their faces.

"Don't stand there doing nothing. I need your help," grunted Stumpfegger.

"What do you want me to do?"

"Cover the bodies up with something, and help me carry them to the garden."

What difference would covering them up make? she wanted to ask him. The young man and woman were Hitler children, the ones who grew up without religious beliefs and would have preferred to be buried like Adam and Eve. But she didn't want to argue with him and went downstairs to look for a piece of cloth to serve as a shroud. She couldn't find anything suitable and came back with the linen tablecloth that covered the dining table.

As she helped him carry the bodies into the garden, she heard what she thought was a steady drumbeat, growing slowly in volume.

"What's that noise, Herr Stumpfegger?" she asked him, pointing east.

He listened and shook his head disbelievingly. "It's the sound of artillery," he said.

Now she could hear shells exploding, and they were coming one after the other. She thought it was the German troops battling the Americans, but the sound was coming from the east.

"It's the Russian tanks. I've to go and join my unit."

"What unit?"

"I am in the *Volkssturm*, woman," he said curtly, walking toward the basement. "I've to go."

She knew what the Volkssturm was, for Goebbels had been calling all males between the ages of fourteen and sixty to join the last-ditch effort to stop the Russian enemy from entering Berlin. Only two days ago, she had seen two boys in uniforms that were too big for them, strutting up and down the street with rifles over their shoulders and bragging about what they would do to a Russian soldier if they caught one.

Stumpfegger suddenly reappeared before her, clad in his First World War uniform and carrying a rifle, a dagger, and a *Panzerfaust*. She wondered how he was going to stop the tanks with these futile weapons from another era as he thrust a bunch of handbills toward her and asked her to distribute them to "everyone you see in the street."

"OUR FÜHRER IS STAYING IN BERLIN," she read. "HE IS NOT GOING TO RUN AWAY, AND HE EXPECTS ALL BERLINERS TO DO THE SAME. JOIN THE VOLKSSTURM, AND WE WILL DRIVE THE RUSSIAN HORDES AWAY!"

"What will I do when the Russians come?" she asked him. "I don't know where to go. I don't know if any of my friends are alive. I don't know if they too have lost their homes."

"You knew this was coming. You've been warned again and again. Why didn't you go somewhere else? Why did you stay in Berlin?"

"For the same reason you are staying here, Herr Stumpfegger. I'm a Berliner. We don't leave our city."

He wrinkled his forehead and thought over that for a few seconds. "You can stay in the basement, woman," he said without enthusiasm. "You can sleep on the couch for the next few days."

"Everything I owned is inside that rubble," she said. "I have no money with me. I would only be a burden to you."

"You may be, at that," he said with an evil smile. "I'm not doing this for you but for Herr Doktor Dresdner. He asked me to help you if you're in trouble. He's a generous man."

She was shocked by his words and wanted to run after him as he goose-stepped away to the red glare coming from the east. She wanted to ask him how he knew about Emil and her. They had met in the utmost secrecy, and on the nights he had stayed over, she had made sure that the coast was clear before she took him to her apartment. Even more puzzling to her was why Emil Dresdner, the scholar turned healer, the gentlest, most sensitive man she had ever known, would want to ask this strutting fool, whose faith in his Führer and Wehrmacht was that of a fanatic, to keep an eye on her.

Dawn was breaking around her. A boy riding a bicycle stood in front of the steps of the building, gave a surprised look at the rubble, tossed a *Völkischer Beobachter* at her feet, whistled, and went on his way. She had heard the Nazis had stopped distributing the newspaper even though they were still printing it. She then noticed the message someone had scrawled in red ink on the front page: "Today at 4:00 p.m., meet us in the basement of our office in Alexanderplatz."

Holding the paper gingerly, trying to minimize contact with the disgusting Nazi rag, she walked back to the garden. The three bodies were lying there amid the crushed red and yellow tulips, and Marta Ritter's white teeth gleamed as though she was modeling for toothpaste. Hannah felt like crying and hastily averted her eyes. Blindly, she went down the wooden steps to the basement and went inside. It was dark there, and the air was stuffy. She kept the door open, found the extinguished the candles, and relit them. She felt very tired and wanted to sit down somewhere. She looked around and saw the couch that was going to be hers for the next few nights below the obligatory portrait of the Führer in his SA uniform. The couch was made of brown leather and was showing cracks here and there. There was a beer mug next to it on a small table, and a pack of playing cards. The ace of spades was on top, and Hannah idly picked it up and let it fall to the floor. It fell face down, and she saw a picture of a naked woman squatting, her vulva spread apart. She put the card back on its deck with its face up, thinking that she knew very little about Stumpfegger. What was he? A plainclothesman for the Gestapo? Or an ordinary German who tattled occasionally to get a reward? She wandered around the room and then into a bedroom obviously reserved for Stumpfegger's use. The walls were covered with Nazi insignias and pictures of the higher-ups. There was an SS dagger autographed by Himmler and a picture of Eva Braun playing with Hitler's dog, Blondi. Her eyes fell on two battery-operated radios lying on the floor next to the unmade bed. She turned on the first one and quickly realized it was a Nazi radio—it had only one channel, used exclusively for broadcasting the party line.

"Today is the Führer's birthday," she heard. "Our beloved leader will turn fifty-six today. Unlike previous occasions, there will be no mass celebrations. The Führer, fighting for the survival of the Aryan race, is preoccupied with the war spawned by the Jewish international bankers and the Bolshevists in Russia. He—"

She turned it off and looked speculatively at the other portable radio. She switched it on, twiddled the dial, and stopped when she heard a speaker with a pronounced French accent saying, "Deutschland, your fight for *lebensraum* has turned Germany into a burial ground." She turned to another channel and heard an announcer from the BBC speaking in fluent German. He was asking the German public to cooperate with the Allies. "Hitler did this to you, and you have suffered enough. Do not resist us, but act with us to put an end to your suffering."

She stretched out on the bed and imagined she was in a small boat in the middle of a stormy sea, unaware of where she was and getting confusing signals from various sources on her radio. It was only a week ago Goebbels was assuring Berliners that victory was around the corner, for General Wenck's army was on its way and would repel the Russian hordes. Now it looked like the British, the French, the Russians, and the Americans were all marching inside Germany, converging toward Berlin. This was a repetition of what had happened twenty-six years ago, in the last phases of the First World War, when Field Marshal Ludendorff and his cohorts were declaring they were winning the war even though it was obvious that Germany had no chance of victory. Soldiers had deserted in droves, and sailors had openly rebelled against the state. Soon the kaiser had been forced to abdicate, and a new republic had been born and along with it the new Weimar culture. She belonged to that new culture, with Bauhaus as its epicenter, influenced by new ideas, new faces, new social mores, and new artists—Paul Klee, Wasilly Kandinsky, Piet Mondrian, Josef Albers, Oskar Schlemmer…but that was a quarter of a century ago. The icons had all left Germany, and she felt alone, in a wasteland, without a friend—her son was fighting somewhere in Russia, her half brother was in a detention center, and her lover was helping wounded soldiers at the front.

She collapsed into the bed and pulled the smelly sheets over her head.

She was woken up by a man's angry voice.

"What are you doing in my bed, woman?" Stumpfegger was shouting, angrily waving the *Völkischer Beobachter* she had left for him on the doorstep.

"I got tired; I fell asleep," she said groggily.

"I made it clear that you were to sleep on the couch," he said. "Don't crawl into my bed again."

She didn't miss the sexual connotation—she was a woman; she needed a man and was offering her body to him. Was there any point in telling him she found him disgusting? He would only think she was saying it because she was scorned.

"What time is it, Herr Stumpfegger?" she asked, hiding her resentment.

"It's noontime. There's a lot of work to be done. The three bodies have to be buried in the garden. And I've to assemble the Werwolves and tell them to drag out and shoot the traitors who are flying white flags in front of their houses."

"Werwolves?"

"They are our guerillas who would fight enemies of the Third Reich and cause havoc among the occupying forces. Haven't you heard Herr Goebbels talk about them on the radio?"

"No, Herr Stumpfegger. I don't know much about what's really going on. Why can't we make peace like they did twenty-six years ago, when the kaiser abdicated and a new government was formed?"

"Your question shows your ignorance, Frau Müller. The Führer is not going to abdicate. We aren't going to be defeated. There may be temporary setbacks, but there won't be a second defeat. General Steiner and General Wenck will drive off the Russians. Do you understand what I'm saying?"

He was condescending, but she decided to let it go. She moved past him toward the dining room, and he said, "Make something to eat, woman. I've potatoes, bacon, and dried peas in the little pantry next to the kitchen."

So that's the deal, she thought. I am going to be the cook and the maid while I live here in the basement. She was too hungry to be resentful and headed toward the pantry. Its walls were lined with many shelves, and she estimated there were provisions adequate for two people for two or three weeks.

She boiled the potatoes on the small coal stove in the tiny kitchen and grilled the bacon. She went looking for Stumpfegger, but he was not in the bedroom. She ran upstairs and saw him dragging the bodies to a newly dug grave. A wave of nausea gripped her, and she went to kitchen sink and retched. She felt better, drank a glass of water, and waited for Stumpfegger to finish his work.

He tramped in a few minutes later, took off his jackboots, and looked at her interrogatively. Thinking he wanted food, she went to the kitchen and placed the bacon and potatoes on the dining table.

"No bread?" he asked.

"I couldn't find any."

"I forgot to get my rations. I'm so busy these days," he said.

He fumbled in his pockets, brought out his ration card, and gave it to her.

"You will get the rations for me," he said. "If anyone asks you where you got the card, tell them you're my guest."

He sat down at the dining table and chewed his food noisily while she moved to the sofa and wondered how and where she could take a bath.

"You aren't eating?" he asked suddenly.

"I am not hungry." She lied because she didn't want to eat with him.

"You should eat something. You've a lot of work to do."

"What kind of work?" she asked, thinking how their relationship had changed overnight from tenant and landlord to that of serf and overlord.

"You are a painter, and I want you to paint some slogans on the walls in the neighborhood. The words are on this piece of paper. There are red paint cans and brushes in the workshop behind the kitchen."

She looked at the slogans and had to control herself from laughing at their absurdity.

"VOLKSSTURM IS THE SYMBOL OF GERMAN UNITY," read one. "VICTORY DEPENDS ON YOU," read the next. The third one simply stated, "LONG LIVE THE FÜHRER!"

"You still think we're going to win this war, Herr Stumpfegger?" she asked meekly, in order not to offend him.

"The Führer has secret weapons in his arsenal, the V-2 and the V-4 rockets," he explained, as though she were a child. "Also, it stands to reason that the British and the Americans are likely to join us in our fight against the Russians to save Western civilization from the Bolshevists. The Americans have crossed the Rhine and met with little resistance from us. They will be in Berlin shortly. In the next few days, the war is going to take a U-turn. We will drive the Russians back to the Urals with the help of our American and British allies—and the Führer will have won a terrific diplomatic victory."

"You've explained everything so clearly, Herr Stumpfegger," she said with a straight face.

"Now take the can of red paint and a couple of brushes, and start painting the slogans on the walls."

"If there are any walls left in our neighborhood," she said and immediately wished she could take back her words, but Stumpfegger didn't seem to take offense.

"There are plenty of walls left, woman," he said. "Also store shutters...and bus stands...and kiosks. You will find that traitors from within have been painting lies about the Third Reich on every available space. They say the war is lost and the Nazi Party is dead. Paint our patriotic slogans over them. And if you see white flags hoisted on houses, note down their street address, and the Werwolves will take care of them tonight."

With those parting words, he stomped off to join his comrades in some basement in Alexanderplatz to make plans to redeem Germany's honor. Hannah, pushed and pulled by contradictory feelings, didn't know whether to laugh or to cry. She hated the Third Reich, but she loved Germany, its land, and the culture that had nurtured her, long before the Nazis arrived on the political scene. Now the stage was set for the final act, for the immolation scene in *Gotterdammerung*. She didn't want to be a witness to it and regretted that she hadn't gone to America like many of her colleagues at the Bauhaus had—she didn't want to leave Johann, her half brother, and had stayed on in the hope that she could somehow shield him from the fate that was in store for him, but she hadn't been able to do that either and could never forgive herself for not giving him the sanctuary he had asked of her.

She suddenly got scared, a pang of fear that gnawed her insides as she saw a rat streak by and disappear into a mysterious hole somewhere. The ceiling of the basement creaked, and she prayed it would cave in and put an end to her life. She crawled back onto the lumpy couch and lay there shivering from the drafts that seemed to come from the door that Stumpfegger had forgotten to close properly. She was too tired to get up and shut it and, closing her eyes, drifted into sleep.

TWO

ZHUKOV'S ARMIES AND KONEV'S TANKS

Washing herself as best she could using the water coming out of the kitchen tap, she set forth to do the tasks assigned to her by Stumpfegger. She found the can of red paint in the tiny workshop behind the kitchen and two brushes with wide, hard bristles. And after a little searching, she found a duffel bag to carry the rations home and some cash in a desk drawer.

When she came outside, the sun was shining into her eyes, and it hurt. She squinted at the massive mound of rubble in front of her and looked the other way. The entire Schöneberg area to the east and south of her seemed devastated by the bomb attacks. She wished she could capture the scene for posterity in the manner of surrealists like Giorgio de Chirico or Salvador Dali, even though her style of painting was quite unlike theirs. What she could do more easily—if only she could retrieve her camera and darkroom equipment from the heap of plaster, wood, and steel lying before her—was to make photomontages in the manner of Hanna Hoch of the Berlin Dada group, with whom she had worked for a while before going to Bauhaus.

A small plane was flying overhead, and she saw a red hammer-and-sickle sign painted under its wings. Obviously, the Russians were surveying the damage the Americans had inflicted on Berlin and taking pictures of it.

With hesitant steps, she moved west to Potsdamer Strasse. Kleistpark on her left was completely in ruins, and the only structure left standing was, ironically, the air-raid shelter on its northern side. Dead bodies lay sprawling on the ground, and sometimes she had to step on them or over them, against her moral scruples. Walking north, she looked at the familiar streets—Pallasstrasse, Winterfeld Strasse, Bulow Strasse— and saw ramshackle heaps of plaster and wood where there used to be houses. The Sportsplast, where the Führer had given his dramatic speech three years ago and Goebbels had asked the Berliners if they were ready for a "total war" to the accompaniment of cheers from the crowd, was in ruins, and so was the Hofbräuhaus next to it, where the SA used to carouse and molest young men and boys after parades.

On Kurfürsten Strasse, which was not as badly damaged as some of the other streets, she saw the "broom girls"—young Jewish girls and Russian women soldiers captured during the war—picking up the debris and sweeping the streets. Dressed in rags, they looked dirty and malnourished, deliberately keeping their eyes on the road and never making eye contact with passersby, fearful of the SS guards who stood watching them, ready to intervene if someone offered the girls a bun or an apple or stopped to have a kindly word with them.

She walked down a side street, looking for a produce market that she used to go to, but it was shut down. A few doors down, crowds were looting from a general store that had its doors blown open by the bombing. She stood in line, and when her turn came, she took a toothbrush and a bar of soap. "Look, there are bottles of honey and jam in the back," a man carrying an armful of stolen goods said to her. She left two marks for her purchases in front of the cash register—which stood untouched by the looters who would never dream of stealing money, even when no one was watching—and left the store.

Where to go next? She thought she would walk toward the center of Berlin to see what was going on, but as she neared the Tiergarten, she noticed that SS men were hurriedly erecting barricades across several streets.

An old woman standing across the street with a grocery bag came hobbling over to her and said in a whisper, "They say the Russians are firing artillery and rockets at the Reich Chancellery. That's why these guys are putting up barriers."

"What's the Führer going to do?"

"I don't know. The Russians will occupy Berlin in a couple of days, and we all have to become communists then."

My mother would have liked that, thought Hannah. Those early days of the November uprising in 1918 came to her mind vividly, as did the fights with her mother, who would drag her to speeches given by Rosa Luxemburg, Karl Liebknecht, and other leaders of the German left.

"Let me stay home with Johann, Mutti," she would plead when her mother would insist on taking Johann to the meetings and parades.

"Let him learn. Let him watch a working-class revolution. Let him see the red flag flying over the kaiser's palace," was her response.

Her mother was never the same after the November revolution had fizzled out. Rosa Luxemburg and Karl Liebknecht had been killed soon after by the Freikorps, and the working class lost its revolutionary fervor and walked into the waiting arms of Adolf Hitler who won them over with his patriotic rants about the stab in the back by the "November criminals" that had caused Germany to lose the war and the need to fight the Bolshevik and Jewish international conspiracy determined to destroy the purity of the Aryan race. Now, a quarter of a century later, it looked like the Bolshevik and Jewish international conspiracy would end up being the winners, and the red flag would be flying over the Reich Chancellery; in the end, der Führer had accomplished nothing but disaster and defeat.

As though reading her thoughts, the old woman mumbled, "I wish Bismarck was still alive. He picked his fights carefully, unlike Hitler.

He would have never sent our troops to Russia. Bismarck was a shrewd man, and Germany was safe under him."

Hannah didn't want to get into a political discussion with this woman.

"Where did you get your rations from?" she asked, with a smile. "I didn't find any stores in Schöneberg."

"Go two blocks west to Cornelius Strasse, and you will find stores there," she said and hobbled away to talk to someone else in the street.

There were lines in front of the grocery store in Cornelius Strasse, and Hannah had to wait twenty minutes before she was able to buy potatoes, bacon, butter, and ersatz bread and coffee. When she asked for milk, the shopkeeper abruptly brushed her off by saying, "No milk," and turned to the next customer. The woman next in line told her, "Goebbels promised milk for our babies, but no store carries it. Our kids are dying from not drinking milk."

Hannah nodded sympathetically and walked out of the store. The sun was still bright, and the rays glinted from the handlebars of dozens of bicycles stacked in a row across the street in a bicycle rental store. On an impulse, she decided to rent a bicycle and ride around for an hour to see the damage suffered by her city from the last bombing raid.

Leaving her bags at the bicycle store in lieu of a deposit, she got on a bicycle and took off in a southerly direction toward Steglitz. Only after a few minutes did she realize that she hadn't asked herself why she was going to Steglitz, and she immediately came up with the answer. She wanted to see if Emil's home was still standing and his wife and children—whom she had seen only in photographs—were unhurt.

There was now gunfire coming from the south, and she wondered if the Russians were coming from all directions, squeezing Berlin by forming a cordon around it. Steglitz had been damaged as badly as Schöneberg, she noticed. Kaiserallee, where Emil lived, was reduced to smoldering ruins, and Hannah was scared of riding her bike through it. She dismounted and looked at the street from the corner of Rheinstrasse. The fashionable women's boutique owned by Johanna Koenig, whom she had seen at artists' parties, was wrecked as a result of a direct hit by a bomb. So was the wine bar next to it. And all that remained of the apartment building where Emil and his family had lived on the top floor was a gap and a pile of debris.

What happened to the huge fish store on the ground floor, where I used to watch the turtles swim in water tanks? was her first incongruous reaction, for she felt more empathy for the turtles than the dead people she saw lying in the street. We brought this on ourselves, she thought, surveying the carnage, and we got what we deserved. But she made an exception for Emil and wondered if anyone had notified him of the wreckage. When he returns from war, he will have nothing, she thought. Nothing other than me, that is, if he still wants me.

She couldn't get the image of the dead turtles out of her mind as she rode the bicycle north, toward the Zoo Berlin. She was hoping that she could go in there, as she had done a hundred times before, and be soothed by watching the leaping monkeys, the eternally pacing tigers and lions, and the pelicans and herons meditating before stagnant water. She circled around the bicycle path around the zoo and noticed that several tall trees had been knocked down to the ground by bombs. "What did the trees do to you to hurt them like this?" she asked the unknown assailant—in her mind a pilot wearing an American or British uniform. The gates were closed, and getting off her bicycle, she stood near them, listening for familiar roars and shrieks, but the only sound she could hear came from the periodic bursts of Russian artillery. She wondered if the animals had been removed to a safe place or had perished in the air raids, and she looked for a zoo employee to chat with but couldn't find anyone.

She mounted her bike and rode away from the zoo, making a right turn at the *Bahnhof* and reaching Breitscheidplatz. Her heart thudded against her ribs when she saw that the Gothic spires of the Kaiser Wilhelm Memorial Church—the Berlin landmark portrayed in a thousand posters—had been blown off by bombs, making it look like a huge carnivore baring its fangs. Not far from it, damaged beyond recognition, was the Romanitsche Café, her favorite hangout in the early twenties. Every night she would be there with the Berlin Dada group, a twenty-four-year-old girl with short-cropped blond hair and bright-red lipstick, waiting for a smile or glance from the stars of the Berlin art world—George Grosz, Hannah Hoch, Jean Arp, and Kurt Schwitters. Hannah Hoch had taught her how to create photomontages and also to love both men and women, dissolving boundaries of gender, race, and class in the universal sea of human warmth. Hannah's composite montages of nude women had opened up a new world of art to her, as did Hannah's first kiss on her lips. And Kurt Schwitters had taught her how to make art free of realism, political sentiment, and conventions fostered by the doorkeepers of the academy and to be true to one's instincts. Those years were her years of freedom, during which she had managed to acquire the inner strength to resist her mother's urges to join the left wing and her uncle Werner's equally strong pull to join the right and become a true German. Even though the whole Dada experiment had crumbled after four or five years and Bauhaus had replaced Berlin as the artistic center of Germany, the sight of the ruined café revived forgotten memories and the faces and gestures of her various artist friends. They loved me, she thought, for I was one of them, bound together by the notion of changing the world through art.

She bicycled eastward on Tauentzienstrausse, stopping only when she saw a huge gaping hole in the street. Cautiously she peered down and saw dead bodies lying on the subway platform. A large bomb or missile must have created the hole and killed the people who had gathered for shelter in that subway station, she surmised.

She moved the bicycle to the other side of the street and pedaled on to Nollendorfplatz, where Russian refugees, numbering tens of thousands, used to live twenty years ago, and there was an array of restaurants lining the streets where one could get blinis, shashliks, and borscht and have one's fortune told by gypsies. Sometimes she would go with her mother and Paul to the Café Leon, where Russian intellectuals hung around drinking endless glasses of vodka. There would be heated discussions about Lenin and Trotsky, and Paul, an emotionally volatile man, would get into violent arguments with his equally combustible compatriots. She saw in her mind's eye, as in an old family photo, her beautiful mother with her hair worn loose and her full breasts bouncing under her coarse linen blouse, putting her arm around Paul, trying to calm him down after one of his tirades. The image vanished quickly, for the Café Leon no longer stood in its accustomed place, and all she saw was the remnant of a wall with shards of glass scattered around it. "The old Berlin I knew is gone," she said to herself. "My past, embodied in the streets and buildings of this city, has disappeared. So has my identity. I have no money, no studio, no loved ones, no place of residence. The life I had lived once exists now only as tendrils, ethereal plumes of memory that are easily wafted and carried away."

She returned the bicycle to the rental place on Cornelius Strasse and walked to her house, carrying the heavy bag of groceries and the sack containing the red paint and brushes on her shoulder. She thought she would dump the latter somewhere, but then her eyes rested on a white remnant of a wall standing on a side street, like the jagged tooth of a prehistoric monster dug out from the earth. She stood next to it and painted "DEATH TO THE FÜHRER!" in large letters.

As she was walking off, pleased with herself, a shadowy figure suddenly materialized before her and said, "I've never seen you before. What group are you with?"

Taken aback, she walked away from him, but he followed her, saying, "We are your friends. Come and join us tomorrow night. We are going to celebrate the death of the Third Reich."

He must belong to the Berlin underground, she thought, one of those leftwing radicals and artists who were now coming out of the woodwork.

"Are you an artist?" she asked.

"No, a movie director," he said. "We make documentaries and send them abroad. We have a party meeting tomorrow, and some of our comrades returning from exile in Russia will be there. Why don't you come? It's in the basement next door to the Saint Ludwige Kirche."

"I will try," she said with a smile and walked away from him.

But she had no intention to attend a Communist Party meeting and felt the same resentment toward the man that she had experienced toward radical groups at Bauhaus who used to pester her to show more commitment to the left. She belonged to no party, and she followed no dogma. She was happy forming her own idea of the world from what she saw and heard around her and wanted to make her own decision about events and persons. As Kandinsky had once told her, politics was the serpent in the artist's Garden of Eden—it seduced you and made you lose your bearings. His was a voice of authenticity, for she knew he was speaking from his own experience.

She gazed at the several piles of debris on her street, and it took her a few minutes before she recognized the mound of wood and plaster that used to be her house. Going down the steps, she opened the door to the basement and saw a group of men standing around, listening to Ludwig Stumpfegger. They were all dressed in makeshift uniforms and carried old rifles. None of them were young or in good physical condition.

She figured they were members of the Volkssturm present at an impromptu meeting. Stumpfegger was pointing a pencil to a large hand-drawn map of Berlin that he had tacked onto a wall.

"Marshall Zhukov's armies are closing in from the east and the northeast," he said, "and Marshall Konev's tanks are massing up in the south of Berlin. It will take many weeks before the Americans reach Berlin. I am told that Stalin wants a total victory over Berlin before May Day."

"What do we do next?" asked a man with a large Adam's apple, wearing thick glasses.

"We may have to fight them from the rooftops if they start patrolling the streets. We will provide you with rifles."

"There are only a few rooftops left in this neighborhood," said another man with an unshaven face and a cynical expression.

"Kill Ivan when he patrols the street at night. Use grenades and bombs on cordons of soldiers; set booby traps with sticks of dynamite."

Nobody responded, and their glazed eyes wandered here and there until they settled on her, with questioning looks.

"That's Hannah Müller," said Stumpfegger. "She is my tenant and lives in the basement, for the time being, as my guest."

One of the men raised his cap and bowed, but the rest paid no attention to her.

"We need refreshment," said Stumpfegger to her. "Give us something to eat, woman. There's food in the kitchen."

He's making my role clear to these numbskulls, Hannah thought. She controlled her anger and went into the kitchen. On the counter, there was a large bag of sausages, two pumpernickel loaves, and a dozen bottles of schnapps. He must have gotten them from the black market, she thought.

She felt hungry and cut herself a piece of the pumpernickel bread. She lit the stove and heated the sausages on the grill. She ate a sausage and thought it was very good. Then she took a tray with bread, sausages, and bottles of schnapps to the sitting room.

"The golden pheasants are leaving Berlin, I understand," she heard a man say. "They're heading west to escape the Russians."

It took her a moment to figure out that he was alluding to top Nazi Party officials, the bureaucrats who had been running Berlin for more than a dozen years. It didn't surprise her that they were leaving. They wanted to move west to be in the American-occupied part of Germany. Once there, they would deny they had anything to do with the Nazis and cut a deal with the conquerors.

"The Führer is staying," said Stumpfegger. "That's all that matters to me."

He stretched out his hand in a Hitler salute, but none of the other men responded. Stumpfegger became angry, and he vented his rage on her.

"Why are you standing here, woman?" he asked her.

"I came here to bring the food," she said, pointing to the tray.

She turned her back on them and went into the kitchen to unpack the groceries she had brought in. She was still feeling hungry. She ate another sausage with a chunk of bread and drank water from the tap. She brushed her teeth with the newly brought toothbrush and washed her face with the new cake of soap. She wondered if she would be killed by Zhukov's armies or by Konev's tanks. In a way, she was glad that the curtain was going to fall on the Thousand Year Reich. She felt very tired and wanted to lie down somewhere. The couch was out of the question because some men were sitting on it. She stretched herself on the kitchen floor and fell asleep.

THREE

"Voyna Kaput"

W hen she awoke, it was dark in the kitchen even though her wristwatch—given by Emil and set in a gold bracelet—said it was six o'clock. There was no one else in the basement.

The men must have gone to set their booby traps, she thought.

In the sitting room, there were empty bottles of schnapps and remnants of food served last night. She lit the stump of a candle on the dining table and found a note from Stumpfegger next to it.

"I am on a mission," it said. "I don't know when I'll be back. You've to do without my help. You're on your own."

She smiled, thinking of the connotations contained in the few words. It was presumptuous of him to think she was dependent on him, but he was a fool.

She cleaned up the living room, made a cup of coffee, and washed her hair using the water from the kitchen tap. She was surprised by the accumulation of dust and grime in her hair and wondered if they contained toxic or cancer-producing chemicals.

Drying herself, she went to Stumpfegger's room and turned on the Nazi radio. Goebbels's high-pitched, excited voice was asking the Werwolves to rise against the enemy.

"Berliners, have courage," he shrieked. "Berlin will be free. We will win this war. The Führer is not going to abandon you. He is in the Reich Chancellery, directing the course of the war."

The other radio carried a broadcast from the Russians.

"We will free Berlin in two days," it said. "We will arrest the Nazi war criminals. Berliners, you have nothing to fear. Your government, and only your government, is responsible for the atrocities committed on the Russian people. We do not believe in collective guilt."

What did all this talk mean? She had a sensation of being crushed between two huge rocks, one with a swastika painted on it and the other with a hammer and sickle. All her life she had wanted only to paint and had never been able to do so except for her interlude at Bauhaus. Wars, famine, riots, secret police, torture—these seemed to be the norms of existence in her universe. And she had a premonition that her life was moving from one inferno to another. She had no illusions about Russia because Kandinsky, living as an exile in France, had written to her about the fate of artists and writers who had crossed the party line set up by Josef Stalin. She did not want to live in another police state, and she wondered if she could persuade Emil, after his return, to move elsewhere. What shall I do about my brother? she asked herself, feeling lost, confused, and powerless in the vortex of events.

She didn't want to sit around and feel sorry for herself, so she looked for things to do. Her wet hair had dried, and casting her eyes around, she found a tortoiseshell comb in the bedroom. It had Stumpfegger's red hairs on it, and she rinsed it under the tap before running it through her hair. She then got dressed in her old work clothes and went outside to the street.

Mixed with the acrid smell of bombs, there was the scent of spring flowers—lilacs and sweet pea and marigolds—from innumerable small gardens in the area. She saw a blackbird flying around, chasing its mate. Nature seemed to carry on, oblivious of the carnage inflicted by humankind.

She finally plucked up courage to face squarely what her eyes had been avoiding—namely, the huge gray-and-brown mound before her. She wondered if she could dig a hole from the side and somehow stumble upon the steel case in which her paintings were kept. She ran over to the garden and brought back a spade. She tried digging on the side where she thought the studio had collapsed, but the chunks of plaster and pieces of beams were too heavy for her to move. In despair, she was ready to give up the project when she sighted the boy who had delivered the *Völkischer Beobachter* a day ago. This time he had a package for Stumpfegger, and he brought it over to her.

"What is in this package?" she asked him. "It's heavy."

"I think it's a machine gun, Frau Stumpfegger," he replied, and she couldn't suppress a smile at the absurdity of being labeled as Stumpfegger's wife.

The boy was about fifteen and built strong, and an idea came to her.

"What's your name?"

"Walther," he said.

"Can you dig through this pile and look for something that belongs to me, Walther?" she asked him. "It's a black steel case, and it must be on the side where I'm standing now."

"I'll give it a try," he said.

"I don't have much money, but I can give you a new bottle of schnapps. A bottle of *Fürst Bismarck*. You can sell it to someone."

"Schnapps is as good as cash," he said with a smile.

He climbed up the mound and started digging, but it didn't seem to be an easy task. The plaster had hardened and clung to the chunks of wood and metal. The boy was tired after a few minutes and came down.

"I'll bring my friends Franz and Gunter. They're bigger and stronger. With their help we can drag out the box."

"I don't have any more schnapps to give," she said.

He looked disappointed, but it was only for a moment.

"Maybe you can give us something belonging to your husband. A dagger or a pistol will be great."

"I don't know. Let me look around. When will you be back with your friends?"

"It won't be until tomorrow morning."

"Can't you come back later today?"

"We have to report for duty soon," he said, puffing up his chest. "We're in the Boy's Battalion. We're being trained to kill the Russians."

The Russians will kill you first in all likelihood, she thought as the boy left with the bottle of schnapps. Only fifteen years old, and you will be sacrificed to appease the Nazi demons.

She was about to go downstairs when the side of the mound nearest to her cracked and heaved, and a huge chunk fell off. She saw the handle of a box and, without thinking, ran up the mound and pulled at it. When she brought it down, she realized the box didn't belong to her. It was locked only with a clasp, and on opening it, she saw a new pair of shoes, a sweater, two blouses, a skirt, and a pair of slacks, all neatly folded. It must belong to Fraulein Ritter, and she must have packed her clothes to go on a trip to a foreign country with her boyfriend, since women weren't allowed to wear slacks in Germany by order of the Führer. These clothes would fit me, and the sweater and slacks would be welcome additions to my nonexistent wardrobe, she thought, even though they're meant for a younger woman.

She took the box downstairs, removed the clothes, and placed them under the couch. She was wondering what to do with the box when the entire basement shook, and she heard explosions all around her. American bombs? British bombs? Russian bombs? She no longer cared. They were all welcome to put an end to her life.

She opened the last remaining bottle of schnapps and had a drink to steady her nerves. She turned on the radio and learned that

American B2 bombers had dropped incendiary bombs in Tiergarten and Schöneberg areas and that a water tank had been hit. She went to the kitchen and turned on the tap, and it spewed forth some brown stuff, sputtered, and stopped. Were they going to kill all Berliners by cutting off water? It would be collective punishment in its most extreme form, she thought, worse than the incendiary bombs and the disruption of food supplies.

Feeling frightened inside the basement, especially of the rat, she decided to go for a walk, even if it meant being killed by a bomb or a bullet. She changed into the sweater and pants belonging to Fraulein Ritter, which fitted her perfectly—the sweater was made of cashmere and silk, and the pants were Merino wool—and she thought she looked good for a forty-five-year-old woman with a 50 percent chance of being found dead in the clothes.

When she climbed the stairs and reached the garden, she noticed that the mound was gone, replaced by charred, burning lumps. Her street had been firebombed, and there was nothing but smoking ruins as far as her eye could see. A few women were coming out of basements here and there, wandering around to see the damage done to their street. We've been reduced to a nation of basement dwellers, she thought—all that's needed is to disrupt the supply of candles, and we will have to live like moles.

She walked up the street for a while and stopped when she saw a young woman dressed in a Frauenschaft outfit with a Hitler button pinned to her breast making signs to her from across the street.

"The Russians have reached the east of Berlin," the woman said. "They'll be here by tomorrow."

"I don't care anymore," said Hannah. "I just want the fighting to stop. Look at the damage done to Berlin."

"You wouldn't want to talk that way if you knew what the Russians are like," said the woman. "I spoke to a refugee from Silesia yesterday, and she said the Russians were beasts."

"So were the Nazis."

"I wouldn't talk that way if I were you," the woman said with a grim smile. "Two blocks down, in Kreutzberg, there is a man hanging from a tree. The Werwolves hanged him for collaborating with the Russians."

"I am no collaborator," said Hannah.

It has come down to this now, she thought. We're all going to accuse each other of being traitors.

"Be careful what you say, and don't wear pants if you want to stay alive," said the woman spitefully and walked away to her own subterranean abode.

Rattled by the manner in which the woman had spoken to her, Hannah walked the two blocks to Kreutzberg to check out what she had said. Ten minutes later she came across a small crowd staring at a man hanging from a tree. Pinned to the tree was a handwritten placard saying, "TOMAS BUTSCH WAS A TRAITOR AND DESERVED TO DIE. BERLINERS BEWARE!"

Nausea seized her, and she hurried away, taking a northern route. "Think pleasant thoughts," said Hannah to herself. "Think of your childhood in wonderful Schwabing, the kind people in your mother's circle, the marzipan sweets they brought for you, and the games they played with you." But nostalgia didn't work this time, and Hannah trudged along, finding a path amid the debris all around, stopping only when she saw a Russian soldier.

He wore a greenish-khaki uniform with a closed collar and brass buttons on his front and on his epaulettes. He had light-blond hair covered by a peaked cap and carried a machine gun. He looked like her son from a distance, and she assumed he was from Ukraine, where many people were of German stock.

The soldier was surveying the wreckage and paid no attention to her. He must be on a reconnaissance mission, she thought. It was hard to think of him as an enemy, and she wanted to accost him, to ask him questions about the war. But he merely looked around, ignoring her completely, and walked back eastward.

There were leaflets trailing in his wake, and she realized the soldier must have strewn them around. They were in red and white and had a hammer and sickle sign in the middle. They warned that the end of war was near and asked ordinary German citizens to cooperate with the Russians in identifying the Nazis and turning them over. Next to them, and muddied by the feet of passersby, she saw leaflets with swastikas in black and red threatening to imprison Berliners who read or distributed enemy propaganda. Hannah picked up both leaflets and put them inside her sweater. I'll save these as historical records, she thought.

She turned south in the direction of Tempelhof, but there were too many barricades, and she went the opposite way, up Prinzenstrasse. There were markings on walls, giving directions to the Volkssturm, and she wondered if Stumpfegger was going to fight the Russian tanks on the southern front. A few shops were still open, and there were women standing in long lines in front of them to buy potatoes and butter.

"The Russians are in Nikolasee," she overheard one of them saying. But a few feet away, another woman was saying they were in Müllerstrasse. So they are streaming into Berlin from the south and the north, Hannah thought. But to make the situation even more confusing, a burst of Russian artillery lasting several minutes came from Oranienstrasse in the east.

The women fell flat on the street as shells exploded, and Hannah followed suit. The impact of the fall hurt her palm and elbow. She lay on the dirty street, with the dust blowing into her face, while planes flew over her, firing machine guns. She didn't know who they were aiming at, and the sound of rushing feet made her look up. She saw German soldiers, unshaven and dirty, running away from the enemy fire, stumbling and panting, looking very different from the golden warriors who had marched behind Panzer tanks through these same streets a year ago.

A few minutes later, the women got up and methodically went back to their prior positions in the food queue. Hannah too got up and noticed with chagrin a huge black smudge on her newly acquired sweater. She didn't want to walk around with that stain and decided to go home. She turned to a side street and walked rapidly, afraid of another artillery attack or air raid. It was a narrow street cluttered with debris, and when she climbed over a mound, she stumbled on the body of a dead messenger boy, with his bicycle still between his legs. He was lying on his face, and from above he appeared to be in his early teens, and this was confirmed by the Hitlerjugend armband he was wearing. She pushed aside the blond hair matted with blood, and on turning his face toward her, she saw it was Walther, the newspaper boy whom she was supposed to see the next morning with his two friends. Impulsively, she kissed his forehead and mumbled, "Rest in peace, Walther." As an afterthought, she took his bike away from him and the small pistol that was in a holster on his belt.

She pushed the bicycle through the debris-laden street until she reached the relatively uncluttered Alexandrinenstrasse, when she got on the bicycle and rode homeward. She had never ridden a man's bicycle before and had trouble maneuvering it, but pedaling it was easy. Several women stared at her as she went down the street, and she realized they were trying to put two and two together in figuring out what she was up to—for she had a large ugly patch on her sweater, she was wearing pants, and she was holding a pistol in her hand.

She put the bicycle in the garden and went down to the basement. She hid the pistol under the couch and took off her sweater. The two leaflets fell to the floor, and she picked them and put them on the kitchen table. She washed her sweater with water she had saved in a jug earlier and was pleased to see the large patch disappearing as she scrubbed. She hung it out to dry in the kitchen and boiled two potatoes while she changed her clothes to the outfit she had worn in the morning.

Going into Stumpfegger's bedroom, she turned on the short-wave radio. The smooth, urbane voice of the BBC announcer merely recapitulated what she had already guessed—namely, that the Russians would take over Berlin in a matter of hours. The voice calmly asserted that Germany would be divided into four zones, with the eastern half going to Russia and the western to the Americans, British, and French. And Berlin also would be divided likewise.

So, my city is going to be cut into four pieces, thought Hannah. A wave of despondency overcame her, and she cried for a while, after which she felt exhausted and closed her eyes.

She was woken up by the sound of a woman's scream.

"There's someone in your bed, Ludwig," she heard a woman yell.

She saw a buxom blonde who reminded her of the slatternly dancing woman on beer mugs sold all over Germany, singing, "*Froh beim bier Das lieben wir.*"

A moment later Herr Stumpfegger rushed in with a gun in his hand and, on seeing Hannah, said in angry voice, "I've told you not to sleep in my bed, Frau Müller."

"Who is this woman, Ludwig?" the blonde asked.

"She's an artist who used to live on the third floor. I gave her permission to sleep on the couch, and now she has taken over the bedroom."

Hannah got up and walked out of the bedroom.

"She isn't my girlfriend, Liebchen," she heard Stumpfegger tell the blonde. "I let her stay here as a favor to her boyfriend, Herr Doktor Dresdner."

"Are you sure you aren't making this up?" asked the blonde.

"No! I'll ask her to leave the house if her presence bothers you."

"Forget about her. Let her stay tonight, and we'll decide tomorrow what we will do with her."

"Ja, let's go to bed. I am tired," said Stumpfegger.

Hannah, still drowsy, stumbled out of the room and went to sleep on her couch. Hours later, she was woken up by sounds coming from the bedroom—a rhythmic creaking of the bed and grunts and screams—and remembered the arrival of the blonde last night. Stumpfegger likes women on the plump side, she thought. She wondered why humans made so much noise while copulating, while animals were quiet even at the height of sexual frenzy. On the whole, she did like the sounds; there was something positive and life affirming about them, she thought. It was like the thumping rhythms in the opening movement of *The Rite of Spring*, and it drove away the images of death and destruction all around her. The blonde enjoyed life; she was like mother earth—unlike Hannah, an artist who was incapable of immediacy in feeling other than through paint and brush and had to go through convoluted mental processes to classify and process emotional experience.

That is the way it goes, she thought. We're what we are, and we cannot be someone else.

She again drifted into sleep.

A loud banging on the door to the garden woke her up with a start, and when she looked up, she saw two stocky Russian soldiers with machine guns standing a few feet away from her. They were not like the soldier she had seen yesterday. These had Mongolian features and coarse, oily black hair.

"Why are you here, standing and looking at me?" she asked them in Russian.

They were taken aback by her words.

"Where did you learn Russian?" asked the older one, staring at her with suspicion.

"From my stepfather," she said. "He came from Moscow."

"What was he doing here?"

"He was a sculptor."

They looked at each other for a few minutes, uncertain of the next step.

"*Voyna kaput*," said the old one in Russian—the war is over.

"We're the victors," said the second one.

She got up and, out of habit, looked at the watch she kept next to her, wound it, and put it on her wrist. It was past nine o'clock.

The Russians moved close to her. The older one pointed to the watch and said, "Give."

"It's mine. It was given to me as a present."

The older soldier grabbed her elbow tightly as the younger one took the watch off her wrist. She screamed and struggled. The Russians were gentle with her, but they wanted the watch and took it off her.

The bedroom door opened and Stumpfegger, in red pajamas patterned with the sig runes used by the SS, rushed out, holding his pistol in his hand. Instantly, the younger soldier turned his machine gun on him. The older one looked at Stumpfegger closely.

"Who's he?" he asked her in Russian.

"A friend."

"Is this his house?"

"Da, da."

"Is he a Nazi?"

She hesitated before answering. "I don't know," she said.

"What are you jabbering?" asked Stumpfegger, turning to her.

"They want to know if you're a Nazi. I told them I didn't know."

"I am a Nazi and proud of it," he said, and gave the Hitler salute.

The older soldier now leveled his machine gun at Stumpfegger and asked the younger man to search the bedroom. The soldier went there and quickly came back.

"There's a woman sleeping in there," he said with a smile. "Do I wake her?"

"No. Go see if there's anything that shows he's in the SA or the SS."

The soldier went into the bedroom and soon returned with Stumpfegger's Nazi Party card that he had taken from his wallet.

"This is what I found," he said.

"Cover him," said the older soldier and took the card from him. He spat on it and threw it on the floor. He then took down Hitler's picture from the wall and stomped on it with his dirty army boots.

This was too much for Stumpfegger. He fumed, he cursed, he shouted, and he rushed forward, cocking his pistol. A burst of gunfire came from the machine gun, and Stumpfegger lurched and fell dead on the floor with a heavy thud.

The blonde came out of the bedroom, still sleepy and disheveled. One of her breasts was popping out of her chemise, and her plump thighs were bare up to her crotch. The two soldiers stared at her, mesmerized.

The blonde peered at Stumpfegger's body and gave a cry of anguish. "He's shot," she said. She looked at the soldiers and said, "You killed him."

"Explain to this woman that he pointed his pistol at us, and we had to shoot him," the older soldier said to Hannah, in Russian.

"These men are Russian soldiers. I saw Herr Stumpfegger raise his pistol at them," said Hannah to the blonde. "They had no choice but to shoot him."

The blonde looked at Hannah for a few seconds, struggling to understand the sequence of events.

"Ask them to take this corpse away," she finally said and went back to the bedroom.

Hannah translated the request, and the soldiers reluctantly carried the heavy body up the steps and into the garden. She saw them dig a shallow grave and place Stumpfegger in it. After they had covered it, they looked around, and their eyes fell on the bicycle that she had acquired the day before. They wheeled it away, and she saw the younger man trying to ride clumsily on it.

She was relieved that they were gone and thought she had seen the last of them. But they were back two hours later, drunk, with machine guns dangling from their shoulders.

The older soldier went into the bedroom, and she heard him say, "Frau, *komm.*"

But the young man, she noticed, was coming toward her, and in a quick movement, he grabbed her and laid her on the couch. He unbuttoned his trousers, pulled down her underwear, penetrated her with a quick, hurting thrust, and ejaculated inside her after a few savage movements. The butt of his gun kept knocking against her knees, and she thought it would break her kneecap.

He soon got off her, buttoned his pants, and walked out of the basement. Soon the older soldier followed him, giving her a wink.

She got up and slowly walked to the kitchen, wanting to wash—she felt so unclean. There was brownish water dripping from the tap, and her mind revolted at the thought of using it on her body. She went to the bedroom and saw the blonde cleaning herself with one of Stumpfegger's shirts, and she followed suit.

"Who knew it would come to this?" the blonde said with a sneer. "An Aryan in the morning and a Mongol in the afternoon. I might as well set myself up as a barracks whore."

The blonde's name was Ilke, and her words were prophetic.

FOUR

DEATH OF THE FÜHRER

During the weeks that followed, Hannah's Berlin went through a cataclysmic upheaval similar to the one that had taken place when the Nazis came into power. Now it was the hordes from the East who had the upper hand. Russian tanks rolled through the streets of Berlin, pointing their guns at the few buildings left standing; Russian soldiers carrying machine guns were everywhere, marching in twos and threes, drinking in the street, lying in puddles of vomit, and urinating or defecating in public, oblivious of the disgust shown by passersby. They stole everything in sight—radios, bicycles, gramophones, cuckoo clocks, dark glasses, leather jackets, shoes, hats, belts, pens, ties, tie clips, cuff links—and of course, watches, for which they had a special fascination.

The soldiers were dazzled by Berlin women, or rather the idea of the Berlin Woman, thinking of her as far more sophisticated and desirable than their own females—most of them, in fact, looking upon her as a being far superior to themselves, and resorting to rape as the measure that would bring about proletarian equality. The soldiers knew only two German words: "Frau, komm." Old, young, fat, thin, beautiful, ugly—these distinctions didn't matter to them as thousands swarmed over the burned-out, litter-strewn streets and found their way to basements where women huddled together. They dragged them to the nearest bed—or to the floor, when no bed was available—and skewered them, even when their husbands or sons, mutely impotent and seemingly uninvolved, were in the room, a few feet away, crouching down with averted eyes.

The soldiers were mostly men in their late twenties or early thirties, and Ilke was their partner of choice; but the few very young ones, in their teens, invariably made it clear, to Hannah's surprise, that she, and not Ilke, was the object of their erotic fantasy.

"They must have a mother fixation among Russian youth," commented Hannah one day when they were picking up vodka bottles after the departure of the last group of soldiers.

"They are attracted to you because you look classy—you know, tall and slender, with green eyes and dark lashes," said the blonde, "unlike me, the typical Bavarian barmaid."

Ilke was from Munich, the daughter of an SA man who owned a beerhall in Munich. He had taken a bullet meant for Hitler in the Beerhall Putsch in 1923 and was rewarded with the patronage of the party bosses. He saw to it that his daughter was brought up in strict conformity with the Nazi protocol for raising Aryan women. Ilke was in the Bund Deutscher Madel and later joined the Frauenschaft. And, on turning twenty, she married an SS captain who, a year later, was sent off to Poland to supervise a labor camp. Not surprisingly after such an upbringing, Ilke thought Hitler was the greatest man the world had ever seen.

"Look what he did for Germany," she said, after bemoaning the absence of pictures of the Führer on the walls. "He took us out of a depression, made Germany into a world power, built autobahns, created the Greater Reich, and made us into a classless, *völkisch* society. I like to see his picture in my bedroom, above me, so that I can feel he's watching out for me."

Hannah wanted to point out the dark side of her hero. "Look what he did to me and other artists for signing the *Dringender Appell für die*

Einheit, the Urgent Call for Unity that pleaded with the public not to elect Hitler in 1933. Look what he did to my half brother because he was Jewish."

But this wasn't the time to get into an argument with Ilke, and Hannah wisely changed the subject.

"How did you meet Herr Stumpfegger?" she asked.

"He was a friend of my father, and they were in the trenches together in the First World War," said Ilke. "Two days ago the walls of my apartment were torn off by a Russian rocket. Stumpfegger offered me a place to stay."

She spoke in the warm, trusting manner of Bavarians, in a High German laden with speech mannerisms, notably the use of the word "gel" for breaking up clauses and sentences. I like her, thought Hannah, even though she is a Nazi to the core.

They cooked and ate together while the rations lasted and took turns cleaning the house. Ilke spent the nights in the bedroom while Hannah slept on the couch.

By mutual consent, they had declared the bedroom and the couch as off limits for the use of Russian soldiers. Whenever the Russians entered the basement, the two of them would sit side by side waiting to be chosen and went into the kitchen or the small storeroom next to it with whoever said "Frau, komm" to them.

After the first night of revulsion, Hannah resigned herself to the systematic assault on her body. She had lost all sense of feeling in those areas where, in the past, a lover's hands or lips would rouse her to heights of passion. Now there was an enveloping numbness, not only of the body but extending to the heart and the mind. She felt that Hannah Müller, the individual she had once been, had been replaced by a mannequin or a clockwork doll. She was there to satisfy the fleeting lust of these strange, dirty men who used her as an anonymous German vagina and moved away from her as soon as their physical urge reached a climax. She did not speak to them in Russian anymore; she didn't want to know them. They were inhuman, in no way distinct from their Nazi counterparts she knew so well. She only hoped that her end would come soon, that she would be killed by a bullet or a rocket or bludgeoned to death by a sadistic Cossack—or, less spectacularly, from dehydration or starvation, since there was an acute shortage of food and water in Berlin after the arrival of the Russians.

She was perpetually hungry, and so was Ilke.

The morning after their rations ran out, they went in search of bread and potatoes but could find no shops open in Potsdamer Strasse or anywhere in Schoenberg. In desperation, they walked as far as Charlottenburg with the same result. Finally, Ilke suggested that they join the bands of women wandering in the park, looking for nettles and dandelions.

"What do you do with them?" Hannah asked Ilke.

"Why, you make soup with them," she replied.

Every morning they gathered a bunch of young stinging nettles and leaves from dandelion plants. Hannah watched as Ilke washed them, chopped them, and stewed them in water.

"I thought nettles would taste like spinach. But they have a fishy smell and taste like seaweed," she told Ilke.

"If you add cream or broth, the soup would taste better," Ilke replied. "But it's nutritious the way it is."

Hannah liked the undressed dandelion salad better than the nettle soup, but she forced herself to eat what was in front of her in order not to offend the chef.

"Is this how we're going to live out the rest of our lives?" Ilke would ask after each meal.

"I hope not," Hannah would reply, stressing the word "hope."

Indeed, hope was what kept them going day after day and made them follow a dreary routine. Hannah got up early in the morning and woke up Ilke. Their first trip would be to the pump on Potsdamer Strasse to fill with water a large empty green bucket they had found in the garden. They would chat with disheveled and dirty women like themselves, standing on line, the topics of conversation being food or Russians. Everyone had the same problems—there was nothing to eat other than nettles and dandelions, and nobody liked Russian men.

"They're animals," was the most common complaint. "They pin you down and force themselves you."

"Two women, a mother and a daughter living in Steglitz, committed suicide after they were raped," said one woman.

"I am not going to kill myself," said another, "even though I feel filthy."

"It's my aunt that I'm worried about," said a third. "She thinks they've infected her. She cries all the time."

The first thing they did when they got home after the exhausting effort of carrying the heavy bucket of water was to clean themselves as best as they could. There wasn't enough water to take a bath or wash their hair, and they had to content themselves with running a wet towel over their bodies. They combed their hair as best as they could using their fingers, for a Russian had pocketed Stumpfegger's tortoiseshell comb, and another had walked away with the mirror in the bedroom.

"How do I look?" each woman would ask the other.

"Fine," each would reply mechanically and smile wryly.

They then went for their morning walk to gather nettles and dandelions. Sometimes they had to walk far to find a garden next to a bombed-out house or a park that had not been foraged by bands of women in the area. Sights that would have astonished them a month ago—an emaciated dead infant being buried in a garden by a weary-looking mother, an old woman picking up a dead sparrow and taking it home, an occasional SA or SS man looking tired, sullen, and emasculated—no longer deserved anything other than a cursory glance.

On and on they walked, covering one district after another, keeping their minds occupied by doing trivial things. They would count the number of houses still standing in Wilmersdorf or Neukolln and the number of white flags put up by Berliners. Or they would count the Russian tanks they saw parked on street corners, seventy-eight being the highest they had seen on any one day.

After they had gathered enough dandelions and nettles, they would go home and make a salad and soup, their one meal for the day, eating it slowly to make it last longer.

The Russians would come cluttering down the stairs in the afternoon. They never came singly but always in groups, officers and men with bottles in their hands, exultant in victory. Each time a young soldier uttered the mantra "Frau, komm" to her, Hannah would wonder why a man barely out of his teens would want to have sex with an unkempt older woman instead of the Russian women soldiers patrolling the streets, most of whom were voluptuous beauties with high cheekbones and rounded bottoms. Was this a form of revenge? A demonstration of *vae victis*, of inflicting suffering on the vanquished?

Wearily, after each encounter, she would wander to the tiny bathroom and try to wash away the filth. She stopped counting the number of times she had been raped after she reached fifteen. Yet she remembered the comments that the soldiers would make about her—terse, dispassionate, brutal asides made with an air of objectivity, as though a judge were delivering a verdict.

"She's a cold woman," she heard from a gangling youth with a fuzzy moustache.

"These German women," philosophized another soldier, short and chubby, "they aren't like our women. No wonder their men leave home to kill and lay waste other countries."

"She smells," said a third one.

"A dry, cold fuck," said another. "Her roommate is better. She at least puts her arms and legs around you. This one is like an ice woman."

Hannah suppressed a smile at the last comment, amused by the naiveté of the soldier. Ilke, who had nimble fingers, wrapped her arms and legs to lift things from the pockets of the man on top of her. Mostly it was cigarettes, penknives, and Russian coins, but on lucky days she would come up with a bar of Russian chocolate or a bag of candy. Once she got an entire *churchkhela* and another time a bar of halvah. She shared her pickings with Hannah, and they would eat the sweets slowly, savoring every moment of joy that they gave them.

The soldiers never came after sunset, and the two women had nothing to do until bedtime. Facing each other across the dining table, they found ways to while away a few hours before drowsiness overtook them. Ilke had a beautiful contralto voice, and she would sing the songs that she had learned by heart during the years as a Bund Deutscher Madel leader. Some of them were sweet and nostalgic, such as the farewell of a soldier to his sweetheart:

> *Ade, mein liebes Schätzelein,*
> *Ade, ade, ade,*
> *Es muß, es muß geschieden sein*
> *Ade, ade, ade.*

Hannah would clap her hands, and Ilke would smile broadly, the years falling away from her face, her cheeks red like that of an eighteen-year-old Hitler maiden.

Not all her songs were pleasant, and in fact, some were replete with hatred and anger, as when Ilke sang,

> *Wir Nationalen Sozialisten,*
> *Wir wollen keine Reaktion*
> *Wir hassen Juden und Marxisten*
> *Ein Hoch der deutschen Revolution.*

Hannah fought hard to keep her gorge down. Her brother's face would haunt her throughout the night, and the pleading voice, "Hannah, can I stay with you?" would play like a nonstop tape in her head.

She would then wonder why she was staying with Ilke. The same answer would pop up again and again. She and Ilke were roommates because they were afraid of living alone. Having sized up each other, they had intuitively decided to become partners until such time the Russians left, which both knew was not going to be in the foreseeable future.

Ilke, in spite of her breezy, barmaid demeanor, was sensitive to Hannah's mood changes. She would try to make Hannah smile by imitating the Munich *Kindl*—the boy on a white horse leading a mob of thousands to the Theresienwiese—or the drunken dancers at the Oktoberfest or would be quiet for a few seconds and then ask Hannah to tell her stories from her past.

My past wouldn't be to your liking, my big, blond Aryan girl, but I will edit it so that taboo items are excised, Hannah would think as she proceeded to give an account of her childhood in Schwabing.

"This was before the Führer taught Germans the right way to think," she would say with a straight face. "People in Schwabing were rebels. They used to gather at a place called Café Stephanie and talk about freedom, freedom to think for themselves, to experiment with themselves. There were a lot of artists and writers living there who wanted women to be as free as men, who accepted homosexuality as natural, who were against wars and the Prussian military. Some of them went to the extent of saying that women should run the world, advocating *Mutterrecht*. This was before the First World War. Schwabing was never the same after the war."

"Why did you leave Schwabing?" asked Ilke.

"I eloped with Gerhard Müller. He was in arts school with me in Munich. We were eighteen, and we thought it would be fun to elope to Berlin and get married. We had no money. He worked as a housepainter, and I worked for a seamstress, cutting clothes and stitching. It was the summer of 1918, and we had a lot of fun. Then he was called up by the army and sent to France. He never came back. And I was three months pregnant when I got a letter from his commanding officer saying he had been killed by a shrapnel wound. I lost the baby. My mother came to Berlin and stayed with me, and I went to art school in Berlin."

"My father always had money," said Ilke. "The SA would hold parties in his Hofbräuhaus. I had everything I wanted. A car, dresses, an apartment…Once the Führer came to my birthday party…I sat on his lap, and he patted my hair."

Hannah felt sick. There are limits to friendship with a dyed-in-the-wool Nazi, she realized, and quickly changed the subject.

"I'll tell you about Bauhaus," she said. "It was unlike any other art school. The students mixed with the teachers, and there were no set classes. We worked on what we liked—painting, sculpture, textile weaving, or woodwork. We worked hard. We also had a lot of fun—moonlight parties, birthday parties, and Christmas festivals. We had a jazz band. Women cut their hair short. No one wore brassieres. We wanted to be free…to do beautiful, unconventional things. We didn't want another world war. We were against nationalism. We thought we could change the world. It was good while it lasted."

"I can't imagine people living like that. It's un-Deutsch. The Führer wouldn't have liked it."

"Oh, the Führer closed down Bauhaus," said Hannah soothingly. "He didn't think it was good for the country. He wanted a different kind of art, an art that glorified the Aryan man and the Aryan woman. And he wouldn't tolerate jazz bands."

Ilke sighed.

"I wouldn't want to live in a Germany without the Führer," she said.

But the Führer died the next day, by his own hand.

Hannah heard it from the Russians who were drinking vodka in the living room, refreshing themselves after a round of rape.

"The colonel told the captain who told the staff sergeant," said one.

"What exactly happened?"

"We were closing in on the Reich Chancellery. Hitler knew the game was up. He gave cyanide pills to his girlfriend and—"

"Hitler had a girlfriend? I thought he didn't like girls."

"Yes, he did. Her name was Eva. Eva Braun. He gave her a cyanide pill, took one himself. He shot her in the head and then fired a bullet into his head. His bodyguard doused him with petrol and burned him, at his request."

The Russians pronounced "Hitler" as "Gitler," which gave the conversation a bizarre twist, as though they were talking about some mythical monster. Hannah wondered for a moment if they were making it up, because it sounded too good to be true. She had no way of verifying it and thought she would wait awhile before she told Ilke.

In the afternoon, there was another round of Russians, this time three older men, with drunken gait and unshaven chins. One of them had visited Ilke before, and he wanted to do an encore performance. The other two waited, passing time drinking vodka and chatting, while their comrade was taking his turn.

They too discussed Hitler's death, and Hannah could hear them in the kitchen as she leaned against the stove.

"We were able to get parts of his body," one said.

"How do we know it's him?"

"They arrested one of his adjutants and got his testimony," the first soldier said.

"How will we really know?"

"His dentist can tell by looking at his teeth, I guess. The German radio announced his death this morning. It's official."

"That doesn't settle it."

"As far as we are concerned, he is officially dead. By the way, Goebbels also committed suicide. He, his wife, and their brood of children. Good riddance, I say."

When they left, Hannah did a little dance that they used to do at Bauhaus, and as she did the gyrations, she felt as though a curse had been lifted from her and she was free again.

She thought she would break the news to Ilke in the evening, but things turned out differently. Ilke was feeling ill from the repeated sexual assaults of the day and wanted to go and sit on a bench on Kleistpark, even though the park was covered with debris. On their way they heard two older women talking about Hitler's death.

"He died a hero's death," said one.

"He immolated himself, like Siegfried," said the other, mixing up Siegfried with Brunnhilde.

"Who are they talking about?" said Ilke, always curious about what was going on around her.

The women overheard her comment, stopped, and turned around.

"We're talking about the Führer, dear," one of them said. "He died for Germany. He killed Eva Braun and then himself to save Germany's honor."

Ilke froze and went pale. Hannah thought she would collapse on the street.

"Let's go to the park, and we'll find a spot where you can sit down," said Hannah.

"I want to go home," Ilke said, in a barely audible voice.

She walked home stiffly, like a zombie, and Hannah had to help her down the steps and lead her to a chair at the dining table. Ilke didn't say a word for several minutes but stared into space with unseeing eyes. Then two tears trickled down her cheeks, her face made contortions, and she began to howl while Hannah watched her, feeling sorry for the grieving girl. Soon the howls subsided to whimpers, and Hannah went over to her and put her arms around her shoulders. She kissed the top of her head and was put off by the smell of unwashed hair. She dropped her hand and was about to leave when Ilke pulled her down to her lap, embraced her, and kissed her on her lips. Hannah let herself be kissed, even though in their present state of personal slovenliness, such intimacy was unwelcome.

"My breasts hurt," said Ilke. "My insides are bruised. All these men…they are like brutes."

She looked at Hannah like a wounded animal, a blond lioness that had been gored. Hannah kissed her back, and the two women clung to each other for a few moments of human warmth.

FIVE

"RUBBLE WOMEN"

In the absence of newspapers and radios, Hannah had to rely on secondhand accounts to find out what was going on. One day she noticed several women and the few men still around were wearing white armbands. She didn't know their significance until a woman at the water pump explained to her that a ceasefire agreement had been signed by the German and the Russian armies.

The periodic bursts of gunfire and the frightening gull-like screams of the Katyusha rockets ceased after that. The rapes rapidly dwindled and stopped entirely within days. Hundreds of Russian soldiers began to leave Berlin, with a retinue of tanks followed by caravans and horse-drawn carts.

A week later, she heard a tall, intelligent-looking woman wearing a man's khaki shirt and pants at the water pump saying that the German Army had formally surrendered to the Allies.

"They did that at the Military College at Karlshorst, at midnight, two days ago," she said. "Field Marshall Keitel signed the surrender document and handed over our country to Marshall Zhukov and General Eisenhower."

"That's why the Russian soldiers are leaving," said Hannah.

"No more rapes for a while," said a vulgar-looking buxom woman. "Now my pussy can have a rest."

The tall woman ignored her and directly addressed Hannah.

"Germany will be divided into four zones," she said. "Russians will take the east, Americans the south and the west, and the British and the French the remainder."

"Berlin will belong to the Russians, then?" Hannah asked.

"They're going to divide Berlin, but we don't know the details yet. Right now the Russians are our rulers."

Ilke, standing next to her during this conversation, heard every word of it. She turned pale, and her face had a frozen look as they walked back to their basement, carrying buckets of water.

"We won't have a country of our own anymore, right?" she asked, when they reached home.

"It looks like we will be occupied by the Russians and the Americans and the British," said Hannah.

Ilke cried for a while, and this time Hannah didn't go over to calm her down. She felt a sense of relief at the news of the formal surrender of the German Army—something they hadn't done at the end of the First World War after their defeat at the hands of the Allies; instead, they had made the Ebert government negotiate a peace deal without a formal surrender, and after the deal was done, the army had turned on the government, accusing them of "stabbing them in the back," paving the way to Hitler's rise. The Allies are playing it smart this time, thought Hannah. They don't want another Führer to pop up twenty years from now.

"I don't want to be part of Russia," bawled Ilke. "I heard that Stalin sent millions of people to Siberia and let them perish in the cold."

It's nothing different than what we did in our labor camps, thought Hannah.

"Ilke, why don't you go back to Munich, which is under American control?" she asked.

"My husband will return to Berlin from Poland, and he will be looking for me," said Ilke. "I want to be with him."

She looked confused after having spoken those words and blushed as she looked at Hannah.

"I'm late with my period," she said.

I don't have to worry about that, thought Hannah. I haven't had one for months.

"What do you want to do?" she asked Ilke.

"I'll go to a clinic, if I can find one," Ilke replied.

"I heard a woman say there was one in Dahlem. We could walk over there, even though it's a long walk."

"We will see."

Even though the Russian soldiers no longer came down into their basement, there were quite a few of them on the streets. They did useful work—they cleared the bus and tram routes and filled huge craters on the streets made by bombs, some large enough for a man walking in the dark to fall through and crash on a U-bahn platform sixty feet below. Some of the soldiers were billeted in the few houses that had survived the bombing raids. The officers occupied the higher floors—having managed to acquire young, stylish German women as mistresses—and the soldiers camped out in the park or lived three or four to a room in the lower floors and spent their spare time drinking or playing cards or shooting blanks at Germans.

There were heavy rains in May, and the stench in Berlin—caused by the decaying carcasses of animals and humans under the debris and the use of streets and parks as public latrines by the soldiers—became unbearable. The unsanitary conditions led to an outbreak of typhus.

The new government announced that its first priority was to clean up the streets. The job was to be done by Berliners, which meant Berlin women, since there were hardly any men around, and the few available ones were employed as overseers. Hannah and Ilke had to report at seven every morning to a station in Hauptstrasse, where they were given a shovel and a pair of heavy gloves and ordered to join a motley crew of women assigned to clean up streets in the Schöneberg area. Their ages varied from sixteen to seventy-five, and none of them were in good physical condition because of malnutrition, but they did what they were told to do by their supervisor, a German soldier back from the western front, carrying with him an aura of petulance and resentment.

The women dug craters in gardens and filled them with the dead from the street or created huge mounds of plaster and shattered stone from the demolished buildings. They washed bricks, bathtubs, and salvageable ironwork and stacked them in trucks provided by the Russians for transportation to Moscow or Leningrad. Most of them worked in silence, avoiding eye contact with their neighbors. Occasionally there would be an eruption of emotion, and a woman would sit down on the ground and cry silently or curse Hitler, the Russians, the Americans, and the British. The others sympathized with her, for they understood that the Berlin woman was being punished for no crime other than being a German—her home was blown up by bombs and rockets, her babies were wasting away from lack of milk, her body was ravished by uncouth barbarians, and she was forced to join the brigade of "rubble women" to clean up the unsightly mess from the streets.

"If you don't work, you don't eat," was the Russian motto. The wages they were given each day were just enough to buy a loaf of ersatz bread, margarine, and turnips. The women lost weight steadily and had to use strings to tie their pants from slipping down their hips.

Every now and then a band of Russian soldiers would come down beating kettledrums, and an interpreter would shout out an announcement. "Go to the clinic on such and such a street and get inoculated against typhus," he would say. Or "Go to such and such a high school where Comrade Mariana Blakovsky will speak on women's role in socialist society." Normally Hannah paid no attention to such announcements because she didn't want to lose a day's wages by having to stand in line for hours for a bus and a few more waiting for the event to start. But one day she heard an interpreter shout that artists and writers should register their names at an employment office at the *Rathaus*, where work was available for them.

She took off from work the next day, dressed in Fraulein Ritter's fashionable sweater and slacks, and walked to the damaged mayoral building on Martin-Luther Strasse. The employment office was on the fourth floor, and she had to wait in line in a large hall filled with the Berlin underground types wearing corduroy pants, checked shirts, tweed jackets with leather patches at the elbows, and goatees. A month ago, they would not have dared show their faces anywhere near the Rathaus for fear of the Gestapo, but now they were smiling and talking about the future that was in store for German art under Communist rule.

"The first thing we've to do is to establish a school like the Leningrad Institute of Proletarian Visual Arts," said a skinny young man to his neighbor, who wore tinted glasses and cultivated a sneer.

"I agree, Comrade. I'm all for Soviet realism, for art should be for the common man, as Comrade Stalin said," responded the latter.

"No Kandinsky, Klee, or Mondrian for our generation," said the first man.

"As Comrade Stalin said, there's no need for an artist to hide behind abstraction. One's work should be intelligible, clear, and unambiguous to the lay observer."

"I always say they should study Isaak Brodsky's *Portrait of Lenin,* the finest of the Soviet style of portrait painting."

Hannah experienced a sense of déjà vu, for she was hearing the same comments that the Nazis had made when they closed down Bauhaus. Were Stalin and Hitler two sides of the same coin? Was the commissar going to replace the gauleiter as the infallible judge of art?

She was the only woman in the room, and the men cast curious glances at her. Some of them were pointing to her and whispering, and after a few moments, one of them, a burly man wearing a Stalin button on a Soviet Army jacket, came over to her.

"We have never seen you at any of our meetings," he said to her.

"I don't go to meetings," she replied.

"My friends are saying you are a spy, and you have been sent over to infiltrate."

Hannah thought it was ironical that she should be accused of spying for the Nazis. She took a step back as the burly man moved closer to her threateningly. She was about to leave the room when another young man, dressed in a black alpaca jacket and skinny white pants, came to her side.

"You got it all wrong, Franz," he said. "I know her. She's on our side."

Hannah, wondering who her savior was, looked at him closely and recognized him as the film director whom she had met near Cornelius Strasse a few nights ago.

"I remember you," she said.

"How are things with you?" he asked.

"The same as with every other woman in Berlin," said Hannah.

"Raped, starved, and enslaved?"

"All three, like the rest of the women in Berlin."

The burly man, still standing around her, was startled by her remark.

"There may have been a few incidents here and there," he said, "but the German bourgeoisie, taking its cue from the Nazis, exaggerates them in order to paint the Russians in the blackest possible light."

"We'll have this discussion at our next meeting, Franz," said the film director. "In the meantime, why don't you go around and tell the others when and where the meeting is to be held."

Franz walked off with ill grace, without deigning to look at her.

"He follows the party line," said the film director. "He hopes that that the new mayor will appoint him to the arts council."

"Mayor? What mayor?" asked Hannah.

"I see you haven't been keeping up with the news," said the film director. "A contingent of expatriate German communists led by Walter Ulbricht has returned to Berlin. The Russians want them to form a new socialist state in Germany. They've already picked a mayor for

Berlin, but the real power is going to be wielded by the deputy mayor Karl Maron. He is the party man."

"I didn't know any of this. I work nine hours a day as a rubble woman and then go home to sleep."

"We will see if we can get more appropriate work for you. We've a meeting tomorrow night at our usual venue, the basement next to the Saint Ludwige Kirche. Come over, and I'll introduce you to Karl Maron."

He soon left her to join one of his friends who was impatiently waving toward him, and Hannah waited in line patiently until her turn came. A young dark-haired woman with a strong Silesian accent interviewed her, starting with her age, name, and address.

"I've no address. My apartment was leveled to the ground by bombs," said Hannah. "I live in the basement of that building."

"Give us the number and the street, and we will find you," said the woman.

Hannah gave her the required information, and the woman asked her what her occupation was.

"I'm an artist, a painter. But I do other things like magazine layouts, decorating shop windows, and setting up cabarets. Also, I studied shorthand and typing in school, and can work as a secretary," replied Hannah.

"Where did you study art?"

"At the Munich Art Institute."

She wanted to bring in her Bauhaus years but thought better of it in view of what she had overheard some time ago.

"Do you know any foreign language?"

"Russian, French, and English."

"That's all I need for the time being," said the woman. "If an opening comes up, we will get in touch with you. We are busy, and if you don't hear from us, come back here a week from now."

Hannah didn't think anything would come out of the interview and had resigned herself to continuing her routine of manual labor.

But three days later, she found a letter from the employment office stuck to her basement door asking her to report to a Colonel Chernov at an address in Kreuzberg the next morning. She put on Marta Ritter's sweater and slacks and walked over to Kreuzberg, passing lines of laboring women digging or picking rocks. The address that she had been given was that of a stylish three-story residential building that had not suffered much damage from bombs or rockets. The Russians had recently taken over the house from a Herr Kammerer and his nameplate was still on the door. Under its Gothic script, a typed card said, "Office of Propaganda, Commissariat of External Affairs, USSR."

The door opened to a lobby, where a young Russian woman in army uniform was busily clacking away at a typewriter.

"Who do you want to see?" she asked in German.

"I was sent by the employment office to see Colonel Chernov," said Hannah, in Russian.

The woman smiled and got up. "Are you Hannah Müller?" she asked in Russian.

Hannah nodded.

"Colonel Chernov has been called to Moscow for a conference. Captain Grisha Perelman will see you instead. I'll take you to him."

She led Hannah to what must have been the music room in the old days when Herr Kammerer had lived there. A piano stood in one corner of the room, with a stand displaying a musical score next to it, and there were a dozen flutes and oboes on a shelf.

Captain Grisha Perelman was a thin, nervous, Jewish-looking man, with a moustache and a goatee, wearing round metal-framed glasses. His thick black hair was combed backward, and he looked like Leon Trotsky in his younger days.

He rose from an armchair and shook hands with Hannah.

"The employment office says you speak Russian," he said.

"I do," said Hannah.

"I am mentioning it only because most Germans don't speak our language," he said. "But then most Russians don't speak German either."

"My stepfather was Russian. I learned it from him," said Hannah.

He smiled at her and offered her tea from a samovar. She had had nothing to eat that morning and felt grateful as she sipped the strong brew, made tart by the slice of lemon in the glass.

"Are you a Nazi?" he asked her suddenly.

"No," said Hannah.

"Have you ever been a Nazi Party member?"

"No."

"That's what everybody tells us these days," he said wryly. "I had to ask that question because we have been told not to hire Nazis."

He lit up a Russian cigarette and offered Hannah one.

"I don't smoke, thank you," said Hannah.

"I am with the Propaganda Ministry, Comrade Müller," he said. "We need artists. We've been directed to paint Soviet emblems and slogans at every bus stop and subway station in Berlin. In addition, large posters of Stalin have to be mounted at the entrance to public buildings. Unfortunately, in the present state of Berlin, we have to take a more modest approach. I spoke to Colonel Chernov yesterday, and he agreed that we should, as a first step, make use of the walls that are still standing in Berlin. The large projects we will do later."

He got up from his chair and walked to the piano and played a snatch from one of Chopin's *Etudes*. He then turned to her and looked at her nervously.

"I have to do this thing right. I want the right artist for it, but I don't know if you are that person. I'll give you a test. There is a box of pastels in the next room and a stack of drawing paper. I'll give you several posters to copy. Come back in an hour and show me your work."

Two of the posters were realistic depictions of women shouting, "Onward the Soviet State" and "Fight Imperialism and Fascism." The third was an abstraction, a red arrow driven into a black circle in the style of the Russian artist Kazimir Malevich, whose work she was familiar with. Used as she was to Bauhaus's training in copying artwork, Hannah had no trouble in reproducing the three works.

"These are good," said Captain Perelman, after studying them for a few minutes. "Start tomorrow at the Tiergarten, and paint them on the walls that you see in the neighborhood. Try to do at least twenty walls."

Hannah nodded.

"Can you get me a ration card?" she asked.

"You will be eligible for the highest grade, number five. Also, you will be paid three hundred marks a week. You can pick up the supplies you need from the storeroom. We have water-soluble powdered paint and brushes. Also, stencils and backpacks, and pants, boots and helmets. Comrade Katrina at the front will help you."

He turned back to the piano and began to play a mazurka from *Swan Lake*, and Hannah left him, closing the door behind her.

During the next few days, Hannah studied the remnants of walls in the streets around Tiergarten. Those near subways and bus stops were being used as bulletin boards by Berliners for posting notices since there were no other means of communication available to them. "Has anyone seen my mother, Marta Jung?" said one notice. "She is 57, 5 feet 8 inches, and weighs 178 lbs. She was last seen inside her apartment, which was destroyed by American bombs on April 19th." There were many notices like that, but some were in a lighter vein. "Would like to exchange a cute Rottweiler puppy for a bottle of schnapps," said one. "Army boots, SS uniform, and thirty-year-old wife in exchange for a box of cigars," said another.

Hannah wasn't sure whether she had the authority to take down these notices and decided to leave them where they were for the time being. She searched the side streets and, finding some bare walls here and there, went to work on them. After painting Stalin's face

and stenciling "Friend of the German working class and their libera-
tor" underneath it, she felt sick and had to sit down on the street for
a while. Hannah asked herself why dictators portrayed themselves
as benevolent rulers, oozing with the milk of human kindness. She
remembered the similar feeling she had experienced when she had
painted Hitler's portraits—replacing his habitual sternness with
avuncular benevolence—for upper-class German households, at the
request of black-market Berlin art purveyors who had given her assignments on the sly, paying cash and meeting her in out-of-the-way
wine bars and *Konditoreien* to escape the watchful eye of the Gestapo.
She thought of her colleagues at Bauhaus—Oskar Schlemmer, Willy
Baumeister, Georg Muche—who, unlike her, had chosen to do menial work in a paint factory rather than sell their services to the
Third Reich. I did what I did because I had to support my brother,
she rationalized: I would be ashamed to tell my friends at Bauhaus
what I did, but I made a conscious choice, even though I hated what
I was doing.

She had finished the third Stalin portrait on a wall and was taking
a final look at it before moving on when she heard someone cackling
behind her.

"You're painting portraits of our new dictator now?" asked an old
woman pushing a wheelbarrow containing rags and pieces of wood.

Hannah was stung. "I've to eat, and that's why I'm doing this," she
replied and walked away.

The rations under her new card were double the size of what she had
under the old one. She shared the bread, the turnips, and the occasional small cut of meat with Ilke, who had shed several pounds after
becoming a "rubble woman." Now she looked tanned and fit, quite
unlike the bouncy barmaid of earlier days.

After coming home from work, Ilke would talk to Hannah for
hours about the events in her day.

"Guess what I found in the rubble?" she would begin.

"I don't know," Hannah would respond.

Ilke would then display her treasure—a radio, a makeup case, a set of knives, or a Dresden china doll. But one day she found a dead baby covered with maggots, deep in the rubble, and that night she had screaming nightmares. Hannah had to sleep with her in the bedroom and cuddle her until the wee hours in the morning. She wouldn't go to work the next day, and Hannah went to her supervisor and pleaded with him to give Ilke a job that didn't involve digging up mounds of debris. The supervisor transferred her to Tempelhof, where a gang of German women were clearing the blocked runways so that Allied aircraft could land in Berlin.

But Ilke didn't want to go to work and kept talking about the baby that was inside her, in its first month.

"I don't think you're pregnant, Ilke," said Hannah. "You don't have morning sickness."

"I didn't get my period. It's nearly eight weeks."

At Hannah's suggestion, the two of them went that afternoon to the women's clinic in Dahlem for a checkup. They had to wait in line for two hours before they could see the doctor and had to listen to an endless stream of conversation about Russians among women seated next to them in the waiting room. It was no longer about rape, even though most of the women were there at the clinic to assess the effects of its aftermath. Listening to them, Anna gathered that they were more interested in getting a Russian officer for a boyfriend so that they wouldn't have to work with shovel and hammer for eight hours a day.

"I was friends with a major," said one. "Very sweet, even though not very clever. He was called off to Moscow last week. He asked me to marry him, but I didn't want to live in Moscow."

"They want young and pretty women," complained another one, no longer in her first youth.

"I am living with a colonel," said a third, dressed in a form-fitting black gown and wearing a necklace and earrings. "I don't know what to do when my husband comes back."

This confession triggered a chain reaction in Ilke's mind as she remembered her husband in Poland.

"What shall I tell him when he comes back?" she asked Hannah.

The woman in black overheard her and turned her head toward Ilke.

"Tell him nothing," she said. "That's what I am going to do, after I get rid of what's inside me."

Several women nodded in agreement.

A weary-looking young blond doctor examined them.

"You're bruised inside. I'll give you an ointment. Put it on for two weeks, and come back for a checkup," she told Hannah.

Turning to Ilke, she said, "You are not pregnant. You didn't get your period because of malnutrition. Once you start eating properly, you'll be fine."

"I'm not diseased?" asked Ilke.

"You're fine," said the doctor. "What you need to do is eat nourishing food. I know you don't get enough to eat, but the situation will change soon, hopefully."

"Thank you, thank you," burst out Ilke and kissed the doctor's hand.

She was in a good mood after leaving the doctor's office, singing old drinking songs and laughing uncontrollably every now and then. Hannah persuaded her to go back to work and walked with her to Tempelhof. The supervisor was angry with Ilke for not showing up on time but was somewhat mollified when she said she would work harder to make up for the lost hours.

Hannah then wandered off to Mariendorf to search for walls where she could paint the hammer-and-sickle icon. She found a few and marked down the locations in a little notebook. She had already done eighty posters and painted twenty slogans. She wasn't sure if she had a quota and decided to ask Perelman at her next weekly interview.

Perelman was a strange man, alternately warm and cold. He would either answer in monosyllables or break into lengthy monologues, his eyes gleaming and his thick black hair tumbling onto his forehead because of his vigorous head movements. The only time he was completely relaxed was when he was at the piano, playing Chopin or Tchaikovsky.

Once, after playing the polonaise, he said, "My mother used to play this," and stopped abruptly.

Hannah looked at him, expecting him to continue.

He lit his Russian cigarette and, after a long silence, said, "She used to teach music at the Kiev Conservatory. The Nazis killed her. Lined her up with other Jews in front of a huge pit and shot her in the back of her neck."

"I am sorry," said Hannah, wondering why she was offering him an apology.

"She wanted me to be a pianist like her, but I don't have her talent."

He got up from the stool and walked out of the room. He must hate me because I'm a German and therefore responsible for the fact that another German killed his mother, Hannah thought. People project an individual's evil action onto all members of his race or background, even if they know such a generalization is fallacious. She felt very depressed and thought of setting herself on fire with the matches he had left behind, by way of expiation. What good would that do? she reflected. How can my death atone for his mother's murder? Dispiritedly, Hannah waited for him for a while, but he didn't return, and she trudged back to paint more pictures of Stalin.

Two days later, when he came to check her work in Tempelhof area, Grisha Perelman was in a cheerful mood. Hannah was painting a red arrow piercing a black swastika embedded in a white circle and was surprised to see his tall, nervous form looming at her side.

"Good work," he said. "I like its perfect geometry."

"We learn how to create circles within squares and squares within circles at Bauhaus," she said, with a sense of irony. "That's what we do most of the time."

"You never said you were there. All I know is you studied art at Munich."

"I was in Bauhaus for five years," she said.

"Stalin doesn't like the Bauhaus. Our beloved leader doesn't like modernism in art," he said and immediately turned cautious, looking around to see if anyone had overheard him.

"Colonel Chernov will be here next week," he said, in a more subdued voice. "I should say Major General Chernov. He has been promoted. Me too, as a matter of fact. I'm Major Perelman now."

"Congratulations, Major!"

"Chernov would like to see some of your work. We should give him a guided tour of the ruined Berlin walls."

"We can do that."

She thought the conversation was over and was ready to go over to the airfield to meet Ilke and eat lunch with her as she usually did whenever she was in the vicinity of Tempelhof. She packed her paints and brushes and turned to say good-bye to him when he announced he would walk with her for a while.

He talked in his usual disconnected way about the government that was going to be formed in Germany, the weather in Kiev during this time of the year, and the Russian ballet and opera troupes who were going to visit Berlin once the cleanup was done. Passersby stared at them, and Hannah became suddenly aware of the contrast between them. Perelman was wearing his major's uniform, a brown coat with gold chevrons and khaki pants pushed inside knee-length boots gleaming with polish. She, on the other hand, was wearing a baggy old sweater and Russian army pants smudged with paints of varying hues and had a large backpack strapped to her shoulders.

He slowed down his pace to match hers as they walked west to the airfield. And as they made a turn at a side street, Hannah heard her name called and found Ilke sitting on a bench on the other side of the street. With her golden hair loose, her tanned skin, and vivid blue eyes, she looked like a poster girl in Nazi calendars, and the effect on Grisha Perelman was startling. His eyes nearly popped out of their sockets, and his jaw dropped as Ilke rose from the bench and came toward them.

"My roommate, Ilke, and this is Major Perelman, my boss." Hannah made the introductions in German.

A warm flush appeared on Perelman's swarthy cheeks, and Hannah thought he was blushing like a schoolboy. It made her wonder if all the tales she had heard about the irresistible attraction of Jewish men toward blond Aryan girls were true.

"Are we going to the park to eat our lunch?" asked Ilke, appearing ill at ease.

"Let's do that," said Hannah.

"I'll be on my way," said Perelman in German. It was the first time Hannah had heard him speak a language other than Russian. His accent sounded like her stepfather's, and Hannah realized he was really speaking Yiddish.

"Shall I come and see you tomorrow?" asked Hannah.

The major had recovered from his state of emotional imbalance by now and appeared suave and urbane.

"No need for that. By the way, I would like you two ladies to come to lunch in my apartment on Sunday. It's next to my office. My orderly is a good cook, and I can offer a good Russian meal."

"We will be there, Major Perelman," said Hannah, while Ilke, thinking of a three-course meal, gave him a huge smile.

A few moments after he left, Ilke broke the silence. "He speaks funny German," she said.

"He's speaking Yiddish. He's Jewish," said Hannah.

"He's the first Jew I've seen in my life, other than in the movies. Will he rape me, like my schoolteachers warned us in class?"

"No, Ilke. He is a gentleman. He is a charming man. I think he's very much attracted toward you."

Ilke smiled and wrinkled her brow, as though thinking about something.

"I've nothing to wear. I can't very well go to lunch in these," she said, pointing to her dirty pants and scuffed-up shoes.

"You can wear the clothes you wore when you first came to the basement," said Hannah, tactfully avoiding any mention of Herr Stumpfegger for fear of another emotional breakdown.

"They will be too big for me," Ilke said. "I must have lost forty or fifty pounds since then."

"I can tuck them in for you. I'm a good seamstress."

During the next couple of days, she helped Ilke get ready for the big event. Ilke wanted her eyebrows tweezed, her nails trimmed, her shoes polished, and her hair washed and brushed. Together, they did the best to groom her, and on Sunday morning, when they walked up the steps of the basement, Ilke looked, if not stunningly beautiful, attractive enough to turn the head of a young Russian soldier who was patrolling the street.

The lunch was quite a success. Bottles of red and white wine with Russian labels, vodka, and Ukrainian *horilka* stood on a table covered with an embroidered white cloth, surrounded by little dishes of red and black caviar, pickled mushrooms, and smoked oysters.

To make it a foursome, Perelman had invited Major General Chernov, who had returned from Moscow that morning.

"I can't wait to tear into the food," whispered Ilke.

"Don't eat too much, and eat slowly. We've to show class," advised Hannah.

The two officers offered them glasses of wine, pulled chairs for them to sit down, and made similar gestures of courtesy throughout the lunch, to their surprise—they had not been treated as ladies for so long that they had forgotten that men, especially Russian men, were capable of gentlemanly behavior.

Major General Chernov was a short, squat Russian with thick graying hair and bushy eyebrows. He looked like a stevedore in a dockyard or a porter at a railway station, and Hannah was surprised to hear him speak fluent French—he had served as a military attaché in Paris before the war—with a Parisian accent.

The main course was chicken Kiev served with bulgur wheat and boiled potatoes.

"This is our regional specialty," said Perelman.

He was surprised when Hannah, in the proper Russian manner, pierced the chicken breast in several places with her fork to let the butter ooze out.

"You've had this before, I see," he said.

"Before the war there were many Russian restaurants in Berlin," Hannah said. "I used to go to them frequently."

But Perelman didn't pay any attention to what she was saying, for he was busy showing Ilke the correct way to eat the chicken.

"This is delicious," said Ilke. "I've never had anything like this before."

Ilke cut small pieces of chicken and chewed them in slow motion, and Hannah was pleased to see she was heeding her warning. In contrast, Major General Chernov, sitting on her left side, ate noisily and had already finished two helpings of chicken, downed two or three glasses of vodka, and was looking bored.

Perelman, as became a host, took note of his boss's boredom and decided to step in.

"Major General Chernov fought in Stalingrad, ladies. He's one of our war heroes. He was awarded the Order of Kutuzov, First Class, for his offensive tactics."

Chernov smiled and looked pleased, but Hannah noticed that Ilke suddenly froze in her seat, holding the fork with a piece of chicken in midair for a few seconds and then putting it down on her plate. More than any other word, "Stalingrad" had connotations of national defeat and humiliation to Germans in her age group, similar to those associated with Amiens and Versailles for an earlier generation. Hannah remembered the Nazi propaganda during the early days of the siege of Stalingrad, the documentaries showing the devastation of the city by the bombs of the Luftwaffe and Hitler bragging about the imminent downfall of the city and the end of Stalin. The tone changed as the months passed, and finally, in January 1943, Germans were told of the defeat of the German Army and the surrender by Field Marshal Paulus. In Berlin, she had witnessed crowds of angry women clamoring to know why their husbands and children had been left to perish in the bitter cold of Russia while the Gestapo, uncharacteristically, stood by idly, without taking down the names of protestors as they would have done in earlier times. She realized then that Hitler was no longer the military genius the German populace thought he was but a mountebank who had suffered a monumental defeat at the hands of the despised Russians.

Chernov intruded into her thoughts by talking to her in French.

"Perhaps madam doesn't know who Field Marshal Kutuzov is," he said.

"I think I know who he is. He is the general portrayed by Tolstoy in *War and Peace*, the one who defeated Napoleon."

His jaw dropped.

"You've read *War and Peace?*" he asked in Russian. "I didn't think the Germans read Tolstoy."

"Frau Müller is very cultured," she heard Perelman say in Russian.

Hannah thought the situation was amusing because Chernov spoke no German, Perelman spoke no French, and Ilke spoke only German but had a smattering of French. She didn't know how to include all the parties in the conversation and decided to conduct the conversation in Russian.

"Yes, I've read *War and Peace*. In German, that is," she said to Chernov.

"You should read it in Russian," he said. "It's our great national treasure. The greatest novel ever written."

What am I to tell this military man? Hannah wondered. Her step-father and his friends used to discuss Russian literature ad nauseam at the Café Lyon, and the literary genius they preferred was Fyodor Dostoevsky, followed by Maxim Gorky, dismissing Tolstoy's novels as "literature for the gentry and landowner." Kandinsky, on the other hand, worshipped Tolstoy, and it was at his urging that she tried to read *War and Peace*, but the cast of princes, princesses, and counts who spoke in courtly style to each other bored her, and she hadn't been able to finish the task.

"Comrade Stalin adores the book so much that he had chapters of it pasted on walls in Moscow in 1942 during the attack on our mother-land by the Nazis," said Perelman.

Hannah began to think that Perelman was a toady, trying to butter up his boss. In any case, his words acted as a spur on the old warhorse.

"I was in a place where there were few walls in 1942," he said in Russian. "Of course, I am referring to Stalingrad. The Nazis had bombed the city to rubble. But we had surrounded the German Army and cut off their lines of supply, in accordance with the plan drawn up by Marshal Zhukov. That way we destroyed the Romanians and the Hungarians first before getting into combat with the Germans. They were tough, the Sixth Army guys. Even after surrender, some of them hid inside collapsed buildings, and we had to kill them in hand-to-hand combat. It was the worst battle the world had ever seen, with two million dead, three-fourths of them Russians."

Hannah was startled by his last sentence because the German people were never told of the casualties. She felt sorry for all the Russian dead, one and a half million of them, and thought that no punishment meted out to Germans would be too cruel in the light of these revelations of wanton carnage. She shot a glance at Ilke to see her reaction, but she was chewing her food placidly and uncomprehendingly.

The orderly brought out a plate of piroshky and placed it in the middle of the table.

"Stenka, did you make these to honor the general or to gain favor with the ladies?" Perelman asked him jokingly.

"For both reasons," said the orderly, a young large Russian, a Tartar or a Cossack, with a handlebar moustache.

"Very diplomatic answer, Stenka," said Chernov and burst into guffaws.

He drank toasts in French, tilting his vodka glass toward Hannah first and then toward Ilke. Then it was Perelman's turn. He toasted "the heroic general's" health in Russian and then turned to Ilke and, in his quaint German, drank to the health of "the fair one who has stolen my heart." The orderly appeared again with a plate of very thin *blinchikis* with jam fillings and confectioner's sugar sprinkled on the outside. The general proposed a toast to Comrade Stenka, and he, in turn, toasted the "legendary Chernov of Stalingrad" and Comrade Perelman. They all smiled and clapped each other on the back. Hannah was struck by the egalitarian nature of the Russian army and contrasted it with the rigid hierarchy of the Wehrmacht. They've achieved a classless society, she thought, and felt a kind of warmth toward all three men.

Perelman then got up and put a record on a gramophone. It was a Russian dance tune, unlike anything that she had heard before, part drums, part a chanting that sounded like *"Barynya, barynya, sudarynya-barynya."* The three men stomped in rhythm, did squats, and while squatting, moved their legs up and down, while Ilke and Hannah watched with amusement. The men soon got tired of it and came back to the table, ate the blinchikis, and proposed more vodka toasts. Perelman then played a waltz by Tchaikovsky on the gramophone and danced with Ilke. Chernov, having finished his vodka, asked Hannah to dance with him, and Hannah dutifully got up. She became aware of Comrade Stenka looking at her with longing and said to herself, "Here's another nineteen-year-old who wants to sleep with me."

After a few minutes, Perelman waltzed out of the room with Ilke. Chernov told the orderly to make up a bedroom for him. Stenka disappeared, returned ten minutes later, and led them to a room upstairs. Chernov undressed rapidly, putting away his uniform and shoes neatly and folding his underpants and socks before placing them on a chair. Hannah turned her back toward him as she undressed, wondering whether he would be brutal like all the other Russians.

"*Vous n'avez aucune maladie, j'espérez,*" she heard him say.

"*Non,*" she said, even as she was thinking, I am not sick in my body, but I'm sick of being a whore.

She turned to face him and saw his stocky, barrel-chested body covered with dark-brown hair. He reminded her of the uncouth, stumbling Russian Bear shown in hundreds of German cartoons. The Bear pawed her breasts, sniffed at her armpits and crotch, and asked her to turn around and bend. She did what he wanted, bending her back and stretching her arms so that they rested on the bed as he entered her from behind, huffing and puffing. The clutching paws then released her breasts, and the Bear climbed into the bed and quickly began to snore.

Hannah picked up her clothes and walked out of the room. Each step seemed to require a great effort on her part, and as she went down the stairs, she felt she couldn't walk anymore. Sitting on the lowest rung, she put her head down on her knees. She felt sorry for herself, for all the dead Russians, and for the millions of innocent Germans who had been needlessly punished. She wished she could find solace in a haven, as in the olden days, when women could seek refuge in convents when tormented by evildoers. But those days were gone, never to come back, and the age she lived in was shaped more by the devil than by Christ. There was going to be no refuge for her, and she would probably end up like the unkempt, seedy-looking women who used to flock the streets near the Alexanderplatz during the Great Depression, offering services of the most degraded kind. Why didn't she have the courage to die? A loud moan escaped from her, and she, losing all pride, let grief overcome her and broke into sobs.

She was suddenly lifted from the staircase by a pair of arms, and for a moment she thought her prayers had been answered and she was ascending to heaven. A warm breath of air on the back of her neck reassured her that it was a man who had lifted her up and was now carrying her down to the basement. She wondered if she should scream, but a gruff voice she recognized as that of Stenka's told her not to be afraid. He took her to a clean, sparsely furnished bedroom that was in the servants' quarters of the house and deposited her on the bed. He then covered her with a blanket and asked her to go to sleep.

"No one will hurt you," he said and left the room.

It was the first act of human kindness that she had experienced in months, and she was touched by it. She thought of Stenka as one of those gentle, noble characters that Russian novelists were fond of describing, like Alyosha in *The Brothers Karamazov* or the servant Gerásim in *Death of Ivan Ilyich*. She drifted off to sleep and had dreams of witnessing a protracted quarrel between her mother and her stepfather, during the course of which the Gestapo was called in, and Paul was arrested and a number was tattooed on his arm. "They're taking him away," screamed her half brother, and she woke up.

There was a strange man lying next to her, and it took her some time to realize that it was Stenka. She sat up, but he pulled her to his side and very gently stroked her hair with his large, surprisingly soft hands. Strong fingers kneaded her tight neck muscles, and she found herself sinking into his chest. He then worked on her back, and slowly, gently, he caressed her abdomen and then her breasts. He kissed her lips, and his mouth moved to her nipples. He parted her legs and entered her, very gently, and kissed her forehead and her closed eyes as he made love to her. Her body responded even though her mind was in other places, for she was thinking of a July afternoon three years ago, when Emil had asked her to meet at Wannsee, and they had strolled along the lakeside road of Havelchaussee until they reached Grunewald Forest. They had slept in a clearing for a while, the sun beating on them, and then made love, and Emil revealed afterward he had to go east to help the wounded and the sick. But the man now lying next to her was not Emil but a peasant, a boy twenty-five years her junior. He was telling her he loved her from the moment he had set eyes on her. I must be a femme fatale, she thought, someone like George Sand or Isadora Duncan, an object of attraction for younger men, a Freudian archetype around whom they spun their older-woman fantasies.

"*Do svidaniya*, Stenka," she said, a few minutes later, and got out of bed.

"It's so early in the morning," he said.

"I like to walk about early in the morning," she said and, without further exchanges, put on her clothes and ran out of the room.

When she returned from work the next day after painting slogans on a wall near Tempelhof, Stenka was waiting for her at the entrance to the basement with three messages.

The first was from Ilke, and it said, "Hannah, I am going to stay here, with the Russians. I am like a mare stabled with two stallions. Grisha tells me that it's common practice in Russia. The food here is good, and the major general has promised me new clothes. Come and see me anytime you want to. PS: I'm not going to work, so don't look for me at lunchtime."

The second one was from Perelman. It said, "We are planning to erect a huge war memorial sculpture in Tiergarten. I would like you to look at some of the drawings and tell me what you think of them. Please meet me tomorrow morning at the Siegessäule at eleven o'clock."

She felt a little angry at his naming a time because she had no means of telling time—no wristwatch, no radio, no church bell, and no clock tower in her neighborhood. The new government had set Moscow time as standard for Berlin, which meant that the sun rose and set three hours later than usual.

Seeing the annoyance on her face, Stenka stepped toward her and asked her if he could help her.

"It would be nice if you could get me a watch," she said.

She had meant it as a joke and was surprised when he took out a ladies' wristwatch from the pocket of his tunic and gave it to her.

"Actually, I wanted to give you this as a present," he said.

She looked at the gold tonneau watch and liked its rose-colored dial with roman numerals shown in gold. The only drawback was the leather strap was a bit frayed—obviously it had been worn by another woman for several years.

"This is a nice watch," Hannah said. "Where did you get this from?"

"I found it in Mishka's room. Mishka was Comrade Perelman's orderly. He was killed two weeks ago, and I am his replacement."

The watch had stopped, and she wound it and set it to the time on Stenka's watch, which showed Moscow time. Hannah was in two minds about accepting the gift, since it was obviously stolen. I shall accept it and then post a note on walls asking the rightful owner to claim her property, she thought.

"Thank you, Stenka," she said and put the watch on her wrist.

She then opened the remaining note, running to three pages and written in a childish scrawl. It was a declaration of love from Stenka, with awkward phrases bumping and jostling against each other, over-eager to convey genuine passion.

"This is a very nice letter," she told him, and he beamed.

"Do you know how old I am, Stenka?" she asked him a minute later.

"Thirty, thirty-two," he said.

"I am forty-five, twenty-five years older than you."

"I don't believe it," he said. "You don't look forty-five."

"I am telling you the truth," she said.

He looked confused and disoriented. She sensed he had prepared a speech and was disappointed he couldn't deliver it; perhaps he had wanted drama with a climax and didn't quite know how to handle the prosaic revelation of her age.

"Come inside, and talk to me, Stenka," she said.

He followed her and helped her as she made her meager dinner of bread, potatoes, and grilled bacon. He politely refused her offer to share food but watched her eat as he drank a little of the schnapps she had saved.

"Think of me as your friend, and talk to me," she said.

It took him some time to open up, and she waited patiently. And then his past was revealed, first in bits and pieces and subsequently in big chunks. He was a Kuban Cossack, and his ancestral home was in the Kuban region, near the Black Sea. His father had fought with the Red Army during the Russian Civil War, siding against his cousins, who had chosen to join the White Army. His parents were now living in Leningrad, where he had gone to school and taken the preliminary courses toward an engineering degree. He had been in love with a Russian girl whose name was Yulia, but she had found another lover, someone high up in the party. He joined the Soviet Army and fought and raped like his fellow soldiers; he had killed sixteen enemy combatants, one with a bayonet, and raped twenty-seven women. He no longer felt patriotic, he was neither Russian nor Cossack, and the only time he felt like a human being with a soul instead of an army robot was when he saw Hannah and instantly fell in love with her.

"We cannot be lovers, Stenka," she said. "It's out of the question."

He didn't take it well but cheered up after she told him that a handsome young man like himself should find an attractive girl close to his age, get married, and raise a family. He sang Russian songs in a baritone voice before he left, promising to visit again and bring her food from his kitchen.

The next morning, she learned from Major Perelman that Stenka had killed himself by putting a bullet into his head.

They were standing in the Tiergarten, which showed the devastation as a result of continual bombardment by planes, rockets, and tank artillery. There were a number of X signs on the ground, made by Soviet bullets, to indicate that an SS man had been killed there by a Russian soldier.

Perelman looked moody and dispirited.

"The Yanks and the Brits and the French will arrive soon in Berlin. That's what I was told this morning. This is going to change our plans.

Originally, I was going to ask your help in choosing a site for the war memorial. That job is going to be done by someone from the mayor's office. What we want you to do is to paint posters that portray the Yanks and Brits as imperialists who are the enemies of the German people, intent on spreading hostility between the German and Russian proletariat."

"You mean I can create my own posters?"

"My boss says yes. But you should do nothing that would embarrass us—there should be no nudity, profanity, or antiproletarian propaganda. Also, it should be something that the average Berliner would immediately respond to."

"Where in Berlin am I supposed to put up these posters?"

"What I was told was that the Russians would get the largest share of Berlin, the entire eastern half. The Americans would get the southwest of Berlin, and the Brits and French would get smaller sectors in the west and the north. I would suggest you start from the southwest districts and work your way up north."

Hannah followed his instructions and, for the next few days, wandered over various districts, from Wannsee to Wittneau. Some buses were running, but the lines were too long, and often she walked, carrying paints and brushes in her backpack. The streets were mostly clear of debris, and the "rubble women" were now assigned to dismantling small factories and plants and loading the equipment to the waiting Soviet trucks. Hannah saw them removing and carrying lathes, drills, grinders, and other such machines from the automobile-repair shops, printing presses, pill manufacturers, and various small businesses that abounded in the Berlin Mitte. Everything of industrial value that could be gleaned from Berlin would be packed up and sent to Russia, she figured. That was the price for losing a war—the winner could do what he wanted with the loser's people or property.

She hated the Russians and began to feel an uncontrollable anger toward them building up inside her. Why am I working for these tyrants? she asked herself. She knew the answer, but the rage still persisted until she ran into a crowd of German women studying a series of posters pasted on the walls of a building in Nikolassee.

She joined them and saw a series of photographs that initially looked like a pile of trash being pushed by a bulldozer but, on closer inspection, turned out to be a heap of emaciated bodies ready to be tumbled into a mass grave by a tractor. The words "YOU GERMANS ARE GUILTY" were printed on all of them.

"The pictures were those of corpses from the Bergen-Belsen concentration camp," said a gray-haired German man standing next to her.

"I don't believe this, this must be a Russian lie," she heard a young woman in her thirties say to him.

"This is put up by the Americans," said the older man. "They are now the masters of the southern part of Berlin. Actually, I've heard that they force Germans at gunpoint to visit the concentration camps and see for themselves the plight of the survivors reduced to skin and bone. They want to drive home our guilt."

"I never heard of Bergen-Belsen," said the young woman. "I'm from Augsburg. How can I be guilty?"

The phrase "*Diese Schandtaten: Eure Schuld*" in bold letters dripping blood laid the guilt squarely on anyone and everyone born a German, and it made Hannah angry at the Americans.

Her black mood made her paint a poster on a large wall two blocks away in Zehlendorf, copying the style and content of a brush and ink drawing by George Grosz called "Stab in the Back." She drew a fallen German worker clutching a hammer and a sickle, while a hand with "America" written on it stabbed him with a dagger.

After finishing, she looked at her work and thought it was a passable imitation of Grosz, down to the details in regard to hands, folds of clothing, and shoes.

"Good job!" said a youthful, masculine voice from behind her, in German but with a heavy foreign accent.

"You like it?" she responded automatically, an artist gratified by words of praise.

When she noticed that he was stumbling to formulate a reply, she turned around to look at him and saw a tall, dark, curly-haired man, in his mid-twenties, in an American uniform.

"You can speak to me in English," she said.

"Thank you. I'm not fluent in German," he said. "I have seen a drawing like this at a George Grosz exhibition in New York. He now lives in New York, you know."

"I didn't know that," she said. "I knew him when he was here in Berlin, though I wasn't close to him."

"This is a very good imitation of his work," he said and, after a pause, added, "I hate to tell you, but this poster has to come down. This is our wall now, you know. We are responsible for governing Zehlendorf and all the neighboring districts. You can't paint anti-American slogans on our walls."

She was enraged by hearing him say "our walls." She then realized he was using it casually, without any intention to offend.

"I won't get rations if I don't do what the Russians tell me to do."

"Oh, that puts a different complexion on things. I thought you were one of the German communists protesting our arrival."

"Look, I'm a professional artist. I don't belong to the left or the right. I am only doing what my Russian boss asked me to do."

"Hey, I've an idea. We too need painters. I like your style. I can use you. Why don't you come to our Dahlem office for an interview? What's your name?"

"Hannah Müller."

"I'm Eric Grossman, Captain Eric Grossman. I am with the American Propaganda Unit. Say tomorrow, around ten o'clock?"

"I'll see," she said.

"Try to come. I am putting you down for ten fifteen. Here's my card."

She took the card and watched him make an entry in his appointment diary with a gold-plated mechanical pencil. He looks a little like my stepfather, Paul, she thought. The same brown eyes, the same humorous mouth, and the dark curly hair—that's why I probably trust him.

After he left, she masked out her drawing with white paint and went back home. On her way, she ran into a group of women gathered around a newly opened food store, listening to a radio broadcast coming through the open door.

"The Americans have dropped an atomic bomb in Japan, in Hiroshima," said one woman.

"Thousands have died, and tens of thousands have been contaminated by lethal radiation," said another.

When she reached home, Hannah undressed and crawled into the big bed in Ilke's bedroom. She felt depressed about the people of Hiroshima, Stenka, and the state of the world and cried herself to sleep.

The next morning she went to see Perelman but found, to her surprise, that his office was locked. She waited on the doorstep, and a few minutes later, Katrina, the Russian girl who had helped her on the first day, arrived with a dispatch case.

"Where is Major Perelman, Katrina?" Hannah asked her.

"He left early this morning."

"He didn't tell me he was leaving."

"They got a telegram last night to take the next flight back home. Major General Chernov has been made the head of a new agency in Moscow, and he took Major Perelman with him."

"Where is Ilke?"

"Oh, she went with them. She told me she was going to marry General Chernov."

"I see. Who do I report to?"

"I don't know," she said. "Wait, I'll call my boss and find out."

She went in and returned after a few minutes.

"A new agency is in charge of propaganda, and they are going to bring experts from Moscow."

"Does that mean I've no work?"

"My new boss says you should go to the employment office at the Rathaus and file an application."

Hannah went home, washed her hair and body, and, wearing the sweater and pants from Fraulein Ritter's suitcase, left for the address given by Captain Grossman.

SIX

DENAZIFICATION

Two tall sentries with bayonets at the end of their rifles guarded the entrance to the military government office where Captain Grossman worked. They looked at her up and down for a split second and then stared straight ahead, ignoring her completely. She went up the steps, and a soldier stopped her at the door, asking her in halting German to state her business.

"I want to see Captain Grossman," she replied in English.

He smiled, showing relief in not having to struggle with an alien tongue.

"OK, you've to check in at the visitor's desk, ma'am, on your right," he said and opened the door for her.

A young woman with blond curls, wearing a military uniform, sat at the visitors' desk, chewing gum.

"*Sprechen Sie Englisch?*" she asked.

"Yes."

"Hi, I am Samantha. What can we do for you?"

"I am here to meet Captain Eric Grossman."

"I see. Let me check something."

She went through a stack of notes and pulled out a sheet.

"Are you Hannah?" she asked.

"Yes, I'm Frau Hannah Müller," she replied, a little annoyed at the use of her first name, as though she were a kitchen maid, by a girl half her age.

"Captain Grossman wants you to be cleared by security. It's the large room on the left at the end of the passage, past the cafeteria. I'll tell them you're coming. You wait in the screening room, and someone will call your name and explain the clearance process."

The girl had a dazzling smile, and her skin was glowing, and Hannah felt a pang of regret that she too hadn't been born American. Theirs was the land of plenty, she thought. They never had to suffer carnage and deprivation like the Europeans. And, as she passed by the cafeteria and saw stacks of food displayed on stainless steel counters, Hannah, who hadn't eaten all morning, wanted to rush in and help herself to the doughnuts, boiled eggs, and sausages, but the warning sign, "Admittance only for US military government personnel," made her tighten her stomach muscles and move on.

About a dozen German women of all ages were sitting in the screening room of the security department. They were educated upper-class women, as was apparent from their conversation, and it came as a surprise to her that they wanted to seek jobs as maids, waitresses, or even cleaning ladies.

"I can take home some leftover food for my children," said one woman in her thirties.

"We will see if they would let us do that," said a cute young blonde. "I worked for them as a secretary and translator in Munich a couple of months ago, when they had just begun their occupation. They were very mean to Germans. They didn't want to socialize with us. They wanted to starve us as punishment for going to war with them."

"It isn't fair," said a thin older woman with wispy hair. "We didn't start the war. Everyone knows International Jewry started the war."

"Don't talk that way," admonished the blonde. "It's better to keep one's mouth shut if one wants to eat, paradoxical as it seems."

Hannah moved away from them and sat on a sofa at the far end of the room. In front of her, on a glass coffee table, were *Life, Time, Newsweek, Saturday Evening Post,* and other glossy magazines. She passed them over to pick up a few brochures that were placed next to them, intrigued by their titles.

The first brochure was about denazification. Hannah learned that the AMG, the American Military Government, was intent on removing Nazi party members from central and local governments of Germany and outlined steps for achieving that end. The second one had the title "JCS 1067." JCS was the acronym for Joint Chiefs of Staff, and 1067 was the first occupation statute, approved by Harry Truman, calling for the arrest of all Nazi party officials, members of the Waffen SS, the SD, and the Gestapo. It also said Supreme Court Justice Robert H. Jackson would be in charge of the implementation of JCS 1067, as chief counsel for the prosecution of Axis criminality. The third brochure, "Our Nonfraternization Policy," signed by General Dwight D. Eisenhower, forbade American soldiers to make friendly overtures to Germans, explicitly warning serving men not to go out with German women.

The little blonde was right, Hannah thought. The Americans are going to treat us as enemies, quite unlike how they behaved to us at the end of the First World War, when the GIs never put on the mantle of conquerors. Even though they were not supposed to socialize with German women, young men from Kansas or Wyoming or Nebraska, shy and unsophisticated, looked up to *Frauleins* (and such Fraus as were available) to teach them the ways of Berlin, to be their guides to nightclubs, dancehalls, restaurants, and theaters. Hannah used to work part time as a hostess in a nightclub in those days, and she remembered fondly the Toms, Bobs, Joes, and Bills she had taken home after work, overlooking their clumsiness and naiveté in matters of sex because of their kindness and decency, especially toward the German children, who ran after them asking for chocolates and chewing gum. The new generation of Americans was a different breed, she realized, and they were naïve in their beliefs in strict nonfraternization and denazification. Did they really think that young men could be kept apart from desperate young women by a general's orders? And did they think they could flush out all Nazis from Germany? The Germans were cunning, they knew how to dissimulate, they were masters of camouflage, and they could put on more colors than a chameleon.

"Hannah."

She heard her name being called by another girl wearing a military uniform, and she again felt annoyance at the American reluctance to use last names even when addressing total strangers.

"Frau Hannah Müller," she said, raising her hand.

The girl came toward her and gave her a sheaf of papers.

"You have to fill these out. Bring it to me when you're done. You can go into the small room around the corner where there are desks and pens."

The sheaf of papers turned out to be a *Fragebogen*, a questionnaire running to six closely printed pages, comprising 130 questions. It listed a number of Nazi organizations, and she had to check yes or no against each of them to indicate if she was or had been a member. It also asked her to list her occupation, employer's name and address, residential address, and her annual income from 1933 onward—that is, after the Nazis had come to power in Germany. How can I remember these details, thought Hannah, since I was paid in cash by shady intermediaries on behalf of anonymous employers and didn't keep any records? She filled in the form, using words such as "freelance" and "estimated income" to qualify her input, resentful that she was being put in a situation where she had to make up data about her past. Obviously, the questionnaire was designed for civil service employees who had to go through the denazification process and was now used as a filter for anyone who applied for a job with the AMG, but neither she nor the women whom she saw in the waiting room looking for menial jobs were likely to be in that target group.

The young woman who took her completed paperwork led Hannah through a maze of corridors until they reached a closed door bearing the legend "US Army SHAEF." She pushed the door open, walked down another corridor, and knocked at a door with the nameplate "Major Leo Levine, US Army, PWD." Hannah was bemused by these agglomerations of letters and thought that the Americans were as bad as the Germans in their fondness for acronyms.

Leo Levine was balding, round-shouldered, and of medium height and wore a small black mustache with a sprinkling of gray. He didn't rise from his seat or shake hands with her but took the questionnaire extended to him by the young woman and pointed to a chair next to a small round table. Hannah assumed he was asking her to take a seat there, and she put her purse on the table and sat down.

She studied the major's face while he studied her Fragebogen. It was a Jewish face, vulnerable and arrogant at the same time—she had seen that type of face among the numerous storeowners in Kurfurstendamm and in medical and legal offices in Berlin in the old days—and Hannah didn't think it was pleasant or attractive.

She wished Levine would read the Fragebogen rapidly and ask her a few questions so that she could leave and pick up her rations, but it didn't turn out that way. He was interrupted by fellow officers dropping in with brief requests or commands, depending on their rank.

"Major, don't forget we have a senator and two congressmen coming tomorrow to see the concentration camps at Ravensbrück and Sachsenhausen," said a gray-haired, distinguished-looking man.

"I know that, General," replied Major Levine.

"They like to have photographs of themselves watching the horrors, which they can publish in the local press. So make sure we take good pictures of them."

"Yes, sir," said Major Levine.

85

After the general left, the major flipped through a couple of pages of her questionnaire.

"Where did you learn to speak English?" he asked suddenly.

"I learned it in high school."

"You speak with an American accent."

"My high school teacher was an American—Patrick O'Farrell, from Philadelphia, married to a Bavarian woman."

"What high school did you go to? I mean in what city?"

"In Schwabing, a suburb of Munich."

"What were you doing before 1933?"

"I was an art student and then a teacher at the Bauhaus. Before that I studied at the Royal Academy of Fine Arts in Munich. I moved to Berlin in 1918 and worked at odd jobs while trying to get my paintings shown."

The phone rang just as he was about to ask his next question, and after picking it up, Major Levine listened to what the caller was saying, interrupting with an occasional "Yeah." Hannah looked around the room and saw a portrait of Harry Truman on the wall facing her and next to it a photograph of the attack on Pearl Harbor. On a small bookshelf, there were two books with garish dustcovers: *Germany Must Perish,* by Theodore N. Kaufman, and *Germany Is Our Problem,* by Henry Morgenthau Jr. Hannah had no doubt that they contained suggestions for punitive measures to be taken against Germans and was wondering whether she would ever get an opportunity to read them, when Major Levine's harsh voice interrupted her reverie.

"What did you do after 1933?"

"I wasn't allowed to work as an artist or teach art, because I had signed the Dringender Appell für die Einheit, which was an appeal by artists and intellectuals to the German public not to vote for the Nazis in the 1932 elections. After the Nazis came to power in 1933, I could get only odd jobs—decorating offbeat nightclubs, doing magazine covers and layouts, designing furniture and dresses, and painting portraits of children and dogs or of Hitler—and I was paid under the table in cash, to avoid keeping employment records."

"The Gestapo left you alone?"

"I was put in jail for three months. My fourteen-year-old son was taken away from me since I was considered to be an unfit mother for an Aryan boy. After coming out of jail, I had to report once a month to the Gestapo headquarters in Berlin and speak with an agent. He would ask me if I was planning to leave Berlin. He would warn me not to engage in antigovernment propaganda and not to stir up trouble. Since I didn't do any of these things, they left me alone until toward the end."

"What happened then?"

"I have a Jewish half brother. Originally the Nazis had classified him as a *Mischling* because our mother was Aryan. But in 1944 they reclassified him as Jewish because his father was Jewish. They wanted to deport him to a camp in Poland. The Gestapo warned me not to give him assistance, but I used to meet him secretly and give him money. Nine months ago they took him away in a van with several other Jews. I don't know where he is, whether he is dead or alive."

"How about your son? Do you know where he is?"

"He used to send me a card on my birthday. He's in the SS, somewhere in Russia, assuming he's still alive. I haven't heard from him for a couple of years."

Major Levine was about to ask her something when the phone rang again. He listened for a moment, put his feet on the table, and began talking angrily.

"We must have a unified policy among the four Allies with respect to the Germans. In Berlin, where there are going to be four zones, it would be foolish for each zone to have its own policy. You know what the American policy is. The purpose of the occupation is to make certain that Germans can never again be a threat to world peace. We must see to it that Germany will never be a powerful industrial nation like it was before the war."

The door opened, and a tall man who looked like a cowboy actor in a western film, wearing rows of ribbons on his chest, came in.

Major Levine took his foot off his desk, sprang from his chair, and saluted, in well-coordinated choreography.

"I'll call you back, Major Wortley-Mackenzie," he said and hung up the phone.

"The Ruskies want to have a meeting with us tomorrow morning at their office, Major. You tell the Limeys and the Frogs to show up there, at ten ack emma. Is that understood?"

"Yes, sir. I was speaking to the British Security Officer Major Wortley-Mackenzie when you came in. I'll call him right away."

"Y'all do that now, ya hear?" barked the general and walked out, closing the door behind him.

Levine sat down and put his feet back on the desk. He picked up her Fragebogen and listlessly flipped the pages.

"Every German man or woman I've interviewed—and I've interviewed hundreds of them—either denies he or she is a Nazi or says that he or she was forced by circumstances to become a Nazi. In your case, you may be telling the truth—but then again, you may not be. I've no way of checking you out. All I can say is if you've told us lies, you will be punished."

He picked up his phone and spoke briefly and inaudibly into it. A few seconds later, the same girl who had brought Hannah into his office appeared.

"Sergeant, take this woman to Captain Grossman," Levine said, and walked out of his office.

The girl smiled at her and said, "Come with me, Hannah."

She took her through another labyrinth of corridors, past a door marked "AUTHORIZED PERSONNEL ONLY," and knocked on a door with the nameplate "CAPT. ERIC GROSSMAN."

"Come in," said a cheery voice, and she was ushered into the room, where the captain was sitting on the edge of his desk, with newspapers and magazines sprawled all around him. He rose and came toward her with a big, radiant smile and extended his hand. She placed the tips of her fingers in his palm in the German manner, but he squeezed her hand warmly and looked at her face intently.

"You seem tired," he said. "Would you like a cup of coffee?"

"Yes," she said gratefully.

"Sergeant, on your way back, will you tell the cafeteria to send me a regular coffee and a couple of doughnuts?" he asked the girl.

"Sure thing, Captain," she said, smiling flirtatiously.

"How did you make out with Major Levine?" he asked after the girl had left.

"I don't know," replied Hannah.

"He can be pretty rough," said Grossman. "He belongs to the Morgenthau school."

"I don't understand what you mean."

"Henry Morgenthau, our treasury secretary, wanted harsh punishment to be meted out to German people. He had a plan, approved by his close friend, President Roosevelt, to demilitarize Germany, deindustrialize it, and make the German people earn their living from farming and agriculture. He also wanted to break apart Germany into smaller states."

"I can understand why he felt that way," said Hannah.

"That isn't my way of thinking," said Captain Grossman. "I want to punish only those who were in power, those who were responsible for misdeeds. I don't want to tar every German with the brush of criminality."

There was a knock on the door, and an orderly entered carrying a tray from the cafeteria. He asked Grossman to sign a voucher, placed a paper cup containing coffee and a paper bag containing doughnuts on his table, and left.

Grossman took the coffee and doughnuts over to Hannah and looked on benevolently while she ate.

"Until yesterday we weren't even allowed to offer you food. There was to be no sign, not even an overture, of friendliness between us and Germans. Things have changed. The Psychological Warfare Division, which was behind this policy, is going to be assimilated into the Information Control Division. And I am going to wear two hats."

Hannah gave him an uncomprehending look, and Grossman gave her his ready smile, warm and luminous.

"I am currently working for Major Levine, but tomorrow I'm going to be promoted. I will have two functions, both related to propaganda. One is to encourage the establishment of a free press in the areas of Germany that we control. The other is to erase the Führer cult from the German school system. You know what I'm talking about?"

"Yes, I do," said Hannah.

A few years ago, she had been asked by an intermediary to do paintings of Hitler for Nazi booklets for children, and she had reluctantly agreed to do it because she needed the money badly. The booklets were about three themes: the benign, caring Führer, fond of children and animals; the need for maintaining racial hygiene by not having contact with non-Aryans; and the portrayal of Jews as evil enemies of the Aryan folk.

"Two generations of school children have been taught, from kindergarten upward, to hate Jews and idolize their Führer," Hannah said. "You're going to change all that?"

"We are," he said and, pulling out a bunch of publications from a shelf, added, "Look at these!"

They were old issues of training manuals for German boys and girls, with titles like *Beware of race pollution!* and *Why Jewry must be stamped out!*.

"I feel sick looking at them," she said. "The more so because the artwork and layout are first rate, done by first-class artists."

"We intend to produce material just like that with counterpropaganda. That's why we need you."

"Why me?"

"There is a big difference between the layout of German and American magazines. We need German artists to create publications for us in the style the readers are used to."

"But why me? There are other artists available. Why do you want me?"

"I checked you out with George Grosz in New York. He remembers you and said nice things about you. He said you were a Bauhaus artist and that some of the émigrés from Bauhaus would know you better. So, I called Josef Albers and Anni Albers, who teach at Black Mountain College in North Carolina. Both of them, especially Anni, thought very highly of your work and were very interested in knowing about your life here."

Floodgates of memory opened up, and Hannah remembered the days at Bauhaus listening to Josef Albers primly expound his theories of color or sad-faced Anni discuss for hours the tactile aspects of fabrics and the design of wall hangings. Tears welled up in her eyes, and she used the sleeve of her sweater to wipe them away.

"Did I touch a raw nerve?" asked Grossman, leaning toward her.

"No," she said, moved by his concern. "I was thinking of the old days when life was filled with dreams for a new world we would usher in."

"Anni told me why you didn't want to emigrate. She mentioned your half-Jewish brother."

"I keep on hoping I'll see him again...somewhere, sometime."

He gave her enough time to compose herself by busying himself with her paperwork.

"I am not allowed to hire you as an artist," he said. "Germans can be hired by the AMG only as chauffeurs, secretaries, translators, or maids and cooks. It's a pity, but that's the way it is. So what I will do is hire you as a translator. You get paid more that way."

"If you think that's the way to do it—" she started saying, but he rose from his chair.

"Come with me," he said.

He took her to the administrative office and got her a translator's badge, a ration card, office supplies, and a stack of time sheets.

"You will get paid at the end of each week," he said.

"OK."

"You can go home now, and we will lay out a plan of work for you tomorrow. Come to my office at nine o'clock."

He shook hands with her, gave his wonderful smile, and pointed to her the quick exit from the building, along a corridor that went around the back of the cafeteria. She came out of the building into a narrow alley lined with garbage cans and saw dozens of German women going through the garbage, picking out half-eaten sandwiches, leavings of white bread and meat, or pieces of sodden cake. Some were stuffing tidbits into their mouths while others put them in bags to take home to their parents or children. Hannah walked away from them, feeling that every remnant of pride had been stripped away from Berliners, now among the poorest and most famished peoples on planet earth. She hoped that Henry Morgenthau Jr. would be gratified by the spectacle and regretted she didn't have a camera to take a picture to send to him.

SEVEN

THE BICYCLE AGE

The next morning, she showed up promptly at nine o'clock, wearing her badge. The sentries, after a cursory glance, let her through, and she was able to navigate the corridors without help until she reached Grossman's office.

"Good morning, Hannah," he said, with his wide smile. "How are you feeling today?"

"Fine. And you?"

"Great," he said mechanically, his mind apparently elsewhere, busy with calculations and explorations that she wasn't privy to. "We can't have our planning meeting today. Major Levine called me a few minutes ago. He wants you to go with us to a meeting with our allies as his interpreter."

"I've never been an interpreter. I don't know if I can do it."

"Levine's interpreter called in sick. He needs someone who can speak Russian, English, and French. Do the best you can today, and tomorrow we'll have our meeting."

He took her to Major Levine's office, where the general she had seen the previous day was standing at the entrance, looking at his watch.

"You're late, Captain…er…Major," he told Grossman.

"Sorry about that, General," said Grossman, in a casual, indifferent voice.

"The jeep is at the front," said Major Levine.

"Let's go then," said the general.

The driver was a German, a discharged or deserted soldier, judging from his furtive, hunted look. He drove expertly through Steglitz and Neukolln, which Hannah had been told were in the American zone. Past Hermanstrasse, driving through Treptow and Karlshorst, Hannah saw large groups of Russian soldiers and realized they had entered the Russian zone. My poor Berlin, she thought. Conquered, divided, and ruled by foreigners who do not speak our language, know nothing of our culture or history, and think of us only as bloodthirsty monsters.

The driver stopped in front of a large mansion, obviously appropriated from its owner by the Russians for their use. A sentry escorted them to a conference room on the first floor, where military officers from Russia, France, and Britain were seated at a large round table, their aides and interpreters standing behind them. The American officers shook hands all around, were offered cigarettes and glasses of tea by the Russians, and, after much scraping of chairs, took their seats in their preassigned slots.

"I am the chairman of this meeting, and since all the parties are present here, I shall start the meeting," said the Russian general, a beefy man with thick gray hair, in an authoritarian voice.

His words were translated by a chic French woman and a young Cockney wearing a loud checked suit.

"It's your turn, Hannah," said Grossman, behind whom she was standing, looking up at Hannah with amusement in his eyes. "Translate into American so we can understand."

"I am the chairman of this meeting," began Hannah in German, nervously, and realizing her mistake, she stopped in the middle of the sentence and translated the Russian's words into American speech, changing "shall" into "will".

"We've reduced rapes in our zone," said the Russian general. "We've told our soldiers we will not tolerate such behavior. We have started publishing two newspapers, the *Red Chronicle* and the *Crimson Hotline,* in our zone. We are in the process of establishing a local government and have appointed a mayor. The main problem we still have is food shortage and lack of medical supplies. We are counting on our allies to help."

The translation of the general's words took several minutes.

The French general responded that his country was in no position to supply food to the Germans because of shortages of coal, meat, milk, cheese, and wheat. He blamed the brutal German occupation for the losses suffered by farmers and added that the French people would rise up against the government if any help was given to the Germans.

After due translation, the British general said there were shortages of potato, bread, and meat in his country also. Food rationing was in effect in Britain, and women had to wait in long queues to get a loaf of bread or a bottle of milk.

The three generals then looked at their American counterpart expectantly, hoping he would solve the problem.

"There's no great desire on the part of the United States to ship food to Germans," said the American general. "As far as I know, neither the Congress nor the White House has initiated any measures to airdrop food over German cities."

"You forget there are no cities left in Germany," said his British counterpart with a sardonic smile. "Berlin, Munich, Dresden, Hamburg, Nuremburg, Frankfurt—all have bit the dust, literally. Huge mounds of debris stand in place of their vaunted architectural creations, and it will take them at least half a century to rebuild."

The check-suited Cockney tittered and then tried to look solemn.

"They've been reduced to the Bicycle Age," said the Frenchman with a laugh. "The Germans have only bicycles for transportation."

There were widespread chuckles at the plight of Germany, and drinks and cigarettes were passed around the table.

"Let's move on to another pressing issue," said the Russian general. "It has to do with the employment of Germans in our respective zones. Is it possible to come up with a set of rules we can all adopt? Right now, we seem to go our separate ways."

"We want to keep all their key personnel so that they can run things," said the British general. "We don't ask them if they're Nazis. If the press digs up some unsavory story about a man's past, we will take action, but generally speaking, we let sleeping dogs lie."

Hannah watched with amusement as the French and the Russian translators struggled to come up with equivalents for "letting sleeping dogs lie." She thought it was the only streak of comedy in this grim prognosis for Germany's future.

"Our policy is to not hire Nazis under any circumstances," thundered the Russian general and, suiting action to his words, banged his fist on the table.

"It means that all the men who once held excellent technical and managerial posts will migrate quickly to our zone," said the British general, phlegmatically.

"We're at a crossroads," said the American general. "Until now, we've been trying to weed out Nazis using an elaborate questionnaire. The problem is one of verification. We've no means of checking whether someone is telling the truth or not. So we are changing our procedure. We will ask the local police and local community boards to tell us if a person is a Nazi, and if he is, we expect the local courts to prosecute him. Recently we've discovered, accidentally I might add, a card index of eight million members of the Nazi party. We're in the process of sorting things out, as fast as we can. In the meantime, we've made some organizational changes. The Psychological Warfare Division of SHAEF has been dissolved, and its responsibilities have been taken over by the Information Control Division. Major Levine and I have been transferred to the Pacific front to work under General MacArthur in Japan. This is going to be our last meeting, and I want to thank you all for your cooperation."

"Who is going to be our new contact?" asked the Russian general.

"I can't answer that," said the American general. "Perhaps Major Grossman should take a shot at it."

"I'm in the Propaganda Division," said Grossman. "Our mission is to introduce democratic concepts and principles to the German people in our zone, from elementary school students to retired people living on pensions."

"You're going to work independently of us?" asked the British general.

"We will pass on information that will be of common interest. But we will not be coordinating with you. There won't be any more meetings unless an occasion arises."

"We will go our own way," said the Russian general, with finality.

The meeting broke up shortly after that, and Hannah got into the jeep with the others.

"Major Levine and I have an interview with *Army Talks,*" said the general to Major Grossman. "Tell the driver to drop us off in front of their office."

Major Grossman gave instructions in German to drop them off at an address in Steglitz, and Hannah watched, as before, the changing of the zones, the blue-and-gray Russian uniforms giving way to American khaki.

After the two senior officers had been dropped off, Grossman suggested that Hannah should have lunch with him at his residence—a house in Dahlem where he was billeted with ten other officers.

"That would be nice," said Hannah. "I really would like that."

"I'll tell them you're a war reporter from France," he said, with a sheepish expression on his face. "You see, we're not allowed to lunch with Germans. I hope you don't mind."

"Not at all," said Hannah. "I'm hungry, and I don't mind a little deception as long as I can get a good meal."

He laughed good-humoredly and helped her out as the car stopped at a three-story house in Dahlem, the only one among its neighbors to have been undamaged by the air raids. Grossman escorted her up a carpeted flight of stairs to a beautifully furnished dining room. A half-dozen officers were sitting at a large table eating lunch, and they waved and shouted to Grossman.

"Hi, guys," said Grossman, and waved back to them. He took her to a smaller table at the corner of the room and pulled up a chair for her to sit down.

They were served by pretty German girls wearing white aprons and caps, who silently and unsmilingly brought tomato soup and white bread and butter in china dishes—obviously, the property of the owner of the house—followed by steamed frankfurters and brown beans, apple pie, and coffee.

Grossman watched as Hannah ate slowly and methodically, enjoying the taste of the beans and the sausage and the heavenly sweetness of the apple pie.

Every now and then a friend of Grossman would drop by their table to ask him a question.

"Eric, you gonna be at the poker game this evening?"

"Sure, Randy," Grossman replied.

"You wanna go to the movies tonight?" asked another.

"What's playing?"

"*Objective Burma*, with Errol Flynn."

"I'll drop in after the poker game in Randy's room."

The men looked at her casually, without interest, unlike the young soldiers from Russia, dismissing her as a visiting aunt or schoolteacher. Hannah found it soothing to be ignored, to be regarded on a par with the anonymous waitresses and maids who dashed in and out of the room carrying cups and plates.

"I wanted to have lunch with you for a couple of reasons," said her host, after the last officer had left the room. "I thought you might be hurt by the callous way the guys talked about Germany at the meeting. I want to assure you that not all Americans think like that."

"I am not offended, Major Grossman," she said.

"Drop the 'major' stuff," he said. "Please call me Eric."

"What I want to say, Eric, is that Germans treated their conquered people very badly during the last decade. We brought in millions of prisoners from Poland and Russia to do forced labor and starved them to death. And it's common knowledge among Berliners that unspeakable acts have been performed in conquered territories by the SS and the SA. Now the tide has turned, and we are the victims. In my opinion, we are being treated much better than we deserve."

"This is what we call 'liberal masochism' in New York," he said.

She didn't understand what he meant and didn't want to ask him for an explanation. He seemed young, young enough to be her son, and an idealist. She felt the same unease with him that she used to harbor toward those at Bauhaus who talked about spiritual harmony, universal values in art, cosmic symbols, and such esoteric topics instead of sticking to the building blocks of composition—namely, line, color, and form.

"I never talked to you about my background," he said. "I'm a Jew from New York. My parents are first generation Jews, their parents having emigrated from Germany and Austria. My grandfather was an architect, and he passed on his gifts to his son, my father, who is well known in New York. My mother owns an art gallery on Madison Avenue, and she displays the work of European artists like Chagall, Kandinsky, and Franz Marc. My undergraduate degree is in political science, and I have a law degree from Columbia University. My specialization is in international law, and the US Army assigned me to the Propaganda Unit because of my background."

He spoke slowly and clearly, but, even so, Hannah couldn't quite absorb the import of some of the phrases he used. She had never heard of New York's Columbia University before. Nor did she know what "political science" meant. She mentally translated it as "*politische Wissenschaft*," but the phrase seemed like a contradiction to her. Wissenschaft involved discipline and years of study and produced rational, thoughtful men like Emil, while politische had unruly, riotous, and irrational connotations linked to demagoguery, race hatred, and warmongering. But she quickly realized that what might seem a contradiction to her would make perfect sense to someone from America because their political environment was different from those of European countries. She knew vaguely their system of governance—an elected president ruled the country for four years, senators and congressman passed laws, and a supreme court interpreted the laws for the nation, providing enough checks and balances for democracy. Its actual working was beyond the comprehension of a German like her, who knew only authoritarian figures like the kaiser, Ludendorff, Hindenburg, and the man with the toothbrush moustache and guttural voice who was last in the line of autocrats.

"I like to get to the bottom of things," Grossman was saying. "Every German I've spoken to, other than you, blames Hitler for all the atrocities. 'Look at what he said in his speeches,' they would say. 'It's all there in black and white.' I've read his early speeches, and the impression I got was that he was mouthing phrases used by other beerhall orators to work up his audience. I know he spoke of hanging the Jews in public squares, but I don't believe that speeches or books can incite people to mass murder. There must have been an organization behind it, planning and following it through. What I'm trying to say is that there must be a blueprint somewhere, a roadmap drawn up by evil masterminds. I would like to look for that and identify the people who created it. That's why I'm staying on in the army."

His intense, focused expression surprised her. Was he another Don Quixote, a knight-errant on a quest? He doesn't know anything about Germany, she thought. The evil he is talking about has existed long before Hitler. My uncle Werner belonged to the Pan-German League, who advocated the same things that Hitler talked about. When I was a fourteen-year-old girl, sketching plants and flowers in the garden, I would hear him discourse with his friend Heinrich Class, president of the Pan-German League, both seated on deck chairs, on the Jewish question and the need for its resolution. I would hear them say things like "Germany's resident Jews must be covered under an aliens' law" and "We must uphold German racial hygiene and must not allow breeding with Jews and other inferior races." Occasionally my aunt Gudrun, a tall, elegant woman, would join them to give them her moral support.

She wanted to tell Grossman that anti-Semitism was part of the collective German psyche, and it had been held under control under the previous rulers because of the laws in effect. When the Nazis lifted those laws, the malevolent genie was out of the bottle, and all the suppressed hatred was let loose. Berliners taunted and beat up Jews who were herded up in street corners prior to removal to unspecified destinations, and landlords and neighbors eagerly waited for Jewish tenants to be arrested so that they could take over their apartments or houses. Ordinary men and women cheered and did jigs during Kristallnacht, as they watched the shattering of glass in shop windows. None of this was the result of a blueprint drafted by a cabal of Nazis working in the basement of the Reich Chancellery.

Her mind then wandered off at a tangent, and she began to speculate on the need of men like Eric Grossman for defining events as the outcome of plots hatched by conspirators holding secret meetings, just like her uncle's friends believed in the *Protocols of the Elders of Zion* as the blueprint for the Jews to destroy Aryan nations. People everywhere needed conspiracy theories, she assumed, whether they were Germans or Americans.

"What do you hope to accomplish by what you're doing?" she asked him, shyly, hesitantly.

"I'll be doing the world a favor," said Grossman, his eyes lighting up with enthusiasm, "by stripping the hypothetical from the cold-blooded design of evil."

"Where do I fit in this effort? I am not a scholar or an intellectual. I'm just a painter."

"I need a German to work with me, an older person who hasn't been contaminated with the Nazi ideology. Why you? You look a lot like my aunt Amy—tall, blond, and green eyed. I used to adore her. She was an idealist, a close friend of Eleanor Roosevelt—she is President Roosevelt's wife, in case you haven't heard of her. My aunt was a professor of social studies in New York University. She was working with Mrs. Roosevelt toward the formation of the United Nations before she died."

Oh God, I am going to be the substitute aunt to a Jewish boy, thought Hannah. She wanted to tell him he was making a mistake—she wasn't like his aunt, she was not an idealist, she wasn't a scholar, she didn't care for the United Nations, and she didn't want to go on a quest for a blueprint. But seeing the look of eager expectation on his face, she decided she would humor him for the time being, for she was sure he would find out in a matter of weeks, if not days, that she was not what he thought she was.

"We will see how it goes, Major," she said with a smile.

"For the next few days we're going to work on the counterpropaganda I spoke to you about—I need cartoons in the style of George Grosz for the newspapers and artwork for the denazification books for schoolchildren. After that I'm hoping to be transferred to Nuremburg. The Allies are going to hold a war-crimes trial there shortly."

"A war-crimes trial?" She couldn't believe her ears. It would be the first time in Germany's history that a trial was held to prosecute the country for war crimes.

"Yes, Hannah," said Grossman. "They've captured a number of Nazi leaders—Goering, Ribbentrop, Speer, and several others. Didn't you know that?"

"No, we don't have newspapers, as you know. And the Russians stole our radios."

"Well, the captured Nazi leaders are going to be tried in Nuremberg. We've also discovered a huge archive of documents, nearly five hundred tons, and a cache of microfilm. These are being translated and evaluated by our lawyers to see if they can be used in the trial. Actually, word is out that the trial will be based on documentary evidence and not on testimony of witnesses for the prosecution."

"I wish the trial was being held in Berlin instead of Nuremberg. I would love to see them being grilled, especially Himmler."

"Himmler is dead. The Brits arrested him while he was trying to escape, but he swallowed a cyanide capsule and died."

"He followed the footsteps of his Führer."

"He had hidden the cyanide capsule inside a molar. I don't know why the Brits didn't check for it. Next to Hitler, he would have been the most valuable witness."

"He wouldn't have cooperated. He would have found some way of doing away with himself."

"Probably true. Well, if you want to be at the Nuremberg trial, I think I can arrange that."

"I would love that."

"Good. You can't stay at the hotel where we will be staying. No Germans are allowed there. Only Americans and maybe one or two Brits. That's the way it is, Hannah."

"It doesn't matter. I can stay with my uncle."

"The trial is two months away. In the meantime, you should report to the American Documentation Center at Zehlendorf tomorrow. I've arranged a workspace for you and authorized your access to the library there. You should meet the librarian Agnes Hardwick in the morning, and she'll take you around."

Hannah was wondering how she could get to Zehlendorf. There may not be buses, and walking was out of the question. If only she had a bicycle, she thought, it would save her a lot of aggravation.

"Do you think I can have an advance on my wages? It's to buy a bicycle to get to work."

He thought for a moment, took out his wallet, and gave her a sheaf of dollar bills.

"I don't know if you can get an advance," he said. "I'll give you a loan. You can pay it back later, in installments."

She took the money from him, gazing at the strange currency showing unfamiliar images of American presidents, and counted the bills slowly.

"One hundred fifty dollars," she exclaimed. "How many marks is it?"

"A lot, I guess," he said. "The mark fluctuates so widely. What I gave you should be enough to buy a bicycle, because I know a girl at the office who got one for a hundred dollars."

They stared at each other for a few seconds. I can't make him out, she thought. Why is he so nice to me? I don't know what he wants from me.

She extended her hand to him, and he, imitating a scene from a Hollywood movie, clicked his heels together and kissed it.

"I hope I did it right," he said with a smile. "Americans don't click heels or kiss hands, you know."

EIGHT

CARTOONS, OLD AND NEW

The next morning she bought a secondhand bicycle designed for going over rough terrain and rode to Zehlendorf, making detours around huge, gaping potholes and rubble mountains still remaining in the American zone.

She was a little tired from the effort, not having had any food for twelve hours, and was upset when the staff at the Documentation Center answered her questions with reluctance that bordered on rudeness, intimating through body language that they considered her an unwelcome visitor. Miss Agnes Hardwick, prim and spinsterish despite her smart khaki uniform, told her she wasn't allowed to use the ladies' room or eat at the cafeteria. She was given a small airless booth near the library with a desk and a chair and a naked electric bulb hanging from the ceiling and allowed access only to magazines and books kept on open shelves.

She thumbed through old issues of *Lustige Blätter, Fliegende Blätter,* and *Simplicissimus* published during the past decade, looking for cartoons she could draw inspiration from. There were dozens of them on Chamberlain, Churchill, and Roosevelt, but they were of very poor quality when considered as drawings. *Simplicissimus* disappointed her.

It was the first time she had looked at it since it had transformed itself into a Nazi publication sometime in the mid-thirties. Before that she used to read every issue, looking for an essay by Thomas Mann, a poem by Rainer Maria Rilke, a set of cartoons by George Grosz, or a sketch by Käthe Kollwitz. Where did that old Germany, the vibrant, creative haven for artists and thinkers, go? she wondered and felt disgust at the inane cartoons and hate-filled articles that she was looking at. She didn't have to go through this trash to come up with a few cartoons for Eric, she decided.

She sat down at her desk and sketched out a few themes that popped up in her mind. In the first one, a middle-aged German man stands on a chair to replace Hitler's photograph with that of Joseph Stalin, but his wife comes running in with a photograph of Harry Truman and tells him, "Heinz, this is the right picture." In another, Hitler and Goebbels are watching a flattened Berlin from up above, and the former tells the latter, "This is exactly what I wanted the Berlin skyline to look like, at the end of my regime." In the third, Hitler complains to Goering and Keitel, "We would've taken Stalingrad if that traitor Paulus hadn't stabbed us in the back!"

She worked on them for a few hours until she was satisfied with their quality. She then put them in her backpack and bicycled to Grossman's office.

"How are things going?" he asked cheerfully.

"I have three cartoons. I brought them to show you."

He looked at them for a while and, smiling again, said, "These are great. You didn't go overboard. I'll send these to our officer in charge of newspapers and ask him to publish them. It's his decision, but I think he'll go along."

"I'm glad you like them," she said.

"I knew you would do a good job," he said. "Now I want you to work on the layout for the magazines for boys and also do some sketches for the new social studies books for schools. You will find the old books in the education section, and I'll call Agnes and ask her to give you access."

"When do you want them?"

"In a week or so. I'm flying over tomorrow to Nuremburg to talk to the head of the Documentation Center there. I would like to get a feel for what they have. Also, I would like to see if I can talk to the prisoners. You can meet me at Nuremburg when the trial starts."

"I've second thoughts about that. What is the point in my being at the trial? I'll only be a burden to you."

"I have ideas on how to make use of you, Hannah. You can be my translator when I need help with the documents. You can also do courtroom sketches, and we can put together a book on the trial to reach the German public."

The excitement in his voice was contagious, and tiny pulses of enthusiasm traversed up and down her body as she visualized a book containing her drawings of war criminals in the hands of hundreds, maybe even thousands of readers. But it was a momentary feeling, and she quickly relapsed into her usual questioning self.

"Eric, what makes you think the trial will be welcomed by Germans? They are so cynical about courts in this country because our judges always find the defendants guilty. The public would believe the outcome of the trial is predetermined."

"In America, we give the defendant every opportunity to prove his innocence. You'll see that at the trial. The defendants will have lawyers, and they'll have their say in court. When the defendants are under cross-examination by the prosecutors, the pieces of the jigsaw puzzle will mesh, and we will find out who drafted that blueprint for war, devastation, and mass murder."

That blueprint again! Looking at his shining eyes, she was reminded of men she had fallen in love with when she was young, painters in Munich and Berlin after the First World War waving manifestos and directives that would change the world forever. It was then that she had become aware of her own weakness for men with obsessions, would-be heroes bent on quests that would lead them through tortuous ways to some far-out terrain—a no-man's land where they would remain ostracized or in self-imposed isolation for the rest of their days. She had no doubt that the man standing before her was doomed to failure, for he was ignorant of the devious ways of Germans, who were experts in using euphemisms to hide their real intentions; but even as she felt pity for him for undertaking what she thought was a futile effort, she felt a revival of the old impulse to cheer him on, in the same way she used to give support to her lovers in her younger days.

"It will take me a while, but I'll find out what I want," he was telling her. "I have been speaking to some of our British counterparts. They know more about what has been going on in Germany than the Americans. One man gave me a map of the Nazi organizational hierarchy. Now I know who was at the top and who at the bottom. He also told me that even though he had no proof for it, he felt Hitler, Goering, Himmler, and Heydrich—Himmler's deputy and head of the Reich's main security office RSHA—were the ones who should be ultimately held responsible for mass murder. Did you know that the Nazis had eleven extermination centers in Poland and Russia, where they used assembly-line methods to kill Jews? Trainloads of Jews would arrive at these death factories and would be processed into ash, and their body fat would be used for making soap, their hair for making blankets, and their skins to be used as lampshades."

Hannah turned pale and collapsed in her chair when she heard his words, her face covered with beads of sweat. Grossman, confused and startled, went over to her, wondering whether he should phone the medics in the building. But she soon opened her eyes—green eyes with flecks of blue that remained unfocused and uncomprehending at first but quickly changed to a look of shock and disbelief.

"You said there were factories for killing Jews?" she asked, sitting up straight in her chair.

"Yes, Hannah, but I shouldn't have blurted it out like I did."

"It's time that someone told me. The American posters proclaiming German guilt showed heaped up bodies of victims who died in a concentration camp somewhere, and I thought they were political prisoners killed by the Nazis. I had no idea they ran death factories for Jews. Now I don't know what to think. My brother is probably dead."

She sat in silence for a few minutes while he looked at her, thinking that she had the type of beauty that never aged. She was a paradox—seductive and forbidding of intimacy at the same time, vulnerable and unconquerable, within reach, but ungraspable. He wondered if she would let him sleep with her, at the same time speculating on the effect of such an action on the relationship that he was trying to cultivate with her.

"I've made up my mind, Eric," she said abruptly. "I too want to get to the bottom of this. I want to find out if my brother is alive or dead. I will be your colleague and do whatever you want me to do, whether it is working as a translator or doing illustrations for your books."

"I am glad you feel that way," he said with a smile. "I'll be back in a week, and we will work out a plan of action. In the meantime, you finish up what you've begun to do."

The next few days she worked in the dingy room at the Documentation Center, looking at Nazi magazines for young boys and teenagers during the past decade. The cover layout in most cases was near perfect and used, ironically, the graphic techniques developed by the Bauhaus innovators. As an artist she couldn't help admiring the geometric placement of a swastika made of gray blocks on the black cover of *Die Kameradschaft*. But then she saw, in small print, the title *Rass ist Shicksal*. They weren't joking, she thought, when they said race was destiny. *Die Kameradschaft* and *Die Jungenschaft* provided group leaders of *Jungvolk* and *Hitlerjugend* with guidelines on indoctrination of boys from ten to fourteen and young adults. From this it was one step to join the SS or their security arm SD and put *Rass ist Shicksal* into practice. She again looked at the magazine cover, hiding the title with her fingers, and was struck with the genius of the graphic artist who had done the design. In Bauhaus, Gropius and others had urged her and others to create a new art of the future that the world would adopt because it used universally understood symbols. Was the cover the end product of that mission—for there was no doubt in her mind that the artist was trained at the Bauhaus?

She flipped through some more issues of *Die Kameradschaft* and *Die Jungenschaft*, which dealt with such enlightening topics as the goals of Jewry, the need for lebensraum for Germany crushed between Western Europe and Russia, and ended with exhortations like "THERE CAN BE NO SURVIVAL WITHOUT FIGHT." Suddenly, she was startled to see her own work on the cover of *Die Kameradschaft* with the title "THE MIGHT OF THE GERMAN WORKER." She remembered that a sleazy middleman who had represented her in those days had asked her to do an abstract poster glorifying the German industrial worker. She had done it in the typical Bauhaus style, the hammer represented by a black cube ready to make an arc along faint but cleanly drawn lines. The agent wouldn't disclose the identity of the publication, and she didn't press him for it but had instead thanked him for the generous payment he had made in cash. If she had known it was for the *Die Kameradschaft*, she wouldn't have accepted the commission, and now she felt betrayed and defiled. She wondered what Eric would think of her after she told him about it, for there was no doubt in her mind that she was going to show him the magazine.

It was in an angry mood that she set to work on designing layouts for the new magazines that would succeed *Die Kameradschaft* and *Die Jungenschaft*. She sketched out pictures of devastation: a flat landscape called Deutschland with a forked road, one branch carrying the signpost "Democracy" and leading to the horizon and the other ending up in a cemetery showing gravestones with the names of Hitler, Goebbels, and NSDAP. Her anger not having subsided, she copied the swastika that she saw in *Die Kameradschaft* and, using the same geometry and mass, broke it up into uneven fragments, in a new layout.

She worked for several hours, day after day, in that small, dark room, perfecting cartoons, layouts, and banners for Grossman's approval. One afternoon, exhausted by the task of laying out future visions for her ravaged and fragmented native land, she leaned back on her chair and closed her eyes for a few minutes. When she opened them, Major Grossman was watching her from the door, an expression of concern on his face.

"Eric, how long have you been watching me?" she asked him.

"For about five minutes. You looked very tired."

"I've been going through this trash," she said, pointing to the stacks of Nazi publications around her. "I also did some layouts and sketches. Would you like to see them?"

There was only one chair in the room, and he sat on her desk and looked quickly through the artwork she handed him.

"I like all of them," he said. "I think we can make use of them in the next few days. The schools start in September, and General Eisenhower wants new textbooks and teaching material to replace the old."

She looked at his eager, open face for a few seconds and decided that she should tell him then and there what had been bothering her.

"Eric, one of my paintings is on the cover of *Die Kameradschaft*. I don't want to cause you problems later on if someone finds it out."

"Show me the painting," he said.

She brought out the magazine, and he looked at it for a few seconds.

"This is similar to the geometric abstraction in Kasimir Malevich's paintings. I've seen them in New York, in various galleries. I thought the Nazis hated this type of art, and I'm surprised that they used this in their magazine."

"I had no idea they would be using it, either. My contact wouldn't reveal the identity of the publication, and I didn't press him for it."

"I think you're making a big deal about this," he said with a smile. "There's nothing in this picture that indicates you're a Nazi sympathizer."

"You are making fun of an old lady," she said, uncertain of his true feelings.

"You are not old, and I'm not making fun of you," he said. "Look, we've more important things to do. I finally have permission to work as a lawyer at the Nuremberg trial, which will begin in a week or so. I also got permission to hire you as a German interpreter and translator, with a substantial increase in pay."

"I would like to be there," she said in a calm voice, hiding the excitement she was feeling inside.

"As I said before, you cannot stay in the hotel where I'm staying. It's against the rules."

"I'll stay with my uncle."

"Also, you cannot fly with me. And there are no trains or buses."

"So how am I going to get there?"

He thought over the problem for a minute.

"My roommate, Captain Frankel, is going to take a hundred German prisoners to the Nuremberg jail. They will be transported in vans. I can ask him to take you with him. Do you mind?"

"I don't mind sitting with prisoners. It's better than going there by foot or riding my bike."

He laughed and made a notation in his pocket diary. "I'll talk to him tonight and will let you know the time and place of the convoy's departure."

He clicked his heels as before, bowed, and left the room, and Hannah wondered why he was so keen on having her with him. "Why do younger men want my company but not older men?" she asked herself, convinced that there was something strange and unnatural in her personality. I must be sending them signals without being aware of it, she thought, as she stacked up the magazines to return them to the library and cleared her desk.

PART 2

NUREMBERG TRIALS

The hard detail of the Holocaust was supplied not by the chief defendants [of the Nuremberg trials] but by more junior officials and security officers who did have direct experience and knowledge of the programme.

—Richard Overy, Interrogations,
The Nazi Elite in Allied Hands, 1945

Did Hitler in fact have any specific design, a master plan, a definite blueprint...which was to unfold, stage by stage, from 1933 to 1945?

—Milan Hauner, *Journal of Contemporary History*, Vol. 13, No. 1 (Jan. 1978)

NINE

FAMILY REUNION

A convoy of vans stood at Tempelhof at six o'clock the next morning when Hannah went there, and into each van were led shackled prisoners wearing shabby SS uniforms without markings. After they were all seated, an armed American guard entered each van and pulled its door shut. A German driver climbed in and waited for the order to start.

Hannah, with her suitcase (property of the late Fraulein Ritter) and bicycle, stood a few feet away from the convoy, waiting for someone to help her. She was beginning to think that they would be leaving without her when a tall American officer, the one who had invited Eric Grossman for a poker game, came to her side.

"You are the French journalist who's coming with us to Nuremberg?" he asked, offering his hand.

Hannah was about to say no when she remembered that was how Grossman had wanted to introduce her to his friends.

"Yes," she said and shook his hand.

He stared briefly at her bicycle and suitcase.

"We've to find space for these," he said. "I think one of the vans has several empty seats. I'll put you in that."

She saw him poking his head into vans and talking to the guards. Having found what he was looking for, he came over to her, lifted the suitcase with one hand, and steered the bicycle with another. She, used to German men who weren't in the habit of helping women, was touched by the oddly chivalrous gesture, and the latent goodwill that she had always felt toward Americans was rekindled in her heart.

"Here we are," he said, when they had reached the van. He opened the door and put the bicycle against a row of empty seats. He then helped her get into her seat and placed the suitcase next to her.

"This is gonna be a rough ride," he said. "The main roads aren't good, they tell me, and we may have to go around some of them. It'll take at least six hours before we get to Nuremberg."

He closed the door but reopened it again and smiled at her.

"I am Captain Frankel, in charge of this convoy," he said. "If you need me, I'll be in the first van."

The convoy drove west toward Lower Saxony and southeast from there until they reached Franconia. They avoided the main cities and drove through small towns and villages in the heart of Germany, choosing routes that had sustained minimal damage from bombing.

Hannah was thrilled to see the familiar German countryside dotted with farms and churches. A herd of red-and-white Holstein cows placidly standing on a meadow reminded her of days spent on a farm owned by her uncle during school vacations, doing chores assigned to her by the tenant farmer and his wife—collecting eggs from the hencoop, milking cows, or washing and cutting cabbage for sauerkraut. The Germany of my youth is still intact, she thought, untainted and inviolate. But a few yards away, she saw US Army encampments on both sides of the road, and the picture of arcadia quickly vanished. The prisoner sitting closest to her jerked his head back and shifted his feet so that the shackles rattled.

"I was born here, in Lower Saxony," he said aloud.

He was very young, not even twenty, and had a blond two-day fuzz over his pale cheeks. His fellow prisoners, three hard-bitten men in their thirties, stared at him without saying anything.

Hannah wanted to talk to the young man from Lower Saxony but didn't think it was a good idea because she would have to answer questions he might ask about herself. She stared at the floor, and they continued their journey in silence.

Two hours later, the convoy stopped at a wooded spot, and the prisoners were led out to stretch their legs and go behind trees to perform bodily functions. Hannah also got out of the van and walked around for a while, looking at the spectacular landscape that lay before her—the hills, the rivers, the tall trees—and wondered why Germany had not produced great landscape painters. Of course, there were August Bromeis, Jakob Dorner the Younger, and Caspar Friedrich—painters she had studied while she was in arts school in Munich—but none of their pictures had the brooding intensity that she had seen in English and French landscape paintings. Maybe it was because sadness or morbidity had no place in these placid surroundings, she thought—which was the reason why Germany had produced philosophers like Kant and Goethe instead of artists like Constable or Gainsborough.

She heard her name being called, and an American soldier—she didn't know whether he was a corporal or a sergeant from his uniform because she hadn't yet learned to tell the difference—came over to her carrying a sandwich and a bottle of Coke.

"Compliments of the US Army, young lady," he said.

He was in his early twenties, nice looking, and charming. He opened the bottle for her with a tool from his Swiss Army Knife, smiled, and left.

She sipped the strange-tasting gassy drink, not liking the passage of the hissing, savagely sweet, and bubbly fluid down her gullet. She took a bite of the sandwich and gagged at the taste of packaged white bread, lettuce, and mayonnaise wrapped over grilled bacon and turkey meat. But she was hungry and ate the bread, throwing the meat into the woods.

After three more hours of driving through small towns and villages, they entered Nuremberg, the convoy stopping at the prison next to the Palace of Justice. Hannah got out of the van, took down her bicycle and suitcase, and surveyed the surroundings.

Emaciated-looking German women wearing rags were wandering around piles of brick, wood, and mortar that were the remnants of buildings that had stood there for centuries. The Nuremberg Prison looming next to her had been damaged so badly by bombs and heavy artillery that it was boarded up in places to hide huge, gaping holes on its walls, and the stately Palace of Justice—that monument of massive Teutonic architecture, held up alike by the faculty and students of Bauhaus as a prime example of what future architecture should *not* look like—had suffered badly and was being fixed up for the forthcoming trials by captured German soldiers in their faded uniforms, torn and shabby, with markings of rank removed from them.

The sun was bright, and strapping her small suitcase onto the rack of her bicycle, Hannah set forth on a tour of the city she hadn't been in for five years. She remembered that as a ten-year-old girl, staying with her uncle and his wife in Nuremberg, she used to wander in and out of its wonderful toy stores or tramp up and down the great food markets, gorging on gingerbread cookies made by the local guild. The place she loved most was the Altstadt, the old medieval city founded a thousand years ago, with its pink walls, its fabulous fountains, and the majestic Imperial Kaiserburg castle with turreted towers.

Overcome by nostalgia, she pedaled her bicycle westward through Maximilianstrasse and Johannisstrasse—riding warily through a sea of plaster and brick dust—until she reached the loop that circled the old city.

The Altstadt was in total ruins—its numerous wooden houses had been burned to cinders by firebombs, and the castle, the Rathaus, and the old Gothic churches were now charred, blackened heaps. She wandered over to the Pegnitz River that meandered through the Altstadt, hoping to be cheered by the sight of its familiar banks, but the river was covered with debris and waste products, and she bicycled away from its stench through narrow, choked-up streets until she reached the Westtorgraben section of the loop and onto Frauentorgraben.

The mighty Nuremberg railroad station—the Hauptbahnhof at the Bahnhofsplatz—was now a wreckage of steel and stone, with upended girders sticking out of its charred and cloven facade. During her last visit, it had stood there like a neo-Gothic monument for the German railroad industry, housing two dozen platforms and providing a labyrinth of tunnels and underpasses for the pedestrians. Trains to every major city in Europe had stopped at the Hauptbahnhof, and long crowds had lined up at ticket booths or wandered around kiosks and food stalls at all hours of the day. Now the station looked like a decomposing monster covered by mud and slime, and Hannah was distraught at the senseless destruction of a behemoth that had once possessed form and function, albeit in the hated baroque style.

Her uncle's villa was in Luisanstrasse, more than a mile away, and Hannah pushed on to Dürrenhofstrasse and then went down the long stretch of Stephanstrasse, agreeably surprised at the number of relatively undamaged buildings that were now coming into view. A lot of them were flying American flags, and she assumed they had been taken over by the AMG to billet American troops. On reaching Luisanstrasse, she saw stars and stripes flying over her uncle's house and a GI with a rifle standing at the gate.

Where did her uncle go? She got off her bicycle and was thinking of asking the GI if he knew of Herr Werner von Thyssen's whereabouts when she saw a middle-aged woman in a printed summer dress cutting flowers in the small garden on the left side of the house. It took her a few seconds to realize that it was her aunt's close friend Ulrike for she had put on weight, and her hair had turned gray.

"I would like to speak to that lady," she said to the soldier.

He looked suspiciously at her dusty clothes and her battered suitcase tied to her bicycle rack with a rope.

"You wait here. I'll go and tell her," he said.

But Ulrike had already seen her and was waddling toward her, carrying her basket of flowers.

"Hannah, Hannah!" she cried and embraced her.

"You've lost weight, Hannah," she said, looking her over. "I've heard that food is scarce in Berlin."

Obviously you don't have that problem, thought Hannah, because Ulrike had put on at least fifty pounds since she had last seen her.

"You came to see your uncle, Hannah?" continued Ulrike. "That's so nice. He's very moody these days—in fact, ever since we lost the war. He will cheer up when he sees you."

"Where is he?" asked Hannah.

"We live in the basement," said Ulrike. "The Americans have taken over the rest of the house. Oh, don't let's stand here. Let's go inside."

I migrate from one basement to another, like a mouse or a rat, thought Hannah, as they walked through the narrow path in the garden to the steps leading to the basement.

Through an upstairs open window, she heard a baritone voice singing, "I'll be seeing you in all the familiar places." A head popped out of the window, and the singer shouted "*Wie geht es Ihnen,* Frau Ulrike?"

"*Gut, danke,*" said Ulrike, not looking at him.

He was a young, clean-cut-looking blond man, and there was no trace of conqueror's pride or arrogance on his face. He wanted to talk some more, but since he had exhausted his stock of German phrases, he looked at them and smiled until the two women reached the steps and disappeared from his view.

"Your uncle is in poor health, Hannah," said Ulrike as they were descending the steps. "The night when our enemies firebombed the old city, we were staying at the Deutscher Hof Hotel for the sixtieth birthday party of my cousin Heinrich, and your uncle collapsed after seeing the flames from our window. He so loved Nuremberg! He couldn't bear to see its churches and old monuments destroyed. His friend Dr. Fischer, who was also in the hotel, revived him. He told me that your uncle had a heart attack and would have died if he hadn't intervened."

She opened the door, and Hannah noticed that the basement was nicely furnished—a far cry from Herr Stumpfegger's cellar—and she saw her uncle sitting in a rocking chair reading a book—a heavy, leather-bound, and scholarly looking tome—as was his wont. He looked older and thinner, with deep creases around his cheeks cutting across his dueling scars. He put his book down for a moment, took off his reading glasses, and stared uncomprehendingly for a moment at the woman behind Ulrike.

"Hannah, Hannah…my child…you came to see me," he stuttered and broke into tears.

Hannah went over to him, not knowing what to say. She thought of him when he was young—a handsome, dashing man, wearing a monocle and a toothbrush moustache in the style of the Berlin dandy, who used to carry her in his arms and sing to her when she was tired from climbing or walking up rocky paths during their weekend outings. He was the only person who had cared for her as a child—her mother spent her time with one man or another in the free-living environment in Schwabing—bringing her toys and books and taking interest in her activities at school.

"*Alles ist kaputt!*" he said, looking up.

Hannah thought it was a neat way of summing up things. Berlin was now cinders and ashes, Nuremberg was a wasteland, Germany was divided, their national identity was fragmented, and their German pride was deflated.

She was about to say a few words of meaningless consolation when Ulrike intervened.

"Hannah has had a long journey, Werner," she said. "She needs to tidy up and have a little refreshment. She will talk to you later."

They're living together as man and wife, Hannah thought. Her aunt had passed away three years ago, and Ulrike, whose husband, a senior officer in the *Ordnungspolizei,* was away somewhere in Poland, had stepped into her shoes. They seemed happy together, thought Hannah, and she was glad that there was someone who would take care of the old man. Besides, she liked Ulrike for her common sense, practicality, and her ability to make the best of situations. She wondered for a moment if she should intrude into the cozy underground shelter they had built for themselves or look for a lodging somewhere else, preferably close to the Grand Hotel, where Eric Grossman would be staying. As if reading her thoughts, Ulrike put her arm around her and said, "I hope you will stay with us for a while, Hannah. It would make both of us very happy, particularly Werner. There are six rooms in the basement, and you can have the one where Werner keeps his World War One relics."

She took Hannah to the back of the house and showed her a large room lined with shelves containing caps, boots, maps, newspapers, and rows of leather-bound photo albums. It had a desk, two chairs, and two lamps.

"We hardly ever come into this room," said Ulrike. "I'll put a mattress in, and you'll be quite comfortable."

She then led her to the bathroom, explaining to her that they had to use cold water pumped from the nearby well, since the electricity hadn't been fully restored and the heating system hadn't been turned on.

"I like cold water from the well," replied Hannah.

After Ulrike had left, she drank the water by cupping her hands under the tap. She washed her face and body and brushed her hair, letting it hang loose. She then changed her clothes and went to the living room, where Ulrike had spread a repast for her on the coffee table. There was buttered toast, a piece of raisin cake, and lebkuchen cookies—the hallmark of the Nuremberg kitchen—with a pot of coffee.

Hannah was hungry, but she ate slowly in order not to give the impression she was starving.

"How are things in Berlin?" asked her uncle.

I can't tell him the truth, thought Hannah. I can't tell him about the rapes and the corpses strewn all over the Grey City.

"Berlin looks like Nuremberg," said Hannah. "Only a few buildings are left standing. People live in basements. And the city is now divided into four zones, each zone occupied by a conqueror."

Her uncle wanted details of specific districts belonging to each zone and was disappointed to hear that those areas where he and his friends used to live as kids were now under Russian control.

"I can't believe this; I can't believe this," he said, his face clouding with anguish.

"You should be thankful that Hannah lives in the American zone," said Ulrike, in an attempt to cheer up the old man.

"Not only do I live in the American zone, I work for the Americans," said Hannah.

A look of shock crossed the old man's face.

"It's hard to work for the enemy," he said after a while, his lips quivering. "But it's better to work for the Yanks than to work for the Russians, I suppose."

"I worked for the Russians also," said Hannah. "They were in control of the entire Berlin area before the zoning went into effect. They didn't treat me badly when I was working for them."

"People everywhere are the same," said Ulrike. "There are good people and bad people in every country."

"What work are you doing for the Yanks?" asked Werner, fixing his bright, piercing blue eyes on Hannah.

"Officially, I am a translator for Major Grossman of the American Propaganda Service," said Hannah. "He's here to cover the war-crimes trial. My real job is to make sketches of the defendants."

She didn't anticipate Werner's explosive reaction.

"The Allies too should be tried for war crimes," he yelled. "They should be prosecuted for intentionally devastating German cities, for destroying our entire civilization, and for the murder of millions of German civilians. In any war both sides commit atrocities, but one side cannot claim only the other side committed them. They are trying to disgrace and humiliate us by setting up these showcase trials..."

Overcome by emotion, he wasn't able to finish the sentence and started gasping and sputtering.

Ulrike got up, put her arm around him, and pleaded with him not to get excited, stroking his back and shoulders until the old man calmed down.

"Is that why you're here, Hannah?" he asked, after a few moments of silence. "I thought you had come here to see me."

"I took this opportunity to see you. I wouldn't have been able to get here from Berlin if it hadn't been for the Americans. I came here in one of their prisoner vans since there is no train or bus service from Berlin to here."

"Us philosophers have the hardest time accepting reality, I suppose," said her uncle, in a self-deprecatory tone of voice. "I am glad you're here with me, Hannah, regardless of what brought you here or who you're working for."

He means what he says, as always, thought Hannah, and he says what he means. He was always there for me, at my side during my times of crises—and I, I never got over my embarrassment of his being a Nazi, not the brawling, hate-filled Julius Streicher type but the charming, urbane intellectual out to save Germany by persuading his audience that Hitler was the strong leader destined to steer the country out of its dire straits.

"Let's go for our evening walk." Ulrike broke in, practical as ever.

She brought him his heather-mixture tweed jacket, his walking stick, his cap, and a book for reading while sitting on his favorite park bench. There was still daylight, and they walked through narrow streets and lanes until they reached a park next to the playground of a small school.

The trees in the park were covered with a fine silvery dust—caused by the airborne debris from the Altstadt, Hannah assumed—but there were shrub roses and lilies growing in wild profusion here and there, amid unsightly weeds and uncut grass. The old man made his way to his favorite wooden bench, opened his book—Hannah noticed with a twinge of distaste that it was Nietzsche's *Will to Power*—and proceeded to read.

The two women wanted to talk, and in order not to disturb him, they moved to another bench a few feet away. They sat together for a while in friendly silence, staring at the hazy pink sun dipping into the western horizon; they liked each other, even though their backgrounds were as different as the Berliner Dialekt of Hannah was from the Franconian speech of Ulrike.

"He wants to marry me," said Ulrike after a while. "I am still married to Karl, even though I don't know where he is."

"Is he a prisoner?"

"He was in a police brigade that was sent to Poland, as its chief. He was then transferred to Ukraine. I haven't heard from him for three years. I don't know if he's dead or alive. In the meantime, I've been sharing your uncle's bed. I need a man. Life is hard, and I always had a crush on your uncle. Am I being immoral, Hannah?"

Hannah was amused by the question, but at the same time she was touched by the naiveté of the woman sitting next to her.

"War has changed everything," said Hannah. "Berlin has changed; Nuremberg has changed. Our men have changed. Our women have changed. We cannot apply the same rules as before. If you like being with my uncle, don't let moral scruples bother you. We don't know what's there for us tomorrow. I've learned to live for the moment. Only the present counts."

"That's what I think too, even though I couldn't put it in words. How about you? Are you still with Emil?"

"I don't know where Emil is. Somewhere in Poland, I guess."

"I hope you stay with us for a while. Your uncle needs someone with brains to talk to. He has no friends. The Americans have arrested all the Nazis in the area. They left your uncle alone because of his heart condition. He spends his time putting his papers in order. He wants to publish his final book, but he needs assistance in putting it together. Maybe you can help."

"I'll help him," said Hannah, even though she wasn't sure how someone like her could be of help to a scholar like Werner, other than arranging his cushions for him or bringing him coffee.

"We live on the money the Americans pay us for rent," said Ulrike. "Your uncle used to get a generous allowance from the government, but the Americans stopped that."

"I will contribute to household expenses while I'm here," said Hannah.

"I wasn't thinking of that," said Ulrike. "Actually, food doesn't cost that much. My sister Frieda is the housekeeper for the Americans, and she brings us food three times a day from the upstairs pantry."

"Frieda works as a housekeeper? I can't believe that," said Hannah. Frieda was the wife of a powerful army-supplies contractor from the nearby town of Furth and used to live in a mansion in the suburb with captured Russians and Poles for servants.

"Her house was destroyed by the American army during the war. Her husband's factories were razed by bombs. That's why Frieda is working here. Her two daughters also. They work as maids."

Hannah felt that the world had turned topsy-turvy. She found it hard to picture Frieda, who used to own fur coats and diamonds and drove around in a Mercedes, working, along with her daughters, as a domestic.

"How do they feel about it?" she asked.

"The food is good, Frieda says. What she doesn't like is the attitude of the Americans toward her. She says they treat her and the girls as servants."

The nonfraternization policy is in effect here also, thought Hannah, the policy that maintains every German is evil and should be isolated like a plague carrier—such a far cry from the old days, those days at Bauhaus, when people from all over the world came to Weimar to hear the message of universal love and brotherhood that was the credo of the new art, when crowds gathered around Kandinsky to hear him acclaim that the function of art was to be transcendental, and color and line can be used to represent spiritual states of the human psyche. Those days were gone, Hannah realized, just as the Weimar Republic was gone, and the reality was what was before her: everything substantial had been reduced to detritus, and the Altstadt was the appropriate metaphor for the present Deutschland.

Her uncle cleared his throat loudly, looked at her, and said, "Hannah, sit next to me. I want to share a thought with you."

Hannah smiled because this was the way he always used to talk to her whenever he wanted to give her his insights into history, philosophy, and other arcane subjects that were of no interest to her. Dutifully, she got up, walked to his bench, and sat next to him.

"The phoenix rises from the ashes, Hannah," he said. "Germany will rise again and fulfill its destiny. The Americans don't want that to happen and are trying to prevent it by imposing democracy on the German people. Over the years, I've told you how I feel about democracy. I read to you, many years ago, my review of my friend Carl Schmitt's book in which I said that decisive action was possible only in a state led by a Führer. My views and Schmitt's views are more applicable than ever if we don't want Germany to be reduced to a weak, vacillating state governed by Jewish democratic thought."

Does he think I'm an intellectual or that I care for Carl Schmitt's views or about political theories in general? Hannah thought. She sensed she was in for a long stretch of unrelieved boredom and felt her neck and shoulder muscles begin to stiffen. But when she looked at him and saw the noble, silver-haired philosopher clutching his

Nietzsche with trembling hands, she felt a great tenderness toward him.

"I hear you are writing another book," she said and watched the pride of authorship send a diffused glow around his cheeks and mouth as she had expected.

"It's my autobiography, Hannah," he said. "As of now, it's in the diaries I've kept throughout my life. I need help to put it all together."

"Do you have a title for it?"

"I'm thinking of calling it the *Life of an Aryan*," he said, and his eyes, magnified through his spectacles, gleamed like balls of blue light.

They sat in silence for a while, and the older man hesitantly put forth a question. "How long will you be staying with us, Hannah?"

"I don't know how long they would want me here," she replied. "Six months, nine months, I don't know."

"Maybe you can help me put the book together during your spare time," he said. "I would like to finish it before I die."

"I'll do whatever you want me to do," Hannah responded. "I am a good typist, and I can organize things...I can translate from English, French, or Russian, if you want any help there."

"We will see," he said in a pleased tone. "All I can say is that I am glad you're here. It is like a godsend."

When they got back home, Frieda and her daughters, Claudia and Octavia, were there, with trays of food from the American kitchen. They exchanged hugs and kisses, and the two girls, eighteen and nineteen, pressed Hannah for details about life in Berlin.

"I've heard from the Americans that the Russians raped the women in Berlin," said Claudia in English, which the two older women didn't understand.

"We will talk about it later, when we're alone," said Hannah in English. "It's rude to speak in a language that the others don't understand."

The girls giggled, looked at each other, and, seeing the frowns on their mother's and aunt's faces, assumed solemn expressions.

"Aunt Hannah, I want to be an artist like you, and I want to talk to you about it," said Octavia, in German.

"I want to be a playwright," said Claudia.

"Hannah will be here for quite a while, girls," said Ulrike. "There will be plenty of opportunities for you to talk to her."

While waiting to be summoned by Eric Grossman, Hannah spent her mornings with her uncle and the afternoons in the company of the girls. After listening to the old man, in his attempt to give her a foundation in German political history and philosophy as a prerequisite in helping him with his book, ramble on about Wagner, Nietzsche, Treitschke, Houston Chamberlain, and their *Weltanschauung*, Hannah would go for a long bicycle ride to clear her head. On her return, the girls would drop by after lunch was served to the Americans upstairs, ready to show off their work and eager for a word of praise from her.

Octavia's drawings came as a surprise to Hannah—they had the thick outlines that were reminiscent of the expressionists, especially Käthe Kollwitz.

"Where did you learn to draw like this?" asked Hannah.

"I saw that style in a painting of Russian soldiers in *Lustige Blätter*, and I liked it," she said.

This was art that was forbidden by the Führer, but it had found its way into the foremost of propaganda magazines of the Third Reich, thought Hannah. She was amazed that a young girl, a genuine product of Hitler's Germany, should choose to express in the deliberately clumsy, tortured style that was anathema to the art commissars of the Third Reich. No one can stop the insidious power of great art, she realized, not even the Führer. This feeling was reinforced when she heard Claudia talk about her play, *Underground Folk*. It dealt with cellar dwellers scrounging for food, obviously based on what she had seen in the old city of Nuremberg, but the way the characters acted and spoke reminded Hannah of the Dadaist plays she had seen in Berlin after the First World War. These girls, and not my uncle's phoenix of the future, are the new Germany, she thought.

Hannah spent the evenings, after dinner, with Ulrike and Frieda, and the three women would talk about their concerns about the new world they found themselves in.

"It looks like we have to survive without men," said Frieda, whose husband, Hermann, an ardent Nazi, had fled to Paraguay to escape arrest by the Americans. She hadn't heard from him for months and wasn't sure if he was alive.

"Whatever happened to German men?" philosophized Ulrike. "I see them picking up cigarette stubs thrown by Americans in the street. I see them cringe when Americans walk by. They're no longer men but slaves."

"I saw the SS men at the Palace of Justice do the menial work that once was done by slave labor—the Poles and Russians," said Hannah, wondering at her own innate cruelty in twisting the knife in the wound. She wanted to hurt them, she realized, because they had been the proud wives of arrogant Nazis, while she had lived in perpetual fear of being beaten up by the Gestapo or sent to prison. But the women didn't seem to mind her remark and, in fact, were supportive of her.

"It isn't like the old times, for sure, when the Führer was around," said Frieda.

"The last time Hannah came here, Werner was presented with a gold medal by the Führer," said Ulrike. "We watched a huge parade at the Adolf Hitler Platz."

I've suppressed that memory, Hannah thought. Five years ago, Nuremberg had been the quintessential Nazi town, dubbed by Hitler as "the most Aryan of German cities." The Nazis held their annual rallies there, and the Hauptmarkt—the place where the Christmas holidays were so joyously celebrated in earlier years—had been renamed

Adolf Hitler Platz and was the site where the Nazi leaders gave lengthy orations at the end of rallies to the big crowd of vociferously applauding followers.

Her uncle's birthday had coincided with the annual rally, and he had been honored with the presentation of the German National Prize for Scholars at a reception presided by Hitler at the Deutscher Hof Hotel. Her uncle had invited her to a family breakfast at the hotel that morning, attended by his wife, her relatives, her close friend Ulrike Schultz, and Ulrike's sister Frieda. The breakfast had been typically German, very leisurely, with cold cuts, sausages, cheeses, and a variety of loaves and rolls, followed by pastry and cakes, coffee, and liqueurs. Speeches had been made by family members praising the old patriarch's scholarly contribution to the Third Reich, not the least of which was the invention of the phrase "Das Dritte Reich." When it came to Hannah's turn, she, conscious of the fact that she was an outcast and a poor relation, had spoken of her uncle's kindness and generosity to her over the years and the good times she'd had with him and his wife when they went on hiking tours in the Thuringian forest or made journeys down the Rhine and the Danube. The old man had beamed and smiled at her and, when the breakfast was over, apologized to her that he could not take her to see the Führer and hinted that she should depart before the arrival of his entourage at the hotel. Hannah had hugged him, assured him that she understood his predicament, and left with Ulrike, who had wanted to watch the festivities at the Adolf Hitler Platz. They were soon engulfed by crowds of flag-waving Germans cheering the goose-stepping columns of the SS, SA, Labor Service, Hitlerjugend, and the Wehrmacht as they marched by. Hannah had decided she wouldn't cheer, but amid the shouts of "Heil Hitler" from all around her and nudges from Ulrike, she too had had to join the mad chorus.

"We all shouted, 'Heil Hitler!'" said Hannah bitterly, still bothered by that memory.

"The American boys upstairs now shoot at the busts of the Führer with their pistols," said Frieda sadly.

"Werner had filled a room upstairs with Hitler memorabilia—statues, photographs, signed letters, uniforms, and such things," explained Ulrike. "The Americans have made it into a shooting gallery."

"When are they going to go away?" asked Frieda. "When will we get our country back?"

It was a question that was foremost in their minds. Hannah was hoping for the resurrection of her old Germany, the Germany of Weimar and Bauhaus—or even the older one of the Schwabing days. Her two companions, on the other hand, were nostalgic for the Germany of the Nazi era, when they had plenty of worldly goods and held their heads high as members of the ruling class.

"I'm worried about my girls," said Frieda. "They go out every night with different Americans."

"I thought the Americans weren't supposed to socialize with German girls," said Hannah.

"Oh, they go out at night, after eight o'clock, when the military police turn a blind eye," said Frieda.

"With the men upstairs?" asked Hannah.

"No," said Frieda. "Those men are officers, and they keep themselves aloof from us. They date only English, French, or American women. Our girls go out with the enlisted men, like the guards who stand in front of the house. Those men are closer to their age, anyway. The girls, with their friends, wait for them in the park and go dancing and partying all night. They come home late."

"The soldiers give them cigarettes, chocolates, and nylon stockings," said Ulrike. "It's a shame our girls have to do this."

They are doing what I did after the First World War, thought Hannah. A montage of images—jazz music, wild dance steps, and men in uniforms pressing their bodies against her—flashed through her mind.

"Don't blame the girls," she said. "After all, you smoke the cigarettes they bring home."

"And Werner loves the chocolates," said Ulrike with a laugh.

But it was not a happy laugh, for the women sensed that their lives had no direction or purpose, and they weren't used to living from day to day, uncertain what the next day would be like.

That night Hannah took a long time to fall asleep, her mind drifting from episode to episode in the past. She tried to find an uplifting moment or a theme—other than the Bauhaus days—during the five decades of her existence defined by wars, totalitarian states, famines, rapes, humiliations, and loss of faith in the entirety of mankind. She tossed and turned in bed, counted all her lovers, her paintings, her students, her teachers, and the restaurants and nightclubs she had been to—until she grew weary of her past, and blackness engulfed her.

TEN

THE SCREAM

The next morning she had a surprise visit from Eric Grossman. She was sitting in her uncle's study listening to the old man's account of Wagner's influence on Nietzsche.

"Wagner, in his *Religion and Art,* developed a new religion for his countrymen based on Christianity without its Jewish elements. He believed Germany would be doomed if Aryan blood was contaminated by the Jewish race. Germans were the chosen people, and our greatness was to be achieved only by ridding ourselves of the Jewish bacilli in our bloodstream. Nietzsche was influenced by Wagner, but he advocated the transformation of Germany by the creation of a stronger, higher level of man. He rejected all the commonly held values of Western civilization and exhorted men to become hard, to live dangerously, and to wage wars. He had no use for Christian values, declaring that God was dead. His Übermensch was a brute—glorifying power. When the Führer took control in 1933, my philosopher friend Alfred Baeumler correctly predicted that the Germany of the future would be built out of the writings of Nietzsche."

The air in the room is suffocating, thought Hannah. Her uncle had closed all the windows and was wearing two sweaters to keep the morning chill away from his old bones.

"The uninformed say that the Nazis were illiterate thugs and unthinking brutes," continued Werner, his magnified eyes gleaming blue behind his glasses. "Not true, Hannah. Many philosophers, some of them my most esteemed contemporaries, know that to be wrong. The best among them—I am talking of Heidegger, Schmitt, and Baeumler—openly embraced the Führer because they knew that he was the manifestation of Nietzsche's Übermensch."

I don't care, thought Hannah. I haven't read Nietzsche and have no intention of reading him. I can't believe that the scary-looking Hitler and the fat Nazi monsters around him were supermen—they were more like toads or hyenas.

She was wondering whether it was such a good idea, after all, to help her uncle with his book. All sorts of questions were popping up in her mind. Why hadn't her uncle been arrested by the Americans like other Nazis? Did he cut a deal with them? Why did he want to write this book instead of distancing himself from Hitler? And why did he want her to be involved in this gruesome endeavor?

She was startled from her thoughts by the sound of a car coming up the driveway and, on looking up, saw Grossman talking to the sentry.

"Uncle, the American man I work for is here to see me," she said. "I have to speak to him."

She saw his mouth tighten and tried to soothe his hurt feelings. "I will come back after talking to him," she said and left the room.

Eric walked toward her with long strides, smiling broadly.

"The guard didn't know who you were," he said.

"You should have asked to see my uncle, Werner von Thyssen," she said. "My name isn't on the list yet."

"I picked up a few things from the army store," he said, extending a package toward her.

She asked him if he wanted to come in and meet her family.

"Yes, Hannah. We aren't supposed to fraternize with you, as you know," he said. "Nevertheless, I would like to say hello to your folks. What the hell, I can always come up with an excuse if anyone brings up the subject."

She brought him to her uncle's study and saw the two men uncomfortably staring at each other for a few seconds before Grossman stretched out his hand. Her uncle took it reluctantly and said in hesitant English, "How do you do, Major Grossman?" He had spent six months in Oxford to study philosophy under F. H. Bradley when he was a student, and he spoke in the cultivated voice of an Oxonian.

"There's no need to be formal, sir. Please call me Eric," said Grossman.

"You see Nuremberg in a pitiable state, Eric," said her uncle. "It used to be called the most German of all cities, and now it's reduced to dust and ashes."

"The city will be rebuilt, I'm sure," said Grossman. "Not only this city but every other city in Germany."

Hannah liked the way he said it, his optimism kept in check by his awareness to be not overly ingratiating. She began to think of him as a very nice man and a smart one, and this lightened her mood considerably. She looked at him and smiled, establishing a rapport that had never been there before.

"I hear you are about to begin a war-crimes trial," said her uncle, still gloomy and unmollified by the visitor's charm.

"It's going to start tomorrow. That's why I came down here. I want Hannah to get her clearance and her badge so that she can come to the trial with me tomorrow."

"The victor always decides these things," said her uncle sadly. "As they say in Latin, *vae victis.*"

"I don't know any Latin, but you're right about the victors deciding the fate of the conquered," said Grossman. "I wish things weren't that way. After all, the Germans decided the fate of the countries they conquered—Poland, Czechoslovakia, Austria, France. They shot the resisters without trial. We Americans don't do things that way."

Werner's jaw dropped, and his face turned gray. He mumbled something about having to take his medicine and shuffled off, a defeated old man.

Hannah and Eric looked at each other in embarrassed silence for a few seconds.

"I didn't mean to upset your uncle," Eric said.

"I know you didn't mean to," replied Hannah, "but you did. We might as well leave now."

"I guess so."

They sat in the back of the car without looking at each other, neither sure about the other, the earlier feeling of rapport between them having vanished. Eric wondered if Hannah was a camouflaged Nazi, agreeing with her uncle's political views when she was closeted with him in his study and putting on a mask when she came out of there. She, in turn, thought of him as a fan of Henry Morgenthau, the vengeful Jew bent on humiliating the fallen Aryan enemy.

When they reached the Palace of Justice, Hannah was surprised by the number of reporters and photographers who had gathered there. Representatives of every race and nation from the four corners of the world seemed to have assembled on Fürther Strasse to see justice being meted out to Goering and his collaborators. Hannah saw Chinese, Africans, and Jews wearing yarmulkes taking pictures of the bomb-damaged Palace of Justice, of the crowds, or of an occasional German who was willing to be photographed.

"I didn't know this was going to be a world event," said Hannah.

"It's the first trial of its kind," said Eric with a smile. "The world wants to see the evil Nazis."

There was a sudden commotion, and the photographers began streaming like lemmings toward the prison house next door.

"They're bringing in the war prisoners to read the charges to them," said someone in French.

A few minutes later, the prisoners appeared in tandem—Goering, Streicher, Hess, Ribbentrop and the others—arrogantly holding their heads high, in spite of their handcuffs and the prison guards surrounding them. At the sight of their sneering faces, Hannah lost control of herself. All the rage suppressed for years erupted out of her, and she screamed, her first high-pitched cry followed by encores of wordless outrage.

The cameramen turned their attention to her, but Eric shielded her by placing his back between them and her and quickly walked her over to a side street.

She calmed down soon, wiped her tears, and turned to her companion.

"I'm sorry for making a spectacle of myself," she said.

"It's fine with me," he said.

"I don't think I'm right for this job," she said. "I've suffered under these men for too many years. You should get someone else, Eric."

"On the contrary," he said. "Your scream convinced me you are the right partner for me. It will reverberate in my ears for a long time."

The tension between them was no longer there, and it was replaced by a bond of trust and understanding.

"Let's get your badge," he said. "Our work is just beginning."

ELEVEN

THE CHARGES

On the day of the trial, Hannah got up early in the morning. She lit a candle because there was no electricity at that hour and washed herself using cold water from the well. She got dressed in clothes she had borrowed from Octavia—a white blouse, a strawberry-colored sweater, and a gray woolen skirt. She made breakfast without disturbing anyone in the house and, after leaving a note for Ulrike on the dining table, left on her bicycle.

In the hazy November dawn, the devastated city looked grayish, dirty, and sullen, like an old woman indifferent to the feelings she evoked in people who passed her by. "I should paint this scene, capture this mood, this evanescent reality—that's what a true artist would be doing," said Hannah to herself. But she knew deep down that in her present frame of mind she couldn't paint anything other than posters, and even to contemplate the possibility of doing creative work was analogous to a sterile woman dreaming of giving birth to a child.

Old frauen were now coming out of their subterranean lairs to scavenge for food, pieces of coal, or cigarette butts—anything they could use for themselves or for barter with other Germans. They wore rags and looked ill and malnourished, but there was no anger in their faces, only deeply etched lines of resignation.

As she bicycled on toward Fürther Strasse, she saw lots more of them, and even some young women, wearing dresses made from old bedsheets and pillowcases. Just as in the case of Berlin, Nuremberg had become a city of women—the only difference being that these women carried themselves with dignity and did not bear the stigmata of the Berlin rape victims.

As she watched them, the very notion of the Nuremberg trial seemed absurd to Hannah. The war was over, and the Germans—especially the women—had been made homeless and turned into a motley crowd of scroungers and rag pickers. The countless tombstones she saw in the lawns and backyards and in the parks and junkyards around her bore mute testimony to those whose lives had been destroyed by the relentless bombing carried out by the British Lancasters and Mosquitos. There was no need to have a showcase trial that put twenty-one Nazis on the dock to exhibit the fairness and impartiality of the Allied judicial system. Why not shoot them or put them in jail for life on a remote island somewhere? What purpose did a trial serve, since severe punishment had already been meted out to the German people collectively?

It was with these thoughts running through her head that she entered the grounds of the Palace of Justice and parked her bicycle in the space allotted to translators, courtroom artists, and photographers. A couple of Sherman tanks manned by helmeted soldiers stood in front of the courthouse. Behind sandbags, American military police crouched with machine guns, their eyes scanning everyone who was entering the grounds as though they expected the Volkssturm or the Werwolves to suddenly appear with the intent to free the prisoners.

The crowds, however, ignored the tanks and the gunners behind sandbags, and some even jostled against the patrolling GIs. The scene reminded Hannah of a carnival, with loud voices joking or asking questions in a medley of tongues, while hundreds of cameras clicked away, taking pictures for posterity.

The doors of the court opened at nine thirty, and Hannah was swept upstairs by the onrushing crowd to the second floor. A soldier posted at the door looked at her pass and gave her a floor plan and a booklet giving thumbnail sketches of the defendants.

The trial room was built like a Roman amphitheater, with rows of rising seats looking down at the sunken center stage. The walls of the room were paneled in dark wood, and in conjunction with the heavy dark-green drapes and the old-fashioned coffered wooden ceiling, the ambience of the room was gloomy and forbidding.

The press gallery, Hannah's destination, was the nicest part of the courtroom, with seats that could be tilted up and pushed flat against the backrest to ease the passage of new arrivals. Its armrests contained outlets for headphones and had a dial with markings of *S, 1, 2, 3,* and *4.* The man next to her, a Swiss journalist, explained to her that one of the innovations introduced at the trial was simultaneous interpretation in four languages—English, French, German, and Russian—and showed her how to rotate the dial on the armrest to select the language of her choice—*S* stood for the language of the speaker of the moment, and the numerals were for selecting the language of interpretation.

The defendants were led in one by one—Goering first, Hess next, followed by others in a hierarchical order that she couldn't quite figure out. The prisoners, looking old and gray in that glaring light, bowed to Goering, who still conducted himself like the *Reichsmarschall* he used to be, and shuffled across to the wooden benches assigned to them.

"How low have the mighty fallen," said the man next to her.

Indeed, Hannah felt that a morality play was being staged in the courtroom for the benefit of the world at large, with the usual themes of such plays—the victory of good over evil, the downfall of the wicked and their subsequent chastisement, and the triumphant meting out of stern justice.

She, along with others in the gallery, stood up at the entrance of the judges, who solemnly filed into the room and moved to their pre-assigned seats facing the defendants. The marshal called the court to order. A hushed silence followed, and the president of the tribunal, a distinguished-looking Englishman, came forward. He spoke a few words about the unique and unprecedented nature of the trial and reminded everyone to maintain the necessary decorum in the court-room. He was followed by an American, a tall, thin, scholarly looking man, who read the first part of the indictment, the conspiracy by the defendants to commit crimes.

As she heard the details, it became apparent to Hannah that it was Adolf Hitler who was really on trial. The charges that were being read—the rule under the *Führerprinzep*, the institution of a totalitarian regime, the use of the "master race" philosophy that led to the perse-cution of Jews, the annexation of Austria, Poland, and Czechoslovakia, the creation of slave labor in these countries, and myriad other evil deeds—were perpetrated by Hitler and constituted the core agenda of the Nazi Party of which he was the head. The whole world knew that, thought Hannah, and the charge of conspiracy seemed absurd to her. Conspirators were supposed to work in the dark, hiding their intentions from the world until the dagger was unsheathed, the shot fired from the gun, or the bomb exploded inside the left-behind suit-case. Here there were no secrets, since everything had been brought out in the open—the fate of the Jews, the wars against Poland, Russia, and the Western powers, and the role of Germany as the overlord of Eastern Europe—in speeches by Hitler, Goebbels, Goering, and doz-ens of gauleiters.

She stopped listening as the American voice at the podium droned on and occupied herself by making a few sketches of the poker-faced defendants or listening to the indictment in different languages by switching channels, surprised by the fluency of the si-multaneous interpreters in using the right phrases even for technical terms.

When the court adjourned for a few minutes, she declined the invitation of her neighbor to join him "for a smoke outside" but hung around in the corridors hoping to see Eric. She finally saw him in a group of American officers, talking away in his impassioned manner, using his hands with their shapely fingers to make a point now and then. When he noticed her, he excused himself from the group and came over to her.

"Those are army psychiatrists, and their job is to interview the defendants," he said, with excitement radiating from his eyes. "They agreed to let me read the transcripts of their interviews with them."

"No doubt they would turn out to be monsters," said Hannah, teasingly. "Latter-day Draculas from the land of vampires."

"Seriously, Hannah, what I have learned so far is that they have no feelings of guilt or regret about the harm they've inflicted on the rest of the world. That's what bothers me. I want to learn more about them. One of the psychiatrists said he would take me along with him as he visits them in their cells."

"Can I come too?"

"No, Hannah. The rules wouldn't allow that. But I'll tell you my impressions when we meet the next time."

"When will that be?"

"Tomorrow evening, I guess. I am going through a lot of documents tonight that the prosecutors have passed on to me. I am friends with one of them, Thomas Dodd, who will soon be presenting the case for the prosecution."

When Hannah went back to the courtroom, a French prosecutor was going through details of the second count—namely, war crimes carried out by the Wehrmacht, the police, and the SS against the French, Danish, Dutch, and Belgian people. He spoke of countless civilians being murdered and thrown into charnel pits, the deliberate starvation of thousands of others, the enslavement of able-bodied men and women and their subsequent deportation to German factories and camps, and the maltreatment and murder of prisoners of war. He was controlled in his delivery, giving facts and figures in a calm, methodical manner, and Hannah found herself weeping at the crudeness and brutality evinced by her countrymen. She wished her uncle was with her and wondered if he would still quote from Nietzsche about the blond beast of prey, the magnificently amoral man avidly prowling round for spoil and victory, proud of his will to destroy.

The man sitting next to her took her hand and gently pressed it.

"Pretty gruesome, isn't it?" he whispered.

Hannah extricated her hand from his.

"Are you German?" he asked. "You look German."

Hannah ignored him.

"I'm Swiss but come from German stock," he went on. "My grandfather was born in Frankfurt. We Germans are a bloodthirsty lot, aren't we?"

"I wouldn't know. I'm Jewish."

She said it to shock him, and the lie had the desired effect. He shrank from her and moved to a seat far away from her during a break in the court proceedings. I should remember this trick, thought Hannah. It's an effective ploy to drive away people like him who bother me.

The next prosecutor, a Russian, continued with the reading of the indictment and launched into the Nazi massacres in Poland and Russia. Hannah was stunned by their magnitude—four million exterminated in Auschwitz, a million and a half in Majdanek, a hundred thousand in Roveno, two hundred thousand in Odessa, and on and on, until she gave up adding the numbers because they were so large. He didn't say anything in the "j'accuse" mode, and it wasn't obvious who the culprits were, since the defendants were listening impassively and gave no indication that they were responsible for these acts. If they weren't responsible, who was the culprit? The trial seemed like an *Alice in Wonderland* episode, with no witnesses or clear pinning of guilt on an individual. The defendants formed a cabal, the prosecutor said, and the cabal was responsible for the crimes. Hanna thought the idea of calling the defendants a cabal was ludicrous, to say the least. A cabal was a secret political clique or faction, but these defendants were the legally appointed functionaries of a government elected by the people.

The next speaker, another Russian, was more explicit in assigning culpability. He blamed the Wehrmacht for the destruction of Russia—six hundred thousand buildings razed to the ground in Stalingrad, Leningrad, and other cities, seventeen hundred towns and seventy thousand villages despoiled or denuded by the German Army as it marched into the interior of Russia, and twenty-five million Russians, bereft of homes and scrounging for food and shelter, dying of malnutrition and starvation. No wonder the Russian soldiers had gone on a raping spree in Berlin, thought Hannah. They were only avenging the brutal crimes that had been done to their people by the Germans. She sketched the two generals on the defendant's bench, Wilhelm Keitel and Alfred Jodl, as they stared at the prosecutor with expressionless faces.

The proceedings soon adjourned, and Hannah hastily left the courtroom to escape the visions of the dead that had been crowding around her in that dark, mausoleum-like chamber.

She bicycled at a brisk pace until her calf muscles began to ache, when she slowed down a bit. She went around the Altstadt a couple of times seeking old landmarks, and her heart sank at the sight of the black, burned-out ruins where the house of Albrecht Durer, with its intricate motif of crisscrossed red beams over its white facade, had once stood. And the Hauptmarkt, where the Christkindlmarkt used to be held during the Christmas season, was a wasteland of rubble and rotting garbage. As she stood in front of it, trying to superimpose the old layout of the place with the reeking mess that stretched before her, a childhood memory came to her: she was standing in the same spot, thirty-five years ago, with her uncle and aunt, watching the Christmas angel recite a prologue from the gallery of the Frauenkirche prior to the ceremonial opening of the market for Christmas shoppers. The three of them had then wandered over to the food stalls displaying a variety of cookies and cakes, fruits made out of marzipan, and figurines made from prunes—a specialty that the stall owners called the "Nuremberg Plum People."

Hannah had run from stall to stall, trying to make up her mind which cookies to buy from the money that her uncle had given her, to his barely concealed amusement. But that warm, soothing remembrance did not last long and was soon replaced by a darker one of hopelessness and despair caused by the bleakness of her surroundings. We bombed them, they bombed us, and the algebra of war left its equations to be solved by survivors, she thought. She rode aimlessly for a while, ashamed of being a German and wishing she had been born a Congolese or a Tahitian instead of being a member of the "master race."

When she came home, Ulrike, Frieda, and her uncle were having dinner. They welcomed her warmly and asked her to sit down at the table, where a place next to her uncle had been kept vacant for her.

"How did the trial go, Hannah?" asked her uncle, after he offered her a glass of wine, which no doubt came from the American cellar upstairs.

The dreaded question paralyzed her, even though she knew it was the first question he would ask.

"It was very formal and legal, with prosecutors from four countries speaking in three different languages. There were simultaneous interpreters, and you could hear their translations on headphones."

The ladies were curious about simultaneous interpretation—as Hannah had hoped they would be—and the next few minutes were spent in explaining the settings on the dials on each chair and the ease with which one could hear translated words even as the speaker was uttering them.

Her uncle waited patiently and then targeted her with barb-like questions.

"What are the charges?" he asked.

"Conducting aggressive wars, destroying populations of invaded countries, setting up a Führer state, crimes against Jews…"

"How are we different from Russia?" he asked. "Stalin is more of a tyrant than our Führer was. He sent people to correctional labor camps, and more than a million people were murdered in his Great Purge in the early thirties. He probably ran the worst police state in history. He would set quotas for arrests and deportation to gulags for his commissars—"

His anger had risen to a crescendo as he was speaking, and now he was shouting his words. Ulrike, afraid he would collapse, rose from her seat to go over to him, but he controlled himself and waved her down.

"Every country has its own skeletons in the closet," he said in a calmer voice, turning to Hannah. "It was the British who introduced concentration camps doing the Boer Wars at the turn of the century. Thousands died in those camps. They used a scorched earth policy, burning down Boer farms and crops in an effort to create a famine. Did anybody put Lord Kitchener on trial and call him a war criminal? Everybody hates us, we are the whipping boy. You don't seem to realize that."

"The tribunal assured the defendants they would be given a fair trial," said Hannah.

"Mark my words, Hannah. They're going to hang every one of them," he said.

Hannah didn't want him to go on like this, his face red, his eyes glinting like icebergs behind his glasses, his silver hair rising at the back of his neck like that of an arctic wolf.

"I don't know politics or history like you do, Uncle," she said softly. "I am only doing the job of a courtroom artist, making sketches of the defendants most of the time, especially of Goering. He has lost a lot of weight, and he looks fit and tough."

The two women were fascinated by Goering's loss of weight.

"The last time I saw him in Nuremberg, he looked like a baby elephant wearing white trousers," said Ulrike.

"The last time I saw him, our Hermann was literally bursting out of his uniform," said Frieda. "How did he lose all that weight?"

"I don't know. Maybe it's his being in prison. He couldn't get his big meals there."

"Maybe I should go to prison too, if it would make me look thin," said Ulrike. "But Werner wouldn't like me if I got thin."

They all chuckled, including Werner, whose glare gave way to a roguish twinkle, and the tension between them vanished.

"It's hard to believe," said Frieda, "but I once had a body just like my daughters. My waistline was twenty-seven inches."

"I was always a little on heavy side," said Ulrike. "Unlike Hannah, who hasn't gained an ounce over all these years."

"Hannah takes after my aunt Mathilde," said Werner, with a tinge of pride in his voice. "Mathilde looked tall, straight, and slim even in her seventies. She was an aristocrat, and she looked the part. Her mother—that is, my grandmother—was a daughter of the von Herbersteins of Austria. Did you know that, Hannah?"

She had heard it a hundred times before, but to please the old man, she shook her head. He launched into their genealogy, going two centuries back, while the women, bored but not wanting to show their boredom, made appropriate interjections and went on eating their food. After the last glass of wine was finished, Werner rose from the table and went to his library, and the three women began to clean up the dining table and put away the uneaten food.

TWELVE

JACKSON SPEAKS

Hannah rose late the next morning and got to the courthouse just as the trial was resuming.

She found a vacant seat in the rear of the press gallery and turned on the headphones to hear the defendants plead guilty or not guilty to the charges of the indictment. Goering was called as the first defendant by the judge. He proceeded to make a speech, but the judge didn't allow him to continue. So Goering pleaded *nicht schuldig*, and this refrain was followed by the rest of the defendants.

The judge then asked the prosecution to present its case. A man who looked like Perry Mason—Hannah was an avid fan of Erle Stanley Gardner's and had read all his novels, beginning with *The Case of the Velvet Claws*—walked to the podium and began speaking in a mellifluous voice. She learned from her neighbor that the speaker was Robert H. Jackson, a Supreme Court justice of the United States.

Her first impression of him was that he was from another century—he wore a pinstriped suit with a vest and carried a pocket watch with a gold chain looped through a buttonhole, and his thick black hair was parted neatly on the side and swept back. All he needed was a monocle to pass for a German banker straight out of *Buddenbrooks*.

This impression was fortified by the slow, measured cadences of his speech and his use of language, which reminded her of Edmund Burke's parliamentary speeches she had studied in Patrick O'Farrell's English class.

"The wrongs that we seek to condemn and punish have been so calculated, so malignant, and so devastating that civilization cannot tolerate their being ignored, because it cannot survive their being repeated," she heard him say and remembered a similar quotation from Burke: "All that is necessary for the triumph of evil is that good men do nothing."

Jackson did not present tables and statistics like the French and Russian prosecutors had done before him but spoke in a loftier vein of the evil that had enshrouded Germany during the Nazi years. "Never before in legal history has an effort been made to bring within the scope of a single trial the developments of a decade covering a whole continent and involving a score of nations, countless individuals, and innumerable events," she heard him say.

She felt soothed by his voice as it rose, crashed, subsided, and rose again, like the waves rolling out on a beach. Initially she paid no attention to the actual content of his words, captivated as she was by his oratorical flights. She then caught on to certain themes, patterns of thought that were not present in previous arguments by the prosecution. One was that only the top officials of the Nazi party, and nobody else—not the millions of party members at large, and certainly not the German people—were the guilty ones in the eyes of Americans. The other was that the Nazi elite had drafted a sinister master plan, a blueprint for the conquest of vast territories in the east for occupation by the master race, following the enslavement of the native populations and the extermination of Jews in those areas. He said he had documentary evidence of such a plan, and Hannah was pleased to hear that. Eric's quest will soon be over, she thought, and he would have the gratification of knowing that his conjecture had been proven right.

When the court adjourned for the day, she saw Eric waiting at the door with his usual cheerful smile.

"What do you think of Jackson?" he asked her.

"I like his oratory, but I'm confused by the message he is sending."

"You're not the only one," he said.

"He says the guilty ones are the top-level Nazis, and the German people do not share their guilt. He says that's the way the Americans feel about it. If that's the case, how does one explain the nonfraternization policy toward Germans? Or the posters proclaiming German guilt pasted everywhere? And in regard to punishment, he says only the top-level Nazis will be punished. But you know that the whole country has been punished already by the destruction of its cities, by starving its people, and by carving it up into zones."

"I wouldn't take Jackson seriously, if I were you," said Eric.

"What does that mean?" responded Hannah.

"We will talk about it—not here but over a drink at my hotel," he said.

They got into his car and drove to the Grand Hotel, past the slag heap that once had been the queen bee among German railway stations.

"I don't like staying in this hotel," said Eric as they got out of the car. "It's too stuffy for me. Only officers are allowed to live here. Every morning, at breakfast, I see through the glass windows hungry Germans scrounging for food in garbage cans, and it makes me sick."

"Am I allowed to come in?" she asked him.

"You have a court pass," he said. "The sentries have been told to admit anyone with a court pass."

They were now at the entrance near the Marble Room, and sounds of revelry mingled with the loud playing of Hollywood tunes on an accordion greeted them.

"Can we go elsewhere?" she asked him, for she didn't want to be in a place where German guests were unwelcome.

"It's too noisy here, anyway," he said, sensing her reluctance. "Let's drive around and find a place where we can talk."

He went to the bar, got two bottles of beer, and got back into the car with her. They drove past the old city, where homeless folks were cooking meals over wood fires.

"It's pathetic," said Eric. "I've never seen anything like this before."

"I guess not," she said. "You've never had such large-scale devastation inside your country."

They drove on in silence until he found a bench in a small park. He opened the beers with a Swiss Army Knife that he had in the pocket of his uniform and asked her if she minded drinking from the bottle.

"Berlin women are used to it," she said.

The beer was without taste, and looking at the label, she saw that it was an American brand. She felt nostalgic for beer from Munich or Düsseldorf, something she had not tasted for months.

Seeing that her companion was moodily playing with the neck of his bottle, she asked him, "You said you wanted to talk to me, Eric. Isn't this the right time?"

"I guess so," he said. "Your comments about Jackson are right on the mark. All he has to do is to look around to see how Germans have been punished for the misdeeds of the Nazis. The US policy until now has been one of collective punishment for collective guilt. Jackson doesn't want to acknowledge that. He wants to come up with a justification for an international trial of the defendants, and he's put together a set of counts that have no legal standing in international law. Jackson didn't go to law college and doesn't have a degree in law. In America, men of his type are called country lawyers. Jackson rose in his profession because he's a crowd-pleaser, but the problem with him is that he gets carried away by his own rhetoric. Many members of the American law team are disturbed by his way of conducting this trial."

"I thought you would be happy to hear Herr Jackson talk about the Nazi master plan," she said.

He laughed.

"What's funny?" she asked. "Why did you laugh?"

"It's the way you refer to him as Herr Jackson instead of Justice Jackson...it's so strange."

"I can see why it may sound strange to you. To continue with my point, Justice Jackson did say repeatedly that he had documents that will prove his case."

"He wasn't being truthful. My friend Thomas Dodd doesn't think there is any master plan. He thinks Hitler did things on the spur of the moment. Jackson, after reading *Mein Kampf*, has convinced himself that the Nazi elite has drawn up a plan to implement the ideas contained in that book. In fact, he had written an earlier report to President Truman talking about a Nazi master plan. I was shocked by his repeated reference to it in his speech yesterday to prove his charge of conspiracy."

"But how about the documents?"

"He doesn't have any documents to prove his case. Thomas Dodd says all that Jackson has is the Hossbach memorandum, which deals with the minutes of a meeting that took place in 1937 between Hitler, Goering, Von Neurath, and others on Germany's need for living space, raw materials, oil fields, and the like. Hitler did most of the talking. The minutes were written by a Colonel Hossbach but not signed by him, and Dodd doubts its value as evidence."

"Nothing else?"

"No. We couldn't find any plans for enslavement of millions of Poles and Russians or for the mass murder of Jews, in spite of what Jackson was saying. I'm sure there is a blueprint somewhere, but we haven't been able to find it. We've to search for it, and eventually we'll locate it."

They sat there in silence for a while in the dark November night, watching fireflies dancing a few feet away from them. Hannah felt sorry for her young knight errant and hoped that something would turn up that would boost up his mood.

After few moments, he offered to drive her home.

"My bicycle is in the courthouse," she said. "I need it to get to work tomorrow."

"I'll have a driver pick you up tomorrow," he said as they walked toward his car.

THIRTEEN

COURTROOM FATIGUE

The next few days of the trial were given to a lengthy and boring discourse on the history of the Third Reich, delivered by various prosecutors in snippets—the beerhall meetings of the twenties, Hitler's building up of the Nazi Party, the failed Kapp putsch and Hitler's arrest for participating in the putsch, which made him known to millions, the publication of *Mein Kampf,* Hitler's emergence as a national figure, and finally, the misdeeds and atrocities of his twelve-year rule.

The recital of these events began to sound like a litany after a while, and Hannah caught herself falling asleep, waking up just in time to catch her sketchbook dropping from her hands to the floor. Then she heard the prosecutor drone the familiar slogans: "The party is above the state. The party is above the Wehrmacht. The party is above every individual. The Führer is the supreme authority within the party. Those unwilling to accept the leadership of the Führer are enemies of the state."

I lived through the horror, and my life was destroyed by it, she thought with a shudder, as scenes from the past surfaced in her mind: the rowdiness at the beerhall meetings where her uncle would take her, against her will, to see the new Siegfried who would resurrect the

German nation; the endless torchlight processions with goose-stepping SA men cheered on by shouting crowds; and the arrival of the Führer in his Mercedes, with his plastered hair and toothbrush moustache, a ghost of a smile appearing on his stern, cruel face as he waved to the crowds, acknowledging their worship of him as *der Held des Landes*. The hero of the land had closed her Bauhaus, had thrown her artistic friends in jail, and had the paintings of Kandinsky, Mondrian, and Klee put up for ridicule by his adherents. The Gestapo had put her in a concentration camp along with other enemies of the state. And when she had come out, she had to go through life as a nonperson, living like a cockroach in the crevices and interstices found in the walls of the Nazi state.

She moodily sketched the defendants as they sat there in front of her, nodding and winking to each other, perhaps under the impression that the charges against them could not be proven and would be dropped. They were so used to annihilating other people's lives that it never occurred to them that they themselves could be destroyed by others. Hannah watched their smug, cynical faces as the prosecutors showed a documentary film on the life and death of inmates in concentration camps, made by American and British army photographers. It started with prisoners being burned alive by the SS in a barn in the Leipzig concentration camp, followed by an endless sequence of images of human figures with sticklike bodies and skullike faces lying on the floor before being picked up and thrown into mass graves by the SS guards. In some cases, they used bulldozers to move the corpses toward the cavernous burial hole. The prisoners, the documentary narrators said, were Belgians, French, Russians, Poles, and Hungarians. They looked like Jews to Hannah, and she wondered why such an obvious fact wasn't mentioned. Maybe everyone looks Jewish after countless beatings and days of starvation, she thought. Their noses become bigger, their eyes bulge out of their sockets, and their unwashed, scruffy bodies give them a Job-like appearance; or maybe the documentary makers didn't want to bring up the issue of anti-Semitism because that would dilute the feeling of compassion on the part of many viewers.

The film consisted of several reels and ran for nearly an hour. Hannah heard retching noises from some of the audience. She, on the other hand, felt nothing, not even disgust, having been immunized by the countless dead bodies with gaping mouths and gunk-covered eyes that she had seen daily on the streets of Berlin. She had also seen similar scenes in the "GERMANS ARE GUILTY!" posters put up by the Americans in Berlin, and all she could think of was how the stills shown on the film reminded her of Cezanne's piled-up bathers, *Les Grandes Baigneuses*, done by the master using the pyramid motif, their skinny bodies turning blue from the cold, their eyes expressionless, huddling over each other to seek warmth.

"I'm dead inside," she said to herself. "I am not a German anymore. I am not an artist anymore. I am just a living corpse."

When the film ended and all the lights in the courtroom were turned back on, Hannah saw several tearstained faces. The president of the tribunal, in a shaky voice, announced that he was adjourning the court. And as they were trooping out, Hannah heard voices in three languages cursing all Germans and threatening to kill them en masse. She had stolen quick glances at the defendants as they were watching the film: Ribbentrop had kept his eyes averted, not daring to look at the screen; Streicher had a smile on his face; Hess had looked like an imbecile, as though he was wondering whether he was being shown a movie or a documentary; and Goering leaned on the rails, his face wooden and immobile.

While she was waiting outside the courthouse to meet Eric, she noticed the German POWs assigned to sweeping the environs of the courthouse, all of them SS men, stooping every now and then to pick up cigarette butts that they put carefully away in a pouch, unaware of the drama that had taken place inside. There is a parable in this somewhere, she thought, as she saw them obsequiously stepping aside for the American military police who were in charge of controlling the crowds. But feeling emotionally drained, she was not inclined to be philosophical and did not pursue the deeper meaning or implication of the moral lesson.

When Eric came out to meet her, he seemed a little flustered, which was unlike him. "I have spoken to one of our psychologists who is going to interview the prisoners right now, and he has given me permission to accompany him," he said. "I'll meet you at the park bench in about an hour and a half."

Hannah agreed and got on her bicycle. She rode slowly, checking out different parts of the old city. She saw that a few trolley cars were running, carrying German workers who were working for Americans—overcrowded trolley cars, with passengers hanging outside. She stopped in front of the opera house, which was the only building in that neighborhood unhurt by bombs. It was now showing American movies on the ground floor—she saw a billboard proclaiming *The Clock*, starring Judy Garland and Robert Walker—and its top floor was being used as a dance hall for GIs. She heard the strains from a saxophone coming from there and stood listening to it for a while, but there was a powerful stench of death in that area, coming from unburied or half-buried bodies in the rubble all around the opera house, and she moved on. The soldiers—youngsters, most of them nineteen or twenty, with *fräuleins* hanging on their arms, smoking cigarettes—didn't seem to be bothered by the enveloping odor, sweet and fetid, reminiscent of smells in zoos. They were busy with each other—obviously, the non-fraternization policy was ignored by them, for they were acting like young people everywhere out for a good time, and Hannah watched them for a while, thinking once more about the young soldiers she used to go out with just after the First World War—guys named Art and Hank and Chuck who kept their hands clasped behind them or folded across their chests when they were walking. What happened to their lives? she wondered. Were they now insurance salesmen or rental agents or used car dealers in Peoria, Illinois, or Wichita, Kansas, or Oneida, New York? Did they ever think of her?

She went on to the park and sat on "their" bench, looking at the bright-yellow and red leaves of the trees around her. Some of them already had shed all their leaves and stood there in bare-limbed grandeur, symbols of decline and renewal, of death and rebirth. She heard someone play music on a flute from behind a pile of rocks, a tune from a Mozart opera. She wasn't sure if it was *Figaro* or *Don Giovanni*. A minute later, an elderly laborer—she thought he was a Lithuanian or Estonian migrant—came out in view and walked by her, tipping his hat as he went by.

Eric arrived a few minutes later in his car. He seemed preoccupied as he offered apologies for keeping her waiting.

"You must be hungry, Hannah," he said, after looking at her intently for a few seconds. "I brought along two K rations boxes and hot coffee in a thermos for our dinner."

She opened the olive-colored box and saw some biscuits, a chocolate bar, a small pack of cigarettes, chewing gum, a wooden spoon, and a metal can with a key to open it with. She twisted the key around and found thinly sliced white meat of chicken and baby carrots.

She gave the cigarettes and the chewing gum to Eric and also the can containing the meat.

"It's good chicken," he said. "You should eat it."

"I will be fine if I eat the crackers and the chocolate and drink coffee," she said. "I don't feel like eating meat."

They ate in silence, with Eric finishing both portions of the canned meat. He then lit a cigarette and smoked for a while.

"A very interesting day," he said.

"How did the interviews go?" she asked.

"The defendants told us they had nothing to do with the operation of the camps shown in the film. They didn't plan it, they didn't hire the personnel, and they didn't give the orders. They never even saw any of these camps. It was Himmler and the people who worked for him who are responsible for these atrocities, they said."

"And Himmler is dead."

"Unfortunately, yes. If we had kept him alive, he would have blamed someone else."

"Eric, Justice Jackson implied that all defendants were somehow implicated in the running of the camps."

"As I said before, there's no evidence to make that assumption. Tom Dodd says that they have witnesses coming up who will talk about the murder of millions of Jews in camps in Poland. Those witnesses are SS officers who will give us a different picture of how these camps were set up and how they were run."

"I don't understand this," Hannah said. "If that's the case, why did they show this film now?"

"Jackson wanted to show that there was a plan to murder political prisoners as part of the conspiracy count against the defendants. That was why the film was shown. He likes courtroom drama."

Hannah was disgusted by the hide-and-seek games played by prosecutors and defenders alike.

"Will anybody ever tell us the whole truth, Eric?" she asked.

"If they won't, I'll find out," he said. "Don't you have any faith in me?"

"Yes and no," she said. "I know you will try. I don't know if you will succeed."

"You shouldn't talk that way, Hannah. I thought you were my ally."

She realized that she should not have spoken that way to him.

"Don't mind what I'm saying, Eric," she said. "Watching that film was hell."

He forgave her for doubting him and was glad to make amends. "I know," he said. "Hans Frank was crying when I interviewed him. Shows what a hypocrite he is. He was the governor of the General Government in Poland. You know that?"

"No, I don't know anything about the General Government in Poland," she said.

"Hitler broke up Poland into three pieces—a German section, where ethnic Germans were going to be resettled; a Polish section for Poles under German rule, called the General Government; and a Jewish section in the east for resettling Jews from Germany and Poland."

"I very rarely listened to German broadcasts," Hannah said. "Occasionally, when no one was watching, I would listen to the BBC, and that was it."

"Coming back to Hans Frank—he was telling us he didn't approve of all these massacres. He spoke of his love of music. He's a gifted pianist, he says."

"Don't believe what these people say, Eric," she said. "They're very good at lying."

"I've learned that by now. Goering seems to be the only one who has the courage to stand by his Führer. All the others are running away from him."

"You spoke to the Reichsmarschall?" asked Hannah, her eyes widening. She felt a twinge of fear as she imagined Eric standing next to the onetime head of the Gestapo.

"I did. He was charming and pleasant. It was amusing in a way. He thinks that he has done nothing illegal and is going to be acquitted."

It began to drizzle a little bit, and they got up from the bench.

"I'll drive you home," he said. "I'll put your bicycle on top of the car and strap it."

"I don't mind bicycling in the rain. Actually, I would prefer that."

He seemed a little put out, and Hannah smiled at him. "I'm used to the outdoors," she said. "I can weather wind and rain."

He got in the car, turned on the headlights, and watched her as she rode away on her bicycle, a tall, slim figure with blond hair gleaming in the light thrown by his car. He wondered why he was attracted to her and whether they would ever be lovers. What was it about her that made him want to possess her, to make her his own? She was twenty-one years older than him, old enough to be his mother. He had never gone out with an older woman before. And her slenderness was in striking contrast to the women he had loved in the past—girls with hourglass figures, large bosoms, and curvy behinds. He couldn't understand why he felt a surge of raw emotion he had never experienced before whenever his eyes met those enigmatic green eyes of hers. Some part of him wanted to reach out to her and touch the hidden core of her, in spite of his misgivings about getting drawn into her orbit.

"This would come to no good," he said to himself. Guiltily, he thought about Deborah, his fiancée, his mother's best friend's daughter, and assistant curator at the Metropolitan Museum of Art—they were well matched in every way, looking good together, popular as a couple, compatible in terms of interests and temperament. But as he watched the speedily retreating woman on the bicycle, he realized the truth about himself and Deborah—it was all show, put on for the benefit of others; he found her dull and uninteresting, and he wasn't sure she was the right person for him.

Hannah found the next several days of the trial extraordinarily tedious as prosecutor after prosecutor talked about Nazi machinations to plant agents for staging insurrections by ethnic Germans in neighboring countries to provide excuses for invading them. They read detailed minutes of meetings between Hitler and his generals and even sections of *Mein Kampf* to emphasize the premeditated nature of such provocations. The long, repetitious list of murder and torture, enslavement, and brutality made her and other listeners weary, and the judges advised the prosecutors to cut short their marathon narratives. But the advice was ignored, and the prosecutors droned on and on until their hearers were numbed by the piling up of travesty on travesty and horror on horror.

November gave way to December, and the trial was adjourned for the Christmas holidays, to the relief of all. As she got on her bicycle in the failing winter light, Hannah asked herself if she had learned anything memorable from the trial so far and concluded that what stood up most vividly in her mind were the words of Himmler quoted by one of the prosecutors: "What happens to a Russian, or to a Pole, is of no interest to me. What these countries can offer us in the way of good German stock, we will take from them, by kidnapping their children and raising them here with us, if necessary. Whether the rest of the population starves to death or survives is of no concern to me, beyond the fact that we need them as slaves for our Kultur. If ten thousand Russian females fall down from exhaustion while digging an antitank ditch, that is fine with me if their work is finished in time."

That's not the way my uncle would have phrased it, she thought as she rode through the death-smelling streets of Nuremberg to his house to set up the Christmas tree—he would have been more humane, even though he loved Germany more than Himmler ever did.

FOURTEEN

CHRISTMAS DONE THE "OLD WAY"

Ulrike and Frieda wanted to revive the traditional German Christmas celebrations replete with a Christmas tree hung with angels, stars, and baby Jesus dolls and an Advent wreath of holly with four red candles, but her uncle was against the idea.

"The Führer wanted to stamp out all Jewish references from our ancient winter festival," he lectured the women. "He replaced Jesus with Odin and banned the use of stars as ornaments. The six-pointed stars reminded him of the Star of David and the five-pointed ones of the star used by the Bolsheviks. They are not part of our old Nordic tradition of the Yule festival—and now you're trying to undo the work of the Führer."

"We want the way things were when we were kids," said Ulrike. "We used to leave our boots outside the door on Nikolaustag, and we would find them filled with presents the next morning."

"And we used to make the pastry dolls, the *Christbaumgeback*, and hang them on the Christmas tree," said her sister. "We would then wait for the arrival of the Christkindl."

"What do you think, Hannah?" asked Ulrike, turning to her. "Do you think we should celebrate the old way?"

The last time Hannah had celebrated Christmas the "old way" was when she had been in Bauhaus. The memory of that event sent electric ripples through her body—the fir tree cut in the shape of a perfect equilateral triangle; the colorful cubes, spheres, and cylinders that hung from it; the tablecloth and napkins woven by Gunta Stölz; and the gingerbread cookies in black and white, shaped like tigers and dragons—so strikingly attractive one didn't want to eat them but kept them in one's purse until they disintegrated.

There had been no Christmas for her after that. In her Berlin apartment house, Herr Stumpfegger would hold Nazi winter solstice festivals in the lobby, with cookies in the form of red-and-black swastikas, and runic symbols and grenade-shaped baubles hanging from a fir tree, urging everyone to drink to the health of der Führer.

"What do you think, Hannah?" asked Frieda.

I'm an atheist, and I don't care how you celebrate Christmas, was what Hannah wanted to say. But she knew she couldn't say that to the two women who looked up to her in many ways.

"This is my uncle's house. It's not for me to say how it should be run," she said diplomatically.

Her uncle was pleased, and nothing more was spoken about the subject until a week before Christmas Eve, when the senior-most officer among the Americans living upstairs, a Colonel Walter Knapp, born of German parents in Indiana, told Frieda he wanted a traditional German Christmas dinner, with roast goose and dumplings, served with red cabbage, Christmas Stollen, and a gingerbread house. The army technicians had already put up a huge tree at the entrance to the house with traditional red, blue, and white ornaments, and a bunch of German carol singers came there every night to sing "O Tannenbaum" and "Es ist für uns eine Zeit angekommen."

Uncle Werner exploded when he heard about this but gave in graciously after his spasm of rage was over. He called the three women into his study, asked them to be seated (a rare honor, thought Hannah), and told them to celebrate Christmas anyway they wanted.

"I'm looking to drink some *Glühwein*," he said. "In the old days, we used to mull the wine at home, but that was before they started selling it in shops during Christmas."

He looked at the three women, one by one, and the women looked at each other. Glühwein needed spices—lemon, cinnamon, cardamom, and cloves—and there were no markets to get them from. Frieda then remembered Colonel Walter Knapp's request for Christmas Stollen and figured that she could get the spices from the US Army food store using her card. She winked at the two women and said she would make the mulled wine.

The old man was pleased. For the next few minutes, he reminisced about Christmas in 1941 in Munich, when he had been a guest of the Führer, and he and his friend Doktor Karl Haushofer had sat at the table next to him at the Lowenbraukeller in Munich.

"The Führer was so gracious. He sent us a bottle of Dom Pérignon that was part of our booty from the invasion of France. He then came over to us and made toasts. He drank only mineral water, but he knew that Haushofer and I loved champagne. He was such a considerate man."

The women looked at each other despairingly because they knew they were in for a long story. Fortunately, they were saved by the ringing of the doorbell.

"Your young Jewish captain is here to see you, Hannah," said Ulrike, who had gone to open the door.

Hannah, wincing at the look of disgust that had passed over her uncle's face, went to greet Eric, who was still standing at the doorway.

"Why didn't you come in, Eric?" she asked, after shaking his hand.

"You know, it is the nonfraternization policy, Hannah," he said, giving one of his radiant smiles. "I've been warned to stay away from Germans with a Nazi past."

He was dressed in a gray woolen suit, with a white shirt and a blue-and-red-striped tie. It was the first time Hannah had seen him out of uniform, and she thought he looked very handsome, with his brown eyes and brown curly hair.

"I have some Christmas goodies for you," he said, pointing to a large cardboard carton that was on the doorstep. "I wanted to deliver them in person."

He brought the box inside, and Hannah, on opening it, gave a cry of surprise. There were groceries she hadn't seen in a while—two boxes of cocoa, rounds of cheese, a jar of peanut butter, another of apple sauce, boxes of pasta, raisins, an entire baked ham, a bottle of vinegar—along with bars of chocolate and four bottles of wine.

She wanted to ask him, "Why are you doing all of this for me, Eric?" but suppressed it, thinking that it would be construed as a flirtatious remark. Instead she said, "Thank you, Eric," and looked at him fully in the face.

His eyes were beseeching her, and she was reminded of Stenka, the Russian boy, and his tragic end. I need an older man, she thought, like Emil, and not someone who is young enough to be my son—but I cannot rebuff Eric.

"Wouldn't you like to sit down and talk to my family for a couple of minutes?" she asked him.

"Not this time, Hannah," he said, disappointed by the lack of warmth in her eyes. "I've to meet my family today at the airport. They're coming here for two weeks."

"Your parents?"

"And my fiancée," he said.

On hearing that, she was relieved, and her affection for him showed in her face. "Where are they staying?"

"I found two rooms for them at the Grand Hotel," he said. "I would like you to meet them, Hannah."

"Me?" she asked in dismay. "Do you think they would want to see me?"

"I want them to meet you, a German woman, cultured and intelligent, who suffered under Hitler's rule," he said.

His mouth was set, and she knew there was no point in arguing with him. "When do you want me to meet them?" she asked.

"Tomorrow we will be going to Dresden, where my mother's parents came from. After that, we will go to Budapest, where my dad's uncle used to live. We are planning to be back by New Year's Eve. Why don't you spend New Year's Eve with us?"

"I can't do that. The folks in this house wouldn't like it if I went off by myself. They're planning to celebrate Silvester the old way."

"Sylvester?"

"S-I-L-V-E-S-T-E-R. That's what we call New Year's Eve, named after the fourth-century pope Sylvester I. This will be the first New Year's Eve without having to hear Goebbels's speech on the radio. Ulrike and Frieda are planning to celebrate it the old-fashioned way, and they're excited about it."

"We will see you then the next day, when the court reopens. Actually, that'll be a bad day for me because I've to meet with some of the other officers. Let's plan on meeting January third, and I'll meet you after the court adjourns."

"Are you sure you want to do this? Your family may not like me," she said in a small voice.

"Leave it to me, Hannah," he said. "Everything will be fine."

He smiled reassuringly, clapped Hannah on the shoulder, got into his car, and drove off. Hannah stood in a daze for a few seconds, watching him drive away. Why does he want his family to see me? she wondered. She could sense that there was some motive lurking in his mind, and it frightened her. "Shall I sleep with him once and let him get over this obsession with me?" she asked herself. It wouldn't end there, she knew. She toyed with the idea of telling him that she couldn't reciprocate the emotions he entertained toward her, but she knew that the consequence of such a move would be that she would have to give up her job. Even so, the situation shouldn't be allowed to continue in this mode, she thought, as she stood at the door figuring out if there was any action she could take that wouldn't create adverse reactions.

She was interrupted by an exclamation of surprise from Ulrike, who had come into the front parlor.

"Look at that box!" she cried. "Your captain brought all that?"

"He did. He is one rank higher than a captain. He's a major."

"Cheese, chocolate, and ooh…look at the strawberry jam. Your uncle would love it."

"We better not tell him where it came from," said Hannah.

"You're right. We will tell him we bought it in the black market," she said.

Her uncle's face lit up when as he saw the jam during teatime, and Hannah smiled as she saw him spreading it over a slice of toasted bread and eating it slowly, savoring the taste that had been denied him for months, without asking questions.

During the next couple of days, Hannah helped the two ladies with the holiday preparations. They made gingerbread houses and baked cookies for decorating the Christmas tree, they made the Advent wreath and laid it flat on a table with four red candles in the middle, and they prepared mulled wine for the old man. On Christmas Eve Frieda brought over a roast goose, dumplings, and red cabbage from the American kitchen, and the four of them sat around the dinner table in a cheerful mood.

"Where's Claudia and Octavia?" asked the uncle. "I thought they would be here for dinner tonight."

"They're at a party," said Ulrike.

The two girls were never at home, spending nights with newfound friends among the nineteen- and twenty-year-old GIs. They jubilantly brought their mother and their aunt—and Hannah too, occasionally—presents they got from their admirers—a shawl, a pair of nylon stockings, a bottle of perfume, and the like.

"They shouldn't be going out with the enemy," said the uncle querulously, his old lips trembling with shame and outrage. "They should go out with German men."

"Not many German men are left here, Papa," said Ulrike. "They're all gone—either dead or rotting in Russian prison camps."

A tear stole down her face, and Hannah knew she was thinking of her husband; and a fleeting image of Emil, unshaven and wearing a shabby army doctor's uniform without markings popped up in her mind as she wondered whether he too was a prisoner.

"We are women without men," said Frieda. "Just like it was twenty-five years ago, after the First World War."

"Wars do no one any good," said Ulrike. "They kill people and destroy countries."

"Why does Germany get into war after war? Why do we do this?" asked Frieda.

"A country goes to war when it feels threatened," said her uncle. "It's a matter of geopolitics. My friend Doktor Haushofer has made it very clear in his books. You women should read them instead of asking questions that have been answered already by our great thinkers and philosophers."

The women looked at each other and tacitly agreed not to say anything that would provoke the old warhorse into one of his rages. They finished their meal in silence, broken by the sounds of revelry coming from upstairs.

"I hope they don't damage our furniture," said Ulrike.

"I shall go upstairs and speak to Colonel Knapp," said Frieda.

She quickly went up the stairs and came back with a broad smile on her face.

"They're all drunk. Half of them are on lying on the floor. As for Colonel Knapp, he was in tears when I approached him. He misses his family in Florida and asked me to keep him company."

The women laughed, but the old man wasn't amused.

"You're silly!" he shouted at them. "You think it's funny when a man thinks you're a whore."

He stalked out of the room. A few seconds later, the lights went out as they periodically did in Nuremberg. The women sat in the room for a while, in the rays shed by the red candles of the Advent wreath, drinking wine until the bottle was empty.

Ulrike wondered out loud what the girls were doing.

"Octavia is hanging out with a black GI, says Claudia," said Frieda. "He takes her out to the nightclubs run in basements."

"I too used to hang out with one, in Berlin, after the Great War," said Hannah. "He taught me how to dance the cakewalk. The band would play ragtime..."

She trailed off because she heard Frieda sobbing.

"The girls are going to leave me. And I don't know where my husband is. I'll be all alone. I never thought my life would end up like this."

The two women put their arms around her, but Frieda's racking sobs did not cease, and they, sharing the same premonitions of loneliness, deprivation, and misery that dwelt in the recesses of their psyche, joined her in collective grief over their shattered dreams.

For the next couple of days, Hannah, who liked to describe her mental states in metaphors, was in the land of the shades. I'm Eurydice, waiting for my Orpheus to get me out of here, she thought. The weather wasn't helpful, being cloudy and rainy, but she didn't let it prevent her from wandering outdoors. She went bicycling wearing Ulrike's gardening cap and sat on park benches in the drizzling rain, where she, usually not given to introspection, analyzed her life, viewing it like the reels of a film. Her childhood in Schwabing had been happy, for her mother, beautiful and vivacious, had made her feel warm and secure, even though she had spent most of her time with her friends and lovers. After Schwabing, there was life at the Munich Art Institute, and she had loved those days because of the camaraderie and the bonhomie she found among her fellow students. She thought of the closeness she had with Gerhard Müller, the slender, athletic, blond-haired boy-man or man-boy who had loved her and then left her a widow. Then came years of struggle in Berlin with a young son to take care of, until the arrival of her impulsive, generous mother, who offered to bring up the boy so that Hannah could go to

Bauhaus. And, in Bauhaus, she had finally found the environment she had been seeking all her life, learning from the masters—Kandinsky, Klee, Mondrian—about line, color, and form, and she had experienced a rebirth as an artist and as a person. But Bauhaus had turned out to be like Thomas Mann's *Magic Mountain*, destroyed in a flash by the Nazis, and her friends and mentors were put to flight. Mann could write in exile because a novelist could write even when he was buried in an attic in a strange city or on the run, carrying his manuscript in a battered suitcase from country to country. Artists were different animals; they needed the company of other artists. They needed to exchange ideas and work in groups. She asked herself if she was dead as a painter and would ever come back to life.

As she sat on that desolate park bench with the rain blowing around her in soft white streaks, she speculated about what her fate would have been if she had been born in another country—Britain, France, or America. Would she have had the freedom she wanted, freedom from the oppressive German masculinity that had been all around her throughout her life in the form of a Kaiser Wilhelm, Erich Ludendorff, or Adolf Hitler? She kept thinking about the words of Justice Jackson, so different from those she had heard all her life from Germans, and she wondered why Germany never produced anyone like him. Every German male she had spoken to—even those who hated the Nazis—believed in strong leadership, military superiority, discipline, regimentation, and the subordination of women to men. Jackson's use of the word "evil" popped up in her mind, now and then, like a porpoise surfacing in the ocean. In Germany, nobody used that word—neither the rulers nor their victims. Whatever was done was in the nature of "historical necessity"—that favorite word of the German male—such as the need for survival, the need to protect oneself from past, present, or future enemies, or the need to eliminate undesirable elements from the nation. She had initially thought of Jackson's use of the word as a rhetorical device, but now it was echoing inside her head in a staccato drumbeat, and she understood what he had been trying to say. "It's wrong to hurt others and justify it as done for the good of the country," he was saying. "It's wrong to enslave and kill the weak and brag that you're doing it for the sake of the nation." In Germany, no one—not even a priest or pastor—had said words to that effect. Maybe it's because he's an American, she thought. They are different. She thought of the dozens of American journalists—fresh faced, with a humorous twinkle in their eyes—she had seen at the courthouse and came to the conclusion that there must be something in America—their history, their culture, and the wide-open spaces of that vast land—that gave them an innate moral sense, sharp almost to the point of righteousness. She should have gone there six years ago, she thought. She should have accepted the offer of a job as an art teacher that her friend Anni Albers had found for her at an art institute in South Carolina—or was it North? Hannah was never sure about names of American states—but she hadn't wanted to leave Germany because of Johann and Emil. One of them is probably dead, she thought, and the other rotting in some jail in Poland. Did Jackson ever experience anything like what she had gone through? she wondered. The Old World—meaning Europe—was a purgatory, and no one from the New World could really understand what it did to the psyche of a person who had the misfortune to wander through its carnage-filled and rubble-choked streets.

A large dog, very wet, appeared from nowhere and stood next to her. It looked like a Munsterlander, its black coat speckled with white patches on its chest, legs, and tail. It's probably hungry, she thought, cold and hungry. She wished she had something to offer him as he looked at her speculatively for a while, rubbed his wet nose against her knee, swished his white-tipped tail, and moved away. I hope it's an omen, she thought, a portent of better things to come.

But the sun didn't emerge from the clouds as the holiday season dragged on. Ulrike and Frieda looked mournful as they darned old clothes or snacked on Christmas cookies. Her uncle drank his mulled wine in silence, occasionally broken by random questions about this or that defendant—"How did Hess appear in court?" or "How did Rosenberg respond to the charges?" Hannah knew he was friends with several defendants, but she wasn't sure of the nature and extent of his friendship. She knew he read about the trial because she saw, in his study, week-old copies of the *Stars and Stripes*—the only newspaper available in Nuremberg—that he must have picked up by rummaging the trashcans belonging to the Americans. She had a suspicion he didn't trust what the American reporters wrote about the trial and wanted to interrogate her in detail about what was happening in the courtroom. Yet something prevented him from doing that—perhaps the fear that she would only confirm what he had read about or, worse, make negative comments about his friends that would only make him more pessimistic about the outcome of the trial.

It snowed on New Year's Eve, and they had to periodically clean the stairs that led down to their basement apartment to avoid falls. Hannah made snowballs and tossed them to Ulrike, who giggled and pretended to eat them as though they were scoops of ice cream. Soon it grew dark, and they sang old German songs while her uncle brooded over his glass of wine.

Just as they were sitting down to dinner, Octavia and Claudia came in, accompanied by two young corporals, nineteen or twenty years old, tall, handsome, and athletic looking. One was black, and the other had Jewish features.

"Hi, I'm Rider Elroy from Camden, New Jersey," said one.

"I'm Gene Frankel, from Pittsburgh," said the other.

"This is my husband," said Octavia, linking her arm with Rider.

"This is mine," said Claudia, putting her arm around the other young man.

"Your *what?*" said Frieda, squeaking like a mouse. Her face had turned grayish, and she looked bewildered.

"We got married today, Mutti," said Octavia. "We are leaving for America tomorrow."

"We came to say good-bye," said Claudia. "And to bring our Christmas presents."

She nodded to the boys, who went out and came back with several boxes, neatly wrapped and tied with ribbons. Each girl placed a box in front of Frieda, Ulrike, and Hannah, smiled, and wished them a happy New Year. They then moved toward Werner, but his chair was empty—obviously, he had walked out of the room after seeing the two young men—and they left his presents on the chair.

"Good-bye. We will write to you when we get there," said Octavia.

She was about to say something more but stopped when she saw her mother was crying. Both girls went over to her, kissed her, and embraced her.

"Octavia, Claudia," sobbed Frieda. "Don't go. Don't leave your mother all by herself."

"Our husbands want us to leave with them," said Claudia. "They've finished their service and have to go back."

"But this is your *vaterland*. You belong here...this is where you grew up."

"I don't know how to tell you this, Mutti, but we don't want to live here," said Octavia. "A week ago, we saw an American documentary with our husbands. It showed what the Führer did to the rest of the world. He tortured and massacred millions of Russians, Poles, and Jews. It made me think of this country as the land of sadists and murderers, and the Führer as an incarnation of the devil. I hate this country now..."

"Out! Get out of my house!" roared a gargantuan voice. Her uncle was standing at the doorway, shaking with fury. "How dare you talk that way about our great nation? There would be no Europe without our thinkers and our scientists..."

He walked threateningly toward the girls, who stuck their tongues out at him and ran out of the house. Their mystified husbands lingered to look at the old man, shook their heads, and then sauntered along.

A minute later, Hannah followed them to the army jeep parked in front of the house.

The girls, still laughing at Werner's behavior, kissed and embraced her.

Hannah looked at the young men and smiled. "You guys can give your aunt a hug and a kiss," she said in English.

"Sure thing," said one.

"We're all family now," said the other.

The two men embraced her and pecked her briefly on the cheek.

"Hannah, we would like you to come and see us," said Octavia.

"We will give her a good time," said Gene.

"We can show her the Empire State Building," said Rider.

"We can drive her to Niagara Falls," said the other.

"I know some good clubs in New York City," said Rider. "Like the Hurricane Club, where Duke Ellington plays."

"It's a good idea," said Gene. "But she might not like jazz."

Hannah smiled at them and said, "I was introduced to jazz before you kids were born. I love jazz."

The young men looked at her appraisingly.

"Hannah is an artist," Octavia said. "She studied at the Bauhaus."

Snow was falling in thick flakes. The young men didn't know anything about Bauhaus and didn't care. One of them looked at his army watch, with its radium dial and khaki strap.

"We gotta leave before the roads are all snowed up," he said.

"Have a nice trip to America," said Hannah. "And good luck to all of you."

"Hannah, I'll miss you," said Claudia. "You can use the clothes we've left behind, since you are the same size as us. Take what you want, and think of us when you wear them."

"With the snow falling on your blond hair, in your flannel gown, you look like a Valkyrie, Hannah," said Octavia fondly.

"I wish I was, my child," said Hannah. "It's better than being a mere mortal."

The two girls cried a little, and Hannah consoled them. But she noticed the young men were getting impatient and left them without further adieus.

Her three housemates were seated at the dinner table, eating the roast lamb, mashed potatoes, and peas Frieda had brought from the American kitchen upstairs.

No mention was made of the two girls or their husbands.

The four of them soon finished their entrée and then ate a loaf of fruitcake, followed by bars of Hershey chocolates. After that, they drank the two remaining bottles of wine and then reeled off to bed, stultified by the surfeit of food and drink.

They were all sick the next morning, blaming it on the wine. Early in the afternoon, one of the German kitchen maids working under Frieda brought down a jar of pickled herrings and a few raw onions—the well-known German cure for hangovers—and it did its magic. They were able to walk around by evening, and at night they had a supper of barley soup and pumpernickel bread, which restored them completely.

FIFTEEN

A FAMILY ERUPTION

The girls had given Hannah a silk blouse, a silk scarf, and a white wool sweater as Christmas presents, and Hannah decided to wear them to the courthouse. She found a matching pair of pants in their wardrobe, which was now hers, and was pleased with the overall effect she saw in the full-length mirror in their room.

At least I won't embarrass Eric when he presents me to his family, she thought, as she rode her bicycle in the gray wintry morning.

Because of the time she had spent in getting dressed, she was later than usual in arriving at the court. She heard the judge bang his gavel while she was taking her seat and soon saw a new prosecution witness—a pleasant-looking, clean-cut German in his late thirties named Otto Ohlendorf—being sworn in. A large organization chart, apparently drawn by him, was on display, and Hannah resigned herself to a few hours of tedious exposition on the inner workings of the Nazi bureaucracy. Indeed, during the first forty minutes, Ohlendorf explained the Reich Main Security Office (RSHA) organization under Heydrich, with Himmler as the boss, and answered questions by the prosecution whether Mr. X or Mr. Y was part of this or that division. The prosecutor then asked him to describe his function in the organization, and on hearing his response, Hannah sat up with a jolt as though a heavy electrical current had coursed through her body. Ohlendorf said he was the commander of a special group (called Einsatzgruppen D), deployed during the invasion of Russia. There were four such groups, he said, and they had received oral instructions from Himmler to "liquidate" Russian Jews. The army unit in which his group was implanted (the Eleventh Army) was aware of his mission, from Commanding Officer von Mannstein down to lower levels.

He was then asked about his method of operation, and he described it calmly and methodically, without any trace of emotion. First, with the help of Jewish elders, they registered all the Jewish residents in a region and then packed them up into a staging area, using the pretext they were going to be relocated to another part of the country. They were then transported in closed wagons to a place of execution, where they were shot, in military style, standing or kneeling. Their bodies were buried in trenches dug by able-bodied Jews, who were subsequently executed.

"Were women and children executed in the manner you described?" asked the prosecutor.

"Until the spring of 1942, we killed everyone using the same method," said Ohlendorf. "We were then ordered to kill women and children in gas vans."

He added that his men didn't like to use gas vans because of the "foul mess" made by the victims in the throes of death.

"How many persons were liquidated by Einsatzgruppen D, under your direction?" he was asked.

"Ninety thousand Jews, between June 1941 and June 1942."

"Did you see liquidation statistics, from time to time, from the other Einsatzgruppen units?"

"Yes."

"Were their liquidation numbers the same as yours?"

"Einsatzgruppen A, B, and C showed liquidation numbers greater than my group."

"Did you have scruples about carrying out these liquidations?"

"Yes, of course. I had scruples."

"How is it that you carried out these liquidations regardless of your scruples?"

"It was inconceivable to me that a subordinate like me should not carry out orders given by the Führer through his ministers."

This was the face of the Third Reich Hannah had never seen before: a calm, soft-spoken, unemotional mass killer so different in appearance and personality from the Nazi Party bosses with their cross-belts, jowls, potbellies, and medals, who used to strut about in the streets of Berlin during party conventions.

Hard to believe this clean-shaven, nice-looking man standing before her had killed nearly a hundred thousand people who were total strangers to him and had done no harm to him or to his country. His superiors had told him to kill, and he had obeyed their orders. Was he right in doing so? She couldn't decide. One part of her mind was convinced he was not to blame for doing what he did, and the other part took the opposite view. She felt that all human actions were inherently dual sided and, hence, too ambiguous and elliptical to be judged by other humans. I would be a poor juror, she blamed herself. I wouldn't be able to decide if a person is guilty or not, and I wouldn't be able to cast my vote in favor of or against conviction—I don't have a moral compass like Justice Jackson has.

"The next witness to be called by the prosecution is Dieter Wisliceny," she heard the voice of a court official announcing over the microphones in four languages.

A smooth-looking, round-faced man in his early thirties was sworn in and described his background, which was similar to that of Otto Ohlendorf. Hannah wondered if he too belonged to an Einsatzgruppen and had killed a hundred thousand Jews, but his narration was even more bizarre. He said that a special section had been established under Himmler to resolve the "Jewish question," and the resolution took place in four stages: the forced emigration of German and Austrian Jews; the ghettoization of Polish Jews; the liquidation of all European Jews using death marches, labor camps, and gas chambers; and the concealment of the evidence of such liquidation. Dieter had worked for Adolf Eichmann, who was responsible for the transportation of all Jews in Europe to meet their grim destiny in Polish camps and had subsequently absconded to South America along with Martin Bormann and other Nazi leaders.

On impulse, she jotted down some notes in question-and-answer format.

"Did you see any executive order regarding the annihilation of the Jews?" asked the prosecutor.

"Eichmann showed me an order from Himmler in the summer of 1942," said Wisliceny.

"What exactly did he show you?"

"Eichmann took a file folder from his safe and showed me a letter from Himmler to Heydrich. The letter said in effect that the Führer had ordered the final solution of the Jewish question, and it was their responsibility to implement it."

"By whom was it signed?"

"By Himmler."

"And you personally examined this order in Eichmann's office."

"Yes, I did."

"Did you understand the meaning of the phrase 'final solution' as used in the order?"

"Eichmann explained it to me. He said it was a code word for the physical extermination of the Jewish race."

"Do you have any knowledge of the total number of Jews killed under the final solution?" asked the prosecutor.

"Eichmann estimated between four to five million. My independent calculations show the same number," Wisliceny responded.

"When did you last see Eichmann?"

"In Berlin, in February 1945. He told me if we lost the war, he would commit suicide."

"Did he say anything about the final solution?"

"He said he would leap into his grave laughing because he had done his share in ridding the world of five million Jews."

After the court adjourned for the day, Hannah got up slowly from her chair and walked toward the exit. She was feeling sick and was reminded of an identical sensation when, during her first flight, the airplane had run into severe turbulence, and she had retched into her airbag. All she wanted was to go home, pull down all the blinds, and lie in darkness for a couple of hours.

She then remembered that she was to meet Eric's family that night.

I'll tell him I can't do it tonight, she thought, just before her eyes fell on a US soldier standing near the courthouse door carrying a cardboard placard with her name written on it.

"I'm Hannah Müller," she said to the soldier.

"I've a letter for you," he said.

It was from Eric.

Hannah,

I was with my family in the visitors' gallery today. After listening to Dieter Wisliceny's testimony about five million being killed, my fiancée, Deborah (actually, I should refer to her as my ex-fiancée, since we broke up a couple of days ago), became sick, and we are going back to our hotel. I still would like you to come there this evening. My mother is very interested in meeting you. Sergeant Swoboda will drive you to the hotel. Do not bring your bicycle. We will take you home.
Eric

She shrugged and looked at the soldier, a very young man with humorous brown eyes and a fuzzy growth on his lips.

"Let's go, Sergeant," she said.

His jeep was parked right in front of the courthouse, and he courteously helped her get into it.

The cold wind made her shiver as he drove fast down Maximilianstrasse, made a U-turn effortlessly, and went on to Frauentorgraben and from there to the Bahnhofstrasse, where, after passing by the monstrous wreckage of the railway terminus, she shivered, closed her eyes, and shrank into a corner of her seat. Soon the car stopped in front of the Grand Hotel, and the driver helped her down and guided her through the lobby filled with officers to a small dining room at the back of the hotel. The door was closed, but she could hear voices raised in argument. The sergeant bowed and turned to go, his eyes and his twitching mouth suggesting the inherent possibilities of comic relief behind the closed door.

Hannah smiled at him. "Thank you, Sergeant," she said and extended her hand.

He took it and kissed it gallantly. He then smiled at her, turned, and left.

Hannah knocked on the door. The voices in the room suddenly became quiet as Eric opened the door and welcomed her with a big smile.

"Happy new year, Hannah," he said. "*Frohes neues Jahr!*"

"Frohes neues Jahr," said Hannah.

He took her by the elbow and introduced her to his mother, Phyllis; his father, Saul; and his fiancée (or ex-fiancée), Deborah.

"We were having an argument about Ohlendorf and Wisliceny," he said. "My mother thinks the two decided to confess because they felt what they had done was wrong. I told her it was to curry favor with the Americans that both of them came forward as witnesses for the prosecution."

"What will they gain from it, Eric?" asked his mother, a tall, slender woman with curly red hair and blue eyes, dressed in a well-cut gray suit.

"My understanding is that they hoped to get jobs as advisers to the American government," he replied.

"I would like to know what advice these two ex-Nazis can give our government," challenged Phyllis.

"Probably on how to exterminate American Jews," said his father, a burly man with a thick mop of gray hair, wearing black-framed glasses. He was grinning, and Hannah, remembering the anti-Semitic jokes her stepfather, Paul, used to make, realized that Jewish humor often had elements of self-mockery and self-laceration.

"This is not something to laugh about," said Eric's fiancée, Deborah. "Especially after the testimony we heard today."

She was a dark-haired, full-figured beauty in her middle twenties, with the olive complexion found in many Mediterranean Jews. She looked very distressed, and Hannah assumed it had to do with the broken engagement. She didn't seem to be pleased with Hannah's presence and avoided saying hello to her when introduced.

"It was pretty bad news, Debbie," said Phyllis. "But we all knew something like this had happened, even though we didn't know its scope or magnitude."

"Yeah, the devil is in the details, as my friend Ludwig Mies van der Rohe says all the time," said the older man, with a wink to Eric.

"In this case we've to find the devil," said Eric, smiling. "His name begins with *H*—Hitler, Himmler, or Heydrich. We don't know which one."

"We will know when we meet them in hell," said his father.

Eric laughed, and he and his father goose-stepped around the room, exchanging Hitler salutes and grinning.

They can laugh about these things, thought Hannah. They can make jokes even when someone leads them to the gas chamber.

Phyllis, seeing the expression on Deborah's face, decided to change the way the conversation was heading. "Hannah knows who Mies van der Rohe is, I'm sure, having been in the Bauhaus for many years. Ludwig is now in Chicago, and my husband, who is an architect, is a good friend of his."

"I know Mies van der Rohe, but I was closer to his predecessor, Walter Gropius," said Hannah.

"I have seen Walter Gropius but never talked with him," said Saul Grossman.

"I've heard he's a lovely man," said Phyllis.

"He was very nice to all of us who worked for him," said Hannah.

The conversation was interrupted by the arrival of a man wearing an apron, who said in German, with an Upper Silesian accent, that dinner was ready.

Hannah looked around and saw a long table covered with trays and dishes at the other end of the room. Obviously, it was going to be a buffet dinner.

"Let us eat," said Saul.

Hannah followed the four of them and watched as they filled their paper plates with warmed-up K rations—spaghetti and meatballs, lamb stew, peas, beets, and carrots. The smell of canned food made her slightly nauseous, but she didn't want to offend her hosts and took small portions from each tray and two slices of the packaged white bread.

She joined them as they sat around a small table on the other side of the room, between Saul and Phyllis. There was tension between the young people opposite them, and they could sense it.

The father, in his jocular way, tried to liven things up a little. "We've come down a little, haven't we, Phyllis?" he asked. "In Dresden we had champagne and caviar that the Russians so generously gave us. Now we have to eat spaghetti from a can."

"The Russians were very gracious to us," said Phyllis, turning to Hannah. "They provided us with English-speaking guides to take us around the old city, where my parents were born. Dresden is nothing but rubble because of the firebombing by the British. They used these blockbuster bombs, each weighing nearly a ton, and they destroyed entire city blocks. The firebombs caused deadly fires that burned down thousands of homes in the old city and in nearby suburbs."

"Henry Morgenthau would have loved to see it," said Saul with a chuckle. "Someone told me he was collecting pictures of all the destroyed cities—Cologne, Dusseldorf, Berlin, Nuremberg, Dresden, Leipzig, and so on."

"My dad went to high school with Henry Morgenthau, Hannah," said Eric from across the table.

"We were in the same class at Cornell also," said Saul. "Henry started out as an architecture student."

"I hate to see cities being destroyed like this," said Phyllis. "After all, Dresden was a cultural center, with all its galleries, bookshops, and museums. It takes centuries to build a city but only two days to destroy it."

"After what they did to us, I wouldn't regret it if the entire Germany was destroyed," said Deborah, with rage and bitterness in her voice. "I have no use for Germans. I don't care if they starve and die."

"Not all Germans are bad," said Phyllis.

"Hannah, sitting quietly over there, had been persecuted by the Gestapo," said Eric, putting his arm around Deborah. "You should realize that there are many people like her in Germany."

"I am tired of hearing about Hannah day in and day out!" Deborah screamed. "I'm fed up."

She got up from her chair, threw her paper napkin and fork on the table, and walked out of the room. Shocked, Eric rose and followed her. His parents looked at each other in stunned silence.

Hannah thought it was time for her to leave.

"Nice to have met you," she said to both of them. "Hope we will meet again."

"Don't go, Hannah," said Phyllis. "I would like to talk with you for a while."

As though taking a hint, Saul got up and said he would have couple of drinks at the bar downstairs with "the boys."

After he left, the two women stared at each other for a few seconds, afraid of articulating their thoughts, each waiting for the other to speak. Phyllis, finally, decided to break the ice.

"Deborah came with us to fix a date for the wedding," she said. "She and Eric have been engaged for a year, and she was hoping to get married this summer. Eric told her he didn't want to go through with it. She was stunned, to say the least."

"These things happen," said Hannah. "She will get over it. She is young and very attractive. There will be no dearth of suitors."

"That's what I told her also. I think she's embarrassed to tell her friends and family that the wedding has been called off. I can understand her feelings."

They were silent for a few minutes, playing with their food.

"Hannah, I don't like beating around the bush, and I'll ask you a direct question," said Phyllis. "Is there anything going on between you and my son?"

Hannah had a feeling that she would be asked that question but hadn't prepared a reply in advance. "I work for him. I think of him as a friend," she said, after a pause. "I am not emotionally or physically involved with him. Does that answer your question?"

"The only reason I asked was because he was talking about you all the time. He is so excited that he met you and persuaded you to work with him. My son is compulsive in his behavior. Right now he has two obsessions—the first is to find out the plan behind the mass murder of the Jews, and the second is you."

"I don't encourage him. I am old enough to be his mother. I am going to be forty-six soon."

"I am fifty-four," said Phyllis. "I think I understand the situation now. I am worried about my son, though. He won't take no for an answer from anyone. I don't know where this is going to end."

They sat there in comradely silence, in sympathy with each other, until the object of their concern burst into the room with his characteristic energy.

"I'm glad you're still here, Hannah. Sergeant Swoboda will take you to your home and will also drive you to the courthouse tomorrow."

"How is Debbie, Eric?" asked his mother.

"She is resting now. I gave her a couple of aspirins and had the restaurant send up a pot of tea. She should be fine."

"Do you think I should go and sit with her?"

"No, Ma. She and I have to discuss a few things. I came out to take Hannah downstairs to the car."

Hannah got up and said good-bye to Phyllis.

"We have so many things to talk about, Hannah," Phyllis said. "Unfortunately, we're leaving tomorrow morning. I would like you to come to New York, and my gallery will sponsor your visit. You'll see a lot of your compatriots there—Gorge Grosz, Bertolt Brecht, and many others."

"Let's wait for a few months and see what happens," said Hannah.

"I liked some of your drawings and posters that Eric showed me. I think I can sell them in New York. And I'll put the proceeds in a bank account in your name. Is that all right with you?"

"Go ahead. It's such a long time since I've sold my work. Maybe it'll get me back into painting."

"I hope you do get back to painting," said Phyllis. "Wish me luck, Hannah."

The two women warmly embraced each other, and Hannah went downstairs with Eric to the crowded and noisy lobby of the hotel.

Eric looked moody and distraught as he opened the car door for her.

"I'll see you tomorrow at the courthouse," he said distractedly. "Thanks for coming."

"Thanks for asking me," said Hannah and got into the car.

The sergeant didn't know the way to her house, and she had to give him directions—a difficult task since there were few streetlamps, and she couldn't see very well from the backseat. She finally asked if she could sit in front with him so that she could see better. He reluctantly agreed—it was against the rules, he said—and she was able to guide him through the outskirts of the old city to her house despite the lack of recognizable signs or street names.

Sixteen

Moving Out

That night and the next morning, Hannah spent a considerable amount of time thinking about her course of action toward Eric. She wanted to be his friend and also to finish the project they had started, but she didn't want to have any deeper relationship with him, even though she didn't intend to pull away from him—it wasn't in her nature to be cold, and besides, it was difficult to be distant with him because he was an open and cheerful person.

They met most evenings after the courthouse closed, discussing the day's events. After the explosive testimonies of Ohlendorf and Wisliceny, the trial was going through a humdrum phase during which a medley of less significant charges against the defendants was presented by prosecutors from all four Allies. One day the prosecutors would talk about Goering and Rosenberg looting art from the galleries of conquered nations, and the next day they would accuse Ribbentrop of persuading Japan to enter the war and for being a party to crimes against humanity. These would be followed by charges against Field Marshal Keitel for taking reprisals against relatives of French nationals fighting for Russians and accusations against Rosenberg for reviling Christianity and promulgating Neopaganism.

"The trial is losing its tempo," said Eric gloomily, while they were having a beer at their park bench. "They're throwing everything, including the kitchen sink, at the defendants."

"Perk up, they may be saving their best salvo for the end," said Hannah.

"I don't feel like perking up, Hannah. I'm in a bind. I don't like living in the Grand Hotel," he replied. "It's too noisy, and the guys drop into my room at all hours. I'm writing a book, and I can't concentrate."

It was the first time she had heard him talk of writing a book. All along she had thought he was going to write a verbatim report of the trial with drawings by her to be disseminated to the German public as a countermeasure to the Nazi mythologization of Hitler.

"What kind of book?"

"A historical work on the planning and implementation of the massacre of European Jews. Its title is *Blueprint for Extermination of European Jews.*"

Here we go again, thought Hannah. He'll never give up his pursuit, his idée fixe.

"You're frowning," he said. "I thought you would be supportive."

"Maybe there is no blueprint, Eric; maybe things happened without a plan," said Hannah.

"There must be one, Hannah," said Eric reassuringly. "You heard Dieter Wisliceny's testimony. Millions of Jews could not have been transported to Auschwitz without a plan. A German train carries about a thousand passengers. To carry a million, you require a thousand train journeys. This was done over eighteen months, adding to five hundred and forty days, which means several journeys per day during wartime, when trains are needed to move soldiers and material. This needs a lot of coordination and scheduling. There must be a plan somewhere, locked up in a bureaucrat's safe, unless they've destroyed it."

"There's logic in what you're saying," admitted Hannah.

"I know I'm right, Hannah," he said. "If I dig deep, I'll find it."

She instinctively sensed that it would be best if she didn't ask him questions and changed the subject.

"Is your family back in New York now?"

"Yes. They were flown from Berlin to London in a transport plane. They spent a week in London, and then they went back on the *Queen Mary*."

They sat in silence for a while, each afraid to step into the other's mental territory. Eric's mother had told him of the conversation between her and Hannah, and he didn't want to alienate her by talking about his feelings for her. She, on the other hand, was afraid that he would say something to her that would force her to break with him.

"This morning an army doctor I know told me he is going back to the States," Eric said. "He and his wife—she too is a doctor—have been living in a rented house in Stephanstrasse, and he wanted to know if I would take over the lease. He showed me the house, and it hasn't been damaged by bombing. The only things I don't like about the house are the awful oil paintings hanging on its walls and the heavy furniture that clutters up the rooms. I was thinking that perhaps you could modernize the house, since you've worked as a decorator."

Hannah's first thought was that Stephanstrasse was too close to her house—it was only a fifteen-minute walk. Her second thought was that Eric was playing a deep game, drawing her into his life step by step. She looked at him speculatively for a few seconds and decided he was sincere in his request for her help.

"I have to see the house first, Eric," she said. "I don't know if I can do anything to it until I see it in daylight."

He took her to see it the next day, when the court was in recess for a couple of hours. It had been built in the late nineteenth century—a house designed by an amateur who had relegated aesthetic considerations in favor of sturdiness and solidity—and seemed a perfect specimen of what the people of Bauhaus used to call "vernacular architecture." Hannah had Eric remove the heavy mahogany and ebony furniture in the house to a storage room in the basement and take down the paintings—mostly hunting and pastoral scenes—from the walls. The rooms began to look different, the high ceilings now coming into play and the moldings and ornaments standing out as things of beauty. The living room had a Persian carpet with light-red and pale-indigo arabesques, and Hannah advised Eric to keep it. As for his study, a room with a large rear window, Hannah got rid of the dark curtains and promised Eric she would paint pictures that would enhance the light-filled airiness of the room.

The next week she painted large pictures—imitations of Gunta Stolzl's rectangular grids in pale red and yellow—in her house, using the paints left by Octavia, and was gratified to see the joy on Eric's face after she had hung them up.

"I feel I can work in this room now," he said. "It feels comfortable. It makes me think of you even when you aren't around."

"I'm not doing this for love, Eric," she said softly. "I am doing this for money."

His face fell, and he took out a few twenty dollar bills from his wallet and gave it to her.

"I hope this is enough," he said.

"It's better than nothing," said Hannah, with a smile. "It's a good feeling to get paid for my work. I wish I could get more work of this kind."

"Don't you like working for me, Hannah?" he asked.

"I'll finish this project, Eric. After that I've to think of picking up my career as an artist."

He asked her to stay and have a drink with him, but she excused herself and went back to her uncle's house. I think I did the right thing with him, she thought, making it clear to him the nature of our relationship. Nevertheless, she felt she had acted churlishly, against her own true nature.

The trial crept along like a local train stopping at every little station on its way. Every morning Hannah would see the same sights—army photographers taking pictures, *Stars and Stripes* reporters talking to the attorneys, and Madame Falco, the wife of a French prosecutor, making sketches—and she would look carefully at the defendants, trying to memorize their facial expressions for her drawings. After opening, the prosecutors would reel off their charges like actors in a play, accusing one defendant of selling dead women's hair and ground human bones and another of the annihilation of the Freemasons in Czechoslovakia and Poland. These actions aren't the result of any blueprint, thought Hannah. It is German greed and German vindictiveness that's the root cause.

February crept on to March, and the worst of winter was over. The days were getting longer, and there was an abundance of flowers peeping through the desolation all around her. This made Hannah happy, and she sometimes sang on her way to work—lieders from Schubert and Schumann she had learned from her mother when she was growing up in Schwabing.

But in the middle of March, an event took place that changed her life drastically.

It began with the suicide of Karl Haushofer, the Nazi philosopher and close friend of her uncle. Haushofer had been interrogated by the Americans to determine whether he should be arrested and put on trial. On the night of March 10, he and his wife committed suicide by drinking arsenic. Her uncle heard the news two days later, when one of his old cronies came to visit him. The effect on him was devastating—he sat at the dinner table like a Parkinson's disease victim, the soup drooling from his mouth, his hands shaking as he lifted his napkin to wipe his chin. The next day he had recovered somewhat but still was very angry during dinner, ranting at the Americans for poisoning a great thinker.

"Americans don't poison people, Uncle Werner," said Hannah, hoping that she could calm him down. "They would give him a fair trial."

"What do you know of Karl Haushofer?" he shouted. "He would never take his own life. And he would never persuade his wife to kill herself. I am told that a Jesuit priest called Edmund Walsh was the American agent who interrogated him. They are cunning, the Jesuits. Mark my words, Haushofer and his wife were murdered, and there's a conspiracy behind it."

Spoken like a true German who sees a conspiracy in every action or incident, thought Hannah.

"There's no reason to believe that the Americans were engaged in a conspiracy to kill your friend, Uncle," she remonstrated, hoping that her words would make him change his opinion. Instead it had the reverse effect on him.

"Traitor!" he shouted at her. "You work for the enemy, and now you praise them. Have you no pride? No shame? They killed my best friend, one of Germany's finest sons, and you're trying to defend them."

Hannah kept quiet, hoping that his anger would wear off quickly. But Frieda intervened, making matters worse.

"The Americans treat us much better than we would have treated them if we had won the war," she said. "I agree with Hannah. I don't think anyone poisoned Professor Haushofer. He and his wife committed suicide for reasons known to themselves."

"The Yankees have corrupted our women!" he shrieked. "Would you have talked this way if the Führer had been around? All our leaders are gone, and now women have come out of the kitchen to tell us what's good for the country."

He threw his glass of wine on the floor and walked out of the dining room and into his study.

"This is no good," said Ulrike. "His friend's death has upset him. They were very close, you know."

Hannah and Frieda drank their wine without saying anything.

"I hope you aren't offended, Hannah," said Ulrike. "Don't pay any attention to what he said. He loves you very much."

"I am not offended," said Hannah. "I can understand his anger. Nevertheless, I think it's time for me to find a place of my own."

"Don't do that," said both women simultaneously. "We love it when you're in this house."

"This the third time in my life he has yelled at me. First was when I decided to go to art school. He didn't want me to do that. Second time was when I joined the Internationaler Sozialistischer Kampfbund and gathered signatures to vote against Hitler in 1932—you know, the Dringender Appell. It took eight or nine years for him to forgive me."

"But you know, Hannah, he worked very hard to see that the Gestapo didn't put you in jail. He and Haushofer went to see Hess—you know that both of them were close friends of Hess—and pleaded with him to ask the Gestapo to go easy on you."

"I didn't know that," said Hannah. "I had often wondered why they gave me a bit more laxity than other artists. I thought it was because of Emil, from what Stumpfegger told me. I had my doubts, for Emil didn't have that kind of power, even though he may have given Stumpfegger some money to keep a watchful eye. I should have guessed it was Uncle Werner all along."

"Your uncle looks at the old albums with your pictures all the time. You were the daughter he wanted to have but never had."

"I know he loves me. But he doesn't like it when I say or do something that he doesn't approve of. He doesn't want me to work for the Americans. Under the circumstances, it's best that I find my own place."

"But where will you go?" asked Ulrike.

"I've some money saved. As I bicycle around the city, I've noticed a number of places where they will take me in as a lodger. Don't worry about me; I'll be all right. And I'll come and visit you every week."

The next day Hannah felt as though a heavy burden had been lifted from her shoulders. It had been quite a strain living with her uncle, going home each day after hearing the litany of crimes against his cronies and associates to listen to the old man reminisce about his Nazi days, and sometimes she had been on the verge of breaking out hysterically and shouting at him, "What did you know of all these heinous crimes?

Were you part of the team, like your friends Heidegger, Schmitt, and Baeumler, who fortified the Nazis with doses of philosophy that justified war and mass slaughter as admissible moral acts?" She felt it was time to move out, to prevent a blowup on her part that would lead to an unhealable rupture between her and her uncle.

"Can I have a couple of days off?" she asked Eric the next day.

"You certainly can, Hannah," he said. "Is anything wrong?"

"I want to find a new place to live. I've stayed too long at my uncle's house, and it's time to make a move."

"I've a suggestion," he said. "Why don't you rent the upstairs rooms in my house?"

"I can't afford that. I am looking for a single bedroom."

"Pay what you can, Hannah. All I am saying is that I hardly go upstairs, and the rooms are unused."

"I don't think it's a good idea for me to live in your house."

"You will be my lodger. There's nothing wrong in that."

"I don't know. I still don't think it is a good idea."

He didn't press her after that. For the next two days, she went looking for a suitable place to live and was disappointed with the results. She visited three houses that had spare rooms to rent but was turned off by the women with whom she spoke. They were typical Nürnberg Frauen—they had been members of the Bund Deutscher Madel, their husbands, all SS men, had not returned from the Eastern front, and Hannah could see the vacant space where Hitler's photograph used to hang in their living room walls—and they stared at her with tight-lipped hostility after learning she was a Berlin artist working for Americans at the Nuremberg trial.

"Have you found a place yet?" Eric asked her when they met after the court had adjourned.

"I checked out three, but I didn't like the people who were renting the rooms," she said.

"Hannah, why don't you rethink my offer? It will be the best for both of us. I have a cook and a maid—both middle-aged German women—a chauffeur, and a gardener. We can eat our meals together, and I can use your help in writing my book."

It was a good offer, she thought, as long as there was no sexual quid pro quo. She didn't know how to phrase her thoughts without giving him offence.

"I need privacy," she said.

"Of course, of course," he said, beaming. "You close the door behind the stairs, and you can have the second floor to yourself."

I should have been more explicit instead of seeking refuge in euphemisms, she thought; and, even as she agreed to his proposal, she knew that nothing good would come of it.

His chauffeur helped her move.

She told Ulrike and Frieda that she was going to live with a colleague in a house that was nearer to Palace of Justice and promised to visit them on weekends.

When she went to say good-bye to her uncle, the old man's eyes were moist with tears.

"Hannah, I didn't mean to drive you away," he said. "You're the only relative I have, and I would like you to stay here with me."

Hannah felt the familiar tug as she looked at her uncle's honest German face, with the square jaw, clipped white mustache, and trusting eyes. She remembered all his kindness toward her—an only child, without a father and neglected by her wayward mother—and wished she didn't have to do what she was doing. He loved Germany just as he loved her, and his love was based on an ideal in both cases—the idea of her as the German girl, blond, untarnished, and vulnerable, and the idea of Germany as his motherland, entitled to power and glory—and she could not make him see that ideals had to be given up for corrosive, disfiguring reality.

She cried on his shoulder as she hugged him and promised to visit him every weekend—and tore herself away from him to get inside the waiting car.

SEVENTEEN

MR. AUSCHWITZ SPEAKS

The proceedings continued at a snail's pace, and whole days were spent in rehashing old charges, presentation of affidavits for and against the witnesses by various individuals, or settling technical points raised by the defense counsel. Often, Hannah heard snores from the audience.

All this changed on the fifteenth of April, a beautiful spring day with unusually warm weather. Hannah was thinking of skipping the proceedings after the midmorning break and going for a long bicycle ride. But the appearance of Rudolf Höss, commandant of Auschwitz—brought in by the defense attorneys to prove that the operations of Auschwitz were classified top secret, and hence defendant Kaltenbrunner, the head of RSHA after the assassination of Heydrich by Czech freedom fighters, could not have been aware of them—took her by surprise.

Höss was a coarse, brutal-looking fellow in his late forties, with a brush like mop of hair that he swept back from his forehead. After hearing his Bavarian accent and unrefined way of speaking, Hannah wondered how he had ended up being an *Obersturmbannführer* in the SS. Some sixth sense told her—or perhaps it was the way he stood, like Nachtkrapp, the very embodiment of German evil—that his testimony was going to be the most revealing and the most shocking disclosure that would be presented at the trial.

She took out her notebook and wrote down some of the questions and answers that followed.

"Were you the commandant of the camp at Auschwitz from 1940 to 1943?" asked the prosecuting attorney.

"Yes," Höss replied.

"Were you a member of the SS?"

"Yes, from 1934 onward."

"You went to Berlin to see Himmler in 1941, did you not?"

"Yes."

"What was discussed at that meeting?"

"I was summoned by Reichsführer SS Himmler in the summer of 1941 to receive word-of-mouth orders from him. He told me that the Führer had ordered the final solution of the Jewish question, and it was the responsibility of the SS to carry out the order. He said if the order was *not* carried out quickly, the Jews would destroy the German people at a later date. Auschwitz was chosen as a site for the final solution for three reasons: it was easily reachable by rail, it was a large site, and it was isolated. Adolf Eichmann would come to Auschwitz in four weeks, and I was to receive further instructions from him."

"Did Himmler tell you that this was a 'secret Reich matter,' and so no one, including your own superior officers, was to be told about it under penalty of death?"

"Yes."

"Please describe the measures you took to ensure secrecy in carrying out your work."

"The camp at Auschwitz was three kilometers from the town. About twenty thousand acres of the neighboring area had been cleared for our use. The Birkenau compound where the extermination camp was built was two kilometers from the Auschwitz camp. It was in a heavily wooded area and completely hidden from the view of outsiders. It was a prohibited area, and only those with special passes were allowed inside."

"Did Himmler come to the camp to see that the order for final solution was being carried out?"

"Yes. He came once, in 1942, and saw how we processed the Jews, from their arrival at Auschwitz to their cremation in our furnaces."

"How about Adolf Eichmann?"

"Eichmann came several times, and he also witnessed the operations at Auschwitz."

"What do you know about the medical experiments performed on the inmates?"

"Professor Klaubert and Dr. Schuhmann carried out sterilization experiments, and Dr. Mengele performed experiments on twins."

"How many members of the SS were employed in Auschwitz?"

"Thirty-five hundred, approximately."

"How many members of the SS were employed in all concentration camps?"

"Thirty-five thousand, approximately. In addition, ten thousand men from the Wehrmacht were doing guard duty at the labor camps."

"Witness, you say in the second paragraph of your affidavit, 'I have been working at concentration camps since 1934, first at Dachau until 1938, then as Sachsenhausen until 1940, and after that I was appointed commandant of Auschwitz. I was in charge of Auschwitz until December 1943. At least two and a half million victims were exterminated there by gassing and burning. Another half million succumbed to starvation and disease, making the total dead three million. This three million roughly amounted to seventy to eighty percent of all Auschwitz prisoners, and the remainder was used for slave labor by German industry. The Auschwitz inmates were mostly Jews from Germany, Holland, France, Belgium, Poland, Hungary, Czechoslovakia, Greece, or other countries. From Hungary alone, we executed about four hundred thousand Jews in the summer of 1944.' Is this true, witness?"

"Yes."

"To continue reading from your affidavit: 'Mass executions by gassing began in the summer of 1941 and went on for three years, until the autumn of 1944. I personally supervised executions at Auschwitz until December 1943, when I was transferred to the Inspectorate of Concentration Camps. I was in a position to know that mass executions continued into 1944. All work in Auschwitz took place under the direct order, supervision, and responsibility of the Reich Security Main Office (RSHA) under Reichsführer Himmler. I received orders for carrying out mass executions directly from the RSHA.' Are these statements true, witness?"

"Yes."

"The following is from paragraph six of your affidavit: 'The final solution of the Jewish question meant the complete extermination of all Jews in Europe. In June 1941, when I was ordered to set up extermination facilities at Auschwitz, there were already three other extermination camps in Poland: Belzek, Treblinka, and Wolzek. I visited Treblinka to find out its method of operation. They had liquidated eighty thousand Jews from the Warsaw ghetto in the course of half a year, using carbon monoxide. I did not think that this method was very efficient. So when I set up the extermination building at Auschwitz, I decided to use Zyklon-B, which is prussic acid in pellet form. We dropped the pellets into the death chamber through a small opening. It took fifteen minutes at the most to kill the people inside the death chamber. We waited half an hour before we opened the doors to remove the corpses. Then special commandos took off wedding rings and extracted gold from the teeth of the dead.

"'We built our gas chamber to process two thousand people at one time, in contrast with Treblinka's gas chamber, which could handle only two hundred. The incoming prisoners would be marched past doctors who would isolate those who were fit for work. The others were sent immediately to the death chambers. Children, because they would be no good as laborers, were invariably exterminated by us. Unlike in

Treblinka, the Auschwitz victims never knew what was ahead for them. We told them they had to undergo a delousing process, but sometimes they saw through our deception, and there were a few disturbances and even riots. The characteristic stench from the nonstop burning of corpses permeated the entire area, and all the people living in surrounding districts knew that mass exterminations were taking place at Auschwitz.' Is this true and correct, witness?"

"Yes."

"Did you ever empathize with the victims, thinking of your own family and children?"

"Yes."

"How was it then possible then for you to carry out these actions?"

"My scruples were laid aside in light of the order given by Reichsführer Himmler and the reason given by him for issuing such an order."

When the session closed, Höss was led away by a guard, and Hannah sat there for a while, stunned and bewildered by what she had heard. In the beginning, Höss's Bavarian face reminded her of a face she had seen in childhood, and she linked it to that of her father's cousin who used to visit her mother and stay at their house for short periods. She never liked him because he would grab her, grope her, and tell her he was going to marry her when she grew up. But this memory made her think that somehow she and Höss were biologically linked, that she too was inherently evil, just like him, and under different circumstances, she too would have worked in Auschwitz, feeding corpses into furnaces or pulling gold out of their teeth. Psychic emanations from Höss had come in bursts toward her, enveloped her, pulled her toward him, and made her his partner in his evil deeds. "Are all Germans morally blind?" The question kept on popping up in her head. Was Auschwitz, with its planned, assembly-line installation for seamless murder of innocents, the culmination of all that was evil in the German psyche? She instinctively felt that Emil, the man she had loved for years, had also been in Auschwitz and had participated in sterilization experiments on inmates, since eugenics had been his field of study for years. She now hated him, and she hated herself for having been in love with him and felt polluted by her physical intimacy with him. Her mood worsened as she recalled the reading of Höss's affidavit by Colonel John Amen in a slow, nasal drawl, each paragraph ending with a question—"Is that all true and correct, witness?"—that had the crushing finality of Thor's hammer. She felt that the ghost of her brother, Johann, was leading her through the various Stations of the Cross—the silent condemnation to death by the SS doctor, the stripping of all his garments, the fifteen minutes under the Zyklon-B gas, and finally the oven where he was burned to ashes. The ghost looked at her, and his glance— mute and supplicating—seemed to imply that she could have saved him if she had tried harder.

A guard placed his hand on her shoulder and shook her from her reverie.

"The courtroom is closing," he said in English.

She got up and walked over to the bicycle stand.

The spring day lingered as she rode home, hardly noticing the sparrows and robins that were hopping around in the ruins before her. A blackbird sitting on a flowering twig opened its pink mouth wide and sang as she went by, pleading with her to look at him and admire his notes. Normally she would have stopped and made a sketch of him in her notebook, but she was so distracted she didn't even notice him.

She pedaled furiously until she reached her new home. She took the outside stairs to reach her room on the second floor and ran the bath. Fortunately, hot water was available, and she soaked in the bathtub for nearly half an hour, pouring water over her head to wash away her sins, performing the sacrament of baptism. She remembered her teacher telling her when she was ten or eleven that the Greek word *baptismos* meant "washing." "What sin are you washing now, Hannah?" she asked herself in the mocking voice of her teacher. "The sin of being German," she answered in a little girl's voice.

EIGHTEEN

"DON'T PUSH ME AWAY, HANNAH"

S he felt better when she got out of the tub half an hour later. She dried her hair and combed it in Fraulein Ritter's style, in two loose plaits behind her ears and falling onto her shoulders. She went through her wardrobe and chose Fraulein Ritter's sweater and woolen pants, which she hadn't worn for months, as her outfit.

When she went downstairs, the sweet odor of baking greeted her nostrils. It surprised her because the cook, Frau Brunner, never baked, getting her daily rations of packaged white bread and biscuits from the army depot. Hannah went into the kitchen and saw Frau Brunner giving the finishing touches to a birthday cake.

"Whose birthday is it today, Frau Brunner?" asked Hannah.

"It's Major Grossman's birthday, Frau Müller," said the cook. "I wanted to make him a sachertorte but couldn't get the apricot jam. But the chauffeur got me marzipan and mascarpone cheese from the black market, and I made a good German birthday cake for the master."

"I had no idea it was his birthday today," said Hannah. "How did you know?"

"I asked him when he hired me as the cook," said Frau Brunner. "I ask that question to all my employers."

The front door banged, and the birthday boy walked in, in his uniform, holding his hat in his hand and looking somewhat strained and moody.

"What's going on?" he asked, looking at the cake. "What's the occasion?"

"*Herzlichen Glückwunsch zum Geburtstag!*" said Frau Brenner.

"Happy birthday," said Hannah.

The greetings caught him by surprise. He looked dazed for a moment and then flashed his beautiful smile. "To tell you the truth, I had forgotten today is my birthday."

"I made a special dinner for you, Major Grossman," said Frau Brunner. "Also, I have a bottle of champagne."

"Great!" he said. "Let's open it. Actually, let's all drink together. I'll bring in the guys."

He brought in the "guys"—the chauffeur and the gardener, newly settled German émigrés who had been moved from Poland to Silesia according to Himmler's resettlement plan, but had been driven away from there by the locals after the Russians had liberated that area and were now working in Nuremberg for the US Army as day laborers.

Eric popped open the champagne bottle, and they made toasts. After that, Eric insisted on all of them eating together, and Hannah was struck by his generosity and complete lack of ill feeling toward Germans. He blames the regime and not the people, she thought, unlike me, who blames the people for having elected the regime. She liked him for his naiveté as she watched him playing the host without the least awkwardness or uneasiness at being the only Jew among four Aryans, three of whom were Nazi sympathizers.

Frau Brunner had made a delicious ragout of meat and potatoes, a mélange of spring vegetables, and the inevitable sauerkraut. She had also bought a couple of bottles of red wine from the Württemberg region through her black-market connections.

The domestic staff were uneasy to be at the same table with their employer, Hannah noticed. The two Polish Germans chewed their food without making eye contact, and the cook, sitting at the edge of her chair, nervously turned her head this way or that to see everyone was doing justice to her food.

Eric sensed the tenseness around him and broke the silence. "This is really good ragout, Frau Brenner. You know how to cook."

Frau Brenner beamed at the compliment and said she was worried the food would not taste good because she couldn't get some of the ingredients, but everyone at the table assured her that it was the best ragout they had ever tasted.

More conversation followed, led by Eric, who said they never ate sauerkraut at dinner in America and used it only as a topping on a hot dog. Frau Brenner didn't know what a hot dog was, and he explained it to her.

"Ach, a wiener," she said and giggled.

After dinner, they brought in the birthday cake, and Hannah sang "Happy Birthday," with the others taking up an encore. A large part of the cake was left over, and Eric suggested that they should wrap up a slice for the maid, and the remainder should be presented to the family of the chauffeur, who had a wife and two kids.

The staff left after stacking up the plates in the kitchen sink to be cleaned by the maid the next day, and Hannah and Eric were alone in the living room.

"I spent some time with Rudolf Höss today after the court adjourned," Eric said. "I went along with the psychologist who interviewed him in his cell."

"How could you bear to be next to the beast?" asked Hannah, thinking anyone who sits next to Rudolf Höss would be damaged by the x-rays of evil emanating from him.

"I was interested in the mental makeup of such a man," said Eric. "He feels that he has done nothing wrong. Himmler's words that what he was doing was being done for the survival of Germany was good enough for him. I asked him if he ever sympathized with the victims, especially the children, considering that he has kids of his own. He said occasionally he had doubts about the rightness of what he was doing, but they were quickly erased when he remembered the reason for such action given by the Reichsführer. Himmler was his pope."

He looked at the silent Hannah for a while, waiting for a response from her. When none came, he continued with his side of the conversation.

"It looks like Himmler was the guy who gave orders for the mass murder of millions. What was Hitler's role? Did he agree to a proposal put out by Himmler, or did he give Himmler explicit instructions? We don't know. The more I get involved in this thing, the more I am convinced that a handful of bureaucrats under Himmler planned the entire mass slaughter—and the key figures are all dead or out of our reach. The twenty-one guys on trial did a lot of bad things and should be punished for it, but they aren't responsible for the mass murder. Hitler is dead, Himmler is dead, Heydrich is dead. They were the architects of the final solution."

"Are you saying this trial doesn't address the central issue?" she asked him hesitantly, not sure of her ground.

"I was speaking to Telford Taylor, Jackson's assistant, a couple of days ago. He told me that there would be subsequent trials held in Nuremberg as soon as this trial is over. There will be an Einsatzgruppen trial for the prosecution of Ohlendorf and others like him. There will be a doctors' trial for doctors who experimented on inmates, another one for Reich ministers, and so on. All the guilty parties would be punished, Telford assured me."

"There were hundreds of thousands, probably millions of Germans who either worked in concentration camps or helped in capturing and transporting Jews. Are all of them going to be tried?"

"Obviously not. What you're asking is a good question. Do you punish a train driver for taking the victims to a camp? Do you punish the engineer who designed the gas chamber? I don't know the answer. I still think that many decent Germans were coerced to perform actions against their will and contrary to their natural inclinations. I like to think that the young soldiers who were sent to Russia were like kids in my own country sent to fight a war. They had nothing against the people of Russia, and I would like to separate them from people like Ohlendorf."

Hannah was feeling a little dizzy from the champagne and the wine, and there was weariness in her voice when she spoke. "You don't know how the Nazis corrupted the minds of youngsters. When I read the school books of my son, I used to feel sick. Hitler was a godlike figure, and the Jews were the devils. Russians were Marxists and thus in league with the devils. Killing the devils was a virtue, a necessary moral deed for the sake of the Reich. If you don't believe me, read some of the letters the young soldiers had sent to their moms and dads. Put an ad in the paper, and you will get hundreds of them if you pay a few dollars for them."

He was stunned by her words.

He rose up, came toward her, and took her hands. "Don't let us argue about this, Hannah. I've told you before I don't believe in collective guilt or collective punishment. I want us to work together."

"I will finish the project with you, Eric," she said. "Now I'm tired and want to go to bed."

He kissed her on her forehead, lingering too long, and as she hurriedly rose from her chair, his lips met hers lightly at first and then clung to hers in a passionate kiss.

"Don't push me away, Hannah," he said hoarsely. "You are the birthday gift I've been wanting."

Her head was whirling from the champagne and wine, and she felt sick. She offered him no resistance as he led her to his bedroom and pushed her gently down to his bed. She wished he would go away and let her sleep in peace, but he was undressing her, taking off her pants, her sweater, and her underclothing, and carefully folding each item before placing it on a chair next to the bed. Vague, disturbing memories of Russian soldiers came crowding into her mind, and she subconsciously flexed her body against another rape. But Eric did not rape her. To her dismay, she soon discovered that he was lost in adoration of her. He touched her very gently, he smelled her body, he kissed and licked every part of her, he counted her ribs, and he caressed her toes—it was as though he had never seen a naked woman before. She had never been intimate with a Jewish man but had heard stories about their fondness for oral contact and their masochistic need to grovel before the blond Aryan woman. She had dismissed them as part of the anti-Semitic lore, but now she was convinced that there was some truth in them as he went through another round of kissing her hair, her eyes, her shoulder, and even her armpits before entering her and climaxing in a frenzy. He then lay quietly on top of her and stroked her hair and arms for a while before rolling over and drifting into sleep. After hearing him snore, she got up, her balance a little off because of dizziness. I wish someone would help this old woman get back into her own bed, she thought, as she stumbled her way up the stairs to her room.

NINETEEN

THE EMPTY CANVAS

The next morning, she left early and bicycled to Fürth to kill time before appearing at the courthouse. She felt hungry and had coffee and a roll at the rundown food stall reserved for Germans, who weren't allowed to go into the main cafeteria.

The session was centered on Alfred Rosenberg, the Nazi intellectual who was Hitler's minister for the Occupied Eastern Territories. He was her uncle's friend, though she was not sure of the extent of their friendship. She had seen his books in her uncle's library, and once she had seen them together, talking about their favorite subjects—racial biology, eugenics, the de-Judaization of Germany, the suppression of Christianity, and the acquisition of lebensraum through annexation of Poland and other eastern countries. But that was many years ago, when Rosenberg was a young man, very different from the tall, middle-aged, clean-shaven individual standing in the defendant's box, with a full head of hair neatly parted on the side, professorial and dignified in his appearance and in his mode of speaking.

Hannah felt she was hearing her uncle's voice as his testimony went on and on—replete with references to historical and cultural icons from Homer to Schopenhauer—in spite of repeated requests from the judge and the prosecutors to shorten his speech. Toward the end of the session, through the thicket of learned words, she managed to understand what he was getting at—he was a "good guy," and despite the fact he had written extensively about the Jewish peril confronting Europe, what he had wanted was a "chivalrous solution" to the Jewish problem and not the one implemented by the likes of Himmler and Heydrich, even though he didn't explain what a "chivalrous solution" to the Jewish problem would be like in simple terms a layperson would understand. Numbed by the length and turgidity of his exposition, Hannah sat with her head down in the courtroom after adjournment until a guard asked to leave. But there was no place for her to escape to, no haven where she could seek shelter. That morning she had been thinking of going back to her uncle's house, but after listening to Rosenberg all day, she decided that she couldn't bear to hear more talk in a similar vein from her uncle.

She rode back to the house on Stephanstrasse, hoping that Eric's behavior on the previous night was an aberration caused by too much wine and champagne and would not be repeated. He was there to greet her, giving her a warm welcoming smile and treating her as though nothing had changed between them. She relaxed, thinking they could return to their old pattern of friendship.

"I've a letter for you from my mother," he said. "She sent it along with her letter to me."

She opened the letter and learned that Phyllis's gallery had sold four of her drawings, and a sum of $500 had been deposited in a bank account in New York in trust for her.

"George Grosz came to the gallery and saw your work," she read. "He really admired it. He remembers you from the old days and sends you his regards."

The next few lines were about the New York art scene, about young American surrealist painters who had been receiving a lot of attention in the media.

"Deborah is now engaged to a man she met at her best friend's wedding. He is a doctor, and they are planning to get married this summer."

The letter ran to several more paragraphs, for Phyllis was one of those six-page epistolarians, and Hannah, intending to read it at her leisure, put it in her purse and went into the kitchen to get a glass of water. The cook had already left, and Hannah saw the evening meal left on a warming tray. She went upstairs and had a leisurely bath and came downstairs for dinner in a calmer mood.

They ate in silence the spaghetti and meatballs in tomato sauce provided by the army food store and the canned pineapple for dessert. After they had finished, Hannah took the dishes to the kitchen and left them in the sink for the maid to clean up.

She came back to the living room and, after saying good night, was about to leave the room when she heard him call out her name.

"Stay with me tonight, Hannah," he pleaded.

She looked at him full in the face and was struck by his look of anguish.

He looks like a Jew, she thought. He is in love with me, and he suffers like a Jew.

Nearly two decades ago, in Bauhaus, she had read Marcel Proust's *Du Côté de Chez Swann* and been mystified by Swann's mental anguish caused by his love for Odette. None of the men she had known had suffered because they were in love, and seeing Eric's face in front of her, she wondered if it was a peculiarity of the Jewish soul to see pain as the obverse side of love and indispensable from it. Perhaps I am trivializing his feelings, she thought. She couldn't reject him, and she walked into his bedroom like a mechanical doll, took off her clothes, and lay in bed.

Last night's adoration scene was repeated, with the difference that her mind was not befuddled by drink. She calmly asked herself why she was submitting to a love that she didn't want and came up with an answer that hadn't occurred to her yesterday. She was the German woman, and he was the Other—the dark, unwanted one whom all Aryans had been taught to hate—and she had to pay a price for the Other's extermination, vividly narrated by Dieter Wisliceny and Rudolf Höss. Hannah justified her passivity as something inevitable, a part of her racial and biological destiny. At Bauhaus, she remembered, they would sit around lit candles and discuss endlessly Jungian archetypes—the anima and the animus within each one of us. One of her favorite remarks from Jung was, "Every one of us carries a shadow, and the denser and blacker it is, the less the individual is aware of it." He was her Jew, her burden that she could not unload that easily, her shadow that would haunt her forever.

He was very nice to her, she had to admit. He was scrupulous not to overstep the boundaries of propriety when they were with others and was careful to treat her with the respect due to a coworker. He built a studio for her in one of the empty rooms on the second floor, where there was plenty of northern light. He asked one of his colleagues who was going to Switzerland on some legal business to bring back oil paints, brushes, and a roll of canvas. He found a German carpenter to build an easel and the four-foot-by-four-foot stretchers she preferred and collected empty cans from the army depot for her to mix paints in.

Now I've to start all over again, she thought, as she stood in front of an empty canvas, stretched nice and tight, thinking of all her best work burned or mutilated inside a mound of rubble in Berlin. She usually began a painting by laying a few patches of color randomly across the canvas. The colors spoke to her, and she responded by moving them around, stretching them, thinning them, or laying another color over them. But nothing happened inside her this time, and she, in frustration, made copies of the works of Bauhaus artists—Willi Baumeister, Georg Much, and Johannes Itten—and erased them afterward.

"This won't do," she said to herself. "I've to find my own voice."

She realized she had to break away from the Bauhaus mold. "I can't play peek-a-boo behind the grid, like Mondrian did, nor can I nest squares like Josef Albers. Maybe I should give in to my emotions like the older generation of German painters, expressionists like Karl Schmidt-Rottluff and Emil Nolde—which means I've to reinvent my-self as an artist."

She wanted to paint scenes of war, rape, destruction, and the wreck-age she had seen in Berlin, but she didn't how to begin. And she stood patiently in front of the empty canvas, staring through her window on the second floor at the scarred and pitted Nuremberg that stretched on and on, waiting for an invisible hand to guide her, to show her a path in a new artistic landscape.

PART 3

POLAND'S GHOSTS

The terrain of the former extermination camps was ploughed up, trees were planted, and peaceful-looking farmsteads constructed...No traces whatsoever were to remain which might bear witness to the atrocities committed in Belzec, Sobibor, and Treblinka.

—Yitzhak Arad, *"Operation Reinhard": Extermination Camps of Belzec, Sobibor and Treblinka*

Few traces of the physical installations of the final solution remain. One may still see the ruins of a gas chamber and the second crematorium of Birkenau, as well as the ARBEIT MACHT FREI sign and many of the buildings in Auschwitz.

—Richard Breitman, *The Architect of Genocide*

TWENTY

DANIEL

In the second week of June, Eric was asked by the prosecution team to attend a parallel trial that was being held in Poland. Arthur Greiser, the governor of Wartheland, a new gau created by the Nazis after the invasion of Poland, was going to be tried by the Polish government for crimes against humanity.

"The Polish delegation attending the Nuremberg trial invited Justice Jackson to be at this trial. He cannot go, and he is sending my friend Captain Art Rubin, who is an adviser to the prosecution staff at Nuremberg," said Eric. "Rubin asked me to go along with him because of my expertise in international law, and I want you to come along."

"I don't speak Polish. If the trial is in Polish, I shall be of no use to you," Hannah said, hoping that she would be alone for a few days.

He waved away her objections, and they left three days later to Poznan in a Russian aircraft with Captain Art Rubin and his Russian friend Grigori Poliakov, a prosecuting attorney with the Polish team.

As the Russian military aircraft flew over the eastern part of Germany, which was now controlled by the Russians, Hannah was able to see the devastation the Allied bombers had wrought in Dresden and Leipzig. These were the cities that she, as a young girl, had visited with her mother or her uncle to see their old friends or relatives. Now they were a heap of ruins, and she could see people scurrying out of tunnels and mounds like scavenger ants and pouncing on anything edible that came across their way.

The three young men sitting in front of her were pointing out to each other the burned-out remnants that they could see beneath them and were laughing at the destruction caused by the fallen bombs. They spoke in English and Yiddish—the three of them, bonded by their common heritage and ancestry, speaking the latter tongue with identical gestures and inflections—and Hannah wondered if, despite all his talk to the contrary, Eric believed in collective guilt and collective punishment and took delight in the destruction of all that was German.

She felt drowsy and, lulled by the drone of the plane, dozed for a while. When she opened her eyes, they were flying over the River Oder, glinting like a metallic ribbon in the summer light, miraculously untouched and untarnished by the wreckage of land and buildings around it.

Soon they were in Poland and were circling over Posen (Poznan, in Polish), where the trial was going to be held. From above, Hannah saw the old city, damaged by German bombs, but not to the extent of the Altstadt in Nuremberg. She only had a quick view of it and wanted to see it in more detail, but the plane veered toward the Rusałka Lake, where swans still floated, before landing at a military airport.

They were welcomed by a friend of Captain Poliakov, and Hannah tried to follow the exchanges between the two men, but her knowledge of Polish was rudimentary. Poliakov turned to them and said in German that the one available hotel in Poznan was fully occupied, but they had arranged rooms in private houses for the American guests.

A Soviet Army car drove them to the house where Art Rubin would be lodged, and a few blocks down the road, the car stopped at a small two-story house where Hannah and Eric would be staying as guests. The driver told them in broken German that he would pick them up at nine the next morning for the trial.

A full-figured blond woman in her late thirties, dressed in black, greeted them in halting Russian. Hannah asked her if she could speak English, French, or German.

"Ja, ja, all Polish people in Poznan speak German," she said. "I also speak a little English."

Eric soon won her over with his characteristic charm, and she livened up quite a bit. She gave them some bread and cheese to eat and also brought out a bottle of Zywiec, a light pilsner beer that tasted warm and soothing.

The woman's name was Olga. She was a widow whose husband had been killed by the SS. She hated Germans for what they had done to Poland, she said, and she loved Americans—in fact, her cousin Alicia was a dress designer in New York, and she was going to go over to meet her there soon after things had settled down in Poznan.

Olga showed them their rooms, taking them up two flights of rickety stairs to an attic which had been partitioned into two sections by a heavy red drape. Each section was furnished with a camp bed, a shelf, a coat stand with a wire hanger, and a lamp on a small table.

Seeing the fleeting disappointment on the faces of her guests, Olga sighed. "This is the best I can do for you," she said. "The second floor, which I didn't show you, has two bedrooms, but the walls and ceiling are so damaged by gunfire by the SS men who came to kill my husband that I decided to put you up here."

"Being an artist, I'm used to living in attics," said Hannah.

The woman ignored her.

Eric said that the rooms were fine, and the woman gave a pleased smile.

"The bathroom is downstairs," she said to him. "I go to work very early, and you can make breakfast in the kitchen."

She turned toward the stairs and started going down, and they followed her to the living room. There was still light out, and a restless Eric suggested going for a walk, with Olga as their guide. They set forth, Eric in the middle, toward the main street, which was only half a mile from the house.

"Poznan is a very old city," Olga said, "founded seven centuries ago. It has an old town, a castle, and a wall built around it. It is the capital of the Poznan province, and the Nazis had made it the capital of the Wartheland. They wanted to make Wartheland a habitat for Aryan folk. Only blond-haired and blue-eyed Poles had been allowed to stay in Poznan. The dark-haired Slavic-looking ones had been expelled to the neighboring General Government administered by Hans Frank or shot and killed when they resisted, as in the case of my husband."

Here she broke down and cried for a while, and Eric put his arm around her and offered his handkerchief to wipe away her tears. They resumed their journey after the outburst of lachrymosity had subsided and walked on Święty Marcin—the main street of Poznan—toward the Old Town, Olga leaning against Eric and looping her arm around his, while Hannah trailed behind, looking at the ruined buildings on either side of the street.

"The Battle of Poznan took place here, last year," said Olga to Eric. "Hitler had named the city a *Festung*, and the Nazis resisted the Russians till the very end."

"What's a Festung, Hannah?" asked Eric.

"A stronghold," she replied, still lagging behind.

The Warta River, a short distance away, glinted and beckoned, and they walked across its western bank for a while, at Hannah's request. When it was getting dark, Olga suggested they turn back.

They had a simple dinner consisting of beet soup, sausages, black bread, and a bottle of Zywiec. During the meal, Olga told her life story in bits and pieces, switching back and forth between English and German. She had been a high-school chemistry teacher before the war. Her husband had been the principal of the school. The Nazis dismantled their educational system, banned the Polish language from schools, and wanted Polish children to be taught the bare minimum necessary to obey simple commands from their German masters—to count to ten and learn a few German words. Olga and her husband, along with other teachers, held clandestine classes for students in private homes, but the Germans got wind of their effort and put an end to it.

"The man who is going to be tried is the vilest man on earth," she said to Eric. "He used to strut around here with his SS guards, kicking Poles out of his way. We had to give up our seats in trams and buses to Germans. We weren't allowed to eat in restaurants. They put up signs saying, 'No dogs or Poles allowed.' And when that man was arrested and brought over here, the prosecutors put him in a cage, and people lined up to see him. I too went, and I wanted to spit in his face, but the guards pulled me back. He is a beast, a mass murderer…"

I wish she would talk to me, thought Hannah. I really would like to get to know her.

But Olga had eyes only for Eric. After a while Hannah, pleading tiredness, got up, climbed the creaking stairs and went to her room in the attic. She undressed in the dark, hanging her clothes on the antler-like hooks, and fell asleep in her bed.

A few hours later, she was woken up by Eric climbing into her bed and wrapping his arms around her.

"I was hoping you would spend the night with Olga," she said sleepily. "She seems to like you."

"You're the only one for me, Hannah," he said. "Olga wants to move to America, and she was hoping that I would take her. I told her I was going to marry you."

Her body went stiff, and as his hands and lips moved over her erotic zones, her reaction was that of tundra-like frigidity.

The trial of Arthur Greiser was held on a Saturday at the Posen University, built by the Nazis to train future generations of Aryans and to house a Center for Aryan Historical Research by scholars in good standing with Greiser, Himmler, and other leaders. Its Great Hall had been hastily converted to a trial room, modeled after the Nuremberg courthouse, with capabilities for simultaneous translation into several languages.

Greiser, bald and wearing glasses, stood at the dock wearing clothes that were too big for him. Unlike the defiant Goering or the suave Speer, he had a scared and nervous look about him as though he was expecting someone from the audience to put a bullet into him.

"He looks as though he has gone through a wringer," she heard an American voice behind her exclaim. "Last time I saw him in Berlin, he was the epitome of the cocky, strutting Nazi."

The courthouse was packed with Poles, and they were a raucous lot. Hannah saw only a handful of Americans and Russians and hardly anyone in a British uniform.

The trial was presided over by Kazimierz Bzowski, the president of the Supreme People's Tribunal—a temporary court set up for trying Nazis for war crimes. Using the Nuremberg trial as a model, Greiser was charged by the prosecutor with conspiracy to wage war, crimes against peace, war crimes, and crimes against humanity. Just as in the Nuremberg trial, there were stacks of documents that established the guilt of the defendant; in addition, several witnesses were called to testify for the prosecution, and it was obvious to everyone that the verdict would be death by hanging.

Hannah experienced the same sense of boredom that she had felt at the Nuremberg trial. The prosecution didn't specify the atrocities committed by Greiser but charged him with the same broadly defined crimes that had been brought against the twenty-one defendants in Nuremberg, even though Greiser was too low in the Nazi hierarchy to be held accountable for those. The only excitement in the trial was provided by the testimony of Daniel Neumann, a Polish Jew who had been a professor of economics at the local university. He was brought in as a prosecution witness, and he described calmly and meticulously the brutality of the Greiser regime, from racial segregation of the Jews to their ghettoization and subsequent liquidation at the Chelmno camp.

Hannah and Eric got to know him by chance at the courthouse cafeteria, where he was sitting next to them, reading from a trial transcript. Eric, in his characteristically friendly fashion, asked him to join them. Daniel was a man of medium height, thin, with refined aquiline features and thick gray-streaked hair, combed backward. He had a cultivated voice and spoke German and English fluently.

"We heard your testimony," said Eric. "It was very moving and powerful, even though they gave you only twenty minutes."

Daniel looked at their faces searchingly and gave an enigmatic smile. "Are you Americans?" he asked.

Eric introduced himself and Hannah.

"This trial comes short in many ways, as does the one at Nuremberg," said Daniel. "Neither trial addresses the central issue, which is the genocide of the Jews."

Hannah and Eric had never heard the word "genocide" before, and seeing the puzzled look on their faces, Daniel proceeded to explain.

"The word was recently coined by my friend Raphael Lemkin, a distinguished Polish jurist, from *genos*, the Greek word for 'race,' and *cide*, which is Latin for 'killing.'"

He stopped suddenly and gave a sheepish smile. "Forgive me for sounding pedantic, but I've been teaching for twenty years, and it is hard to escape one's past."

"We learned a new word, Daniel," said Eric. "We should thank you for it."

"The prosecutors at the Nazi trials are reluctant to use that word—neither the British nor the Americans used it in Nuremberg, except once in passing, and the Poles are not using it here either. Instead they use euphemisms like 'crimes against humanity' or 'crimes against peace.' While it's true the Nazis killed millions of Russians and Poles, they didn't do so on racial grounds. The genocide was only against the Jews, and the Americans and the British and the Russians and the Poles do not want to admit it because of the anti-Semitism covertly or overtly present in their own countries."

Hannah, who was by now quite familiar with Eric's thought processes, sensed that Daniel's words had made a deep impression on him and set his mind on new track of exploration, analysis, and hypothesis formulation.

"Daniel, please have dinner with us tonight, and tell us what happened to the Polish Jews," he pleaded.

They met at a nearby café later on in the evening; it was very warm, and they sat outdoors, drinking beer and eating sausages and black bread.

"I was arrested, my house and valuables were confiscated, and all of us—my wife, my two sons, and my sister who was living with us—were sent to the Lodz ghetto," said Daniel. "Lodz, before the war, had a large and thriving Jewish population, with some very rich men and a number of highly skilled artisans. Immediately after the Nazis conquered Poland, they divided it into three gaus. Arthur Greiser was the *Reichsstatthalter*, or the governor of the Warthgau, which was planned to be incorporated into Germany as a new gau. People had to bow to Greiser when he walked by. The Poles, especially the darker ones, were treated like slaves by Germans. The Jews were forced to wear yellow armbands and were quickly rounded up and sent to a ghetto in Lodz. Their assets were seized, and their houses were taken over by the Nazis. The ghetto was soon sealed—that is, barbed wire fences were built around it to prevent the escape of its inmates. There was no electricity or water supply and no sewage disposal; food was scarce, and disease was rampant—I don't want to go into details because they would only make you sick. Some of my friends in the ghetto kept diaries which are part of the evidence at the trial, and these are available for inspection. I survived because I worked in the factory in the ghetto where they used skilled Jewish workers to produce spare parts needed by the German Army. My father owned a foundry in Lodz, and I used to work there during my summer holidays, becoming adept in handling machine tools. Little did I realize at that time that learning the machinist's trade would be my passport to survival."

He stopped to drink his beer, and Hannah liked the way he put his mug down on the table gently instead of slamming it. The fingers wrapped around the mug were slender and strong, with clean, scrubbed nails. Hannah's eyes moved on to his arms, tanned and muscular and covered by light-brown hair. She stared at them for a few seconds, thinking their latent sense of tension and power reminded her of Leonardo da Vinci's drawings of arms.

"More Jews arrived at the Lodz ghetto from other parts of Europe until it became so overcrowded that Hans Biebow, the administrative head of the ghetto, refused to admit anymore arrivals," Daniel went on, unconscious of Hannah's scrutiny. "But Hitler wanted the remaining Jews in Germany to be sent to Poland, and Himmler insisted that they should be put into the Lodz ghetto. Greiser made a deal with Himmler—he would admit one hundred thousand Jews into the Lodz ghetto if he were allowed to kill an equal number of the current ghetto residents. The deal was agreed to by Himmler and presumably by Hitler. Originally Greiser's plan was to take the Jews to a nearby ravine and shoot them. But that was changed in favor of building an extermination camp at Chelmno, the first one of its kind in the Third Reich, for murdering Jews by herding them into large trucks and using the exhaust gas to asphyxiate them. I was one of those who were taken there for extermination, but they gave me a job as a mechanic to do welding jobs to make sure the exhaust pipes of the trucks were working properly. They killed a hundred and fifty thousand Jews there. A few of us, serving as either mechanics or *sonderkommandos*—they're the ones who buried or burned the dead Jews—still remained, when Greiser was told to close the camp. The SS guards told us to tear down the camp and leave no trace of its existence. We knew, after we had done that, the guards were planning to shoot us, but we got the better of them and escaped."

He stopped and was about to lift his beer mug to his lips when his eyes met Hannah's. She stared into those deep brown pools of suffering and felt she was going to drown in them. I am falling in love, Hannah thought, and it has never happened to me this quickly before.

Shyly, gently, she spoke to him. "You must hate Germans for what they did to you, Daniel."

"I don't hate all Germans, only the ones who tried to humiliate us and kill us. We were not human beings to them but a lower species like the apes. At the Lodz ghetto, we would periodically get throngs of German visitors, gawking at us, laughing at us, taking pictures of us as though we were animals inside a zoo. The German guards, most of them in their teens, didn't think we were flesh and blood or had feelings or experienced pain the same way Aryans did. We were like vermin, and it was not a moral offense to spit on us, kick us, or even set us on fire. I used to wonder what made these young German guards act the way they did. Did they go to a special school, or was it their innate brutality that had been denied outlets when they were in their own country? It will take me hours to tell you the subtle inventions of physical and psychological torture they managed to inflict on us. As I said before, these are documented in the diaries that are part of the trial proceedings. Would I do the same thing to Germans if the opportunity were given to me? The answer is no. Can I wipe out from my memory all the incidents from the past and think of Germans in the same way as I think of the French or the English? The answer is no again."

Hannah knew exactly what he was feeling and admired him for expressing his thoughts so vividly. A deep gloom settled over her. His worldview would always be polarized, she thought, which meant they never could be friends.

"Doesn't the trial lift up your spirits?" asked Eric, hoping that Daniel would agree with him that justice would be served by punishing the guilty.

"I wish I could agree with you, Eric, but I cannot. There were thousands of perpetrators, and most of them got away scot-free, like

Friedrich Übelhör, the governor of the Lodz District, who first proposed the creation of the ghetto in Lodz. I know that you can't put thousands of Germans on trial, but there is no point in executing a few people if many guilty ones go unpunished."

This man thinks like me, thought Hannah. He is not like the smug Americans who think their system of justice is applicable to a complex situation brought about by millennia-old resentments and hatreds. She looked at him openly, admiringly, and he glanced at her, surprised at her interest in him.

Eric seemed to be in a trance, completely oblivious to what was going on around him. Hannah sensed that he was trying to make up his mind about some new course of action.

She was right because, a moment later, Eric addressed Daniel. "I would like you to take us to Lodz," he said. "Also, I would like to see what's left of Chelmno. And after that, Warsaw. And finally, Auschwitz."

"The Nazis have erased the Lodz and Warsaw ghettos," said Daniel. "The only signs you will see there are the remains of tenements. As for the extermination camps, Chelmno and Treblinka have been dismantled by the Nazis. The only ones that have been left intact are Majdanek and, to some extent, Auschwitz. I don't really know what you could gain by making the trip you suggested."

He means well, but he doesn't know his customer, thought Hannah. When Eric wants something, he isn't going to be dissuaded by reasoned argument.

"I would like to make the trip, Daniel," he said. "I'll arrange a car and a driver, and I would like you to be our guide."

Daniel gave a quizzical, tolerant smile—the gesture of submission by an indulgent father to a wayward, willful son.

"If you're determined to go, I won't stand in your way," he said. "Please make sure we carry sleeping bags and food supplies for three or four days. The area we will be traveling through has been hard hit by the war."

Two days later, the court decided unanimously that Arthur Greiser should be given the death penalty. His execution would be carried out in public, in front of the ruins of the Poznan Citadel. Hannah and Eric didn't want to witness the hanging, and bidding farewell to Olga, who tearfully embraced and kissed Eric on the lips in front of others, they left for Lodz.

The route they took ran parallel to the Warta River, and Hannah glimpsed every now and then through the car window the wide ribbon of water. She was struck by its color—it switched back and forth from a dark to a light blue, with an inner light coming from it—and marveled at the complete, almost mystical, union between the river and the verdant Polish landscape around it.

"I've never heard of the Warta River, since geography isn't one of my strong points," she said to Daniel, who was sitting next to her in the back of the car. "I had no idea that the Polish countryside was so beautiful."

"The Warta is a tributary of the Oder River and runs for five hundred miles through Poland before it empties into the Oder at the border with Germany," replied the professor with the encyclopedic mind. "It touches nearly two dozen Polish cities and is the most important river in Poland, after the Vistula."

He discoursed on the history of Poland, its early accounts by Ptolemy and Tacitus, its various proto-Slavic tribes, its numerous civil wars, and its partition and governance by Teutonic Knights and Russian tsars. She had trouble following his tortured and fragmented narrative, but she liked to hear his voice and listened passively while looking out the window, her eyes taking in the dozens of small towns they went by, each with its own steepled church, medieval castle, and statues of legendary warriors who presumably fought against the Teutonic Knights. She then dozed for a while, her head resting against Daniel's shoulder. When the car stopped, she woke up, smiled, and apologized to Daniel for leaning against him.

"It's my fault that you fell asleep," he said. "I shouldn't have bored you with all those details of Polish history."

They were in a small town that, judging from its appearance, seemed to have fallen into hard times.

"This town is called Kolo," said Daniel. "The driver stopped because he needs someone to tell him how to get to Chelmno from here. I told him I would direct him. The Jews from the Lodz ghetto were first brought to Kolo and kept in a synagogue here and then sent to Chelmno using the railway line."

"I thought we were going to Lodz first," said Eric.

He seems moody and a little annoyed with Daniel, probably because I have been talking to him, thought Hannah.

"Lodz is about forty minutes away from here by car," said Daniel. "I thought it was easier to see Chelmno and then drive south to Lodz."

"OK, if you say so," said Eric.

"I can guide better if I sit in the front," said Daniel.

Eric acceded and climbed into the seat next to her.

They sat in silence as they drove through the lush countryside, with the River Nerem, a tributary of the Warta, on one side and the vast Polish plain on the other. Daniel stopped the car when they reached a small church, painted white. They climbed to a nearby knoll and surveyed the peaceful landscape around them.

"You won't believe that this was the place where the Jews had to wait before they were carried by trucks to the killing center, which was an old manor house that Arthur Greiser had seized from its owner," said Daniel. "It was completely hidden from view by trees. They also built a wooden wall around it, which provided additional concealment. The new arrivals at the killing center were told to undress in the great hall. They were then led along a corridor to the front door and asked to get inside a truck. They were told that the truck would take them to a bathhouse. When the truck was full, an SS guard locked its doors, its engine was started, and carbon monoxide was pumped into the truck through an exhaust pipe. It took about five minutes before the cries and shrieks of the victims died down. The truck was then driven to a wood, and the Jewish sonderkommandos buried the corpses there."

He stopped for a while, and it was obvious that he was trying to control his emotions.

"Now this area bears no traces of the killing center," he resumed in his usual cool, cerebral style that Hannah liked. "Himmler made sure that there would be no traces of genocide. All that remains of the manor house are a few foundation stones here and there. The thousands of corpses buried in the woods were dug up and incinerated in specially built ovens that were subsequently dismantled and removed. I am an eyewitness, a victim, and a survivor who can attest to the mass murder of my compatriots. Yet I am faced with a dilemma: the absence of evidence of such a horrendous event would be taken by many to mean that the event itself didn't take place. But I know it took place—not only here but in Belzec, Sobibor, and Treblinka, all of which have been dismantled by the perpetrators."

Eric didn't reply. Instead, he went back to the car and took out his field glasses from his army kit. He stood on the knoll and surveyed the areas pointed out by Daniel. He then gave the binoculars to Hannah, who, through its powerful glasses, saw a brown-and-white hare sitting on its haunches and a few birds—larks and woodcocks—circling around trees. Nothing was seen of the Chelmno camp, and Hannah thought for a moment that the camp was a figment of Daniel's imagination, a nightmare so vividly imprinted in his memory that he mistook it for reality.

"My next painting will be called *Ghosts at Chelmno*," she said to him. "Give me a few minutes to make some sketches."

The men ate their lunches and drank coffee from a thermos while she deftly made a sketch of the white church and the woods. They offered her a sandwich and coffee, but Hannah, who was feeling queasy, said she wasn't hungry and would eat later. After she had finished her work, they got into the car and reached Lodz in half an hour.

The day was bright as they strolled through Piotrkowska Street—the Champs-Élysées of Lodz—which still displayed wealth and grandeur, though wearing the signs of war. Daniel said the city was ushered into the industrial age by Jewish entrepreneurs, especially one Izrael Poznanski, who had set up textile factories that made Lodz the center of the clothing industry in Poland. His name was seen everywhere in Lodz—his huge mansion was now a textile museum, and his mausoleum in the Jewish cemetery, as big as a house, was a tourist site.

"The Jews changed Lodz from a nameless small town to a vibrant industrial city," said Daniel. "Poznanski, Goldfeder, and Silberstein practically built the city. Before the war, they had a thriving Jewish population here—and now they're all gone, gone with the wind."

There were tears in Eric's eyes, and Hannah noticed a transformation taking place in front of her—a hardening of his features, a tightening of the jaw muscles. He feels it in his guts, Hannah thought, as if he's in the process of creating a Jewish identity for himself. She didn't know whether it was good or bad—as for herself, the years at Bauhaus had washed away all feelings of ethnicity and nationalism, and she thought of herself as just another human being tossed up and ravaged by the maelstrom of world events: in fact, her Aryanness, when she thought of it, seemed to her like a hideous birthmark, a curse from which there was no escape.

The two men started walking ahead of her, somehow linked to each other. Hannah didn't hurry to catch up with them but took her time looking at the architecture around her—it was a mixture of the baroque and neoclassical, neither exciting nor boring, and the phrase that came to her mind was "forgettably provincial."

The men stopped and waited for her, still talking to each other.

"I agree with you, Daniel," said Eric. "A separate Jewish state is the only solution, but I don't know if it is achievable."

"We are trying hard, especially my friend David Ben-Gurion. He is from Poland, you know. His real name is David Grün before he changed it to Ben-Gurion, after the medieval historian Joseph ben Gorion. We are going to have a meeting in December, and we are going to put pressure on Britain and America for the creation of a Jewish state in Palestine."

Two men with missions, Hannah thought. She admired them and wondered what her mission in life was. Probably to satisfy Eric's sexual obsession with older women, she thought, without bitterness.

They soon entered the Lodz ghetto area, and Daniel pointed out the location of the Gestapo post that controlled all exits and entrances. The tenements that comprised the ghetto had been pulled down, and there remained only vast stretches, showing remnants of walls and fences. Daniel would every now and then point to a location where a ghetto landmark had once stood—a Jewish cemetery, a market street, a building where the Nazi police was housed, the central prison where Jews were tortured, or a small park where they were executed for the crime of eating food thrown over the barbed wire fence by a kind-hearted Pole.

On and on they walked, passing Saint Mary's Church—built by none other than the ubiquitous Izrael Poznanski for his Catholic workers—and, next to it, the red brick building that used to be the headquarters of the Gestapo, until they reached the notorious Radegast Railroad Station, the place the Nazis called the *Umschlagplatz* of Lodz—the site where Jews were assembled prior to being shipped out to the gas vans of Chelmno.

They waited at the railroad station for the driver to pick them up, as previously arranged. Eric and Daniel discussed what they should do next—whether they should spend the night on one of the park benches in Lodz or drive on to Warsaw, where Daniel was sure they could find sleeping accommodations at the house of a friend. They finally decided on the latter course, and Daniel, sitting next to the driver, guided them through the heart of occupied Poland, from Arthur Greiser's Warthgau to Hans Frank's General Government territory. Hannah, feeling tired, closed her eyes and soon fell asleep, her head resting on Eric's shoulder. When she woke up, they were in Warsaw, eerily reminiscent of Berlin because of the destruction wrought upon it by air and ground offense by the enemy—in this case, Germany. There was still light in the streets even though it was close to seven o'clock, and Hannah was stuck by the sight of buildings all around her with huge holes in their walls or roofs blown away and bricks, mortar, and wood piled up in heaps everywhere. Kids in rags were jumping up and down on the rubble, and they yelled at them in Polish as the car crawled past them. On the main streets, however, there were men wearing suits and women in summer dresses, going about with an air of fortitude and self-reliance that showed their determination to rebuild what had been damaged and to revive what had been given up as dead.

"I had no idea Warsaw would look like this. This is like being in some of the German cities," she said to Eric.

"I am as shocked as you," he said, holding her hand.

He is claiming his rights over me, thought Hannah, for he senses he has a rival.

"Eighty percent of the city was destroyed by the Germans," said Daniel. "Initially it was from the bombs. Then, after the uprising in the ghetto, Himmler wanted the entire city to be razed to the ground. The Russian army arrived in time to save what was left of the city."

She wanted to know more about it, but since he was busy giving the driver instructions to get to his friend's house, she decided to wait until the next day to ask him questions.

Soon the car came to a halt in front of a house with its top floor missing. Daniel went to the front door, which was opened by a short man resembling Vladimir Lenin because of his goatee and bald dome. They greeted each other in the Polish fashion by kissing each other on the right cheek, then on the left, and an encore on the right. Some devilish impulse prompted Hannah to say, "Heil Hitler!" but she controlled it in time.

"Pan Grossman, Pani Müller," said Daniel, by way of introduction. "This is my friend Pawel Szymanski."

"*Dzie dobry*," said Szymanski.

"My friend speaks French and Russian and of course Polish," said Daniel. "He knows German but isn't fluent in it."

"Hannah speaks Russian and French fluently," said Eric. "I speak neither language."

"Daniel or I will interpret," said Hannah in Russian.

"Good. Am I mistaken in thinking you are a German communist?" Pawel asked her, in the same language.

"No, just an artist blacklisted by the Nazis," replied Hannah.

That was good enough for him, and he was beaming as he took them into his living room, where the walls were covered with pictures of Marx, Stalin, and Marshal Zhukov, and the floor was stacked with books on socialism in three languages.

"Pawel teaches Marxist philosophy at the Warsaw University," said Daniel.

Hannah realized with a shock that Poland was under Russian control and hoped her host wasn't going to lecture them on how Comrade Stalin had saved the world, but that was exactly what he did during the repast of beer and sausages he provided for them. Hannah gathered he was a Polish communist—the Nazis had arrested him, and if it hadn't been for the timely arrival of the Russian army, he would have been shot or sent to a labor camp for his political beliefs. His wife, whose mother was Jewish, was put in the ghetto and, six months later, sent to Treblinka.

Hannah washed dishes and made coffee while the men went on talking at the table—gesticulating, vociferating, ridiculing. Daniel had no love for communism, branding it as another form of fascism, while Pawel despised Zionism as an escapist bourgeois fantasy. As for Eric, he seemed to be out of his league amid these polyglot, doctrinaire eggheads, smashing and returning arguments like expert shuttlecock players.

"I am tired and want to go to bed," she said to Pawel after a while.

Still arguing with his opponent, he rose from his chair and led her upstairs, with Daniel following them, to a room with a bed and a chair in it. The room had a gaping hole, the size of a dinner plate, on the wall facing the street.

"This used to be my wife's room," said Pawel. "There is a bathroom next door, but there is only cold water available. I am sorry that's all I can offer you."

"It's good enough for me," said Hannah.

The men left the room, closing the door after them, but Hannah could still hear them arguing as they were going down the stairs. She quickly fell asleep but was wakened a couple of times by the noises coming through the gaping hole—the staccato bursts from a motorbike without a muffler and the loud singing of a drunken man.

She slept later than usual, and after washing in ice-cold water, she went downstairs. The men were assembled in the kitchen and were eating *nalesnikis*, the Polish pancakes made by Pawel, who was an expert chef in addition to being a Marxist philosopher.

They greeted Hannah with smiles and cheery "good mornings" in three languages. Pawel placed a mug of coffee before her and proceeded to make a new batch of pancakes.

"Apple sauce or cherry jam?" he asked.

"A little bit of each," she said, knowing it would please him.

Indeed, he was all smiles, hovering over her as he placed tarnished silverware and a chipped plate in front of her. But the pancakes were excellent, and so was the coffee.

After she had finished eating, she asked Eric what they were planning to do that day.

"Pawel will show us the Warsaw ghetto—that is, what is left of it. We will then walk around the city for a while. And we will drive to the Majdanek extermination camp after that. From there we will go to Krakow and stay the night there, and tomorrow we will see Auschwitz."

The ghetto was in the old town, and they drove north with Pawel in the front directing the driver and Hannah wedged between Daniel and Eric in the back. After a few minutes, they turned west and drove through a maze of streets until they reached the ghetto. Parking the car on a side street, they began their tour from the Nozyk Synagogue with its neo-Romantic façade, scarred by gunfire and arson but still interesting because of its Byzantine and Moorish motifs. Facing it stood a tall, sparse-leafed tree, a mute witness of the synagogue's desecration by the Nazis, who, according to Pawel, had used it as a stable for their horses.

Pawel was a good guide, giving them a palpable sense of the place by showing them remnants of the ghetto walls here and there and a couple of tenements—brick structures damaged by gunfire—still standing in Prózna Street.

"The place now looks as innocuous as a battlefield from which all bodies and weapons have been removed," he said. "But Jews were packed into this area like sardines three years ago. Try to visualize them living in a crowded, filth-covered slum behind ten-foot-high walls. My wife was inside these walls, and she was sent with thousands of others to Treblinka…I loved her very much."

"She was the kindest, gentlest woman I have known," said Daniel. "Let's observe a moment of silence for her."

"Let's observe another moment of silence for all the Jews who were gathered in this ghetto and then sent to their deaths," said Eric.

They stood in line, hands across their chests, with a bright-blue sky over them and a wind gust from the Vistula River scattering shreds of yellowed paper and dried grass around their feet, while the ghetto— known variously as Warshauer Ghetto or Getto Warszawskie—rose, walled and brutish, before them, in their collective imagination.

They then resumed their walk in the city, traversing its main thoroughfares—Krakowskie Przedmiescie, Nowy Swiat, Marzscalkowaska, and so on—all of them in ruins, leaving the viewer to conjecture the grandeur of the old baroque structures from the charred and battered vestiges. A few years ago, before war had ravaged it, the city must have been beautiful, Hannah thought, and she realized with a start how ignorant she had been about her eastern neighbor.

The Germans had no awareness of the cultural heritage of the Poles and thought of them as helots, good at building roads and working in factories under the supervision of Aryans: it never occurred to them that their eastern neighbors were gifted in other ways, capable of building cities as imposing as any in Germany.

As though reading her mind, Pawel, walking next to her, began talking to her in Russian.

"Even before the start of the war, the Führer wanted to tear down all our beautiful buildings and rebuild Warsaw in the model of a small German town, with a population of a hundred thousand Aryans," he said. "Such was his hatred of everything east of the Oder River. They dropped hundreds of tons of firebombs into the center of this city and then bombarded it with artillery."

"The same thing was done to us too," Hannah replied. "You ought to see Nuremberg and Berlin. They are in far worse shape than Warsaw and Lodz."

"The war was waged by and for the sake of armament manufacturers, Hannah," he said. "Marx foresaw the overproductions of weapons. So did Lenin. Hitler was a pawn of the German industrialists."

Here we go again, thought Hannah. I've heard all this stuff before, for every communist I know lectures me in a pedantic voice about Marx's insights.

"Fortunately, our system will win because of its historical inevitability," he went on. "Europe is on our side; the only force that is resisting us is the Americans. Eventually, they too will come around."

I used to hear about "historical inevitability" from my stepfather, Paul, thought Hannah. She tried here the strategy that she had successfully used against him, which consisted of smiling and saying nothing. It worked, because after a monologue that lasted three to four minutes, Pawel lost interest and said he was hungry.

They went to a farmers' market on a side street and picked up bread, cheese, sausages, and beer. They ate their lunch at an orange grove at the Lazienki Park, watching ragged kids climb a German tank that had been abandoned there by the SS. The kids were pretending to be Nazis and shouting to each other in German to kill the Jewish swine.

"Time for us to leave," said Daniel after a while. "I told the driver to meet us at the main entrance to this park."

The driver crossed to the other side of the Vistula and continued on a road parallel to it for a while. Soon they left Warsaw and its suburbs and traveled along the far-stretching Polish countryside, more lush and fertile than the Rhineland, and ready, after the harvest season, for the plow or the tractor to make furrows on it. The land, expectantly waiting for seeds to be planted, made her think of a woman needing to give birth every year as an affirmation of her fecundity. She now understood why the Germans dreamed of lebensraum, for next to their fatherland was this huge area of agrarian tract, richer and more bountiful than any in their native environment and ready to be annexed if the Poles would concede their ownership peacefully—or seized with bloodshed if the Poles chose to fight.

Hannah nodded off and dreamed Daniel had married her, and she was living in Poland, becoming part of this beautiful, placid nation. When she woke up, she saw that Erich's hand was on her thigh, and the man in her dream was explaining to the driver the best way to reach Majdanek.

"Head to Lublin," he was saying. "Majdanek is a couple of miles away from the city limits of Lublin."

Half an hour later, she had a glimpse of Lublin's Old City, with red roofs, looking even more Gothic than the *Altstadt* of Heidelberg or Tübingen. High on a hill stood the Royal Castle, ornate and majestic, and Hannah was sure that it had been there for centuries.

"The Nazis used it as a prison for Polish insurgents," said Pawel. "Lublin was governed by the Russians before the war. The Germans then took control, and they decided to make it into a Jewish ghetto, along with Lodz and Krakow. And, of course, they built extermination centers near each ghetto."

Daniel stopped the car a few yards away from Majdanek. Pawel pointed out the watchtowers and the white stucco house where the camp commandant used to live.

"The Russians didn't give the SS enough time to dismantle the camp, as in the case of Treblinka and Chelmno," said Pawel, as they walked along a stretch of dried-out grass to the forced-labor workshops and the warehouses used by the Nazis for storing property taken from the dead.

The gas chambers were close to the warehouses.

"The Jews were stripped of all their belongings—clothes, caps, gloves, shoes, watches, glasses—before being sent to the gas chambers," said Pawel.

They were standing in front of a chamber made of brick with a tightly fitting metal door. A guard let them inside, and Hannah saw a cave-like structure, about thirty feet long and fifteen feet wide. Its walls were stained with shades of gray ranging from almost black to greenish, and Hannah's first impression was of an abstract mural done by an artist to depict the colors of death, the symbolism of the final solution.

"The stains on the walls are caused by Zyklon B," said Pawel with a cynical smile, as he watched Hannah looking at the walls.

I don't like this man at all, thought Hannah, but she didn't say anything.

"The Zyklon B pellets are dropped through holes in the ceiling," he said. "They then blow hot air, and the pellets turn into cyanide gas."

Hannah imagined herself inside that chamber, naked, her flesh pressing against other bodies, screaming with them, flaying her limbs with them, and wailing with them before the final enduring silence. I'm being a hypocrite, she thought, in pretending to experience something beyond the realm of my imagination. And, perversely, she thought of herself as a female guard, disguised as a nurse or a bath attendant, escorting the resisting victims into that chamber, closing the door, and giving a signal to the pellet dropper. The image made her ill, and she went out of the room to get a breath of fresh air. She walked around the barracks looking for something that would take her mind off her German heritage—but she could see nothing but overgrown brownish grass. There were no flowers, no trees, no birds—not even bees or squirrels.

"Hannah, are you all right?" She heard Eric's voice. "We are now going to see the crematorium."

She went over to where they stood, and they walked up a long slope toward the crematorium behind the barracks, five brick ovens that looked like equipment for baking giant loaves of bread.

"These are fired by coke," said the knowledgeable Pawel. "Each oven can accommodate two bodies, which are put in from the rear side of the oven. The ashes are collected from the front. Our Soviet comrades took pictures of these ovens, with heaps of ashes next to them. We can see them at the museum site."

Hannah didn't want to go to the museum site. A few yards away from the crematorium, there were huge ditches where gassed corpses had been dumped, doused with gasoline, and burned. She looked at them intently for a while, and started seeing skulls and bones picked clean as in Death Valley. I must be sick in my head, she thought, and retched violently, her body shaking in great spasms. A friendly guard saw her and brought her a can of water and stood by her while she drank some of it and washed her face with the rest.

When she rejoined them, she learned the men had made plans for the rest of the day. They would walk in the Old City for a while, have dinner at one of the cafés, and then spend the night at the University of Lublin, where Pawel's friend—the rector of the Socialist Studies Department—had made sleeping arrangements for them in a dormitory.

It was a warm summer afternoon, and they trudged along, with Pawel as guide and Hannah and Daniel taking turns as interpreters, from one end to the other of the Old City. They climbed the Trynitarska Tower, admired the Lublin Cathedral, stood before the Krakow Gate, and ambled through the main street, the Krakowskie Przedmiescie, all the way down to Lithuanian Square. They bought the usual Polish fare of bread, cheese, sausages, and beer from a food store and went to the nearby Saxon Park to have their evening meal.

There was no one else in the park. Eric took out his field glasses and scanned the trees for birds.

"There's a woodpecker," he said, passing the glasses to Hannah and to the two men.

The sight of the black-and-white bird with its red underbelly, clutching the upright tree trunk and tapping away, cheered her.

"I wish we could sleep in this park," said Hannah. "There seem to be plenty of empty benches. We can bring our sleeping bags from the car and spend the night here."

"Good idea," said Eric.

But after it was translated to him, Pawel looked at the sky for a few minutes and predicted rain by midnight.

"See the clouds over there?" he said pointing north. "They're cirrus clouds. The wind is from the northeast, blowing to the south. I'm pretty sure it's going to rain within the next six or seven hours."

Eric was skeptical, but nobody in the group wanted to take a chance of getting wet in the middle of the night. So they trooped over to the university, where they were given beds in adjoining rooms in an empty students' lodge.

The next morning they gathered at the rector's residence for breakfast, with the ubiquitous pictures of Stalin, Lenin, and Marx glaring at them like a demented trinity. His housekeeper, a grim-faced, middle-aged Polish woman dressed in black, brought in breakfast—boiled eggs, a basket of rolls, a plate of mild yellow cheese, and coffee in a beautiful ceramic coffee pot.

The rector, a short, powerfully built man, spoke very good English. After getting an idea of his guests' backgrounds and immediate plans, he lost no time in proving he was a good spokesman for the Soviet Union.

"The war's origins lay in imperialistic and capitalistic governments," he said. "The British and the French have colonies, and Hitler wanted colonies. The Americans joined the fray because they didn't want Japan to be their rival in the economic sphere. Of course, the arms manufacturers in all countries were enthusiastic in their applause. Marx prophesized things would happen this way and the Soviet system would prevail in the end. He was right, even though he didn't predict the enormous damages done to Europe by tanks and planes."

"Not to speak of the massacre of our populations, Comrade Antoni Ponikowski," said Pawel in a toady's voice.

"Thank you for reminding me, Comrade Pawel Szymanski," replied the rector. "It was unpardonable of me not to mention the millions of Poles who died in extermination camps at Chelmno, Treblinka, and Auschwitz."

Eric, sitting next to Hannah, was startled by his words.

"The millions who died in extermination camps were Jews from all over Europe, not Poles," he said.

"The party doesn't want to distinguish between Jews and non-Jews," replied the rector. "We want to stress that millions of civilians were exterminated as part of the Nazi policy."

"That's what I heard from the Russians at the Nuremberg trial," said Eric. "I don't agree with them. Why hold a trial if the issues aren't clearly brought out?"

"Don't forget that the Soviet Union was the primary advocate for holding the Nuremberg trial," said the rector. "Churchill wanted to shoot the Nazi cabinet and top generals without a trial. We were the ones who wanted to bring out the horrors done by the Nazis to innocent civilians. And I'll make this prediction: after hanging the Nazi defendants at the trial, the Western governments are going to let many perpetrators go free; instead of prosecuting them, they are going to turn on us and announce we're the real enemy."

Eric was about to say something in response, but Daniel intervened.

"We have a long drive ahead of us, Eric," he said. "The sooner we leave, the better."

"You're going back to Lodz?" the rector asked, pleased with himself for having scored points against his opponent.

"No, we're going to Auschwitz," said Daniel. "And we will spend the night at Krakow. Tomorrow Eric and Hannah will fly from Krakow to Nuremberg. I will take the bus to Lodz."

"You can stay at one of the dormitories at Krakow University," said the rector. "I'm sure there will be empty rooms. The rector is a good friend of mine. Shall I send him a telegram saying you will be coming?"

"No, thank you," said Daniel. "I was thinking that we could sleep outdoors, in the Jordan Park. Hannah would like that, I'm sure."

"That's a good idea," said the rector. "I too love spending time in Jordan Park. But if you change your mind, give me a call, and I'll be happy to arrange sleeping quarters for you."

The drive took about four hours through the Polish countryside—fields and farmyards followed by forests and stretches of agrarian land with farmers driving horse-drawn wagons. The roads were bumpy and narrow in some of the small towns they had to pass through. Often, they would encounter trucks and had to park their car on a side street to let them pass. The four of them would then get out of the car, and while the men talked politics, Hannah spent time looking at the picturesque churches, town halls, and houses painted in blue and red that were built very close to the streets. I love Poland, she thought, more than I love my native land—nature loves it more and has blessed it. The dream of living the rest of her life here came to her again, but it was darkened by the fear of living in another autocracy, with people like Pawel telling her how to think. I shouldn't be thinking of any future for me right now, the way the world is, she mused. Sighting the bluish-indigo gleam of the Vistula River a short distance away, she wished she could be in a boat and float down to wherever the river would end.

Finally, after an hour's drive, they arrived at Auschwitz.

Hannah was a bit scared as they entered the wrought-iron gates with the sign of ARBEIT MACHT FREI stretched across it. Having heard Rudolf Hoss's testimony at the Nuremberg trial, she had thought of Auschwitz as being a hell on earth or close to it, and it was with great trepidation that she cast her eyes around her. She thought she would still see huge heaps of rotting dead bodies and lingering flames from the ovens, but the path that lay before her was straight and wide, with beautiful tall trees on either side. True, the camp was fenced with barbed wire, and red brick army barracks loomed before her, but beyond those she could see green fields stretching out to the woods.

"This doesn't look like a death camp. Who planted all these trees?" she asked Daniel.

"The SS did. The Germans love nature, as you should know," he said, with a tinge of sarcasm.

Hannah looked around some more and saw, next to some poplars and birches, a set of wooden structures on a field, like goalposts in a soccer field, but taller.

"They are gallows for hanging prisoners," said Pawel, when she asked him about it. There was a touch of mockery in his tone, as though he was laughing at her for being a woman who could not tell apart gallows from goalposts.

Hannah's mood dampened, and she dropped behind the three men, with a foreboding that something would happen that would crush her psyche, that some unseen hand from beyond the grave would clutch and choke her, leaving her gasping for breath.

"The SS began evacuating Auschwitz when they saw the Russian army advancing toward them," she heard Daniel say to Eric. "Most of the prisoners were sent on a death march through frozen terrain to Upper Silesia. This was in January 1945, and very few survived that march through the icy countryside. The SS then proceeded to dismantle and destroy the camp. They managed to blow up the gas chambers, the ovens, and the huts where they kept the prisoners—but they weren't able to do a thorough job, and we can still see the remains.

The Soviet troops arrested the SS who were guarding the camp and liberated the remaining prisoners. My cousin was one of them. He had survived by hiding under a mound of corpses."

"We should walk over to Camp Birkenau and show them the remains of the extermination center, Daniel," said Pawel.

Hannah followed them, wondering why she was inflicting pain on herself as her eyes fell on the sinister railroad tracks that led directly to the lethal chimneys.

Pawel stopped at a warehouse that stored the worldly goods taken from the gassed victims—thousands of shoes, eyeglasses, chamber pots, suitcases, and even prosthetic limbs. Salvador Dali would have loved this, she thought, this heap of artificial limbs, these lenses from myriad glasses flashing in the sunlight, these images that are so reminiscent of his *The City of the Drawers* or *The Metamorphoses of Narcissus*, and perhaps living proof that random acts by mass murderers could sometimes turn into replicas of imaginative works by great artists.

"Millions of Jews were brought here from all over Europe," she heard Daniel say to Eric. "About seven thousand were found alive by the Russian army. The survivors showed the Russians the remnants of gas chambers. The ovens had already been dismantled and shipped back to Germany."

It strained one's credulity to see that the world's foremost death factory, with its gas chambers and ovens, its sinister medical laboratories using humans as guinea pigs, its slave labor camps and its torture chambers, had been turned into an idyllic Polish landscape with meadows, trees, bushes, small ponds, and gamboling deer and hare. The survivors were now dispersed throughout the globe, the captured SS shipped out to Russia to work in their labor camps, and if it hadn't been for the front gates and the railroad tracks, the gallows and the warehouse, and the remnants of gas chambers, there would have been a total erasure of the dark deeds done by evil men during three years in this secluded environment. "Hide your sin, and you are absolved" seemed to be the dubious moral imperative to be learned from the undoing of such a heinous action.

She walked away from the men toward the line of poplars, stopping only when she felt something crunching under her foot. She looked own and picked up what appeared to be a human bone, probably the tibia of a child. Holding it in her hands, she knelt down and mumbled a Latin prayer that she had learned in middle school: "*Réquiem ætérnam dona ei Dómine; et lux perpétua lúceat ei. Requiéscat in pace. Amen.*"

She didn't feel any better after that. I'm an atheist, she thought. Prayers don't work for me. Her uncle's favorite quotation, "God is dead," ran through her mind, repeating itself like a Gregorian chant. If he was alive, why was this unthinkable, unbelievable act of evil allowed to happen? If he was alive, why were innocents like the child whose bone she had held a moment ago in her hands allowed to die? The only answer she could think of was that worldly events did not take place under divine control but occurred randomly, and theological notions of good and evil, right and wrong, were irrelevant to any analysis of cause and outcome.

She stood up, wiped her eyes, and ambled over to a large tree, leaning against it for comfort until the others joined her.

"The Polish government is going to build a museum here," she heard Daniel say. "They are going to rebuild the barracks, the jails, the gas chambers, and the ovens. They will also display photographs, handwritten documents, and artwork by the inmates."

"Will they even mention the genocide against the Jews?" Eric asked. "Or will they follow the party line and dedicate the museum to all Polish people who were killed here by Germans?"

There was an edge to his voice, a bitterness she had never noticed in him before. The poor boy must be suffering, she thought, because of what he has seen and heard in Poland—the ghettos, the camps, the forced labor, the atrocities.

"Comrade, one shouldn't take a narrow view of such important matters," said the autocratic Pawel. "We in the party like to avoid racial classifications. We never mention the Jewish ancestry of Marx, Engels, or Trotsky. We never refer to Stalin as a man from Georgia. We like to view people without reference to racial identification."

Eric turned red, and Hannah was afraid the two men would get into a fight. She was relieved when he controlled his temper and, taking out his binoculars, scanned the sky for birds.

"There don't seem to be any birds flying around," he said, handing his field glasses to Hannah.

She looked through them and saw a crane, a beautiful, stately bird with a tiny red tuft on the top of its head, flying like a ballerina across the blue sky—neck outstretched, legs folded parallel to the ground. I wish I could fly like that, thought Hannah and wanted to watch it forever, but it suddenly dived into the woods and was gone from sight.

"I saw a crane, but it disappeared into the forest," she said, handing over the binoculars to Eric.

"They say birds never fly over Auschwitz," said Pawel with a snicker. "I've been here three times, and I don't recall ever seeing a bird. But Hannah sees things that others don't see."

"Hannah is the most honest person I know," said Eric, turning on him savagely. "If she says she saw a crane, it must be so."

"Sometimes you have to believe another person's account of what he or she saw, Comrade Pawel," said Daniel, trying to mediate. "After all, we believe that torture and assembly-line executions had been carried out in this place even though we did not witness it."

"I believe in collective testimonies, not an individual testimony that is contrary to my own experience," said Pawel hotly.

"You should then, as a historian, be prepared to challenge historically accepted testimonies given by individuals," said Daniel.

The two of them went over the subjective versus objective views of history, like dogs fighting over a bone, throughout the bumpy, jostling, uncomfortable ride to Krakow.

The car dropped them off at the Market Square in the old city. Krakow had a magical quality about it, Hannah thought, because it seemed untouched by the war. Through her car window, she had glimpses of its medieval buildings, its parks and squares, and they looked as though they had been kept in a time capsule for generations as specimens of Gothic architecture untouched by Renaissance or Slavic influences.

"The city is built on the Vistula River, in a valley at the foot of the Carpathian Mountains," said Pawel, who had been born in Krakow and raised there. "The Nazis made it the capital of the General Government, and Hans Frank ruled from the Wawel Castle. They arrested all the intellectuals and academics and sent them to Dachau. They then rounded up the Jews and put them in a ghetto before sending them to Auschwitz. The only good thing that happened was that they didn't destroy Krakow like they did Warsaw."

He beamed at them and looked at them with eyes full of conceit— like a bald poodle after performing a trick.

"You need several days to see the historical wonders of this place," he went on. "But my understanding is you'll be leaving tomorrow. Am I right?"

"Your understanding is correct," said Eric with an amused grin.

"I will give you a short tour, then," he said. "We can spend some time at the Wawel Castle, and from there we could walk through the old Jewish neighborhood of Kazimierze. Or we could spend time here at the Market Square—the Rynek Glowny, as it is called by us—looking at the wonderful church of St. Mary, built in the fourteenth century, and then wander through the markets."

"I would like to go to the castle and then walk around the Jewish neighborhood," said Eric.

"What about you, Hannah?" asked Pawel.

"I would like to look at the church," said Hannah, "and you can meet me there later. I will wait for you at the main entrance in three hours."

The men agreed to do that, but as they were about to leave, Eric had second thoughts about leaving Hannah alone.

"She doesn't speak a word of Polish, and these people have no love toward Germans," he said. "I don't want to take chances."

"No one is going to hurt me," said Hannah, but Eric was not convinced.

"I'll stay with Hannah," volunteered Daniel.

Eric looked at him searchingly for a few seconds, trying to read his true intentions. He didn't raise any objections, however, and left quickly with Pawel.

The church fascinated Hannah because it was built in the Gothic style using red brick, in contrast to the cathedrals with limestone facades commonly found in Europe.

"Take a look at the church towers, Hannah," said Daniel, "especially the taller one with the gilded dome. Every hour, instead of ringing bells, a man plays a tune on a trumpet, the *Hejnał mariacki*, from the top of the tower. They do that to honor the memory of a thirteenth-century trumpeter who was killed by an arrow from a Mongol while he was giving the warning signal of an enemy attack on the city."

As if on cue, a window opened at the top of the tower, and a man popped up like a jack-in-the-box, wearing a blue dress and a blue cap. He started playing a doleful five-note tune on a trumpet, broke off in midstream, and closed the window.

"You know why they break off in the middle?" Daniel asked.

"I can guess. It is to remind us that that the trumpeter was killed in the middle of his life."

They looked at each other intently and smiled. His hand stole toward her and grasped hers. The simple act of touching made her tingle all over her body, and she sensed she was blushing. I'm not a young girl, she thought. I'm too old to fall in love and should watch my step.

"Shall we go inside, Daniel?" she asked softly.

The first thing she noticed when they entered the church was a gigantic Gothic altarpiece carved in wood, showing life-size scenes from the Bible.

"This is the work of Wit Stwosz, Europe's greatest sculptor during the latter half of the fifteenth century," said Daniel. "The Nazis took it away from here and kept it hidden in Nuremberg. The wood carving was brought back after the end of the war, and it took a lot of work to restore it."

I've never heard of Wit Stwosz, thought Hannah. At the art school in Munich, they taught us about the great German sculptures of the fifteenth century, especially the *Mourning of Christ* in Jakobskirche, but I never learned anything about Polish art.

She looked around and saw wonders everywhere—ornate stalls displaying baroque woodwork and exquisite stained glass in the chancel. And on the walls there were magnificent paintings—the work of the Krakow painter Jan Matejko, Daniel informed her.

"I am a painter and an art teacher, but I never heard of Jan Matejko," said Hannah. "I like the way he paints crowds. His brushwork and sense of color are truly amazing."

"He is one of our national heroes," said Daniel. "It doesn't surprise me you didn't hear of Matejko. Artists are judged everywhere by their race and nationalities. I wish it weren't so. I wish there would be a universal art that trespasses national boundaries."

"We at Bauhaus tried to do that," said Hannah. "But we failed."

"I know, Hannah," he said. "I've read about them, and I admire them. They had a showing of Kandinsky and Klee in Warsaw many years ago, and I was spellbound by their work. It was liberating art, universal art."

"Klee used to say, 'I paint for all mankind,'" said Hannah.

"I had a print of his *Red Balloon* that I cut out from an art magazine in my study," said Daniel.

We have similar tastes, Hannah thought, for that picture of Klee's is one of my favorites. Moving close to each other, hand in hand, they spent nearly two hours at the church. After that they walked through old streets of the Market Square, admiring the architecture of old buildings. The Polish street names—Szczepanska, Jagiellonska—fascinated her, and she made Daniel repeat them a few times, to his amusement.

Hannah felt a great sense of comfort in being with him yet didn't feel close enough to ask him questions about his life—whether he had a wife or girlfriend or what he was planning to do now that the war was over. Being together with him was enough, and the present was all that mattered.

They rode in a horse-drawn carriage driven by a liveried driver, and Hannah realized she had never felt such happiness since the early days of her youth as they clip-clopped through Polish streets— Zwierzyniecka, Franciszkanska, Dominikanska—crowded with buildings that were from another age, steeped in a history that was completely closed to her as a German.

As they were driving on Grodzka Street, they sighted Eric and Pawel walking toward them, engaged in friendly discussion. They paid the cabdriver, got off, and waved to them.

"What did you see, Eric?" she asked him.

"We didn't see the castle," he said. "We spent some time in the Kazimierz district, which used to be the old Jewish neighborhood. Then we walked over to Podgorze, on the other side of the Vistula River, to see what has been left of the Jewish ghetto. There was little to see other than the remains of the wall because the ghetto was liquidated after the Jews were sent to Belzec and Auschwitz."

He paused for a few seconds and looked at Pawel.

"Pawel gave me a short course on the history of the German occupation of Poland," he said. "You know, they made Jews wear armbands, and even young boys had to wear them. And there was armed resistance in the ghetto. Jewish groups, helped by the Polish underground army, conducted attacks against the Nazis. Nothing came of it, however."

They walked back to the market square, checking out its stalls, outdoor cafés, and wandering performers. The trumpet was blown again from the top of the church, and Hannah heard once more the story of the arrow shot by a Mongol archer. Young people were dancing the Krakowiak in the square, mimicking the gait of horses, while older folks watched them from the sidewalk. Hannah liked the flouncy red-and-white dresses worn by the girls and the way they did their hair in braids.

"That's a nice place to have dinner," said Pawel, pointing to an outdoor café across the street.

The owner apparently knew him and gave them a table from which they could watch the crowds. Pawel ordered traditional Polish fare—piroshkies, herring, kielbasa, and kasha—and a jug of Zywiec.

Toward the end of the meal, Pawel brought up sleeping arrangements for the night—they were going to sleep in Jordan Park, he said, and he was sure they could find four benches in a secluded area in the park.

"I'll buy some bread and cheese and apples for our breakfast from the stalls here," Daniel volunteered. "And a couple of bottles of Zywiec."

The sky was cloudless, and they walked around the square for a couple of hours in the lingering daylight. They then drove to Jordan Park and took out their sleeping bags from the car. Pawel found four benches in the park, and they soon went to sleep under the light of a crescent moon.

Hannah woke up hearing the sound of the quacking of ducks. She sat up, yawned, and looked around. She could hear the sound of a river flowing nearby, and the quacking came from there. She then saw a note from Eric next to her. "Going birdwatching with Pawel," it said. "Will be back before noon. We should be at the airport by four." There was no sign of Daniel, and she thought he might have also gone with them.

It was a warm, beautiful morning, and Hannah decided to go and look at the ducks. She walked along the bank of a river whose name, she learned from a nearby plaque, was Rudawa, a tributary of the

Vistula. The bank was damp and yielding, and she assumed that there must have been heavy rains here recently, causing the river to overflow.

There wasn't a soul around, and on an impulse, she stripped herself, put her clothes on a jutting rock near the bank, and got into the water. She washed her body and face and then swam for a while, slowly and leisurely, floating on her back, her long hair spread out on either side of her.

"You look like a Rhine maiden," said a voice behind her.

She turned around and saw Daniel standing on the rock where she had left her clothes. She greeted him with a smile and wave of the hand.

"Can I join you?" he asked.

"If you want to," she said.

He undressed quickly, and Hannah saw a trim, muscled body with matted chest hair turning gray. He swam rapidly toward her, aided by the current.

"The water is cold," he said. "It must be because of the rains."

"I like cold water," said Hannah.

They swam in silence for a while and then turned around, swimming against the current. When they reached the rock, Daniel said they should dry themselves in the sun. They climbed up the rock and stood together for a minute, gazing into each other's eyes. Hannah suddenly became aware of his maleness and took a step back, in fear of another rape. He hates Germans, she thought. He is like the Russians, and wants to take his revenge on a vulnerable German woman.

She felt weak at the knees and sat down on the rock. He lifted her up, and she looked into his eyes; she intuitively knew he was not a violent man, and he wanted her because he loved her. She put her hands over his neck and kissed him, and he stroked her lingeringly, as one would stroke a kitten, and pressed her to him. She gently guided him inside her, and they stood on the rock, moving their bodies in slow rhythm.

"I would like to live with you, Daniel," Hannah said. "I'll move to Poland. It doesn't matter where we live, whether it's Warsaw or Lublin or Krakow. And if you have a wife, it is OK. I'll be your mistress."

She had never offered herself like this to anyone before, and even though she did not regret what she had said, a doubt rose in her mind whether he would mistake her words as a desperate plea for love and accede to her wishes out of kindness. She did not want that.

He said nothing for a while, avoiding her eyes as he put his clothes on.

"I was thinking what I should say to you, Hannah," he said after a while. "You say you would like to live in Poland, but I find it hard to live here. Like other European people, Poles are very anti-Semitic. Poland had passed laws similar to the Nuremberg race laws. There have been savage attacks here against the Jews, similar to what happened during the Kristallnacht. Poland is a beautiful country, and I love the land, but the sad truth is that Poland doesn't want me because of my race."

Hannah was disturbed by his words, for she had thought of anti-Semitism as a distinctly German phenomenon until then and had no notion that it was endemic in Poland also.

"We can go elsewhere," she said. "I think I can manage to get a teaching position in America. I have money in an American bank from the sale of my drawings. I can support you until such time you get a job there."

"We can do that, Hannah, but this is not the right time. Next week I'm going to Berne with a delegation of Polish Jews to attend a conference on the economic aspects of the creation of a Jewish state in Palestine. Like many other Jews, I am convinced that we need a country of our own, to avoid another mass murder of Jews. I took an oath, after I escaped from Chelmno, that I would do all I can to achieve that goal. That's why I'm going to Berne to raise international financial support for our cause. After that, I am planning to attend the Zionist Congress that will be held in London in December. I am very hopeful that we will have our own state soon, and after that happens, I will go to America with you."

"How long will it take?" asked Hannah.

"People in the know say the world feels guilty about the Holocaust, as the British call it, and the time is ripe. My guess is that next year will see the birth of a Jewish state. I'll come and see you when my task is finished. I hope you will feel the same way toward me when I return."

"I don't know if it will work, Daniel," Hannah said despondently. "Today I'm going back to Nuremberg. As you probably guessed, I'm living with Eric. I don't know what the future holds for me. You have no idea what the war has done to the women in Germany, how it has destroyed all our beliefs and values. I was really dreaming of a Garden of Eden a few minutes ago, when I asked if I can live with you, here in Poland. I fantasized we were Adam and Eve, and that we were going to live in a state of bliss. But after hearing you talk about your immediate mission, I think we should go our separate ways. That's best for both of us."

There were tears in her eyes, and he wiped them with his handkerchief.

"I am an optimist, Hannah," he said softly, "and something tells me we will be together. I would like you to give me your address in Nuremberg."

She gave him her uncle's address, and he took out a small diary from his pocket and wrote it down and then smiled at her.

"I am going to leave now," he said. "You will hear from me, my love."

I'll never hear from him again, she thought sadly, as she watched him walk away from the rock. She dived into the water and swam, thrashing her arms and legs, wanting to wash away all traces of him, and along with it, all hopes of a life with him. She then climbed back on the rock and dried herself in the sun.

When she returned to the park bench, she found the three men engaged in a friendly debate over the political future of the world.

"Europe is no longer in the picture," she heard Pawel say. "The fight for domination will be between two countries—the United States and the Soviet Union."

"We will win in the end," said Eric, "because we stand for freedom of the individual."

"We will see about that, Comrade," said Pawel. "Remember, most countries in Africa and Asia hate colonial powers, and you're regarded as their ally. I would say with certainty that the future belongs to us."

They became aware of Hannah standing next to them, and Eric turned to face her.

"What's your opinion, Hannah?" he asked her. "Do you agree with Pawel?"

Hannah, uncharacteristically, felt resentment toward all three men.

"My country is now under occupation. It is cut in half for all practical purposes. My Berlin is divided into east and west, and most of us are homeless and live like beggars. Our young girls behave like hookers, and our men labor as your slaves. And you want my opinion about who is going to lead the world in the future? I don't care, I tell you. Do you understand? I don't care."

She walked away from them, and Eric and Daniel followed her. She quickly gained control over herself and stopped.

"I shouldn't have spoken like that," she said.

"It's a good thing you got it out of your system," said Eric soothingly. "You've been holding back all the time I've known you."

Daniel didn't say anything but stared at her for a while, feeling a new sympathy for the woman he had been intimate with—and then left.

The rest of the day was somewhat of an anticlimax. Pawel dropped them off at a small military airport in Krakow. They were given seats in a Russian cargo plane delivering milk, cheese, eggs, and poultry to Berlin, and from there an American plane took them to

Nuremberg. Throughout the first part of the flight, she heard the squawking of chickens, and Hannah wondered if they had a language of their own.

TWENTY-ONE

A LUCKY BREAK

I n the heat of midsummer, Nuremberg gave off a stench that was unbearable, caused by rotting bodies of humans and animals beneath
the wreckage of buildings or buried under the rubble that covered
its alleys and side streets. The smell was there even on the banks of
the once-beautiful but now debris-clogged Pegnitz River, where GIs
roamed looking for sex, shouting out offers of dollars or cigarettes to
any attractive woman who passed by them.

As Hannah pedaled along the loop inside the old town, the foul,
sticky air made her feel weak, irritable, and resentful of the forces that
had made her life seem so pointless and irrelevant, a mere flotsam in
the turbulence of violent events. Seeing the dirty and defeated-look-
ing German women crawling out of their caves in search of food, she
wondered what crimes they had committed to deserve this mode of
life and why the victors of the war were giving them no relief or offer
of help. Her political opinions, once inchoate and undefined, slowly
began to take shape in her mind and buzz about like awakened hor-
nets. The individual, she felt, was always punished for actions taken
by the state, even if he or she was against those actions, and the violence done to him or her by the state quickly metamorphosed into the

equally oppressive maltreatment by the power that came after it. These women didn't bring about the war, and Hannah thought it was unfair they were being punished for crimes they weren't responsible for and couldn't prevent from taking place—did anybody care about them or give them a chance to articulate what they felt?

It was with a sense of rebelliousness that she entered the courtroom at the Palace of Justice a few minutes before the war-crimes trial began its final session. The attendance was sparse, comprising mostly reporters and staff, and the judges and lawyers looked weary and frazzled. It must be the heat, she thought, for the courtroom was stiflingly warm.

There was nothing new in what either side was saying. The lawyers for the defense—pedantic-looking Germans who had once proudly proclaimed their faith in Adolf Hitler and greeted everyone with "Heil Hitler"—denied any wrongdoing by their clients and repeatedly pointed out that under the Führerprinzep the defendants had to obey Hitler's orders even if they were against them in principle: they were not allowed to resign and had to stay in office until such time it pleased Hitler to remove them; nor could they express any opinion contrary to Hitler's policies because they would be branded as traitors and punished by death. The defendants were not anti-Semitic, the lawyers stressed, even though they had to take certain actions for the good of the Aryan folk of Germany; they had no knowledge of the extermination centers and were "paralyzed by horror" when, during the trial, they heard of the atrocities at Auschwitz and other death camps.

The defense also had objections based on the questionable validity and legality of the trial itself. They argued that the branding of their clients' actions as criminal under the laws created by the Nuremberg tribunal were not valid in a court of law since they were created ex post facto: that is, the actions now deemed criminal had been performed at a time when such laws were not in force. They questioned the fairness of the hearings, saying that victor's justice was being carried out, and pointed out that even though similar crimes had been committed by the Allies, as in the case of the carpet-bombing of Dresden and the dropping of the atomic bomb on Hiroshima, the defense was not allowed to bring them up at the trial.

The outcome of the trial was no surprise to anyone in the audience, but to judge from the facial expressions of the defendants, ranging from stunned to crestfallen, they must have been hopeful of outright acquittal or short-term imprisonment, as one by one they were brought before the judges and their sentences read to them. Eleven defendants—Goering, Frick, Frank, Sauckel, Keitel, Jodl, Seyss-Inquart, Streicher, Ribbentrop, Kaltenbrunner, and Rosenberg—were given the death penalty, seven got lengthy prison sentences, and three were acquitted.

Eric, like many other prosecution lawyers, was unhappy with the way the trial ended. He thought Jackson hadn't prepared the case properly and was wrong in presenting an indictment based on abstract notions such as wars of aggression and crimes against humanity, which did not have existing legal definitions.

"Julius Streicher was a disgusting man, but he had nothing to do with starting wars or with the running of extermination camps," he said. "And in the case of Goering and others, the defense lawyers correctly brought up the question of the fairness of the trial. Stalin was a mass murderer, but his actions could not be brought up by the defense. Nor could his pact with Hitler, under which huge chunks of Eastern Europe became part of the Russian empire. These were definitely acts of aggression and crimes against humanity perpetrated by the Russians."

He and Hannah were sitting in the small garden at the back of their house, drinking bourbon and ginger ale he had picked up from the army depot. The roses had long died, and the stems of the bushes were turning brown.

"What's the point of the trial?" he asked, and Hannah could see the struggle he was going though, trying to come to terms with what he had seen and heard. "Jackson had repeatedly said in his opening statements that there was a master plan behind the Nazi actions. He didn't produce it during the course of the trial. In fact, I can definitely assert that I have seen no evidence of a plan for genocide of the Jews, or one for world conquest, in the supporting documents prepared by the prosecution. I am not sure how or where or by whom the genocide was started. Was it by Arthur Greiser in Warthgau, where he built the first extermination camp at Chelmno, or by Friedrich Jeckeln in Kiev, where he killed thirty thousand Jews, including women and children, and threw them down into the Babi Yar ravine? The Russians captured, tried, and executed Friedrich Jeckeln in Riga a few months ago. I've read the transcript of the trial, and I believe that he, with help from the German Army and police, was responsible for the massacre. His defense was that he followed orders and did what he did for the sake of Germany, but the judges didn't buy that argument. What I am saying is that the Nuremberg trial should have been about provable heinous crimes rather than conspiracies and master plans."

Hannah, who was in total agreement with him, could sense his disappointment and frustration for having participated in a wild goose chase.

"What is your next step, Eric?" she asked, hoping to hear he was planning to abandon his quest for the blueprint and returning to New York.

"Telford Taylor, who is Jackson's right-hand man, is now in charge of conducting more trials here in Nuremberg," he said. "He asked me to stay on as a prosecutor."

"I didn't know there were going to be more trials," said Hannah.

"Otto Ohlendorf and other Einsatzgruppen leaders are going to be tried in Nuremburg by the Americans. So are the top cabinet members and ministers and the doctors who did criminal experiments on prisoners. Rudolf Höss is going to be tried in Poland, along with his Auschwitz associates."

"So you are staying on for a while?"

"Yes, Hannah. I would like to get to the bottom of this mystery. How did the Jewish genocide come about? From the top or from the bottom? From Berlin or from the conquered territories in Russia and Poland? Who were involved? The SS, the Wehrmacht, the German police, or the gauleiters? Right now there are more questions than answers, and I intend to find them."

He is fighting a losing battle, thought Hannah, because he's looking for a rational explanation. Germans were not rational when it came to the Jewish problem, a chimera created by them to justify their aversion toward the Jew. She remembered the roars of applause that punctuated Hitler's or Goebbels's speeches after each anti-Semitic tirade and the crowds of cheering onlookers as the SA kicked Jews in the street or dragged them out from their homes and put them in vans that would carry them to a nameless destination known as the East— the Nazi euphemism for the fiery furnaces of Gehenna. Germans had no sympathy for these *Untermenschen* and looked upon them as "useless eaters," to be eradicated from the surface of the earth in the time of war and hardship. And the man sitting before her had no idea of the persistence and intensity of their hatred.

Eric gazed at her speculatively, as though he were debating within himself to bring up a topic that was likely to be touchy.

"Will you continue working with me, Hannah?" he asked hesitatingly, hoping she would agree to his request.

She didn't want to turn him down, but she knew it was wrong to go on living with him.

"I don't know, Eric," she said. "I made a promise that I would stay with you through the Nuremberg trial, and now that it has come to an end, I would like to do something else."

"Is it because of our relationship?" he asked, with a twinge of pain in his voice. "I don't want you to say something that will make me feel good. I want the brutal truth."

"Once we used to be friends," she said. "I liked that. You then started making love to me. I cannot reciprocate, and it isn't fair to you."

She could see that she had hurt him, and she hated herself for doing so. But there was no turning back.

"What do you want to do, Hannah?" he asked her, after a few moments of silence.

"I don't know," she replied. "I would like to leave Nuremberg, maybe Germany. It's hard for someone to hate one's country and one's own people, but that's what has happened to me. I want to have a new life, start all over again."

He didn't say anything for a while but sat there looking at the dying roses.

"If I may make a suggestion," he said tentatively, unsure how show she would respond, "I would like you to stay with me till such time you decide what you want to do next. You can finish the drawings you've made for my book on the Nuremberg trial. The US Army is going to print it. My mother has written to me saying there's a demand for your drawings in the United States, and I can send some of your work to her. She also asked for some of your paintings. What I'm saying is you can get steady income from your work. And if you want to emigrate, I'll help you in every way I can."

She was touched by his generosity, by his innate goodness.

"Thank you, Eric," she said, with tears in her eyes.

Her daily life, from that day on, followed a different routine. After Eric went to work early in the morning, she had the house to herself. She got up at eight, chatted with the cook while eating breakfast, and wandered around the house for a while before going up to her studio.

She then sketched or painted for several hours, but not in the style she had been working with until then. Bauhaus was behind her, and the world it represented was gone. "Paint what you want to paint, and not what you were taught to paint," she kept on telling herself. At first she drew scenes from fairy tales—Cinderella, the Frog Prince, the Little Mermaid, and the like—but the drawings, good from a technical point of view, did not satisfy her. "I'm painting like Marc Chagall, escaping into childhood whimsy. I want to draw something else, but the censors in my mind wouldn't let me do that," she said to herself. But one day the censors relaxed their vigil, and she found herself drawing guard dogs tearing the flesh of bearded Jews, armed guards cracking open the skulls of little boys with rifle butts, and emaciated figures screaming in gas chambers. She was surprised at the violence that seemed to radiate out of her drawings and debated whether she should destroy them. "This is not me," she pleaded with herself. "I'm not a violent person." She felt like a punctured balloon, and a feeling of total emptiness overwhelmed her. To escape it, she bicycled all over Nuremberg, still wearing her summer clothes, even though an early autumn had replaced summer and the biting winds from the east made her shiver.

On her way home, she rode past her uncle's house and decided to visit him, little knowing that the visit would make her life take on a new and unexpected course.

Ulrike greeted her warmly as she entered the house and complimented her on her appearance.

"You look younger than before," she said. "We are the same age, but look at me, fat and frumpy, like a typical German hausfrau."

"Bicycling keeps me fit," said Hannah.

"Ach, I've no time for exercise. I've to take care of the house and look after your uncle."

She led her to the dining room and placed a plate of lebkuchen cookies and a glass of sherry before her. It was very good sherry, and Hannah figured Frieda must have pilfered it from the cellar of the Americans living upstairs.

"How is my uncle?" asked Hannah.

"I've never seen him like this. He's very angry and bitter ever since he read about the sentences given out at the Nuremberg trial. He went to see his friends Rosenberg, Hess, and Frank at the jail, and for a couple of days he walked around in a total daze. He then began ranting at the Americans and the Russians, without letting up."

"Is he in his library now?"

"No, Hannah. He is in the park. He sits on his favorite bench. He has a folding table that I carry in the morning, along with a sack containing his papers, a sandwich, and a thermos of coffee. He edits his material there, and I go over to bring him back in the evening."

"Why can't he work here?"

"He says he can't work here as long as the Americans are upstairs. He wants them to leave, but there's nothing he can do about it."

"Shall I go and see him now?"

Ulrike looked embarrassed.

"I would leave him alone right now. He's very angry at you because you're living with an American, a Jewish American. He feels betrayed by his own family members—Octavia, Claudia, and now you."

"I'm sorry he feels that way. None of us thought our lives would end up like this."

"He really loves you, Hannah. I think he'll get over his anger in a few days. I know him. He has been angry at me on several occasions for doing things he didn't approve of. But he gets over his bad moods."

"How are the girls doing? I mean Claudia and Octavia?"

"They're doing fine. Octavia's husband has a good job as a garage mechanic. And Claudia has moved to Los Angeles. Her husband's father died recently, and he has inherited his father's business. That reminds me, Hannah—there's a letter for you from Claudia. It came three days ago."

She went to her room and returned with a large yellow envelope stuffed with papers. It was the first time in her life Hannah had received any mail from the United States, and she looked at the stamps with curiosity. They showed Roosevelt celebrating the four freedoms—of speech and religion, and from want and fear. She was used to seeing the stern, grim-looking image of the Führer in the postage issued by the Deutsches Reich, and the sight of the American stamps kindled hope in her heart—hope for nations of the world and hope even for the German people. Ideas do matter, she thought. Words matter, and the vision of a great leader can change a country, and even the world, for good as well as evil.

She opened the envelope and took out a three-page letter and an application form from the US Immigration and Nationalization Service. She read the letter, written in English in Claudia's tiny script.

Seeing the surprised expression on her face, Ulrike gave her a questioning look after she had finished reading.

"There's good news," said Hannah. "Claudia is pregnant. She's living in a beautiful house in Los Angeles. Her husband, Gene, has inherited his father's talent agency business in Hollywood, and he's working hard to make it a successful operation. His father was a Jew from Austria, and his clients are mostly European Jews in the motion picture business in Hollywood who immigrated to America after Hitler came into power. Gene has a hard time dealing with them, since he doesn't speak German or Russian. Claudia wants me to go there and help him temporarily since I speak English, French, and Russian. She has offered me a job as an assistant to Gene and wants me to file the application papers. She also says she would like me to be with her when the baby arrives—there's no one else she can ask since her husband's mother is still angry at him for marrying a German and has refused to come to their house."

"Claudia is right, poor thing," said Ulrike. "Frieda can't go and see her because her husband wants her to join him in South America. And I can't go because I've to be with your uncle."

Hannah put the letter back in the envelope.

"I've to think about this," she said.

She stayed for a while longer with Ulrike until it was time for Ulrike to go to the park and bring the old man home.

That night she showed Claudia's letter to Eric.

"What do you want to do, Hannah?" he asked her. "Do you want to go?"

She had been debating the issue in her mind until that very moment, and suddenly the answer came to her, clear and incontrovertible.

"Yes," she said.

She did not give him any further explanation, and he, sensing her mood, didn't press her.

"If that's what you want to do, that's what you should do. I will help you with the application."

She thought she could detect a sense of relief in his voice. He has probably met another woman, she thought, and is waiting for me to leave. The thought didn't disturb her at all and, in fact, quieted her guilty feelings about leaving him.

The next day, Eric filled out the immigration forms for her, wrote a letter describing her work and giving her a character reference, and had a military photographer take passport pictures of her. She signed the form and mailed the completed application to Claudia.

Hannah went back to her painting routine, working several hours at a stretch, and over the course of the next four weeks, came up with a portfolio of twenty drawings and a dozen oil paintings. Kandinsky wouldn't like them, nor Paul Klee, she thought, because of the violence displayed in my work—but then they hadn't seen and experienced what I had seen and experienced.

She was so wrapped up in her newfound creativity that she forgot all about Claudia's offer and was surprised when Eric came home one evening with an official-looking envelope that he handed to her. Inside it, she found a visa to the United States, allowing her to work there, along with a welcome letter from the Department of Immigration and Naturalization.

"I've arranged for your flight from Berlin to New York in a military aircraft," Eric said. "You are still on our payroll. Your job with us will come to an end when you've finished proofreading our Nuremberg trial book. My mother will meet you in New York, at the airport. And she will make arrangements for your train ride to Los Angeles."

She could smell another woman's perfume emanating from his uniform. He really is in a rush to get rid of me, she thought, as she went through the papers he had given her.

"When do I leave here?" she asked him.

"At eleven tomorrow morning. An army car will pick you up from here and take you to the airport in Berlin."

"I've a request to make, Eric," she said. "I want you to send me a cable if you hear any news about my brother, Johann Gruenwald, or my friend Dr. Emil Dresdner."

"Sure, Hannah. I'll let you know as soon as I hear anything."

He took out a little book from his pocket, wrote down the two names, their ages, and personal identification details, and left the room. She could hear him taking off his clothes and splashing about in the bathroom. He's washing off traces of his new girlfriend, she thought.

At dinner an hour later, he was calmer and more like his usual self. He talked about the coming trials and his new promotion to the rank of colonel. He then moved on to other topics, telling her how pleased his mother would be to see her and advising her to be careful in Los Angeles.

"You meet quite a lot of operators there," he said. "They try to sucker you into all kinds of schemes."

He was speaking abstractedly, in an obvious effort to make conversation. She found it unbearably embarrassing.

"You're acting strange, Eric," she said. "I know you've been with another woman. Do you feel guilty about it?"

"How do you know?" he asked, shocked.

"I could smell her perfume on your clothes when you came in," she said.

"I have been seeing a woman lawyer working for Telford Taylor," he said after a few moments' hesitation. "Her name is Naomi Bressler. She is from New York. She's very nice, but I'm not sure I love her. And to answer your question, I do feel guilty about it."

She walked over to him and placed her hands on his shoulders.

"Don't feel guilty about me," she said. "I don't mind it in the least. I'm glad you are with someone."

He had recovered his emotional balance and was smiling at her.

"Let's drink to that," he said.

He brought out a bottle of champagne that someone had given him on New Year's Eve, opened it expertly, and filled two glasses. They toasted each other, kissed briefly, and after putting the dishes away for the maid to clean the next morning, they went to their separate bedrooms.

Hannah woke up a little later than usual the next morning and found that Eric had left for work by the time she came downstairs. She found a note for her from him, propped up on the dining table.

Dear Hannah,

I apologize for my odd behavior last night. To tell you the truth, I was very disturbed at your leaving, but I didn't want to let on that I would miss you—hence, there was a conflict between passion and restraint that resulted in my strained attitude yesterday.

You've made an indelible impression on me, Hannah. You've changed me in many ways. I don't know if you've read any of Henry James's novels, which deal with the theme of Old Europe corrupting young America. When I came here, I was a quintessential young American in the sense that I believed that if Germany had our form of government, with its checks and balances and free elections, the country would have followed a different path. I believed, with Justice Jackson, that the twenty-one Nuremberg defendants were solely responsible, alongside of Hitler, Himmler, and his henchmen, for all the evil done by Germany. You've always taken a different view, even though you never fully articulated it. You believed that the evil lay in the hearts of the German people, and they were cooperating with the government as it carried out the unspeakable acts they subconsciously yearned for against Jews. Believe it or not, I am coming to the same conclusion after hearing the testimonies of Ohlendorf and Höss and listening to Daniel Neumann and Pawel Szymanski on the German atrocities in Poland. Hannah, I saw you at Auschwitz looking at that small bone belonging to a child and noticed the expression on your face, and I knew you were grieving at the inherent evil of the countless Germans who destroyed life without regret. And it changed me forever.

I know you don't love me, and I, who used to believe that sex without love between two people is an abomination, have come to your way of thinking—I've been going to bed with Naomi, even though I've no feeling for her, experiencing no shame or regret.

I will write to you, Hannah. Maybe we will live together again. If we don't, I won't cry over it because I've become like you—someone who accepts the world as it is and has learned to swim, instead of thrashing about, in a turbulent sea.
Eric

Poor boy, mused Hannah, he thinks he's become like me, even though he will never know what it is to be like me, living through two terrible wars, with no sense of hope or redemption—living in a tunnel, with no glimmer at the end. He has never listened to the Kaiser rant about his ambitions for world conquest or the lying General Ludendorff blaming the Jews for his military collapse, accusing them of stabbing the army in the back. He will never understand that mendaciousness and denial of responsibility are integral parts of the German soul—why they could never admit they lost the First World War because of their ineptitude and had to find scapegoats or why they could never confess that they had been Hitler's willing henchmen. He has never seen Germans as they really are: he has never watched them banging on tables with beer mugs while Hitler spouted hatred at beerhalls or heard the frenzied squeals by German women of "Heil Hitler" at every Nazi rally in Berlin or Nuremberg. He has never seen the SA spitting on Jews or kicking them while crowds stood around with huge grins on their faces. He will never have an understanding of what my inner self is like, bruised beyond repair, incapable of ever hoping for a new dawn, the redeeming light beyond.

Her thoughts made her feel distracted and edgy. "Thank God I'll be out of here for a while, maybe forever," she said to herself. She quickly drank her coffee and ate a piece of toasted white US Army bread, marveling at its insipid taste.

She tipped the cook and the gardener and went upstairs to pack her belongings in a suitcase, not forgetting to include the portfolio of her new paintings.

"You can have my bicycle," she told the gardener, as he helped her down with her luggage.

The military car was waiting for her at the door, and she got into it, waving good-bye to Nuremberg.

PART 4

RED SCARE

We will not be driven by fear into an age of unreason if we...
remember that we are not descended from fearful men, not
from men who feared to write, to speak, to associate, and to
defend causes which were, for the moment unpopular.

—Edward R. Murrow

Most of them don't know what communism is, could not pick it
out of a lineup. They only know what anticommunism is. The
two are practically unrelated.

—Barbara Kingsolver, *The Lacuna*

TWENTY-TWO

NEW YORK

S he was the only woman on the plane, other than two stewardesses, and the only one not wearing a uniform. She was given a seat in the back of the plane with a window facing the Tempelhof airport—by now all repaired and spruced up.

She watched officer after officer with insignias and medals on their uniforms climb up the steep ladder—some of them puffing from the exertion—into the plane. She couldn't tell their rank because she didn't know what the chevrons on their sleeves or the colored stripes on ribbon bars meant. Signs are meaningless if they are not universally recognized, she remembered someone in Bauhaus telling her. To her, as an artist, the coded colors meant nothing other than what Kandinsky had drilled into her as "warm" and "cool," with yellow and blue at the two antithetic extremes of the color spectrum.

Two men sitting in front of her were talking in loud voices, and she heard them say that they were flying in a Douglas Skymaster, and the plane would make two stops—Prestwick in Scotland and Gander in Newfoundland—before landing in Idlewild airport in New York. Geography wasn't her strong point, and she was beguiled by the names of places she had not heard of or read about. She wished for a moment that Eric was with her so that she could ask him to explain why Prestwick and Gander were chosen as the start and end points of a transatlantic flight or where Idlewild was in relation to Manhattan.

The propellers began to whirl, and the plane began its long and bumpy trip across the runway. Soon they were in the air, and she saw Berlin's ruins from above as the plane circled, gaining height. The dome of the Reichstag still had a huge hole in it, the Brandenburg gate was still smashed up, and the Kaiser Wilhelm Memorial Church had stumps for steeples. She averted her eyes when she saw the wreckage of Potsdamer Platz and the huge manmade mounds of rubbish, under one of which, in all likelihood, the remnants of her paintings and those given to her by her colleagues lay buried.

She wished she had brought a book to read and was going to ask an airhostess if they had newspapers and magazines on board when she heard someone say, "*Sind Sie Deutsche?*" She turned to the side and faced a man, a new arrival, sitting across the aisle from her.

Her first response was to say "Ja, Ich bin," but she didn't want to conduct a conversation in German in the plane.

"Yes, I am," she said.

"Going to the States?" he asked.

He was in his forties, a beefy, red-faced man with thick gray hair, with a row of medals and ribbons on his chest.

"Yes," she replied, unenthusiastic about interacting with this unprepossessing stranger.

"I'm Colonel Parkington," he said, extending his hand. "Ralph Parkington."

His hand was clammy, and Hannah, suppressing a shudder, felt that she was squeezing a warm, slimy reptile.

"Are you headed toward Washington, Frau Müller?" he asked, his eyes wandering over her face and body. She was beautiful, aristocratic looking, and aloof, and he wasn't sure whether she was on some mission to Washington or one of those German women on their way to meet their husbands hiding somewhere in the United States or Latin America.

"I'll get off at New York," she said reluctantly.

He was now sure she was on some secret mission on behalf of Germany, and he wanted to show that he was on her side, unlike many of his cohorts.

"I was an aide to General Patton when he was the military governor of Bavaria," he said to her. "He is a great man, a visionary, and he ran into trouble because he didn't want to pursue the denazification policy of our government. I agree with Patton's views one hundred percent. Our real enemy is not the Nazis in Germany but the Russians."

He held forth for a while on the failure of the American government to see the real threat to freedom: Patton wanted to fight the Russian army with the help of the German soldiers, and Churchill wanted to do the same thing with Allied soldiers, but the Democrats in Washington were eager to hand over half of Europe to the Russians.

It was the first time she had met an American who openly advocated a lenient policy toward the Nazis, and she thought there was something incongruous about it. And soon it became clear to her that he was hoping to get a positive response from her, a resounding affirmation of his views.

"We don't have the old Germany anymore," she said, unable to bear his eager, persistent, questioning look. "We are divided into zones."

He was happy that she had thrown him a sop and talked nonstop for several minutes, blaming Morgenthau, Hollywood, and the Jews for wanting to punish the Germans and to demonize them in the minds of the American people. Soon it dawned on her that he was talking like an anti-Semite, and she was a little surprised because, in her mind, anti-Semitism was strictly confined to the shores of Europe, and Americans were immune from it.

"They own the newspapers and the radio stations," the colonel said. "They own the banks and brokerage houses. They own Hollywood. You had the same problem in Germany, until your Führer put an end to it. Don't you agree with me?"

He gazed at her with the expectation that her answer would be a look or a word of encouragement.

"Ich bin ein Jude," she said.

As soon as the words were out of her mouth, she asked herself why she was lying again about her identity. Did she subconsciously want to be Jewish? Maybe it's because the two men I've slept with recently are both Jews, she thought. Our bodily intimacy might have changed me in some way and made me want to identify with them.

She saw the colonel's jaw drop, but the expression of surprise was quickly replaced by a glare of hatred. She thought he was going get up from his seat and smash his fist into her face. However, he quickly controlled his emotions: his features became stern and frigid with disapproval, and he looked straight ahead for a few moments; he then got out of his seat and moved to a vacant one four rows away.

They were flying over the North Sea, and Hannah busied herself scanning the dark blue expanse under her, alive with mystery and replete with signs and wonders, until the plane began to circle down for landing. Soon the church steeple, the railway line, and the main street of a small town came to her view. The town had a sunlit, inviting beach, and Hannah could see fishing trawlers and sailboats in the ocean.

There was a waiting period of an hour at Prestwick, and Hannah bought a sandwich and an apple from the food counter. She walked around and, seeing a small bookshop, went in to browse the Penguin, Pelican, and Vintage paperbacks stacked up on cheap wooden shelves. After some searching, she chose Agatha Christie's *Murder on the Orient Express* over Ford Madox Ford's *The Good Soldier*, unable to resist her craving for a good Hercule Poirot mystery.

The plane was a bit more crowded on the transatlantic leg of the flight, and the seat next to her was occupied by an English military man in his late forties, with a clipped moustache, monocle, and a green lanyard looping around the shoulder of his khaki uniform. He looked at her through his monocle, frowned, and, taking out his *Times* newspaper, became engrossed in solving its crossword puzzle.

Hannah looked out the window for a long time, mesmerized by the ocean, the boats, and an occasional liner on its way to some unknown destination. Once she saw a whale rise out of the water and descend with a splash, and the lingering spray refracted light like a rainbow.

"I say, do you mind closing the window? I would like to take a nap," said the colonel or brigadier, whoever he was, sitting next to her.

She acceded to his request and opened her Agatha Christie mystery. Soon she was entirely absorbed in the locked-room murder of millionaire Samuel Edward Ratchett despite the occasional loud snores emanating from the man next to her. She read slowly, savoring the descriptions of the Russian princess, the count, and the beautiful, mysterious woman. And her beloved Hercule Poirot did not disappoint her as he unraveled the mystery using his "little gray cells."

Her eyes became tired, and she fell asleep, soothed by the drone of the propellers.

When she woke up, the plane was circling over Halifax. The colonel had woken up and was at his unfinished crossword puzzle. She opened the window and noticed that the sky, the sea, and the land were all one stretch of gray in the early-morning light.

The plane soon landed in Newfoundland, and once again the passengers were herded to the airport and given coffee and donuts.

They reboarded half an hour later, and the plane was on its way to New York. The bright light from the rising sun bounced off the sea below her, and she wondered why she had avoided the sea, and even the color blue, in her paintings. I am a land person, she thought. But then a second thought came to her, replacing the first. She realized she had a fear of the color blue. In fact, she could only think of one painter, Fra Bartolomeo, who was a master of that color, extracting the subtleties that it offered in all its tonal variations from indigo to cerulean.

There were numerous fishing boats and freighters crisscrossing the ocean, and once in a while, she caught a glimpse of the jagged coastline of North America that jutted out, only to pull back after a couple of minutes, as though the sea and the land were in a perpetual struggle for space.

Soon they were flying over New York City, and her first impression was one of bewilderment. It's built by extraterrestrial kids playing with Meccano sets, she thought, putting buildings too close to each other in an attempt to see who can create the most number of tall structures in a narrow space. She knew that its nickname was "Skyscraper City," but she had no idea that its architecture would be such a medley of neo-Gothic, art deco, and wedding-cake styles, with each tall building nestling against its neighbor and clamoring for recognition.

"Er, is this your first visit to New York?" asked the brigadier or major general next to her. Gray stubble was beginning to show on his face, and his eyes were bleary from lack of sleep.

"Yes," she said.

"It's unlike any other place in the world. People rush, they're rude, and they don't even bother to say sorry if they bump into you."

"Have you been here many times?" she asked.

"Oh, yes. Got a desk job here two years ago. Before that was a Royal Marine Commando. Was wounded in the leg at Tripoli, fighting the Italians."

"How's your leg now?"

"A bullet went right through it, tearing up the calf muscle and breaking the shank. The doctors fixed it up. It still hurts on cold days."

They were readying for landing, and the colonel seemed to be debating with himself about something.

"Er, if you care to see me, I'll be staying at the Waldorf Hotel. Ask for Colonel Trevor-Brown. Don't push myself, normally. Saw you looking out of the window and watched the emotions on your face. Wife was killed in London by a Nazi bomb in forty-one. First time I found anyone interesting, after that."

Hannah looked at him—a pale-blue eye gleaming through the monocle, the incongruous stubble on his face, and the trace of hidden grief and loneliness on his bent shoulders—and felt sorry for him.

The plane had landed with a bump and was racing on the runway toward the disembarking area.

"I'm on my way to California," she told him. "Thanks for the invitation."

He nodded, stood up, and walked toward the exit. Hannah followed him a couple of minutes later.

Her papers were checked by an immigration official who said, "Welcome to the United States." She picked up her suitcase from a room next door and was quickly cleared by a customs official.

In the arrivals area, she saw wives and girlfriends hugging and kissing their returning men. A feeling of desolation came over her. This was a new country, a new life. She felt disconnected from the place and the people around her. Maybe I should have gone with the colonel to the Waldorf Hotel, she thought and smiled at her sense of irony.

"Hannah!" She heard someone call her name, and a moment later Octavia had her arms around her.

"I'm so happy to see you, Hannah," she said.

She looked as though she had put on weight, and it took Hannah a couple of moments to figure out she was pregnant.

"How did you know I was on this flight?" Hannah asked her.

"Claudia called me on the phone yesterday," she said. "Your boss, Colonel Grossman, had sent her a cable about your arrival."

"That's how we knew when you'd be here," she heard a man's deep voice announce.

She turned around, and it took her a few seconds to recognize Rider. He was wearing a brown leather jacket over a black cotton T-shirt, complemented by black jeans and heavy boots. His hair was longer and thicker and covered his head in thick, bushy curls.

"How are you, Rider?" she asked, giving him a hug and a kiss on the cheek.

"Things aren't bad, Hannah," he said.

"He's a foreman for the repair shop of a trucking company," said Octavia. "And he works at night as a cabdriver. I hardly ever see him these days; he works so hard."

"I gotta do it, babe, being a family man. We'll have one more mouth to feed in four months," said Rider.

He had an infectious smile, and Hannah and Octavia found themselves grinning.

"You are going to live with us for a few days, aren't you, Aunt Hannah?" asked Octavia.

Before she could respond, she heard someone else greet her, and on turning around, she saw Eric's parents coming toward her. Phyllis looked elegant in her tailored suit and well-coiffed hair. Hannah felt ashamed of her creased and worn-down clothes (property of the late Fraulein Ritter of Berlin) and her old clunky walking shoes. I must look like a caricature of the refugee woman seeking asylum, she thought. But her embarrassment was quickly dissipated by the warmth shown by Phyllis.

Hannah made the necessary introductions and was quick to notice the range of expressions—surprise, discomfort, and put-on heartiness—that passed through Saul's rugged countenance. The blacks are the Jews here, the Untermenschen, she thought, and she knew she was right when the grin faded from Rider's face and was replaced by a look of wariness.

"We would like you to stay with us, Hannah," said Phyllis, after hugging and kissing her.

Hannah saw a questioning look on Octavia's face as though she was uncertain what Hannah's response would be.

"I am going to stay with Octavia," she said. "But I'll come and see you, and we will spend some time together."

"That will be fine," said Phyllis. "Come to my gallery first, and we will make plans. It's on Madison Avenue at Sixty-Seventh Street. It's called the New York Atelier."

She and her husband left after effusive farewells, and Hannah and Octavia followed Rider through the halls and corridors of the airport to a parking lot. When they came out into the open, Hannah inhaled deeply the air of New York, equating it with freedom, a blessed escape from Europe devastated by pillage, rape, and carnage.

Octavia and Rider lived in the basement of a brownstone in Greenwich Village. The house belonged to a Mrs. Greene, an elderly lady who had inherited it from her rich husband, a real-estate developer. Rider and Octavia were given the basement apartment rent-free with the understanding that he would perform the functions of handyman and janitor, and she would clean the house and do the laundry for the lady.

"We got this place because of Rider's mom," said Octavia. "She and Mrs. Greene have known each other for a long time. Both were chorus girls on Broadway."

It was a nice, spacious apartment, with an extra bedroom for a guest. My destiny is to live in basement apartments, thought Hannah, as memories of the days with Stumpfegger and Ilke came to her mind. But she had no time to brood over her past because Octavia wanted to do things with her in the city right away. The two of them strolled through the narrow, cobblestone-paved streets of the Village and sat in a park watching street musicians, dancers, and chess players and eating pretzels, hot dogs, and Italian ices. In the evening Rider took them to nightclubs where jazz was played, and during the weekend they made long walks, at Hannah's request, up and down Broadway, looking at the buildings—Georgian, neoclassical, Victorian Gothic, art deco, and the mongrel skyscrapers known only by the names of their corporate owners, Woolworth, Singer, Equitable, AT&T—lining the streets, each building intent on asserting its own uniqueness without paying any attention to its neighbor's facade or structure. Why did they build this way? Shouldn't architecture be subject to aesthetics? She wished she was at Bauhaus, participating in an open classroom discussion with Gropius and his fellow architects about the role of entrepreneurs and corporations in the shaping of a modern city.

"This street reminds me of Fritz Lang's movie *The Metropolis*," she said to her two companions as they walked down Wall Street from Trinity Church to Water Street. "The looming buildings dwarf the pedestrian, and I feel as though I'm walking inside a cavern inhabited by giants."

"I've never seen *The Metropolis*," said Octavia, while Rider looked puzzled.

"It's a silent movie made in the late twenties and regarded as a classic by many in my generation," said Hannah. "You didn't see it because the Nazis blacklisted the director Fritz Lang after he mocked Hitler in *Das Testament Des Dr. Mabuse.*"

Octavia's expression changed as though she had been slapped on the face, and Hannah intuitively felt that she wanted no references to her Nazi past. Maybe she doesn't want the past to come between her and her husband, she thought—that was why she hadn't asked any questions about her mother or Ulrike.

She made a mental note not to bring up or make references to Germany in future conversations, even though she yearned to talk about Fritz Lang and Lion Feuchtwanger and the prophetic forebodings of the two great German artists of the twenties regarding the Nazi state. She wished someone of her own generation, say her Polish lover, was by her side—an intellectual with a sense of humor, walking with her in these surrealistic streets—instead of these two children who didn't know and were indifferent to the artistic renaissance that had taken place in Weimar, similar to the ones in Florence, Venice, and Rome some four hundred years ago. A sense of dislocation, both spatial and temporal, came upon her as she walked like a marionette between her niece and her husband, listening to but not quite understanding their chatter about names for the baby due to arrive in four months.

Phyllis called her the next morning and invited her to come to her gallery, after closing time. She offered to send a car and pick her up, but Hannah insisted on taking the subway and got the necessary directions. She left the house shortly after ten o'clock because it was Octavia's cleaning day, and even though she offered to help, Octavia declined it and hinted she would only be in the way.

Hannah took the portfolio of her latest paintings that she had brought from Germany and, after consulting the New York City map that Octavia had given her, walked to Bleecker Street to take the Lexington Avenue line.

The underground stations in New York operated quite differently from the Berlin U-Bahn, she learned quickly. Discovering a new subway is always an adventure, she thought, as she put a nickel into the turnstile, walked up the platform, and bought the *New York Times* from a news vendor. She never got to read it because the train arrived in a few seconds. The faces she saw inside the subway seemed to cover the entire ethnic spectrum from Nordic to Mongolian, and fascinated, she studied them surreptitiously while pretending to read the paper. I wish I could paint them, she thought. I wish I had been born in New York instead of Munich.

She got off at Grand Central Station and walked up Fifth Avenue amid the hurrying throngs. It was a beautiful day, with an occasional white cloud drifting across the sky. She explored the side streets one by one, looking at the clothing stores and restaurants and comparing them to the ones in Berlin and Munich during the Weimar days. There is no grand architecture here, she thought, no plazas, no great churches, no palaces, but only skyscrapers like unicorns standing upright, jostling against each other. She did not hate skyscrapers—in fact, she was hoping that one day New York would build one using the Bauhaus styles proposed by Mies van der Rohe and Walter Gropius—but the Gothic piles that she saw before her, one looming behind another, drove her crazy because of the chaos they caused on the skyline.

As she walked on, her eyes fell on a painting displayed at an art gallery window on Forty-Seventh Street, and she was startled to see that the picture was a visual representation of the images that had been going through her mind. The painting was of Manhattan skyscrapers, very realistic to the casual observer, but to her trained eye, she saw touches of German expressionism, hints of smoke and fire, of looming apocalypse waiting in the wings, to remind the viewer of the fragility of all manmade things. She couldn't make out the name of the artist on the painting and decided, after some hesitation, to ask someone in the gallery.

"Yes?" asked a modishly dressed young woman, obviously not impressed by Hannah's sartorial getup.

"Who painted that picture at the window?"

"George Grosz," said the woman, without looking at her.

"Really?" asked Hannah in surprise. "I know him, and I've seen his work in Berlin. His style is completely different from the painting in the window. Are you sure it's by George Grosz?"

"The artist is here today. Why don't you ask him if he painted the picture?" the girl said brusquely.

She pressed a button on her desk, and a male voice said, "Yes, Carole?"

"A woman says she knows George Grosz and wants to see him."

A few seconds later, a side door opened, and a bulky middle-aged man came out. He looked around and then came toward the receptionist, who whispered to him and pointed to Hannah.

He looked at Hannah for a few seconds and spoke in German. "I know you from Berlin. You used to hang out at the Romanitsche Café."

"I used to do that," said Hannah with a smile.

"Yes, I remember you," he said, recognition dawning on him. "You were a friend of Hanna Hoch. You had short-cropped hair and wore bright red lipstick and green eyeshadow. That was a long time ago, in the twenties."

"You were the star of the Berlin Dada in those days, Herr Grosz," she responded. "I was one of the young girls waiting to be noticed by you. But you never did, and I went to Bauhaus."

"I did notice you. I thought you had a lot of talent."

The two of them stood there looking at each other, hoping for the past to come alive again. He's a middle-aged German mensch with a beer belly, she thought, and I'm the living symbol of a refugee: the past can never be recaptured, nor can it be reconciled with the present.

She was about to bid farewell to him when he smiled at her and held out his hand.

"You know, I haven't heard anyone talk about the Berlin Dada in decades," he said. "What's your name?"

"Hannah Müller."

"I remember now. A year ago Phyllis Grossman was asking about you. I couldn't recall your face, but I remembered seeing your work in Berlin galleries. I thought they were very good. Now that I have been able to link the name with the face, let's go somewhere and celebrate. It's time for lunch, and I'm hungry."

He hailed a cab, and they went up Fifth Avenue. On her left, Hannah saw Central Park and made a mental note that she should walk through it on her way back. The cab went up to Eighty-Sixth Street and turned east toward their destination, an unpretentious German restaurant whose owner greeted Grosz as a long-term customer and led them to a quiet booth in the rear. Soon a waiter placed a pitcher of dark German beer and two mugs at their table.

Grosz filled his mug and took a long, deep swallow.

"Nothing like good German beer to slake one's thirst," he said.

He looked at her and asked her why she wasn't drinking.

"I would like a glass of white wine," she said.

He went to the bar and came back with a glass of Riesling, and they toasted each other.

The waiter returned, ready to take their order.

"Bratwurst with sauerkraut and fried potatoes," said Grosz.

"I'll have some bread and cheese, please," said Hannah.

Grosz's mood became expansive after a few draughts of beer. "How are things in Berlin, my fellow artist-in-exile?" he asked, with a wide smile.

"Berlin is in ruins. The Romanitsche Café is gone, and the Kaiser Wilhelm Memorial Church is badly damaged. So are the Berlin Zoo and the Tiergarten. So are my studio and my paintings, all converted into a heap of rubble."

He looked sad and said nothing for a while.

"You know, I am always a German. I tried hard to become an American, but I gave up. One has to be born here to be a true American. Transplanting oneself in another country doesn't work. So here I am, a middle-aged demoralized German, constantly asking myself, 'How did my country end up this way?'"

He conveys what he feels so well, Hannah thought. I wish I had that gift, the gift of self-analysis and self-expression.

The sausages on his plate had disappeared, and Grosz turned to the platter of bread and cheese.

"Sometimes, in the company of artists from other countries, I am so conscious of my Germanness that I can't even look them in the eye," he said. "A few months ago, I was with Piet Mondrian at one of his gallery showings. He looked slim, fit, and cheerful, and his art had taken a turn for the better after living in New York. In my case, it's the reverse. My art has lost its edge, and my paintings are second rate."

"Piet Mondrian is here in New York?" asked Hannah, surprised to hear that one of her heroes, the one she admired most after Kandinsky, was living in this city. She should waste no time in visiting him, she thought.

"He used to live on Fifty-Fourth Street on the west side," said Grosz. "He died a few months ago."

"Ach nein!" exclaimed Hannah as those moments with Mondrian in Bauhaus—him explaining the theory of reduction of painting to the bare essentials of the grid—quickly flitted through her mind.

"He was getting on in years, but he was very creative," said Grosz. "In fact, of all the Bauhaus painters, he and Kandinsky succeeded in advancing their theories on painting late in life, unlike other artists like Josef Albers and Lionel Feininger who got stuck in a rut and were unable to move forward. An entire museum, the Museum of

Nonobjective Art on East Fifty-Fourth Street, is devoted to Kandinsky and Mondrian. The curator is Hilla Rebay. You know her, don't you?"

"Hilla Rebay?"

"Hilla von Rebay, the baroness from Alsace-Lorraine. She used to be Rudolf Bauer's mistress."

"I remember Rudolf Bauer. He was in the avant-garde movement for a while. I remember the beautiful poster he designed for *Der Sturm*, during the First World War. I kept a copy of it for many years. I didn't know Hilla Rebay was his mistress. I now remember seeing her with Kandinsky at Bauhaus. I thought she was friendly with him."

"She was friendly with a lot of men. Now she is the mistress of Solomon Guggenheim, the man who owns copper mines. He fell in love with her while she was painting his portrait. He founded the museum at her urging and has become, under her tutelage, a collector of Bauhaus art."

"Kandinsky must appreciate it. Is he also in the United States?"

"He passed away a year ago. He died in France."

Tears stole out of Hannah's eyes, and she quickly wiped them away with the napkin. Grosz stopped eating and looked at her with sympathy.

"He was seventy-seven, you know," he said.

"I wanted him to live forever," said Hannah. "He was the biggest influence in my life. He made me see the world in a different light."

"Let's go to the museum and see his paintings," said Grosz. "I'll introduce you to Hilla Rebay."

The Museum of Nonobjective Art was like a church, with artwork set up in gilt frames like altarpieces. The walls were covered with neutral gray velour to emphasize the glowing colors of the Kandinskys and Mondrians.

Hilla Rebay was a tall, elegant redheaded woman in her middle fifties, and after the introductions were over, she offered to take them on a tour of the museum. Grosz excused himself, saying that he had to go back to his gallery to meet a client, and the two women, left to themselves, found out quickly they had a lot in common. Hannah was shown dozens of Kandinskys and several Mondrians, and even though she had seen most of them in Bauhaus, it was quite an experience for her to make their acquaintance again after a period of fifteen years.

"I still can't believe he's dead; he was like a father to me," Hannah said at the end of the tour.

"Who? Kandinsky or Mondrian?"

"Kandinsky."

"I miss him too," said Hilla.

She led them to her office, and they had tea, German style, with a piece of Dresdner stollen taken from a tin.

"Can I look at your portfolio?" Hilla asked Hannah.

"If you want to," said Hannah. "These are my most recent paintings."

Not wanting to watch Hilla while she scrutinized her paintings, Hannah went to the ladies' room.

When she came back, she found that Hilla was wiping her eyes.

"I expected to see nonobjective painting, following the lead of Kandinsky," she said. "But these are so different; these are pictures from hell. Especially *Ghosts at Chelmno*."

"I painted them after visiting death camps in Poland. I *was* in hell."

"I don't want to hear about them," said Hilla, placing her hands over her ears. She looked at Hannah with unease verging on hostility. "Your paintings are very powerful, but I can't use them. Mr. Guggenheim and I have made a commitment to show only abstract art, art that's free of objective representation. Your paintings are about death. If, instead of human figures, you had painted black squares in a gray space as in Kazimir Malevich's work, I would've taken them."

She rose from her chair to indicate the meeting was over.

She is blaming the messenger for the message, thought Hannah. A dirty word—*Du Arschloch*—came to her mind, and she was surprised at her own latent vulgarity. I've been told never to use that word as a kid, she thought, and I wonder what made me think of it.

"I want to say one thing to you before I leave," she said, trying to stay calm. "You've built a temple here for the Bauhaus artists, but it is a mausoleum. Bauhaus is dead. No self-respecting artist living in Germany will ever paint like that anymore."

Hilla glared at her in silence, and Hannah took her portfolio of paintings and left the building. She was tired, her feet were hurting her, and she wanted to go home. But she had promised to see Phyllis that evening and slowly walked up Madison Avenue toward Sixty-Fourth Street.

The New York Atelier was located on the second floor of a brownstone and had large glass windows facing the street. It was holding a group show for New York artists, according to a notice outside the gallery. Hannah climbed a flight of stairs and entered a wide, well-lit space to see Phyllis talking to a group of men in suits, while pointing to various pictures hanging from the walls. They must be prospective buyers, thought Hannah. Will they buy this art? Hannah had never heard of the artists' names, but they appeared to be young American men trying to paint like Spaniards, Russians, and Germans. It's a case of young America stealing from Old Europe, she thought. The first painting was by someone called Arshille Gorky, and it showed, on a neutral gray background, patches of color enclosed by thin, sharply drawn black lines reminiscent of cartoon drawings. The title was *Garden in Sochi*. It reminded her of one of Kandinsky's improvisations, except Kandinsky would not have allowed overt representational motifs in his later pictures. The next one was done by a Willem de Kooning, and it was obviously derived from a Picasso painting of a woman, except that Picasso would never have used the color green so lavishly in his work—European painters usually shied away from green, and even the great Monet in his *Water Lilies* mixed it with gray, blue, and yellow to curtail its untameable garishness.

"Do you like these artists, Hannah?" asked Phyllis, who had come over and was standing next to her, smiling.

She has the same smile as Eric's, Hannah thought—what a wonderful gift to give to one's son!

"They try to paint like the Europeans, but then they put something else in their work, something American, perhaps? To tell you the truth, I don't want to judge them at this stage."

"The critics say they're the best among the younger generation, so I decided to give them a group show. I can't get anyone to buy them. Collectors are still looking for Cézannes and Matisses."

She smiled again, and her smile made Hannah feel good.

"Let's go to my office," said Phyllis. "We've to talk business, and then we will go to dinner."

At the office, she told Hannah that all her Nuremberg drawings had been sold, and there was a credit balance of $3,000 in her account.

"I'll write a check for you right now," she said.

"I don't have a bank account," said Hannah. "I would like to have cash."

"The banks are closed for the day. I'll get the money tomorrow and send the money by messenger to your address."

She took down Octavia's address and then asked Hannah to show her the new paintings.

"You've changed your style, I see," she said, after looking at them for a while. "I don't know what to call them. They could be called expressionistic, for I see some Emil Nolde, but they also remind me of Salvador Dali. Are you going to paint more in this style?"

"I don't know," said Hannah. "I don't even know if I'm going to paint again. I feel like a fish out of water in America."

"You know, many German émigrés say that. I've spoken to quite a few of them, and they've ambivalent feelings. A good number of them moved to California, and they feel worse over there than in New York."

"Is it that bad?"

"I don't think so. Bertolt Brecht is out there, staging plays. Hanns Eisler writes film scores that are very successful. Thomas Mann is a nationally known figure. So, you see, it depends on the individual, I guess."

If I don't like it there, I can go back to Germany, thought Hannah, to the ruins of Nuremberg or Berlin.

"Coming back to your recent work," said Phyllis, "I don't want to give you a show. These paintings touch a raw nerve, and there will be notoriety associated with it. What I would like to do is to show it to private collectors who are interested in this type of work. I think I can get a very good price for them. Is that OK with you?"

Hannah felt very tired. Hilla Rebay tells me it's powerful stuff, but she can't show it, and Phyllis Grossman tells me, in effect, the same thing, she thought. Nice try, but no cigar—as the Americans say.

"You seem moody," said Phyllis, looking at her with concern.

"Do what you want to do with them," said Hannah evenly. "You know best, and I trust you."

"I'm glad to hear that. Some of the artists would have been insulted by my offer. But then Eric has said to me so many times you're so calm and rational, one of the best."

Because I don't show my emotions doesn't mean I don't have them, thought Hannah. She couldn't quite figure out what the woman facing her wanted from her—or for that matter why she was sitting in that office instead of walking out. Like an automaton, she signed the papers placed in front of her without reading them and left her paintings in the gallery without any regret at parting from them.

The two women then walked over to Third Avenue to a French restaurant. It was a small, cozy place, and the owner, who seemed to know Phyllis, gave them a nice table in a corner.

"I come here frequently with clients," Phyllis said. "The *coq au vin* and the *bœuf bourguignon* are quite good. And also, the *baba au rhum*."

The owner brought over two menus and a wine list and asked what he should get them from the bar.

"How's the wine situation, Jacques?" asked Phyllis.

"We are still waiting for the French wines, but we have some excellent reds from South America."

"I'll have a gin and tonic," said Phyllis.

"Me too," said Hannah, even though she didn't care for gin or tonic. What she wanted was a glass of Liebfraumilch, but that was out of the question in a French restaurant.

The menu was written in French, and the owner solicitously asked Hannah if she wanted any help with it.

"I understand French," she replied in that language.

He appeared discomfited after hearing her, and Hannah thought she had somehow let him down—obviously, he had wanted to explain to her the gastronomic subtleties of his cuisine and was disappointed when that chance was denied.

They ordered their main courses and talked for the rest of the meal—Phyllis had a lot to say about Eric, while Hannah listened and gave brief responses.

"He has a new girlfriend, Naomi," said Phyllis. "She is a lawyer and is taking part in the trials that are going on there. He says he isn't serious about her. She is now living in his house, in the room upstairs. She is from Philadelphia, and her parents are doctors. It would be an ideal match for him, but it is not going to happen."

"He told me that he was seeing Naomi," said Hannah.

"My son has an obsessive personality, as I told you before. My feeling is that he had an affair with a German woman, and he's still in love with her. I don't know that for a fact. I'm guessing from a few hints that he's dropped."

"He has dropped a few hints to me also," said Hannah.

"Another example of his obsession is the mass murder of Jews in Europe—the Holocaust, as it's called here these days. He is going to attend what the newspapers refer to as the subsequent Nuremberg trials, some six or seven of them, and also the trials held in Poland. He is convinced that the logistics involved in the transportation and extermination of six million Jews is so complex that it couldn't have been carried out without a centralized plan. He is determined to find out who among the Nazis was responsible for it. He also wants to write a book whose working title is *The Blueprint*."

"I know," said Hannah. "He has talked to me about it, and I wasn't very encouraging, I'm afraid."

"Me neither. I think Naomi is urging him to go ahead with the project. My husband says we shouldn't focus on the past. I agree with him. We should look to the future; we should work for the creation of a Jewish State. I wish Eric would take that attitude instead of digging up the past to find out which Nazi drafted the plan for the final solution."

"Nothing that we tell him will make him change his mind," said Hannah.

"You're right. We should leave him alone, I guess. By the way, my husband wanted to meet you, but this is his poker night. His buddies will be at our house until late, and that's why I didn't invite you. If you are free to come over tomorrow or the day after, we would like that."

"Tomorrow is my last day here, and I want to spend it with Octavia and Rider. I am taking the train to California the day after tomorrow, at five o'clock from Grand Central."

"Maybe I'll come and see you off," Phyllis said.

The two ladies finished their meal shortly afterward, and Phyllis accompanied Hannah to the subway entrance.

The next morning Hannah woke up late, blinking at the sunlight that poured in through a grating in her basement room and was falling on her face. She looked at her watch—the same watch given to her by the Russian Stenka—and found it was nearly nine o'clock. She heard Octavia singing in the other room, a sweet German song that people used to sing in pubs in the late twenties. She must have learned it from her mother, Hannah thought, as she put on a robe and went to the living room.

"Good morning," said Octavia. "There's a package for you from Phyllis Grossman. It was delivered a few minutes ago."

She doesn't speak German anymore, thought Hannah, even though she sings German songs when no one is around.

She opened the package and found a stack of twenty and fifty dollar bills and a letter from Phyllis saying how much she enjoyed speaking with her and promising she would get to work right away in getting collectors to see her new paintings.

She counted the bills, and they added up to $4,000. Octavia was watching her with open mouth, and Hannah, on an impulse, counted $1,000 and offered it to her.

"It's a gift to the baby from Aunt Hannah," she said.

It took Octavia a couple of seconds to fully comprehend Hannah's gesture. She burst into tears and hugged Hannah.

"It is so kind of you," she said in German. "We could use the money."

German words gushed out of her in a torrent. Life was hard here. Rider loved her, she was glad she was married to him. He was so gentle and caring. His mother paid no attention to her. When they visited her, she spoke only to Rider. Rider's friends were embarrassed by her. She felt like an outcast, like a Jude in the old country.

The storm subsided after a while, and she smiled again.

"Today is your last day here," she said to Hannah. "Let's spend the day together."

An hour later, they left the house and walked around in the Village, from west to east and north to south. The cobbled streets and the narrow sidewalks reminded her of German cities, even though the names were in English. Some of the streets were only fifty yards in length before they merged into other narrow streets and assumed different names. Bethune, Bank, Perry, Charles, Christopher, Bedford—the streets seemed to float by her as they crossed over to Washington Square Park and, from there, walked southward into a grimy complex of huge iron buildings that looked like factories or warehouses. They stopped at a tiny Spanish outdoor café and had a leisurely lunch, drinking sangria and eating olives, *croquetas*, and sausages. After that they wandered in and out of shoddy art galleries displaying cheap replicas of modern paintings: copies of Paul Klee's famous *Senecio*, a red-and-orange face inside a circle, Salvador Dali's painting of bent clocks called *The Persistence of*

Memory, Picasso's *Three Musicians,* and the like. Hannah wondered who bought these ungainly reproductions and for what reason. The words of Walter Benjamin, someone who had a lot to say about the mechanical reproduction of works of art, came to her mind. "Even the most perfect reproduction of a work of art is lacking in one element: its presence in time and space, its unique existence at the place where it happens to be." What would he have said about these?

Octavia stopped in front of a small bookstore that displayed a paperback edition of Thomas Mann's *The Magic Mountain.*

"Have you read it in German, Hannah?" she asked.

"I've read only the reviews," Hannah replied.

"I would like to give it to you as a present," Octavia said.

"That'll be nice," said Hannah, even though she doubted if she was going to read another work by the verbose author whose *Buddenbrooks* she had found tedious.

After the purchase of the book, they walked west until they saw a French dress shop. At Octavia's insistence, she went inside and ended up buying a dress, a skirt, and a jacket, and luxury of luxuries—a pair of French shoes.

"I never had any money to spend on clothes," she told Octavia. "At Bauhaus, we made our own dresses, using colors imaginatively, under the supervision of a crafts teacher. It's the first time I have splurged, and it makes me feel guilty."

"I'll make you feel even guiltier," said Octavia, with a mischievous smile, and dragged her to a beauty salon a block away, where they were given the complete treatment—shampoo, conditioning, coloring, styling, a manicure, and a pedicure.

"Eyebrows, ma'am?"

Hannah refused to have her eyebrows plucked.

"I'm happy with the way they are," she said.

The bill came to a hundred dollars, not including the tip.

"I can't recognize myself in the mirror. This isn't the person who used to be me," said Hannah.

"You look stylish and beautiful," said Octavia. "You don't look forty-six."

This is America, thought Hannah—you conceal gray hairs and hide your age. All for what? To have sex with a younger man? To escape the watchful eye of Death?

She felt uncomfortable walking in her new shoes and the new dress, which Octavia kept admiring, even as she was complaining of the baby kicking her in the belly.

On West Fourth Street, they saw a movie theater playing *Notorious* with Cary Grant, Ingrid Bergman, and Claude Rains. Like most Germans, unable to resist the tug of the silver screen, the two of them went inside and soon got drawn into the love triangle between the three famous actors, woven into an improbable plot dealing with a Nazi attempt to smuggle uranium to make an atomic bomb. The photography was good, the direction superb; the only thing that was lacking was conviction, Hannah thought, after they came out of the theater—for none of the actors fitted the roles demanded of them by the awkward script.

It was getting dark when they got out of the movie. They had pizza and beer for their evening meal, and Octavia, like a good wife, took half a pizza home for her husband's dinner.

The next morning, Rider and Octavia dropped her off at Grand Central Station on their way to visit his mother, who lived in Camden, New Jersey.

Hannah's train didn't leave until 5:00 p.m., and she checked her suitcase in a locker at the station. After that she walked uptown, stopping at East Fifty-Seventh Street to look at a row of sleek galleries displaying Miro, Leger, and other European masters. She went inside one and was put off by the purely commercial aspect that was in evidence—the cold, snotty receptionist, the owner in a three-piece suit obsequiously explaining the worth of a Braque as an investment to a gray-haired woman wearing an expensive designer dress. Is that what art really meant? Was it nothing but a transaction between a well-off agent and a wealthy client? Her disillusionment persisted as she passed by other galleries, all in the same mold. But a break came her way when she saw some interesting paintings displayed in a small gallery, not much bigger than a storefront. She went inside and learned that the works were by Stanton MacDonald-Wright and Morgan Russell, two American artists she had never heard of before. At first she thought they were Bauhaus imitators because of the similarity in their use of abstraction and coloration. She then noticed that Morgan Russell's work was done in 1913, long before Bauhaus had been founded. Why weren't these artists, obviously the precursors of modernism and abstraction, not given any recognition in Europe? Their work was even more interesting than that of the Bauhaus abstractionists because of the emotional tension that was latent in their nonfigurative, nonobjective style of painting.

She spoke to the gallery owner, a down-to-earth man wearing khaki pants and a blue shirt, and found out that both artists had studied in France and had had exhibitions in Munich just before the First World War. That was the time when Kandinsky was around in that city, and Hannah was sure he must have seen their work.

"Why don't they get more recognition?" asked Hannah.

"The American art critics don't like them," said the owner. "Especially the *Art World*. Personally, I think MacDonald-Wright and Russell would've been better off if they had called themselves surrealist or abstract painters. Instead they chose to be known as 'synchromists.' Here in America, names matter."

Hannah thought over what he said. What if Picasso and Braque had called their movement "fragmentism" or "deconstructionism" or some other name that was more appropriate to their work? Would the world have walked away from them?

"You know, you're right," she said to the owner. "The name matters."

299

The paintings did not cost much, and she bought a red-and-orange work by MacDonald-Wright for $120. I can't afford it, she thought, but I love it, and that's what matters.

Her next stop was Bloomingdale's, and she spent time wandering from floor to floor looking at the merchandise, the sales people, and the customers who crowded the aisles. She remembered the pleasure she used to get in visiting the department stores of Wertheim and the Kaufhaus des Westens in Berlin before they became targets of Nazi wrath. Mental pictures of brown-shirted SA men blocking entrances and taunting Jewish-looking customers and passersby whirled past her like reels from a film noir. Disturbed, she went out and wandered aimlessly in the strange, crowded streets of Manhattan until she was stopped by a young woman with a clipboard who asked her to sign a petition against dropping nuclear bombs on the Bikini Atoll.

"Who is doing it?" Hannah asked the woman.

"Our government is doing it. They say they have to test these weapons before the Russians catch up. The radioactive fallout is lethal, and the poor natives will have to pay a price."

Hannah signed the petition on the clipboard, even though she wasn't quite sure of the location of the Bikini Atoll. It was the first time she had signed a petition since 1932, and she felt a sense of freedom and elation. The full realization of what the young woman, a plump, dark-haired beauty, was saying came to her only after she had walked away from her. Were they going to test new weapons without any end in sight? Would the whole world be covered with radioactive ash? She had left the death factories and burned-out cities of Europe and now was being told that mushroom clouds, more lethal than cyanide gas, were being released into the atmosphere by mad scientists to soothe the paranoid fears of the new rulers of the world. There will never be peace on earth as long as *Homo sapiens* are alive, she thought, and the sentiment gave her no comfort.

Seeing a diner close to her, she went in and lingered over a cup of coffee until she was soothed by the warmth and coziness of the place. Opposite the diner, a rundown movie theater was playing *A Night in Casablanca*, starring the Marx Brothers. The last one of theirs she had seen was *Horse Feathers* thirteen years ago in Berlin, and she had been captivated by Chico's piano playing and Groucho's singing. She had three hours more to kill, and leaving a dime on the countertop—she did that because she saw a man two seats away who had a cup of coffee also doing it—she went across the street to the theater. It was another movie about the Nazis, but she had a good time watching Chico playing the "Beer Barrel Polka" and a zany swordfight between Harpo and a Nazi, and her mood of exhilaration stayed with her as she made her way down to the Grand Central Terminal.

Her ticket was for a through sleeping car, the porter who carried her battered suitcase explained to her, and she didn't have to change trains at Chicago. The name of the train was Twentieth Century, and its opulence reminded her of the Orient Express. A crimson carpet had been rolled out on the platform, and the passengers, many of them dressed formally, walked to their carriages accompanied by porters pushing their luggage, as though they were going to a gala event at some millionaire's mansion. The porter took her to her car, and she took out her purse to tip him. She didn't know what the right amount was and handed him a dollar.

"This is too much," he said, after giving her a glance of curiosity mixed with sympathy toward the foreigner.

"I don't know what the right amount is," she said.

"A quarter will be fine."

"Oh, you keep the change," she said and went inside the carriage.

She was somewhat unsettled by the transaction and felt like an impostor who had no right to be in this train meant for the wealthy. This feeling was accentuated during the rest of the journey as Pullman porters went by her at regular intervals doing their allotted chores—handing her a cocktail menu, bringing her a glass of wine, handing her a dinner menu, making the bed ready for her, bringing her a nightcap, and turning out the lights—and she, not used to being served upon, felt like Cinderella during the night of the ball.

The dinner consisted of five courses, and used as she was to American food, she was puzzled by certain items she found on the menu, such as crab Louis cocktail, corn sticks, and green apple pie. Afraid of making a fool of herself, she stayed with the familiar and ordered a piece of grilled salmon, carrots, and cauliflower and chocolate cake. Every now and then the lights from the river Hudson (she knew its name from the route map that was printed on one of the napkins) would flash by her. She wondered if she would ever have the same feeling for an American river that she had for the Rhine, Danube, or Oder. Could she get to love this vast, mysterious country in the same way that she loved Germany, Poland, or Austria? Eating her food slowly, she brooded about whether she should go back home before the end of the year or stay here and become an émigré like George Grosz or Hilla Rebay. Neither option appealed to her, and she felt like someone walking on a tightrope stretched across a vast abyss. Diabolical voices spoke to her from the recesses of her brain. Who are you? What's your identity? What are you doing here? Where are you going to? In the past you were a Berliner, an artist, a victim, and a survivor, and now you're on a journey across this threatening continent into the Dreadful Night. Shaking with fear, afraid she would faint, she asked the waiter for a glass of brandy and drank it slowly. The smooth motion of the train as it sped by the dark river soothed her nerves, and she felt she was ready for a long night's sleep.

She woke up early the next morning and took a seat in the observation car. They were going west, and the sunlight coming from behind fell on the long stretch of Lake Erie that lay parallel to their course. After a while, her eyes got tired from watching the lake, and she went to the dining car for breakfast, where she decided to try new things—a glass of pineapple juice, waffles with maple syrup, and a slice of watermelon.

The train was slowing down, and soon they entered the LaSalle Street station in Chicago.

"The Super Chief to Los Angeles starts at six forty-five this evening, ma'am," said a porter in answer to her inquiry. "This carriage is gonna be shuttled to Dearborn Station, which is where the train starts from."

"What am I supposed to do until then?" she asked him, wondering why all the Pullman staff, from porters to stewards, were black and why they were smiling all the time, so eager to please.

"Some people go to the Ambassador Hotel to shower and eat lunch. Others kill time at Marshall Field's, the department store. Some stay in this car and stretch their legs at the station."

She chose the last option and tried to read *The Magic Mountain* but soon gave it up. There were no interesting characters or incidents in Thomas Mann's novels. People talked and talked, and now and then the authorial voice would offer philosophical digressions on time, space, and such abstract topics. Someone had told her many years ago that the book was a parody of Schwabing, where Mann used to live—the sick people in the sanatorium were the intellectuals constantly debating the future of the world, and the rarefied atmosphere that made visitors dizzy was that of the Café Stephanie. Trying to see if this was indeed the case, she dutifully continued reading the book off and on, carrying it with her to the observation car of the Super Chief as it wended its way to Los Angeles via Kansas City, Newton, Dodge City, La Junta, Raton, Las Vegas, Albuquerque, Winslow, Seligman, Needles, Barstow, San Bernardino, and Pasadena. The names fascinated her, and she would repeat them like a mantra whenever they arrived at a new station.

The second leg of the journey was even more luxurious than its predecessor. Delicious hors d'oeuvres were served an hour before dinner, along with cocktails; an elaborate meal followed, offering exotic items such as chicken okra Louisiana-style, avocado salad, new potatoes persillade, pecan pie, and bourbon whiskey bread pudding with preserved guavas.

The portions were much larger than she had expected, but she liked the taste of everything on her plate, and after drinking a glass of vintage port, she went back to her sleeping car, satiated and drowsy. She tried to read some more of Thomas Mann and fell asleep, dreaming of Schwabing—walking with her uncle, young and handsome, in the Englischer Garten and staring at two of her favorite sights, the waterfall and the Chinese pagoda.

She woke up early the next morning and sat in the observation car with a cup of coffee, watching the huge American prairie land rush past her. The landscape then changed to rockier terrain, as the train passed by hills, through paths hewed out of rocks, and then back again to the flat lands.

When the train stopped at Albuquerque, she saw American Indian women selling beads and jewelry on the platform. She bought a silver ring with a turquoise stone from a young girl and a shawl from an older woman.

The next stretch was Arizona—areas of desert, followed by rocky land, sterile and monotonous—and it was with a sense of relief that she welcomed the rising palm trees as they neared Pasadena.

Half an hour later, they were in Los Angeles. Hannah got out of the train and stretched her legs while a porter brought out her suitcase. Moments later she saw Claudia, very pregnant, waddling like a penguin toward her, followed by Gene, who was unrecognizable in his natty blue blazer, white cotton duck trousers, and clipped moustache in the British style—a far cry from the GI in his khaki outfit.

The two women hugged each other and then kissed, genuinely glad to be together.

"*Wie geht es dir, mein Lieber?*" asked Hannah, with her arms around the young woman and felt a stiffening of Claudia's back muscles.

"I'm doing fine," was her reply, and Hannah sensed that German was not to be spoken here also.

They walked to their car, which was parked near the railroad station. Gene opened the backdoor of the Cadillac for her, and she got in and slid toward the end of the seat, making room for Claudia. But Claudia, like a dutiful wife, sat in the front with her husband, and Hannah felt a twinge of disappointment.

"Shall we drive around and show you a bit of Los Angeles?" asked Gene.

Suddenly, Hannah felt weary of it all—the new city, the new relationships to be formed, and the careful dance steps she had to learn to avoid treading on someone's toes.

"I am a little tired," she said. "I didn't get enough sleep on the train."

"We will go home then," said Gene. "We can show you the city tomorrow."

TWENTY-THREE

SANTA MONICA

The guest room where she had slept had french windows that opened to a long stretch of sloping lawn, ending in a grove of orange trees. Their fruit glinted in the rays of the midmorning sun, and Hannah, intrigued by the contrast of colors produced by the foliage surrounding them, walked toward the trees. She picked up a fallen orange and ate it slowly, tasting its overripe sweetness that lingered long after she had spat out the last seed.

Somewhere near her was the sea, because she could hear the slow rhythmic heave and crash of the waves. She turned around, and her eyes rested on rows of brightly colored flowers, flaming yellows and poignant blues she had never seen in Europe. And above them, several red-and-brown birds fluffed their feathers as they tried to get into birdfeeders hanging from branches.

I don't even know where I am exactly, but I like everything here, she thought—the blue sky, the sound of the sea, the fauna and flora that are new to me. The light around me makes me feel like van Gogh in Arles, wanting to paint every color I see—the pale lilac of the garage walls, the faded red of the picnic table on the lawn, the chrome yellow of the canopy on the gazebo. She realized, a moment later, that her paints, brushes, and canvasses were in Nuremberg and wondered how difficult it would be to start over again in this strange city, six thousand miles away from her roots.

"Senora Müller." She heard a voice from behind her. "Senora Müller, I brought you some coffee."

She turned and saw a dark woman in her early thirties, with coal-black hair cut in a bang across her forehead, smiling at her with white, even teeth. She wore a maid's uniform with a white flower in a buttonhole. She looks like someone from a Gauguin painting, Hannah thought. I would like to get her to model for me, if it doesn't present problems.

"Senora Frankel told me you would be our guest," she said.

"What's your name?" asked Hannah.

"It's Camellia, but everyone calls me Camille," she said.

"Yes, I would like some coffee, Camille," said Hannah.

Camille smiled, left, and returned holding a tray that she placed on the red picnic table. She poured a cup of coffee from a pot, looked at Hannah, smiled again, and retreated to the kitchen. A plate of cut-up fruit and freshly baked rolls were on the tray. Hannah sat down and ate slowly, relishing the taste of what, to her, was exotic fruit. This, and not New York, is the real New World, she thought, and I like the feeling of remoteness, of new possibilities after escape from the prison that was the Old World.

She sat at that table for a while, absorbed in watching the flowers and the birds, until she heard voices inside the house. Gene came out, dressed in blue shorts and a white short-sleeved shirt, and stood facing her with a smile.

Everyone smiles here, Hannah thought, unlike in Germany where everyone frowns a lot.

"Did you have a nice long sleep?" he asked.

"Yes, I did."

"Claudia and I've made plans for us for today," he said. "We will go to the beach, then we will give you a tour of Hollywood, and we will have dinner at this wonderful Mexican restaurant."

"I was thinking of walking around for a while to get a feel for the place."

"Nobody walks around in this town," he said with a smile. "Everyone drives a car, including the maid and the gardener. Can you drive?"

"Yes. When I was young, my uncle taught me. He even let me drive his sports car in Munich."

"You have to get a driver's license. I'll arrange for someone to give you driving lessons. Also, you need to get your own car, from a good used-car dealer."

Hannah, not knowing how much it would cost and worried about the state of her finances, didn't know what she should say to him.

"You should also find a place to live," he went on. "Try the Santa Monica area, where many émigré artists have homes. After you get your car, you should drive around and see what's available there."

He has it all planned, thought Hannah. She noticed the change in him from the boyish soldier she had seen in Nuremberg to a tough businessman used to making plans and giving orders without doubting they would be carried out. It has happened so quickly, she thought. His jawline has changed, his posture has become more assertive, his diction more decisive, all because of the few months he spent in Hollywood. She wasn't sure that she liked him anymore. She didn't want to ask him any questions, thinking that she should have a discussion with Claudia first.

But that discussion didn't take place until a week later.

During the next couple of days, Hannah was driven around Los Angeles by Gene and Claudia in their elegant Cadillac Town Car. Streets, avenues, and boulevards whizzed by her—Venice, Sunset, Glendale, Ventura—and Hannah tried to retain some impression of them, but the only image that stayed in her memory was that of a medley of buildings in the Spanish, Venetian, Gothic, Moorish, Tudor, and Mediterranean styles mixed in with parking lots, palm trees, movie theaters, and hot dog stands. They went over hills with houses on either side precariously perched on slopes, seemingly defiant of the next landslide that would crash and sink them into the engulfing mud, and through canyons where rocks, trembling on the verge of anxiety as though they were objects in a still life painted by Cezanne, were ready to tumble over and crush them if there was an earthquake. Claudia, who was uncomfortable sitting for a long time in a car, especially if there were bumps on the road or sharp turns, complained incessantly. They never got out of the car, except once when Gene stopped at Hollywood Boulevard to show Hannah the footprints made by movie stars—the only record of man's palpable achievement in this city with no towers, no battlements, no old town with narrow, cobblestone-paved streets, no medieval cathedrals, and no architectural past.

At the end of the tour, she was mystified and exasperated by the City of Angels and wished she had someone to explain to her why or how it was built. Gene was no help—he was wrapped up in Claudia, holding her hand, kissing her, touching her stomach, or constantly making plans revolving around the baby that was due in a few weeks.

Getting her driver's license was a top priority according to Gene, and a driving instructor showed up in a dual-control car in their driveway the next morning. He was in his fifties, of medium height, lean and fit, clean shaven, with neatly kept hands. He wore a denim shirt, khaki pants, and a red leather belt with an engraved silver buckle, obviously made by Indian artisans. He introduced himself as Randy Stevens and shook hands with her.

"Gene said you are his wife's aunt from Germany," he said with a friendly grin. "Welcome to Los Angeles. Gene says you know how to drive. What we will do is go to a quiet street around here and let you drive around for a while."

From Marbery Road they went to Adelaide Road, when they switched seats.

"I've always driven on the right side," she said. "But I think I can manage if I drive slowly. Please explain the signs to me as we see them, since they're different from the German ones."

They drove through empty streets for a while, and Hannah, nervous behind the wheel, looked out for traffic that might appear unexpectedly from a side street. The man explained to her the rules regarding right of way and the meaning of the unfamiliar signs. After a while, she began to relax a little and smiled at the instructor.

"How are things in Germany?" he asked.

"Bad," said Hannah. "There are only a few buildings left standing in Berlin and Nuremberg. It's the same in Dresden and other cities. People live in basements. Food is scarce. And the country is divided into zones."

He remained silent for a while.

"Do you mind if I ask you something?" he asked.

"Go ahead," she said, wondering if he was going to ask about her marital status.

"Were you a Hitler supporter? Lots of women were, from what I've read. And you look the type, if I may say so. I mean, you are tall and blond, the very model of an Aryan woman."

Hannah laughed.

"I was on Hitler's blacklist. The Gestapo were harassing me all the time. I lived in the shadows, like someone on parole, in Berlin for twelve years."

"Maybe we've something in common."

Hannah was amused by his response.

"What do we have in common?"

"I too am on a blacklist. I used to be a scriptwriter in Hollywood. And the studios fired me because of my political views."

They had reached Griffith Park, and he asked her to slow down the car.

"I haven't had breakfast," he said. "I'm going to get a cup of coffee and a donut from the diner over there."

She accompanied him to the diner, bought a cup of black coffee, and went inside the park with him. He looked around and walked toward a wooden bench where he could sit and eat. There were wildflowers everywhere, and a hundred yards away a line of palm trees stood behind a wall. I've an affinity for palm trees, thought Hannah. I would like to climb one like a tomboy and slide down the trunk.

"I come here quite often," Randy said. "Griffith Park is a huge place. They have a theater modeled on the Greek amphitheater. The battle scenes in the movie *Birth of a Nation* were filmed in this park."

"I don't know much about American movies. I haven't seen *Birth of a Nation.*"

"It is about the Civil War and the assassination of President Lincoln. The movie shows black people in an unflattering, I would even say racist, light."

Hannah groaned inwardly. They hate the blacks the same way Germans hate the Jews, she thought. Does every country have its own pariahs? Why is it always that way? Do humans have the basic need to despise and hate other humans? And what is the solution? Segregation? Extermination? Or the one proposed by my friend Daniel, to get a state for every persecuted group? A state for Jews, a state for blacks, a state for every subdivision of humanity? That notion clashed with her Bauhaus heritage, the dream of a common humanity, the idea of a world without boundaries.

An aggressive pigeon hopped over her foot to seize a crumb that had fallen to the ground from the donut that Randy was eating.

He gave her an amused smile.

"I'm in two minds about feeding birds in the park," he said. "I feel sorry for the poor creatures, but I don't want too many birds in the park. Every situation that we humans face seems to come with its own built-in dilemma."

She was surprised and pleased by his words, which reminded her of the duality in her own thinking. She was about to tell him that she felt the same way when she heard loud voices speaking German from a nearby bench. The people sitting there were a ragged lot, gesticulating and arguing vociferously.

"What's all that about?" asked Randy.

"I think they're arguing about whether they would find a better welcome in the eastern or western zone of Germany, if they decide to go back," she said.

"They're the Jewish refugees from Germany," he said. "I used to see a lot of them in the Hollywood studios during the war years. They were in great demand then. Now, the studios don't want to hire them, and I see them wandering in the park or sitting in groups and arguing."

"It must be awful for them."

"Some of them did very well. People like Hanns Eisler, Fritz Lang, Max Reinhardt, Thomas Mann… They live in posh houses in Pacific Palisades or Beverly Hills."

"I had no idea they're all here in Los Angeles," she said.

"They love this place. They call it an émigré's paradise. In fact, there's an entire German community in Santa Monica called Weimar in Exile. There are German cafés, movie theaters, and cabarets. If you would like to, we can go over there right now."

He let her drive, giving her occasional advice, and taking the wheel from her a couple of times. They went in and out of side streets, and he showed her the rundown house where Bertolt Brecht lived and another equally shabby place where Heinrich Mann, grief-stricken after the suicide of his cabaret-dancer wife, was passing his days in ghostly solitude. Her mother had known both Manns, Heinrich and Thomas, in the old days, in Munich. She wondered whether she should visit them, and…then what? The past was gone forever—those Berlin and Munich scenes of her youth, with Brecht strutting around as the new wunderkind of the theater, and Heinrich, creator of *The Blue Angel,* more famous than his brother, placed on a pedestal as the most eminent man of letters in Germany—and the literary lions of Weimar had escaped unscathed from the Third Reich to live out their lives in Santa Monica, but divested of their claws and manes.

She saw several German bookstores and *Kaffee und Küchen* places and elderly German women walking poodles and dachshunds, like in any suburb of Munich or Berlin. I've left Germany, but I can't escape it, she thought.

"Want to go inside one of these places and meet your compatriots?" asked Randy.

"Not now," she protested. "I will come by myself, later on."

"Let me drive you to the beach, then."

He took the wheel and drove through side streets expertly, and the beach appeared suddenly before her, a long stretch of white-and-brown sand bordering the magical, mystical Pacific Ocean beyond it. I've never seen an ocean before, she thought. The huge body of water tantalized her, mesmerized her, and overwhelmed her. They took off their shoes and walked on the sands, and Hannah enjoyed the feel of the grainy mounds yielding and then spilling over her foot in a cycle of submission and retaliation.

"How do you like it here?" her companion asked her.

"It's wonderful. I've never seen anything like this. It's like being in another world."

"Don't they have beaches in Germany?" he asked.

"Only near the North Sea and Baltic Sea. I haven't been to either. I'm more of a river girl, having gone up and down the Rhine and the Danube many times."

They walked in silence for a while as the sea heaved and surged by their side, like a gargantuan animal futilely trying to climb over a huge ridge.

"I would like to live near here," she said. "That way I can come here every day."

"That shouldn't be a problem," he said. "I too live in this area, in a recently built apartment complex, five minutes by car from here. We can go there now, if you would like, and check it out."

She looked at him fully in the face for the first time, and old memories of platonic men friends came to her, men who had wanted nothing more than affection and kindness from her in return for eternal devotion. Randy was one of them, she guessed, and in a split-second decision, she took him on as a friend.

They spent a couple of hours in his apartment, which he shared with Roddy, a much younger man who was an actor, and the two of them, in synchronized tableaus of hospitality, made Hannah feel like a special guest: they placed, in succession, plates of cheese and crackers, guacamole and corn chips, and guava with cream before her, they brought out their photograph albums and showed her pictures of the trips they had taken together to Machu Picchu and Galapagos, and over glasses of sangria, they related to her hilarious anecdotes about Hollywood celebrities.

The two of them helped her to get acclimatized to her new environment over the next few days, and she quickly learned how to get around the City of Angels by herself. She passed her driver's license test without any trouble because of their coaching, and Roddy found her a used Plymouth Fastback, arranging a loan for her with the dealer under which she would pay for the car in twelve monthly instalments.

She still had not been able to be alone with her hostess, for Claudia suffered from migraine headaches some mornings and would lie in bed for hours. Most of her afternoons and evenings were spent in going to various clinics or doctor's offices—her gynecologist, her obstetrician, her neurologist for her headaches, an osteopath for her hurting back, a midwife for advice on natural childbirth, and a masseuse for improving her circulation, especially on her swollen legs and feet. And during weekends, she and her husband would go on daylong outings with friends of theirs, a set of elegant young Hollywood producers and directors.

She learned these details from Camille, with whom she had struck up an easy friendship.

"The senora is not happy. She cries in the mornings," Camille said.

What was the cause of Claudia's unhappiness? Hannah wondered. Was it her husband? Was it the pregnancy itself, the burden of having to carry a kicking, bouncing fetus in her belly with all the existential doubts and premonitions that went with it?

She didn't have to wait very long for an answer because that same evening, as she was sitting in the patio reading *The Magic Mountain*, Camille came rushing toward her.

"The Senora's masseuse has canceled her appointment a few minutes ago," she said. "I think you can go and talk to her now."

Hesitantly, Hannah tiptoed to Claudia's suite and found the door partially open. She saw Claudia reading a letter, her shoulders heaving in spasmodic sobs. Hannah walked to her side and placed her hand gently on her back.

"What's the matter, darling?" she asked in German.

In response, Claudia handed her the letter she was reading.

It was sent from Paraguay and was from her father, Hermann Winterkorn. Hannah had to wade through several paragraphs of schmaltzy, run-on writing in the German style—how Hermann missed his dearest daughter Claudia, how he wanted to hold his grandchild in his arms and bounce it on his knee while singing "Hoppe, Hoppe, Reiter", how, unlike other Germans, he was not prejudiced in the least and didn't mind if the baby's father was Jewish for he entertained no hatred against anyone belonging to that race and, in fact, thought the Jews were smarter than most Germans, how he wanted to be there when Claudia was giving birth, but, unfortunately, it was out of the question because of his present circumstances, and on and on—before she understood his predicament. A month ago, an order had been issued by the German government for his arrest, and he was moving to Argentina for safety. As a primary supplier to the SS, he had to do what the top brass wanted him to do—the SS generals had asked him to make mats out of the hair shorn from the inmates of Buchenwald and Treblinka and soap from fat delivered to him in vats. He didn't know at that time the fat was from humans, nor was he aware that the parchment they had sent him for making lampshades was human skin flayed from corpses. Some survivors from those camps had unjustly accused him of trafficking in human residues, but he was completely unaware of the true nature of the material that had been given to him. More maudlin outpourings followed, about how the once great Führer had led Germany to ruin by listening to Himmler and Bormann, and their beloved Fatherland, once the most powerful among nations, now lay in ruins because of mistakes made by its leaders. The letter concluded by telling her not to write to him until such time she heard from him, probably under a different name.

Hannah's reaction was one of revulsion at having to read yet another document about German ghoulishness wrapped in the cover of patriotic righteousness, but that feeling was quickly replaced by concern for Claudia, who was studying her face with round, tear-swollen eyes.

"Don't feel bad, darling," Hannah said. "He'll find a safe haven in Argentina."

"They blame me for everything," she responded in German.

She's speaking to me the way she used to speak to me, thought Hannah, but I don't understand what she's saying.

"Who is blaming you?" she asked, afraid of her answer.

"All the Jewish people. Gene's clients, Gene's friends, Gene's mother."

It took a while for Hannah to get to the root of the matter. Four months ago, just after Claudia and Gene had moved to Los Angeles, there had been a newspaper article about German businesses making fortunes from selling byproducts of the death factories in Auschwitz and elsewhere. Hermann Winterkorn had been mentioned as one of the worst perpetrators in this regard. Gene had put Claudia in charge of dealing with his émigré clients, and until the appearance of that article, she had gotten along well with them. One of his clients, a Jewish woman from Bavaria, somehow found out that she was Hermann's daughter, and Claudia's life had become hell after that. Hate mail kept pouring in, there were threatening phone calls, and Claudia had a nervous breakdown. Gene was wonderful, she said. He stood by her and told her not to work for his agency. She had then suggested to him that Hannah should be brought over to take her place, and he had fallen in with the suggestion, albeit reluctantly.

"What exactly does Gene want me to do?" asked Hannah mechanically, her mind in turmoil because of the revelation about Hermann—his daughter will have to carry a burden of guilt and shame for the rest of her life, she was thinking.

"He wants you to take over what I was doing. Gene cannot speak German or French, and the émigrés don't speak English well. He wants you to tell the émigrés about your struggle in Germany and win their trust. After that, you should convince them that there are no jobs for them in Hollywood and that they should make plans to leave."

Even as she was vicariously feeling Claudia's anguish, the émigrés' plight loomed liked a dark cloud in her mind.

"Where will they go? They can't go back to Germany or Hungary or wherever they came from," said Hannah.

"Gene says he can't help them," Claudia replied. "He is a businessman, and it isn't up to him to solve all the problems of the world."

She is no longer the girl I used to know, thought Hannah. America has hardened her, made her into an automaton that speaks a language devoid of human concerns and empathy.

"You want me to talk to them and urge them to stop looking for jobs in Hollywood?" Hannah asked.

"Yes," said Claudia gratefully. "They will listen to you because…" She flushed with embarrassment and didn't finish the sentence.

"Because I'm an outcast like them? Is that what you didn't want to say?" asked Hannah.

"You did what you thought was the right thing, Hannah, and I respect you for it. I wish my dad had done the same thing."

Her words aren't convincing, thought Hannah, they don't seem to come from her heart. It wasn't that long ago she had seen her in a Bund Deutscher Madel uniform replete with Nazi insignia and heard her shouting "Heil Hitler" in parades and sing *Die Fahne hoch* in girls' choruses. She was a product of the Third Reich, her conscience had been surgically removed by Nazi experts, and her mind was an echo chamber where other people's thoughts reverberated. Hannah had no doubt she was now regurgitating words she had heard from Gene.

As though on cue, Gene walked into the room, dressed in tailor-made jeans and a torso-fitting cream-colored shirt. He planted a clinging kiss on Claudia's lips and turned to Hannah.

"You will start tomorrow, Hannah," he said coldly. "I'll fill you in at the office."

Hannah understood it as an order to leave the room and, put off by his rudeness, impulsively decided she would move out of the house as quickly as possible. She picked up a copy of the *Santa Monica Daily* lying around in the living room and went over its rental listings. She then drove over to see Randy and Roddy, and the three of them spent the rest of the day looking at apartments.

They drove in circles around blocks from Topanga to Playa del Rey, with frequent stops at coffee shops, looking at seedy rooms with stained walls and creaky boards, with an occasional roach scurrying into a crevice when the light switch was turned on. Hannah was disappointed with every apartment that she saw and had given up hope of ever finding a place to live when Roddy, who was driving, stopped the car in front of a small white-painted house on Twenty-Sixth Street. He pointed to a "TO LET" sign planted on the neatly mown lawn and suggested they check out the place even though it was a house and not an apartment building.

They were greeted at the door by a middle-aged European woman, tall and elegant in her plum-colored cashmere sweater and white pants. After preliminaries, she took them on a tour of the house, and Hannah was delighted by what she saw. The house was furnished in the modern style, the walls were white, the curtains were white, and the furniture was made of blond wood. The woman was Swedish, as Hannah had guessed. She had been living in the house for ten years, but now she was moving to her daughter's house for a while. She didn't want to sell the house but was willing to rent it to someone who would take good care of it, preferably a single, older woman.

"We've brought you the right candidate," said Roddy, the cheerful, talkative curly-haired partner.

"We've to discuss the rent, Roddy," said the practical Randy.

The woman wanted seventy dollars a month, which was absurdly cheap for that space.

"I don't need the money from this place to live," she said. "As I told you, I want to rent the house to someone I can trust."

"You can trust Hannah," said Roddy.

The woman looked at Hannah for a few seconds.

"The two of us need to talk for a while," she said. "In the meantime, you two men can take a walk around the house and see if anything needs to be fixed. There's beer in the icebox, and you're welcome to it if you're thirsty."

After the men left, Isabella—that was the woman's name—told Hannah that her daughter, an actress, had suddenly and inexplicably become the favorite of Hollywood producers, each one bidding against the other to give her a lead role in forthcoming movies. She had a bought a six-bedroom house in Beverly Hills and was feeling very lonely and miserable in her new environment.

"She broke up with her fiancé, and she wants me to be with her," she said.

It was Hannah's turn next, and she told her story, plainly and truthfully.

"You shouldn't be doing this job," said Isabella. "You're an artist. You should be doing creative work."

"Right now I've no choice," said Hannah. "I've to keep my promise to Claudia."

Isabella was not to be easily dissuaded. She suggested that Hannah convert a large room on the second floor—where there was "plenty of northern light"—to a studio and offered to take her to art-supply stores downtown to buy stretchers, canvas, and paints.

"My sister is an artist," she said. "She lives in Stockholm. I used to help her with priming canvases and mixing paints. I enjoyed doing those chores, even washing brushes covered with paint."

They talked in this vein for a while until the men returned, each holding a bottle of beer.

"We checked out everything," Roddy said. "This place is a steal for the rent Isabella's asking."

"I know that," said Isabella. "As I said before, I am not doing this to make money. If Hannah wants this place, I'll be happy to rent it to her."

She brought out the lease at Roddy's request, and Randy looked it over.

"Looks OK to me," he said.

Hannah signed on the dotted line with a sense of relief. I've my own place now, she thought, a lair where a wounded German woman can hide.

But she soon found out that it was impossible to hide in Los Angeles.

She had wanted to check out the streets in the neighborhood by herself, discover the nearest bookstore and movie theater, and wend her way to the beach without asking anyone for directions. But Randy and Roddy were around her most of the time, doing errands for her, moving the furniture around, helping her buy groceries, and even making meals for her.

What do these guys want from me? Hannah wondered. They're so nice to me, and I would like to know the reason why—but she didn't spend too much time speculating on the reason because there were other matters that needed her immediate attention.

Despite his promise to "fill her in," Gene didn't do much to enlighten her about her exact function in his office. On her first day, after following him in her car as he drove to his office on Labrea Avenue, she had looked forward to hearing details regarding her duties, work hours, and salary. But he had no time to talk to her. The lobby of his office was crowded with Jewish émigrés who tried to get his attention as he walked by. Ignoring them, he led Hannah to a room at the back of the building and gave her the key to it.

"That's your office, Hannah," he said, with an attempt at a smile. "Your job is to persuade these guys to stay away from us. They come here every day looking for work, even though they've been told the studios don't want to hire them."

The room had a musty odor, and Hannah opened the windows and turned on the ceiling fan to its highest setting. It was nicely furnished, with a mahogany table and comfortable chairs. A reprint of Whistler's *Chelsea Wharf* hung on the wall facing the table, and its glimmer of silver and red through a veil of fog seemed to be a metaphor of her own mental state. For a few minutes, she sat on the chair while the fan whirred overhead, trying to figure out what she was going to say to the émigrés.

She was startled when the door was pushed open, and a small man in an ill-fitting suit, grinning from ear to ear, entered the room in a shambling walk.

"We're glad you are here," he said in German, and his accent was pure Berlin.

Hannah sat up straight in surprise.

"Why? You don't know me. Why are you glad?" she asked nervously.

"Anyone who signed the Dringender Appell für die Einheit in 1932 is welcome in our community, Frau Müller," he said. "By the way, the name is Heinz Weingarten."

"How do you know I signed that?" she asked, more surprised than ever.

"We Jews have a network, Frau Müller," he said with a secretive smile.

He wasn't kidding—they really did have a network, Hannah found out quickly. From him and a dozen others who trooped in after him, Hannah learned what was happening in that office. Gene's father, who had migrated from Vienna as a young boy, had helped émigrés from Europe to settle in Los Angeles by finding them jobs in Hollywood. He had also set up an émigrés' welfare association that would provide them with monetary and professional assistance to alleviate hardship caused by sickness or unemployment. Gene's father was the executive director of the association, and until his death, out-of-work émigrés were guaranteed a monthly stipend of eighty dollars from the association's trust fund. Gene, in clear violation of his father's wishes, had cut the stipend in stages, and now it was down to ten dollars a month. His argument was that the money in the trust fund was running out, and the job situation was getting worse for émigrés because Hollywood was no longer interested in producing movies about Nazis.

"Hollywood wants to regain the German market," said one sad man, once a scriptwriter for MGM. "It's all about money."

"So this is paradise?" shouted a wild-looking man with shaggy locks and smoldering eyes, who introduced himself as Heinrich Hellman. "The only paradise I knew was Vienna in the twenties, and after that it has been a travel through Dante's inferno for me."

He had been a longtime collaborator of Bertolt Brecht and had worked with him in silent movies such as the *Kuhle Wampe* in Berlin. And in Hollywood he had worked with Brecht in Fritz Lang's *Hangmen Also Die*, a film about the assassination of Reinhard Heydrich. Brecht was no longer in demand at the movie studios and had returned to staging his dramatic works, leaving Hellman in a lurch.

Hannah soon learned all there was to learn about the émigré community in Los Angeles. The poorer Weimar exiles such as Heinrich Mann, who survived on a small allowance provided by his brother, and Arnold Schoenberg, the great avant-garde composer and creator of the twelve-tone music system, lived in ramshackle houses in Brentwood. The rich ones, such as the movie directors Fritz

Lang and Billy Wilder, lived in mansions in Beverly Hills, close to Marlene Dietrich and Alma Werfel. The successful novelist Lion Feuchtwanger and the equally successful movie composer Hanns Eisler lived in Pacific Palisades, next to Berthold Viertel, the famous Austrian movie director. Thomas Mann also lived in Pacific Palisades, in a mansion with a huge garden. He had been the spokesman for German émigrés before and during the war and was known as the "Goethe of Hollywood." But now his star was on the wane, for the American public had lost interest in his insights about the duality of the German character, the good and the evil in deadly combat in the psyche of the German, the eternal struggle between the warrior and the philosopher to take possession of the German soul, and such lofty themes that he used to dwell upon in his lectures to packed halls during the war years.

All the conflicting strains in human nature became apparent to Hannah as she talked with the men who crowded her office. Some of the émigrés believed in capitalism; others swore by the tenets of *Kommunismus*. Some wanted to return to Russian-controlled Germany; others wanted to stay in America. Some thought that German music, culture, and philosophical thought were the greatest achievements of the human mind, while others believed that European culture was moribund and were looking to the New World for their salvation.

They invited her to their cabarets, their coffee houses, and their chamber music recitals. She felt she was in the 1920s in Berlin, when she heard a singer in a Santa Monica cabaret belt out Walter Mehring's Dadaistic words: "Berlin, your dancer is death / Foxtrot and jazz." The audience of middle-aged couples smiled and applauded, thinking of the good old days when they all had sat in the Romanitsche Café in Berlin and thought that Hitler was a buffoon who would quickly fade into oblivion and obscurity. "How is Berlin after the war?" they would ask her but quickly turned away from her when she said there was no Berlin left, only debris and ruins. Nor did they want to hear about what the Russians had done to the women of Berlin. "The Russian *Kameraden* wouldn't do something like that," they would say, loath to believe anything negative about Stalin or the Soviet Union. Hannah soon stopped giving honest responses about Berlin and substituted generalities such as "War is bad for people" and "It will take some time for Berlin to be her old self," which elicited sympathetic nods and smiles from the old faithful.

The émigrés, rich and poor alike, loved parties, and the same people gathered every weekend at the houses of half a dozen hosts. Once Heinrich Hellman took Hannah to a party given by Salka Viertel, the wife of Berthold Viertel, where she saw a number of Weimar intellectuals—Theodor Adorno, Thomas Mann, Bertold Brecht, Lion Feuchtwanger, Arnold Schoenberg, and a few lesser lights—standing around in a circle drinking schnapps and arguing whether a communist dictatorship was more suitable to the Deutsche temperament than the democratic regime foisted upon Germany by the Americans. Brecht and Lion Feuchtwanger were hardcore Marxists, Schoenberg was apolitical, and Thomas Mann was hard to pin down as they talked without listening to responses, each convinced he had made the right points and won the debate.

"There was a big fight the other day between Mann and Schoenberg," Hellman said, pointing his grimy finger at the bald, shriveled, dour-faced composer and the grim-looking man of letters. "Mann's last novel, *Doktor Faustus*, is about a composer named Leverkühn who makes a pact with the devil just like Faust did. The devil promises him worldly success. Leverkühn invents the twelve-tone system and becomes a celebrity. But soon he goes mad from the syphilis he had contracted earlier in his life and dies from it. Schoenberg was furious when he read the book because he thought future generations would think that Mann, and not he, had invented the twelve-tone system. He didn't mind the syphilis part that much, ha-ha."

The great men at the party talked to her as though she were some-one to whom it was their solemn duty to impart their oracular views on American culture. Theodor Arno, a pompous baldheaded man in a black suit, cornered her when Hellman had left her to replenish his glass and lectured her on the lack of culture he found among the Americans. He didn't like American cities because they seemed hast-ily put together by real estate interests, and he didn't like Hollywood because it measured the success of a motion picture only in terms of its box office performance. But his real vitriol was reserved for jazz.

"But I like jazz," she told him. "I love its rhythms, its chord progres-sions, and its improvisations."

"That's because you don't know what true music is, the music of Mozart and Beethoven," he said. "If you are free next Friday evening, I'll take you to hear Bruno Walter conduct the *Jupiter Symphony* and explain the music to you."

"My mother used to play Mozart's music all the time. I would rath-er go to a jazz concert."

He looked at her for a few seconds as though wondering if she was trying to pull his leg and then turned his back to her and walked away to join his friend Thomas Mann, who had been staring at them with cynical amusement during this interlude.

Moments later, she was approached by Max Horkheimer, an essay-ist and periodic contributor to a locally published German newspa-per, who had views similar to Arno's on American culture. He ranted against hot dog stands, popcorn, chewing gum, girls wearing high heels, and the scattered condoms he saw on the beach carried by the tides from the sewage.

"This is a bankrupt civilization," he said. "It has nothing to offer us Europeans."

"Why do you stay here if you hate it that much?" she asked him, and he glared at her as though he would like to throttle her before shuffling off to the long table at the other end of the room that served as the bar. I know the answer to the question I asked him, she thought.

He's staying here because this is the only country that would have him. Back home, he would have been put in a gas chamber, fed to the flames in a furnace, and reduced to ashes. She felt ashamed for having thoughts like these and shrank into herself like a snail or a tortoise. Pleading a headache to the importunate Heinrich Hellman, who wanted to go the beach with her and watch the stars, she drove home, taking the road parallel to the beach, soothed by the sound of the surf that came to her through the open windows.

Soon Hannah stopped going to these parties. She stayed home listening to jazz music on the radio or went with Randy and Roddy to gay nightclubs that proliferated in the side streets of Santa Monica. She was surprised at the number middle-aged women, like herself, who were in the company of younger men at these clubs. "They're called 'fag hags' because they like to hang around with us," said Roddy, when she asked him about them. The clubs reminded her of Berlin in the early twenties, except that there were no men painted to look like women. Also, the Berlin singers and actors were more talented than the ones she saw in the grubby theaters in Santa Monica—with poor lighting, rickety platforms, and bad acoustics. But she liked the shows because they conveyed wistfulness and innocence, instead of the decadence and sadism that was almost the norm in Berlin. Why shouldn't a man fall in love with another man? Why should he be ashamed of it? Why should he be punished for it? These questions popped up in her mind as she heard the wistful songs or noticed the self-hatred implicit in the parodies. And she was glad to see open displays of affection between Roddy and Randy, now that she was accepted by them as a friend, as the three of them walked on the beach in the dark, their bare feet slipping over the yielding wet sand.

But the happiness she shared with them evaporated when she drove to work and saw the same old faces waiting in the lobby for her arrival. Day after day, week after week, they showed up at that office looking for an assignment from MGM, Warner Brothers, or Universal

Studios. Hellman, Heilman, Frankenthaler, Weingarten—the same interchangeable faces, with the same interchangeable stories. Some said it was unfair of Gene to violate a written agreement and asked her to plead with him. Others threatened to sue him but confessed they didn't have the money to hire a lawyer. A third group didn't want her to do anything for them other than listen to them—and, in return, they gave her old battered copies of their novels and plays published in Munich, Berlin, or Vienna in the twenties. They nostalgically reminisced about the old days when one cried after seeing Phil Jutzi's film *Mutter Krausens Fahrt ins Glück* or roared with laughter at the First International Dada Fair in Berlin in which the German generals were branded as the enemy of the people and sentenced to perpetual exile in a mock trial of the Wehrmacht. They debated which was the best cabaret in Berlin during the Weimar years—was it Max Reinhardt's *Schall und Rauch*, Rosa Valetti's *Café Größenwahn*, or Trude Hesterberg's *Wilde Bühne?*

One day, after hearing that Hellman, who could not swim, had committed suicide by wading into the ocean, Hannah was caught in a spiral of depression. Hellman had left a lengthy note blaming Gene for cheating them and lining his pockets with the money his father had agreed to pay them. Hannah, after hearing the story, realized that she couldn't work in that office anymore. It was exactly a month after she had been there and, a few minutes after she had made up her mind to leave, Gene's secretary, Gwen, a bleached blonde with plucked eyebrows and wearing bright-red lipstick, brought her an envelope.

"Your salary for the month," she said.

Hannah opened the envelope and counted thirty ten dollar bills.

There was something unclean about the money, she thought, as she gave the bills back to Gwen.

"It's yours. I can't take it from you," said the surprised secretary.

"I'm leaving this job," Hannah said to her. "I won't be here tomorrow."

"I'm going to tell Gene this," said Gwen and rushed out.

Without waiting to hear Gene's response, Hannah left the office and went home. She wandered in the house for a while, moving chairs and tables around, and then ran the Hoover vacuum cleaner downstairs and upstairs. She then went into the garden and sat in a chair for a while, her mind drained of all emotions, staring at the fading gladioli, hydrangea, and chrysanthemums, idly classifying their color patterns into yellow, brown, blue, and so on, until she heard someone knocking at the door.

A messenger on a motorbike was at the front of the house, holding out a letter for her. She signed his book and opened the envelope. The letter was from Gene, and she was shocked by its tone.

Dear Frau Müller,

Your behavior this morning was completely unprofessional. Claudia, out of the goodness of her heart, persuaded me to offer you a job, and I was hoping you would convince the émigrés, mostly your countrymen, to abandon their hopes of finding careers in Hollywood. Instead, you walked out on me, leaving me in a lurch. You're aware, of course, that your action would require you to leave the country within a few days because it leaves me with no choice other than to withdraw my sponsorship of you. I'll be generous and take you back if you show up tomorrow, but there will be no further negotiation.

The choice is between going back to work and going back to Germany, Hannah thought. She didn't want to make choices but only to float, without making any decisions. She wasn't going to show up for work tomorrow, she was sure of that. Let Gene do what he wanted, and she would wait for the immigration agents to haul her away.

She got into her car and headed for the beach, driving past Marina del Rey toward Venice, taking in the visual spread of sand, surf, and ocean, the earth colors mixed with myriad shades of blue and gray, and gradually she calmed down.

She drove back home on Venice Boulevard, taking notice of the changing neighborhoods, the hodgepodge architecture with strains and themes from every country in the world, the grotesquely built churches, and the garish storefronts, and she wondered if she would ever understand this country. This feeling was reinforced when she reached home and saw Randy and Roddy sitting on her doorstep, drinking beer and cracking jokes.

"The rebel returns," said Roddy, flashing his white smile.

"We thought you had driven off to nowhere," quipped Randy.

Puzzled, Hannah looked from one to the other for an explanation.

"I called you at work," said Roddy. "We wanted to take you to a jazz concert. The secretary there said you left the place after making a scene. She said you made a fool of yourself."

Seeing the mystified expression on her face, Randy asked her, "What happened at work, Hannah?"

She invited them in, and sitting around the dinner table, she gave them an account of the events of the afternoon. Gene's letter was lying on the table, and she let them read it.

"If you ask me, he's cheating the artists out of their stipends and putting the money in his pocket," said Roddy.

"He sure is," said Randy.

"He'll carry out his threat of deportation," said Roddy.

"We will hide Hannah," said Randy. "I've an aunt in Poughkeepsie, and she can live with her."

"Of course, one of us can marry her," said Roddy, looking earnestly at Randy.

"It won't be necessary," said Hannah, laughing. "I'll go back to Germany."

"No, that's not an option. We want you to stay here," said Randy, and Roddy nodded and smiled.

"Let's go to the jazz concert," said Hannah. "I don't want to think about options for a while."

They went to a downtown nightclub to hear Count Basie and his orchestra, and for a while Hannah was lost in the world of piano, clarinet, and trumpet, wishing she knew how to translate those magic notes and rhythms into lines and colors. The musicians look so joyous and serene when playing music, she thought, unlike me, who suffers when I paint, bringing all my buried angst and trauma to the surface.

After the music, they went to a pub and had beer and burgers, and the two men drove her home, once more offering the sanctuary of an aunt's house in Poughkeepsie or the magic nuptial knot to ward off the threat of exile to Germany.

TWENTY-FOUR

THE EISENBERG GALLERY

The next morning, Hannah felt tired and dispirited. She had woken up later than usual and had lingered in bed, trying to make sense of the jumbled images that popped in and out of her mind as in a peep show—the scene with the girl Gwen, the letter from Gene, the jazz musicians at the nightclub—until they gave way to a question, rocklike and immovable, that confronted her. "What shall I do next?" she asked herself and was at a loss for an answer. She got out of bed, did routine chores, and drank coffee, strong and black. It was a beautiful November day, and the wind was blowing from the west, carrying smells of the ocean. "The snot-green scrotum-tightening sea"—an Englishman she was friendly with at Bauhaus used to tote along James Joyce's *Ulysses* and had pointed out that line to her as an example of Joyce's precision in rendering visual impressions into physically palpable phraseology. She had tried to read the book at his urging but couldn't get beyond the first two pages. What happened to him, the curly-haired youth she had slept with after a wild, drunken Christmas party at Bauhaus? Did he fight during the Second World War? Was he taken prisoner? Was he alive? She let her mind explore the past, identify and confront a face, analyze and deconstruct a scene, mark it as important or dismiss it as inconsequential to her life—and begin anew, taking a turn into another forgotten corridor of her memory; but she wasn't used to these kinds of mental excursions, and some inner mechanism censored her reverie and urged her to get up and start *doing* things. She stood up but was at a loss to act. What should the next step be? She stared out the window, looking at the trees turning color and, on impulse, decided to visit Claudia.

Camille, the maid, greeted her with a big smile.

"You've a lot of mail, Senora Müller," she said. "I was going to bring it over to your house today."

The mail was stacked in a neat pile on a narrow ebony table in the vestibule. There were two packages and a letter from Colonel Eric Grossman, USMOG, a letter from Phyllis Grossman, and another from the Eisenberg Gallery in Los Angeles.

"I'll pick them up when I leave," said Hannah. "Where's Claudia?"

"She's in the backyard, eating lunch."

Hannah found her in the gazebo, staring at the orange trees. Out there in the distance, there was the sound of the sea, the slow, hypnotic roar and sigh of the waves. Claudia looked at her with resentment, and Hannah concluded that Gene must have poisoned her mind against her.

"How are you?" asked Hannah, in German.

"I'm fine," said Claudia, in English.

"You know what happened, don't you, Claudia?"

"I know."

"I couldn't stay at that job, with people clamoring they were cheated of what was rightfully owed to them."

"I don't want to hear all this," Claudia said. "You were supposed to help us out. You turned on us."

"I'm shocked you should say such things. You know I love you."

332

Claudia's face contorted with fury. "Please leave me alone," she said, in German. "The sooner you go back to Germany, the better it will be for Gene and me."

Stunned, Hannah went back to the house and walked toward her car.

"Senora Müller," she heard Camille shouting after her. She turned back and saw the maid bringing her mail. She took it from her, absently thanked her, and drove toward Griffith Park, hurt and confused by Claudia's behavior. She has changed, thought Hannah. America must have transformed her from a vibrant young girl to a rich, morose, unhappy woman—but I may be wrong, perhaps it's her pregnancy that makes her unbalanced in her reactions, and Claudia would return to her old self after giving birth to her baby. The last thought cheered her up as she parked her car on the southwest side of the park and walked toward an empty bench shaded by a large tree.

She opened Eric's letter and saw there was a check for her for $1,500 from the USMOG. The letter itself was several pages long, and she thought she would read it in full later. Glancing through it, she learned that his book on the Nuremberg trial, with her drawings, was ready for publication in German and English. He was sending her both editions, and he wanted her to proofread the German edition. He had, following her advice, put in ads in the newspapers offering to pay cash for letters from German soldiers to their families and friends and had received hundreds of letters, which he was sending to her for a preliminary analysis and review. He was keeping her as a translator and would send her a monthly paycheck.

She looked at the English edition of the *Nuremberg Trial* and saw her name was on the title page, under Eric's. The phrase "With drawings by Hannah Müller" brought a smile to her face because the last time she had seen her name in print was several years ago, when her translation of Kandinsky's book on point, line, and plane was published as a monograph by a Berlin art publisher. Her drawings looked good, and she felt a craftsman's pride in her work. The text, however, disappointed her, because Eric was essentially following the themes laid down by Justice Jackson: the defendants had followed a master plan based on Hitler's master race theories, the guilty were punished by an international tribunal after due process, and the German people were absolved from criminality. Tables showing the number of deaths caused by death marches, shooting of prisoners, Einsatzgruppen killings, and killings at extermination camps were given as appendices.

Hannah put the book away and opened Phyllis's letter. She was surprised when a check for $2,850 dropped into her lap. Phyllis, in her unassuming, matter-of-fact way, informed her that a buyer in New York had bought all her paintings and wanted to know if there were more. Her commission was 15 percent, and she had deducted it from the sale proceeds. She also mentioned that Tad Eisenberg, owner of a Los Angeles art gallery to whom she had sent a catalog of her paintings, was extremely interested in her work, and suggested that Hannah should meet him.

The next letter was from Tad Eisenberg. It wasn't a proper letter but a few words scrawled on the back of a business card. "Artist," it read, "please come and see me. Tad." The business card gave the location of the eponymously named gallery as North Bedford Drive, Beverly Hills. Looking at the pocket map of Los Angeles that Randy had given her, she judged the distance to be about ten miles.

"I'll go see him now and have lunch somewhere afterward," she said to herself, gathering up her books and checks.

The gallery was a two-story building in an opulent neighborhood. There was no window display, and a sign below the nameplate said, "By appointment only." She pushed a white electric button, and a couple of minutes later, the door was opened by a short, powerfully built gray-haired man, who looked her up and down suspiciously while blocking the entrance with his body.

"I'm Hannah Müller," she said, "Phyllis Grossman's friend."

He looked puzzled for a moment and then smiled and stood aside, holding the door wide open for her.

"You're the artist from Berlin, yes?" he said in German, with a strong Austrian accent.

Hannah nodded, and he led her to his suite on the second floor.

"I was making lunch," he said. "Would you like to join me?"

"Is there enough for two?"

He laughed. "There's plenty. It's warmed-over goulash with sausages," he said.

He led her to the dining room, deftly set the table, poured her a glass of Riesling wine, and gave her a plate with goulash, sausages, and crusty rolls.

"You are a very good chef," she said, after tasting the food.

"My friend Bruno is the chef," he said. "He is at rehearsals."

"Is he an actor?"

"He is a cabaret artist," he said. "He sings, dances, mimes…"

Everyone I run into these days turns out to be a homosexual, thought Hannah. Tad Eisenberg was masculine in speech, demeanor, and gesture, and it was hard to believe that he was living with a man.

"I liked your paintings in the catalog Phyllis sent me," she heard him say. "They reminded me of the work of the Viennese expressionists before the Anschluss with Germany."

Oh, the Anschluss, thought Hannah. That day in March, crowds had danced in the streets of Berlin as their beloved Führer announced the happy, long-desired union between Germany and Austria from the Heldenplatz in Vienna, after the Wehrmacht had sent in their tanks to make sure there would be no opposition to the forced merger of the two countries.

"You left Austria after the Anschluss, Herr Eisenberg?" she asked him.

"A week later," he said. "By the way, please call me Tad. We're in America now, where everyone calls everyone else by their first name."

"OK, Tad," said Hannah.

"I left Austria a week later. My dad was an art dealer and owned hundreds of paintings by Austrian and German artists. He made a deal with the Nazis, and they let us cross over to Italy. We chartered two buses and filled them with our paintings. We deposited them in a vault in Milan and moved to England. My dad died a month later, and I came here with the help of my father's friend who had an art gallery here. Soon I set up my own shop and moved all my paintings here."

"Where are they now?"

"In the basement of this building. It has two levels, and I've set it up as a warehouse."

When they had finished eating, Eisenberg removed the plates and put them in the sink. He then poured coffee out of a thermos into two cups—and something about their design made Hannah think of Bauhaus.

"These cups look like they're designed by Hermann Gretsch," she said.

"How did you know?" asked Tad, in surprise.

"I've seen them in Bauhaus."

"These are Bruno's cups. Arzberg porcelain. Bruno likes Bauhaus design. He wants me to buy Bauhaus paintings, but I don't want to spend money on something that I don't like."

"You said you liked my paintings."

"But you're no longer painting in the Bauhaus style—I mean, your paintings convey emotions. They aren't just lines and squares."

They finished their coffee, and Tad stood up.

"Do you have any more paintings, Hannah?" he asked.

"My work was destroyed in Berlin by American and British bombs," she said. "The paintings you saw in the catalog were done a few months ago, in Nuremberg. I've been here for a month and just rented a house. I haven't set up a studio yet."

Tad stared at her for a few seconds, as though trying to make up his mind. "Look, Hannah," he said. "I'll come to the point. The reason I wanted to see you was I need a curator badly. I haven't catalogued the paintings I brought over from the old country. I don't even know what condition they're in. Tell me if you're interested in working for me."

Hannah was surprised by his offer. "You don't know anything about me," she said.

"Phyllis's brochure of your paintings describes your background. Besides, I take pride in my ability to judge a person after talking to him or her for a few minutes," said Tad. "I met Bruno while standing in line at a cinema theater. He was next to me, we started talking, and I made up my mind about him in less than five minutes."

"You must have psychic powers," said Hannah.

"I sometimes think I have them," he said with an impish grin.

"Tad, please listen to my account of how I came over to this country and the situation I'm in," said Hannah.

He nodded, poured more coffee for both of them, and sat down.

After listening intently to Hannah's narration, he rose from his chair and stood facing her.

"I'll ask my lawyer to get a residence permit for you," he said. "He has done it for several other émigrés. You can start tomorrow. As for salary, I'll pay you eight thousand dollars a year, plus a bonus. There is a studio on the first floor that I built for my friend Roland, who's a very good artist. He has moved out, and you can have it for your use. I judge a person by results, and I want you to put the catalog together in about six months."

"You said that most of your artists were Austrians. I know very little about Austrian art."

"I've a library full of art books on the first floor. It's arranged by period. You can dig up information about any artist without too much trouble."

She wanted to talk to him some more, but a young man bounced up the stairs and pirouetted before Tad.

"Your slave, Herr Eisenberg," he said mockingly.

They embraced each other with ardor, and Hannah liked their openness in their need for each other. They aren't discreet like Randy and Roddy, she thought.

"Bruno, this is my new curator, Hannah Müller," said Tad, after freeing himself from the other's arms.

"Sind Sie Deutsche?" Bruno asked.

He was of medium height, blond, with curly hair and hazel eyes. She liked his freckled face and warm smile.

"She's from Berlin, Bruno," intervened Tad. "She was on the Führer's blacklist."

"I was born in Berlin," Bruno said. "But my father took us out of Germany in 1933. I was twelve years old."

They talked for a few minutes about the old Berlin until Tad interrupted them.

"I've a client coming in a few minutes," he said. "I'm hoping to sell him a Gustave Klimt etching."

Hannah excused herself and moved toward the stairs.

"You will be here tomorrow?" asked Tad.

"At nine in the morning."

"We are late risers and sometimes sleep past ten," said Tad. "I'll give you a spare key to the front door and another to the vault downstairs."

Hannah took the keys and left, the two men following her downstairs, arms around each other's waists. She gave them a farewell glance before closing the front door, but they were busy kissing each other and didn't notice her.

TWENTY-FIVE

"AN AGENT FOLLOWS ME AROUND"

Hannah, to her surprise, liked being a curator. Some days she toiled for hours in the warehouse, moving around and photographing the nudes and landscapes by eighteenth- and nineteenth-century Viennese painters, most of whom appeared to her to be less talented than their German or French counterparts. She was fascinated by the painting techniques of some of the Viennese artists, so different from what she was used to, such as their transference of a drawing to a primed canvas by copying it on tracing paper, creating an outline of it on the obverse side of the tracing paper with paint using a thin brush, and then pressing the paper onto the canvas. The old painters also experimented with turpentine from Strasbourg and Venice, to which they added different balsams and worked with rounded brushes of varying sizes to get transparent shadows and opaque highlights. All this seemed a far cry from the Bauhaus artists, who were taught to paint directly onto the canvas and move the paint around experimentally to create abstract or semiabstract forms. She made careful notes of the Viennese artists' techniques, thinking that she would write, sometime in the future, a monograph on the evolution of painting in Europe.

In the meantime, her painting style had undergone an evolution of its own. Whenever she stood in front of her canvas, the color blue loomed before her—the color of the Pacific Ocean with its myriad tonal possibilities, ranging from celestial to ultramarine. Such was its strong pull that she started painting while standing on the beach, varying the time of her painting to catch the changing rhythms of the sea.

"You're going back to abstraction," said Tad, after seeing her work. "I was hoping you would do some more of the paintings you did in Nuremberg."

"Painters change their style when they migrate," said Hannah. "You know that."

"You're referring to Gauguin and van Gogh," he said.

"Also to Kandinsky, my friend and my teacher."

"His was a change for the worse. I liked his earlier paintings."

"He's the father of abstract painting," she said. "The leader who showed us a new world. He had so many ideas, so many ways of working with colors and lines."

"I should talk to you more often, Hannah. That way I can learn how to look at modern art. In New York, so many artists are following the Bauhaus style. I should buy some of their paintings, purely from a business point of view. And yours too, for that matter."

They had some more discussions on the theories of color and light, but Hannah was not able to substantially change Tad's views in regard to Kandinsky and abstract art. He will never understand the language of paint, she thought. He can grasp only the realistic, the recognizable visual image—that's why he likes these old Viennese painters.

Hannah also sensed that he was never fully at ease with her and was unable to understand the reason for it, until one day Bruno showed a photograph of Tad's wife.

"She caused him a lot of trouble, Hannah," he said. "The woman is a Viennese aristocrat and married him for his money. She was so mean to him after their divorce, spreading rumors about him in Vienna. Tad hates her, and all women, by extension."

"Where did you find this photograph?"

"I was going through his album, and I asked him who she was. He was so upset. He told me never to show him that picture again."

"Why did he hire me then, if he hates women?"

"He needs a curator badly, Hannah. He thinks there is going to be a postwar boom in the art market. He likes your credentials. He doesn't get to meet people like you often. Also, he was moved by the story he heard from Phyllis about the way the Nazis treated you and your brother."

"What about my brother?"

"Don't you know? He died in a concentration camp, at Treblinka."

"This doesn't make sense to me," said Hannah, refusing to believe what she heard. "Phyllis could have gotten the news of my brother only through her son, Eric, and Eric surely would have notified me first."

"I've given up making sense of the world, Hannah," said Bruno, shaking his curls and smiling. "Unintended things happen all the time. Eric might have sent a cable, and it might have been delivered to the wrong place. I tell you what. I'll call up Western Union and find out."

He came back a few minutes later, with downcast eyes and drooping mouth.

"It was delivered to Claudia Frankel's address. They read the cable over to me, Hannah, and I copied it," he said, handing over a piece of paper to her.

"RECORDS SHOW JOHANN GRUENWALD WAS KILLED IN TREBLINKA," the cable read. "ALSO, EMIL DRESDNER WAS TRIED AND EXECUTED AT THE POLISH TRIAL FOR DOCTORS. SORRY TO BE BEARER OF BAD NEWS. WILL WRITE SOON. ERIC."

As she read the printed letters, they seemed to dance and waver before her misted eyes.

Bruno took her by the elbow and moved her to the sofa in the room.

"Shall I bring you a glass of brandy?" he asked.

She shook her head and sobbed for a while as he stood watching her. He waited until she lifted up her head and offered her his handkerchief.

"It's over now," she said, even though she knew that nothing was ever over.

Her relationship with Bruno became very close from that day onward. He called her "Mutti" and was affectionate like a puppy whenever he saw her in the hallway or in the dining room. He begged her to see his cabaret act and took her to a dingy club in West Hollywood. The clientele was mostly middle-aged men who slipped money into his side pockets as he danced in panties and high heels while singing gay parodies of popular songs by Frank Sinatra, Bing Crosby, or Perry Como. Several times during the night, he would disappear with strangers and be back after a few minutes with his hands on his hips and an insouciant smile on his face.

"Don't let Tad know I made nearly four hundred dollars today," he told her proudly, unashamed of his promiscuity, unaware of any moral infraction.

She wanted to tell him that she too had earned money that way immediately after the First World War, when every attractive girl in Berlin worked in a dance hall or a cabaret to keep herself from starvation. Let my past stay buried within me, she thought. There is no need to share it with anyone.

Bruno introduced her to his patrons, most of them British expatriates who had come to Hollywood at the start of the war and who were making careers for themselves in the film industry after years of struggle. They would shake hands with her and talk to her as though she were a visiting elderly aunt eager to see the nightlife of Tinsel Town and give her pointers on the best places to catch a glimpse of Hollywood stars, to the amusement of Bruno, who would mimic them later when he was alone with her.

After a while, she began to get tired of these evenings and came up with excuses when Bruno would ask her to go to the cabaret with him. He took her evasions in stride, but a few days later, he would make the same request again, with a smile, and she would accompany him and watch him do his gyrations.

With Randy, her other friend, things were becoming difficult. He had undergone a change, and there was a hunted look on his face. He was nice and polite as usual and greeted her always with a smile, but the smile seemed to be forced. She wondered if he had financial or health problems and was going to ask him outright, but the right moment never appeared during their encounters because of Roddy's presence.

Then one day, when she went to Griffith Park to escape for a few minutes from the tedium of cataloging mediocre Viennese landscapes, she saw him sitting on his favorite bench, reading a newspaper. She greeted him, and he looked up at her, his eyes sad and despondent.

"Is something wrong, Randy?" she asked, taking his hand.

"Read this," he said, passing the paper to her.

The newspaper was the *Hollywood Reporter*, and it carried the headline "THE RED SCARE IS REAL."

"Are the Russians going to attack us?" she asked him.

He laughed at her naiveté, and she liked the way his lips parted, revealing clean white teeth, and the crinkly eyes that shone with amusement.

"They aren't talking about Russians," he said. "They're talking about people like me who are members of the Screen Writers Guild."

"I don't understand, Randy. Please explain to me."

He did that patiently, starting with his own life in a small town in New York State, growing up in the Great Depression, coming to New York City in search of work, standing in line in front of soup kitchens, taking acting classes with the little money he earned doing odd jobs, getting minor roles here and there, and getting his own play produced.

"All of us wrote plays for the masses," he said with a grin. "We had fun. The head of the Federal Theater Project, Hallie Flanagan, wanted us to use themes that would be of interest to the man on the street. She was greatly influenced by the German director Erwin Piscator."

"I know Erwin Piscator. He published one of my drawings in his magazine *Die Aktion*. I saw his play *The Good Soldier Schweik* in Berlin. He, like Brecht, wanted political theater. Everyone in Berlin wanted to be a leftist in those days."

"Here too. In my case, I was a member of the Communist Party of the United States. Lot of us writers felt capitalism was on its last legs, and the only ideologies of the future were fascism or socialism. Of the two, socialism seemed the only choice a decent person could live with. In New York, every man and woman I knew was either a communist or sympathetic to our cause. But then came the break between the Stalinists and the Trotskyites, and the party expelled the Trotskyites, of which I was one. I hated Stalin for the Moscow trials and the murder of thousands, maybe hundreds of thousands of party members in the Soviet Union. I hated him the same way I hated Hitler."

"My stepfather was a communist, as was my mother," said Hannah. "They used to take me to hear Rosa Luxemburg and Karl Liebknecht. My uncle was a Nazi. He used to take me to the beerhalls where Hitler gave his rants. All three tried to convert me, but it was no use. I believe that each person should be allowed to make decisions without regard to party positions."

He looked at her in surprise. "I've never heard you make such a clear statement about any issue until now. You are usually reluctant to reveal yourself."

"I'm getting Americanized, I guess."

He laughed. "We Americans talk a lot, don't we? We reveal too much of ourselves."

They sat in silence for a few minutes, each wondering about the other, the desire for companionship tinged with suspicion and uncertainty.

"What's the Red Scare the paper is talking about?" she asked. "I haven't seen or heard about any leftist uprising in this country."

"The US Congress has set up a House Committee on Un-American Activities, HUAC for short. Two of their top members—Parnell Thomas and John McDowell—are here to investigate the Hollywood Reds. Many writers are going to be interrogated by the committee, including me. FBI agents have come up to our house a couple of times to conduct a preliminary investigation of me. An agent follows me around. In fact, the man sitting at the other end of the park, pretending to read a newspaper, is one of them."

Hannah turned her head slightly to look at the man, a tall, athletic-looking individual with close-cropped hair in a tweed jacket and black wool pants.

"This is what the Gestapo used to do to us in Germany," she said.

"Doesn't it make you wonder why police in every country spend a lot of time keeping tabs on their fellow countrymen? The government wants to act as our thought police. Doesn't it make you sick?"

Hannah knew she was out of her depth when it came to discussions of government versus citizenry, so beloved a topic among the men in her life. She didn't know how to put her inchoate thoughts into words. She intuitively knew that those in power wanted to exercise it to its extreme limits, and it would always be that way.

"I'm only an artist, Randy," she said. "I'm no good as a partner for political debate. Let's go for a drive and walk on the beach for a while."

He smiled, and they walked over to his car. During the stroll on the beach, he talked about the approaching holidays—Thanksgiving and Christmas—and invited her to be their guest on both occasions.

The Red Scare was spreading with the virulence of an epidemic, and Hannah would read in the newspapers or hear on the radio someone being branded as a "Red" followed by a pejorative, such as "traitor," "renegade," or "double-crosser." In Nazi Germany, the term "un-Deutsch" was used to describe anyone in the blacklist maintained by

Goebbels's Propaganda Ministry, and the list included Bertolt Brecht, Hanns Eisler, and many others, including herself. She was surprised to see that similar euphemisms were used by the HUAC and the news media who supported them—especially the Hearst newspapers. "Red Commissar" was used as a code word for a Hollywood communist, while "Premature Antifascist" was used to describe someone who in his younger days had been a party member but had given up his member-ship subsequently. The Screen Writer's Guild was targeted as the cen-ter of a vast conspiracy to undermine American values and to sabotage the American political system. Every day the name of a new writer be-ing branded as a Red would pop up as a headline, provoking outbursts from her friends.

"They got Ring Lardner," fumed Roddy, as he was reading the *Hollywood Reporter* with Hannah and Randy in a coffee shop.

"I knew they would get him, since he was the president of the Screen Writer's Guild," said Randy.

"To call him un-American as this moronic congressman does is travesty," said Roddy.

"Lardner is the quintessential American writer, as American as ap-ple pie," responded Randy. "He was a close friend of Scott Fitzgerald and Maxwell Perkins. Perkins was his editor."

Seeing the uncomprehending look on Hannah's face, Randy ex-plained to her who Lardner was, a man who wrote humorous short stories about American life and screenplays that were widely praised by writers and critics.

"He got an Academy Award for *Woman of the Year*," said Roddy.

"I didn't see that movie," said Hannah.

"You saw *Forever Amber* with us and liked it," said Randy. "He wrote the screenplay for that."

The next victim was Dalton Trumbo, screenwriter and novelist, and another of Roddy's heroes. He was followed by John Howard Lawson and Adrian Scott—two screenwriters who were close friends of Randy. And a week later, at a formal dinner given by one of Tad Eisenberg's

Viennese friends at the Roosevelt Hotel on Hollywood Boulevard, Hannah, who had accompanied Tad as the obligatory female companion for such events, was made aware that the "Red Scare" had spread to the émigré community. The dinner was actually a fundraiser, hosted by Salka Viertel to help émigrés who were victims of the HUAC persecution. Hannah heard that Hanns Eisler, the successful film composer, was likely to be deported, as well as Bertolt Brecht, for their ties to communists.

"We have lived here for several years and have been welcomed with open arms by the people in Los Angeles," Salka said, in a speech following a four-course dinner of cherry soup, herring, goulash served over spaetzle, and chocolate cake. "The tide has turned, and we are now perceived as the enemy. Thomas Mann, until recently the spokesman for anti-Nazi Germans in exile and a favorite of the American liberal establishment, is now suspected of being a left-wing sympathizer, and he's planning to leave for Switzerland. Speaking personally, they view me as an enemy because I helped many artists, including some great ones such as Sergei Eisenstein and Hanns Eisler, in their troubles. The US government has denied me an American passport even though I'm an American citizen."

She went on in this vein for a few minutes, a distraught, gray-haired woman, stunned by events that seemed to arrive out of nowhere and unprepared to handle repercussions that hadn't appeared in her wildest dreams.

She was followed by a dry legal type from Vienna who urged the establishment of a legal defense fund for émigré artists and asked for contributions. A silver tray was passed around for collecting checks or pledges, and when her turn came, Hannah wrote a check for $200.

A Viennese waltz followed—with all the formalities of the old pre-Nazi days observed, except for the white gloves and gowns worn by the ladies. The women sat on chairs arranged in a row while the men stood in front of them, bowing before asking them to dance. The women then stood up and curtsied and followed their partners to the dance floor, where they whirled to the right, paused, took a few measured steps, and whirled to the left, paused, and changed directions again following the beat of the music. Tad was a good dancer, expertly cuing her to do the required gyrations, even as Hannah tried hard to keep a straight face. These people are living in a time capsule, she thought. No one dances this way in Germany or Austria ever since the Nazis banned the waltz, along with the foxtrot and the swing, because they considered them too exhibitionistic. Nevertheless, she found herself enjoying the journey into a bygone era—the chairs with red plush seats and gold-painted legs and the baroque design of the hall with its ornate candelabra reminding her of dancehalls in the Munich of her youth.

They had Viennese coffee and chocolate biscuits afterward and, of course, schnapps—made in Kentucky and tasting sweeter than its German counterpart. Everyone drank to everyone's health, and upon leaving, a drunken Tad wove his car through deserted streets, nearly averting collision with a vagrant crossing a red light. She took the wheel from him and, on reaching his house, helped him up the steps.

TWENTY-SIX

TAKING THE FIFTH

Six months went by quickly, and her work in cataloging was completed. Tad, pleased with her effort in bringing order into his chaotic art collection, asked her to organize an art fair in downtown Los Angeles in collaboration with two gallery owners who were Tad's friends, two Viennese Jews with no-nonsense views about art.

"We shouldn't take any abstract artists," said one.

"Not for us," said the other.

"What sells is surrealism," said the first one.

"But not abstract surrealism like Joan Miro's," said the other.

"Right. We need artists like Dali, Matta, and Max Ernst," said his friend.

"People like them because they work with distorted or displaced visual realism."

Hannah asked Tad to exempt her from running the fair, but he wouldn't hear of it.

"I'm going for the long haul, Hannah," he said. "I admire and trust your ability to judge artists. Also, I want to show some of your seascapes at the art fair."

He spoke to the other two jurors and arrived at a compromise—Hannah was to be in charge of the American modernist section, while they ran the rest of the show. There were dozens of canvases to choose from, sent in by the many art-school students and teachers in the state of California. Of these, a couple of paintings by an unknown artist—they were not surrealist, cubist, or of any school with ties to the Old World—intrigued Hannah at first and then fascinated her. Simple in construction, they showed streaks of yellow and crimson in dark color fields, and after days of looking at them, Hannah concluded they were mental landscapes, with Freudian and Jungian overtones. She felt out of depth because European art, especially Bauhaus art, was concerned with visual effects of line, color, and form and steered away from abstract portrayals of one's interior world. Here the artist, Clyfford Still, seemed to do just that: he was putting on canvas unconscious impulses, metaphors of the mind, and exploring the dark, inexplicable aspects of the psyche. She sent him a note asking him to meet her, and he arrived two days later, a man in his forties, unpretentious and unassuming. When she told him that his work seemed to be a mixture of German expressionism combined with Jungian archetypes, he laughed.

"I'm just a country boy from North Dakota," he said. "I paint images that slowly take shape in my mind."

"That's what I'm trying to say," she said. "You paint the mind."

He smiled and invited her to his studio in San Francisco to see more of his paintings, and she took the train there the next week. He met her at the station, and they had lunch at a farmers' market, sitting outdoors in the bright sunshine with a cold wind blowing from the ocean. They then went to his studio, and she watched him work. She was surprised to see that he got his effects by using a large palette knife, almost the size of a trowel. In her mind, she contrasted the formal discipline she had to endure in the art school in Munich and later on in Bauhaus with the ingenious way this man slapped down paint on the stretched canvas and then scraped it off or shaped it—with his knife or with his hands—over and over again, until he was happy with the result. Was this art by trial and error or art to uncover an image that was playing hide-and-seek? She always knew what she was painting, but this man had no clue what the final result would be, except that he would stop when he saw it.

He is a genius, unlike me, she thought, during the train ride back to Los Angeles, so creative yet inarticulate, unlike my colleagues at the Bauhaus, who loved to talk about art; I can easily fall in love with him if he gives a hint he wants me, realizing with a pang that Daniel had mysteriously disappeared from her emotional horizon.

The art fair was a success, getting excellent reviews from the critics, and a number of paintings, including all her seascapes, were sold at good prices. The only paintings that didn't sell were those by Clyfford Still, possibly because they got bad reviews. Hannah was disappointed by the way the artist was slighted by the critics and thought they had no clue as to what he was trying to do. When she got a check for $10,000 from Tad, she offered to buy the paintings from Clyfford, but he, blaming her for his lack of success, refused to sell them to her. She called him a couple of times, but he wouldn't speak to her, abruptly terminating the conversation on each occasion. She couldn't understand his behavior. I'm his friend, and he treats me as an enemy, she thought. She felt rejected and miserable but soon got over her down mood—for life was very good in her new environment. Her bank account held nearly $20,000—she had never had so much money in her life—and it gave her a sense of security. She bought clothes for herself and presents for her friends and took them to fancy restaurants. But then her sense of discipline asserted itself, and she went back to her routine of curating, painting, and physical exercise to keep herself fit.

The sea and the sun—the two main attractions for people from Mitteleuropa—still fascinated her, and she took every opportunity to take walks on the beach or to paint the sea in its multifarious moods and colors. One of her favorite moments was to stand beneath the pier in Santa Monica Bay during low tide, feeling the damp sand sink under her bare feet, and watch the gulls wade in the puddles left by the retreating sea. The sea hissed when it ebbed, and it roared during the occasional windy days, but mostly it was placid, its rhythms quite unlike the monotonously dull rushing sounds of the Rhine or the Danube. On such occasions she fantasized she would like to live the rest of her life in Santa Monica: she would buy a boat, learn to sail, and make runs from Point Dume to Paradise Cove or the Marina Del Rey and paint the moods of the sea, like Turner and Whistler.

Packs of stray dogs—feral and threatening—wandering around the beach and the mindless faces of girls with plucked eyebrows and scarlet mouths, eternally chewing gum as they strolled by with their tattooed, violent-prone boyfriends, made her return from the land of fantasy to the world of reality. There's no Shangri-La anywhere for me, she thought. This feeling of unhappiness with her surroundings was accentuated as she drove back to Tad's house through stretches of slums where migrant workers from Mexico crowded in filthy houses, through downtown Los Angeles cluttered with hot dog stands and hamburger shacks and mountains of waste piled up in vacant lots. Often she felt confused about this new country, so different from hers. Europe never had poverty like this, even in the worst of times. The contrast that she saw here between the rich and the poor offended her sensibilities, but then she would be pulled back again into her dream world by the ethereal light that shone on the sea, the sound of waves breaking on the shore, and the exotic trees, shrubs, and flowers around her. She never got tired of looking at the flaming colors she saw everywhere: the California poppies, the dwarf sunflowers, the red maids, and the scarlet monkey flower—names she had learned from Roddy, who was something of a botanist, having worked in a plant nursery in between studio assignments.

Occasionally the thought of Claudia intruded into her consciousness, and one day she decided to go over and see her. She had expected to see Camille open the door when she rang the bell and was surprised by the appearance of a red-headed, unsmiling woman.

"Yes?" she asked.

"I'm Claudia's aunt Hannah, and I want to see her."

"You wait here, and I'll see if she's available," the woman replied, in an unmistakable Irish brogue.

Hannah had to wait at the doorstep for five minutes before the redhead reappeared.

"The mistress is not feeling well, but you can come in for a few minutes."

Hannah followed her into the living room, where a tableau-like setting was in place. Lying on the white coach, wearing a white robe, was Claudia, in the supine pose of an odalisque in a French painting, and standing next to her, holding a three-month-old baby, was a young black woman. Images—Manet's *Olympia*, Guido Reni's *Reclining Venus*—rushed through Hannah's mind. Soon reality asserted itself, and she sized up the situation. The baby, a little Jewish beauty with dark eyes and curly black hair, was Claudia's newborn child, and Claudia, with her arm draped around her forehead, was going through postpartum depression.

"How are you, Claudia?" she asked in German.

"Fine," she answered in English and, after a lengthy pause, turned her face toward the wall.

Hannah wanted to ask her many things—why she wasn't told of the birth of the baby, why Claudia was in this catatonic state, why all the staff was new—but she knew that they would remain unanswered. She stood there for a few seconds and then sneaked out of the room.

The grim-faced Irish woman opened the door for her, and Hannah smiled at her, without getting any response from her.

"Is Claudia well?" Hannah asked. "I used to live here, you know. Can you tell me what's going on?"

"Loose lips sink ships, that's what I say," she hissed.

Hannah was on the doorstep when she remembered something. "Sometimes I get mail here. Is there any for me? The name is Hannah Müller."

The old dragon went to a cupboard next to the coat hanger and came back with a stack of mail. Hannah took them from her, stuck her tongue out at her, and went to her car.

There were letters and a package from Eric Grossman.

She didn't open them until she reached home and, even then, had to fortify herself with a nip of brandy first. Lulled to lethargy by her dreamlike life in California during the past few weeks, she had forgotten Germany and its horrors, and it was with trembling fingers she opened the letters.

The first envelope contained photographs of Eric and Naomi Bressler and a check for her salary, for she was still on the payroll of the US Army. Eric missed her terribly, he wrote in an attached note.

The second letter was several pages long and contained particulars of the later Nuremberg trials, some of which had already started and others that were ready to go into court soon. Eric was one of the lead prosecutors at the forthcoming Einsatzgruppen trial, where two dozen defendants were going to be tried for the mass murder of Jews. The defendants were all SS officers, like Otto Ohlendorf, whom she had seen at the Nuremberg trial. The four Einsatzgruppen units, A, B, C, and D, had been responsible for the extermination of nearly one and a half million Jews in Eastern Europe using bullets and, in some cases, exhaust gas from trucks. Yet Ohlendorf and others were pleading not guilty using the argument that they were following *Führerbefehl*, that is, orders from the Führer. In addition, they contended they acted in self-defense since Jews were communists and hence were enemies of Germany.

The prosecution had anticipated these moves by the defense and hoped to stymie them by bringing the charge of genocide as count one in the indictment. "They should have brought this up in the earlier

Nuremberg trial," Eric wrote, "but the term 'genocide' wasn't used in international trials until the Polish lawyer Raphael Lemkin pushed for its use in the trials of Nazis in Poland, as Daniel Neuman had explained to us. The murder of several million Jews would certainly qualify for genocide, and Naomi and I are pressing hard to get that charge in."

Naomi, as seen from the photographs, was a good-looking brunette with a shapely figure. Eric appears to be happy with her in the photographs, thought Hannah, and they seem to blend with each other.

"Naomi thinks she has found the master plan that we were looking for," Eric wrote, "the blueprint for the *Endlösung der Judenfrage*, the final solution of the Jewish question. Please read the plan, which I'm attaching, and let me know if you agree with Naomi."

He had enclosed the minutes of a meeting held in Wannsee in January 1942, under the leadership of Reinhard Heydrich, who had been put in charge of the Endlösung by Goering. Heydrich gave statistics on the Jewish population in every European country, totaling eleven million Jews, using the Nuremberg Law criterion of classifying someone as a Jew if one grandparent out of four was officially registered as a Jew. Heydrich's proposed solution covered all European, and not just German, Jews. Able-bodied men and women would be put to do hard labor, building roads, bridges, and tunnels, until they dropped dead from malnutrition or illness. Those unfit for labor were to be deported to the east (i.e., Poland or Russia), except the old, who were to be moved to the Theresienstadt concentration camp to perish from malnutrition and disease. Ghettos were to be created in all Reich-controlled territories for herding Jews together to facilitate deportation.

There followed a lengthy discussion on mixed marriages and the offspring of such unions—the *mischlinge*, as they were called. Some conference attendees proposed the legal abrogation of mixed marriages and the sterilization of the mischlinge. It was all done in typical German style, with thorough attention to details, and Hannah created a mental tableau of two dozen Nazis in a beautiful villa in Wannsee—her uncle and Emil among them—drinking cognac and smoking cigars, planning the murder of eleven million human beings. Her gut reacted violently. She ran to the bathroom and threw up, cursing herself for being German, for being a blond, green-eyed Aryan, for being the niece of Werner, for having slept with a Nazi doctor, and for being linked by culture and heritage to the Nazi henchmen. She lay panting on the bathroom floor for a while, thinking that she ought to tell Eric that she didn't want to have anything more to do with Heydrich, Himmler, Goering, Goebbels, Hitler, or the genocide of the Jews, and all she wanted was to live in peace in this part of the world, warmed by perpetual sunshine and lulled by the sound of surf at the beach. But evil had its own fascination, and she returned, after a while, to the pages spread out on the kitchen table.

She opened the next letter from Eric, which confused her.

"On second reading, the Wannsee protocols seem more like a manifesto than a plan of action," he wrote. "Its goal is clearly stated— eleven million Jews are to be killed, and Europe was going to be Judenrein—but the means of killing are not specified explicitly, and only euphemisms like 'attrition' and 'deportation to the East' are used. There's no reference to the mass-murder techniques described by Otto Ohlendorf and Rudolf Höss at the Nuremberg trial, and there's no mention of building the death factories in Auschwitz, Treblinka, and elsewhere. The interesting thing here is the territorial expansion of the Jewish problem. Initially it was restricted to the 132,000 Jews in Germany and Austria, and now it encompasses eleven million, covering a stretch of Europe from Great Britain to Turkey. I personally think that this is a grandiose plan designed by Heydrich either to hold on to or to improve his position in the Third Reich. Naomi, however, doesn't think so. She believes Hitler is the architect of the final solution, and the Wannsee Protocols is a plan for its implementation, presented by Heydrich with the Führer's approval. We fight over this all the time, and we're going to write two books—she about the discovery of the Wannsee Protocols and I on the haphazard nature of the plan of execution of the final solution. As far as I can tell, the Third Reich had expanded so rapidly that no one, not even Hitler, controlled it anymore.

In Poland, the General Government under Hans Frank had its own plan for killing Jews by starvation, and in the Warthegau, they had built gas chambers on their own. The only thing I can conclude, after reading the pack of letters from German soldiers I'm sending you, is that every German instinctively hates a Jew and wants to kill him. All this makes me feel confused because I really want to know how and why the Holocaust happened, and I'm nowhere near a resolution."

She opened the package sent by Eric, which consisted of nearly two hundred letters, most of them written by SS men or auxiliaries such as truck drivers, medical workers, and the like. Eric, following her suggestion, had obtained them through advertisements that promised money (and anonymity) for letters from the Wehrmacht and SS personnel to their family members. He wanted Hannah to translate them into English, since his fluency in German was not up to the mark.

The primary theme of the letters was the Jew—his appearance, his demeanor, and his ultimate destiny.

"I was shocked when I saw a bunch of Jews cleaning the streets," wrote a young recruit to his mother on his first arrival in Warsaw. "They looked like carriers of filth, in their dirty, tattered garbs. They bowed from the waist as we passed by and tried to grab our hands and kiss them. We didn't want to be touched by these creatures and drew our pistols. One of them veered toward Oberschütze Luther, who hit him on the skull with his Luger and cracked it open. When I joined the SS, I never thought I would have to deal with situations like this. On a positive note, I have good times in the company of my fellow recruits. The food is good. We have cultural events, and I saw a play by Heinrich von Kleist put up by the *Standartenführer*'s wife. But coming back to the Jewish question—what are we going to do with these creatures?"

A few months later, he was posted to the Lodz ghetto, and he wrote to his mother again. "I am on guard duty, and I visit this hellhole each morning. The stench from the open drains makes me ill. There's a typhus epidemic, and the Jews stack up their dead for burial at night, as required by their laws. Hundreds of German tourists come to see the ghetto every day, and they take delight in watching the stacked-up dead Jews and take pictures of them. I can't wait to come home for my beloved sister's wedding and breathe German air, walk the German streets, and be soothed by the cleanliness and orderliness that's the hallmark of a German life. Each day I am here, I feel I'll turn mad and start spraying bullets into these diseased, sick-looking scarecrows, whom it's impossible to look upon as humans."

Hannah remembered the newsreels of ghettos that were shown in the early forties in Berlin theaters. The sequence of images they presented were identical to those conveyed in the letters, down to the gawking tourists, grinning and making jokes about the ghetto dwellers. She used to wonder about the ultimate purpose of such propaganda, until she saw groups of Jews carrying suitcases at Berlin checkpoints on their way to trains that would carry them to the "East." Goebbels had done his job well—made the enemy look repulsive, numbed feelings of compassion that might exist in the heart of the German viewer, and prepared them for the inevitable final solution. The young recruit who wrote the letters grew up watching newsreels and those horrible films—*Der Ewige Jude, Jud Süß*, and the like—and listening to the daily radio claim of an international Jewish war that was being waged against the *Vaterland*. The air was corrosive, and it destroyed everyone who breathed it including me, she thought: I painted dozens of pictures of Hitler for display in the homes of the wealthy. The Germans like the *Mona Lisa* style of painting, using sfumato—the smudging between background and foreground—and I provided them with that. Kandinsky wouldn't have done it; Mondrian wouldn't have done it: I am worse than a prostitute because I debased my art instead of my body.

She let the feeling of self-disgust run its course and, after a while, rationalized her actions by saying to herself she had no choice, that moral criteria did not apply when one faced starvation. She went back to the stack of letters and read a few from the Einsatzgruppen auxiliaries—bus drivers, photographers, ambulance men, and the like. She learned that hundreds of Jews had been clubbed to death in Lithuania and Latvia by gangs of local convicts released from prisons by the Nazis to do the dirty work for them. The Einsatzgruppen had also rounded up Jews, took them inside sealed vans, and killed them by using the exhaust gas from the vans. In Ukraine, they had forced a group of Jews to lie down at the bottom of a ravine, shot them in the neck, and then brought in the next batch and made them lie on top of the dead ones and shot them the same way—batch after batch, until the ravine was three-fourths full. "How many layers of dead Jews were in that ravine, I cannot tell you," wrote a truck driver from Bremen to his wife. "I stopped counting after twenty, dazed and disoriented by the sight of blood and the screams from the victims. This is no way to conduct a war. Mark my words, we will have to pay for this."

Next came letters from the killing centers, Belzec, Treblinka, Auschwitz, and the rest. The writers complained about the sickly sweet odor of burning bodies, some comparing it to the smell of burned pork, others to smells from a tanning factory.

"I couldn't stand the killings at Kiev," wrote a twenty-two-year-old SS lieutenant to his girlfriend. "I have been told by teachers, parents, and party leaders from the age of seven onward that the Jews are our enemy, and I've heard the Führer say that in person at public rallies. Yet I can't kill them in cold blood, especially women and children. So I asked for a transfer, hoping to be sent to fight in the Western or African front, to do something daring and manly. Instead, my colonel, who doesn't like me, sent me to the extermination camp at Belzec. I can't describe the stench in that place that met my nostrils, and looking around, I found it came from a huge pit stacked with corpses. They bring the Jews here in trains and gas them. They then drag the dead bodies into this pit and leave them there. I assume they would eventually burn the corpses, but right now it's an open graveyard, and every night I dream of the bodies in the pit coming alive and roaming the place like vampires. I wake up tired and sick in the mornings and go into the open countryside to breathe fresh air, but even there I can't escape these ubiquitous trains carrying

Jews. Twice I rescued infants being thrown out of train windows by their mothers, who probably hoped a stranger would take them and bring them up. I picked up the first baby and took him to our medical staff. The doctor smiled at me and said, 'You brought him to the right place. I'll take care of him.' The child was killed an hour later! The second time I walked to a farm and left the baby at the door, rang the bell, and ran away. I hope it's still alive. As you can guess, the new colonel doesn't like me either. He thinks I'm un-Deutsch…"

"A number of German tourists come here, after visiting Warsaw, to watch the show," a young SS private wrote to his aunt from Treblinka. "The trains bring in six or seven thousand Jews per trip, and they are quickly processed. Some of the Jewish females are very talented, and they've organized an orchestra to play music for us. Too bad they have to be gassed. The other day, I gave a bar of chocolate to a young Jewish girl, all bones, with eyes big as saucers. And I was reprimanded. 'No SS man should nurture compassion,' barked an officer. He told me I would be punished if I helped the Jews, who were our sworn enemy, and warned me not to reveal what was going on in this place to any outsider. It's a foolish order because the German visitors know what's going on, and they'll spread the word."

We all knew that something like this was going to happen, thought Hannah. Hitler had said it so many times on the radio. She remembered an incident that had taken place three years ago, on a cold February morning, while she was drinking coffee in a rundown restaurant on Potsdamer Strasse. A customer sitting at the next table had left behind a copy of the *Niedersächsische Tageszeitung*. It had the headline "THE JEW WILL BE EXTERMINATED." She had picked it up and read the Führer's assurances of carrying out his prophecy of *Vernichtung* to the "Old Fighters," who had assembled in Munich to reminisce about the good old days of the Beerhall Putsch and brawls at the various ratskellers. Herr Steinhauer, the owner of the coffee shop—a kind, avuncular man who let Hannah eat there on credit—had seen the headline as he was pouring coffee into her cup. "He means every word of it," he had said. "He will kill them all by starving them, shooting them, or gassing them." The other customers—two older men and a young pregnant matron—had shrugged their shoulders and went on with their meal. Steinhauer had been found dead on the street a few months later, with a bullet hole in his forehead. The street cleaners, Poles and Russians, had taken him away in a garbage truck as Hannah watched.

"I have to decide every day who is to live and who is to die," wrote a doctor from Auschwitz to his mistress. "I've come to the conclusion that Jews pollute our planet, and the sooner these subhumans are liquidated, the better it'll be for the rest of us. Yesterday, at the officer's club, we had a discussion on the Jewish question, and everyone agreed that the Jews should be eradicated like the tubercle bacillus so that the rest of us can breathe more freely."

After going through a few more letters in the vein, Hannah couldn't read any more. For the next few days, she debated whether she should continue translating the letters as Eric had wanted her to do. I feel filthy touching them, let alone reading them, she thought. Yet she felt equivocal about denying Grossman's request. He has done so much for me, she thought, and I wish he would get off his obsession to get to the root of the *Endlösung*. Sometimes, it's best to leave things alone.

Torn between repulsion and feelings of loyalty, Hannah spent some of her free time translating the letters, would get sick with what she was doing, and would then switch over to assignments that Tad had given her. He was planning a huge private sale, and Hannah was in charge of making a catalog of paintings by Viennese artists Oskar Kokoschka, Egon Schiele, Anton Kolig, and Josef Gassler. The paintings were not up to the artists' usual quality, and she found it hard to bestow the requisite words of adulation on them. Yet she did what was expected of her, and Tad, very pleased with her effort, offered her a handsome contract that would make her, after a couple of years, an equal partner of the art gallery.

"Let me think about it," she told him.

She really didn't want to be a gallery owner because she felt it would seriously compromise, even jeopardize, her work as an artist. The money that would come to her if she accepted Tad's offer would make her rich beyond her expectations, but she thought of Clyfford Still and his dedication, despite financial struggles, to his art. She told Tad that she wanted to teach and paint like many at Bauhaus did, and he, gracious as ever, offered to introduce her to the head of an art school in downtown Los Angeles.

"You should do what you want to do, Hannah," he said. "You can always work here, part time or full time. I'll also try to sell your paintings, and you can expect a good income, based on the response we've had to your work."

A day later, he arranged for an interview with a Dr. Preston Clarke, an art critic and historian, who was the head of the art school.

"I'm a painter of Americana," Dr. Clarke said, pointing to a number of paintings hanging on the walls of his office with a sweeping gesture. "I studied under John Sloan. Have you heard of him?"

Hannah shook her head, somewhat mystified by what she saw hanging on the wall—paintings of grandma and grandpa holding grandson's hands, a cow being milked by a buxom girl with yellow hair and cornflower-blue eyes, two fishermen angling in a lake, and a returning soldier being welcomed by his relatives. These are not works of art, she thought. These are illustrations for a fairy tale called American life.

"In my younger days, the big names were George Bellows, Robert Henri, William Glackens, and of course John Sloan. They were founders of the Ashcan school. Have you heard of it?"

Hannah shook her head again.

"Those guys believed in visual realism, and some great paintings came out of that group, like *McSorley's Bar*, by John Sloan. You haven't seen that painting, I assume."

Hannah shook her head again.

"I don't think I'm the right person for you, Dr. Clarke," she said, wanting to get away from him. "I was under the impression that you were looking for someone to give courses in modern European art."

"I was coming to that, Miss Müller. Our students have been clamoring for a new department on modern art. I had a conversation with Tad yesterday, and he said you were the right person to head such a department. But I've to warn you: you will be isolated, because all my colleagues think and paint like me. We know nothing about modern art, and, frankly, we think it is all hogwash."

Shall I walk out of this office and go for a drive along the beach? Hannah wondered.

"The salary is seven thousand dollars," said Dr. Clarke, "and you can start after the summer recess."

"Are you offering me the position?" she asked him, not sure whether he was joking.

"Tad recommends you highly. His word is good enough for me. He's a nice man. In fact, I'm looking forward to showing some of my paintings in his gallery."

Hannah was puzzled and disturbed by his remarks. Was there a quid pro quo between Tad and this man? she wondered. Is that the way the art world works in America? Dr. Clarke hires me, and Dr. Clarke will be rewarded with a show?

"Will I be in full control of my curriculum?" she asked him, determined to end the interview if he said no.

"I leave it all to you, Hannah," he said. "Let's now go to lunch."

She watched him eat two cheeseburgers, with a double order of french fries, and drink two bottles of beer while she ate her cucumber-and-tomato salad. He showed her pictures of his sons and grandsons and his golden retriever, Brandon. If I take this job, I've to listen to him, day after day, she thought. But soon the bright side asserted itself: I can still be in Santa Monica; I can go to the beach whenever I want to, paint, and bask in the sun; I can reach out to new artists like Clyfford Still and make a new career—I can do all that because I was lucky to come here, to this great land, this New World, this haven to Europeans for half a millennium.

But the feeling of euphoria was short lived. The day after she got the formal offer from the Los Angeles Art School, she was visited by a tall, clean-cut young man who introduced himself as Agent Ralph Hildebrand of the FBI.

He looks just like the Gestapo who used to interrogate me in Berlin, she thought, and her body went tense as he took out his wallet and showed his card to her.

"Would you like some coffee?" she inquired, playing the hostess.

"No, I would like to ask a few questions," he replied.

He sat in a stiff-backed chair in the sitting room facing her, while she crouched on the edge of the sofa. He wanted to know about her past in Germany, what she did before, during, and after the war. She answered truthfully because she suspected he knew the answers and was ready to pounce on inconsistencies.

"You made a living by painting portraits of the Nazi leaders between 1933 and 1945?"

"Yes. But I did other work also."

"Such as?"

"The underground movements would ask me to paint posters, and there were small cabarets in Berlin that would ask me to design settings."

"You signed the petition against Hitler, the Dringender Appell für die Einheit?"

"I did."

"Were you a communist when you were in Germany?"

"No."

"But you associated with communists, right?"

"I did. My mother was a communist, and so was my stepfather."

"You worked for the Russians after the war, right?"

"I did."

"You painted posters of Stalin, right?"

"I did."

"You also painted Soviet propaganda posters, right?"

"Yes."

Where's all this leading to? she wondered. She wanted to walk away from him but knew that it would be a wrong move.

"You were at the Roosevelt Hotel recently for a fundraiser for Hanns Eisler, right?"

"Yes."

"You know he's an avowed communist?"

"Yes."

"Yet you decided to support him, right?

"True."

"You're a close friend of Randy Stevens?"

"Yes."

"You know he's a communist?"

"Yes."

"Do you agree with his political views?"

"I don't know what they are. I never asked him, and he never told me."

"But he told you he was a communist?"

"He did say that."

Hildebrand made some notes, and his mood changed suddenly. "I wouldn't mind having that coffee," he said with a smile.

"How do you take it?"

"With milk and sugar, please."

Hannah went into the kitchen and poured two cups of black coffee from the thermos she had filled earlier in the morning. Adding milk and sugar, she brought them to the living room.

"Good coffee," said the man, after tasting it. He stared at her speculatively for a few seconds and said, "Look, you're going to be called as a witness. You've a choice to make—you can be a friendly or a hostile witness. I would advise you not to take a hostile attitude, for your own good."

This was bewildering news to Hannah. "Why do you need me as a witness?" she asked. "I've answered all your questions, and I saw you take down my answers."

"You will make a good impression for the prosecution," he said. "You are what's called a credible witness."

"What do you want me to do?"

"You will get a subpoena from us in two weeks. You will be given a date for the hearing. You must show up and answer the HUAC prosecutor's questions."

"Looks like I've no choice."

He smiled at her, the complacent smile of the victor. "OK, then. You will hear from us."

That night she went with Randy and Roddy to see Bertolt Brecht's *Galileo*, which was playing at a small theater on La Cienega Boulevard, with Charles Laughton in the title role. They didn't like the play because of its pedantic overtones and were in a grumpy mood as they sat down to beer and burgers at a nearby pub.

"Hey, that guy's an agent, and he's been following us," said Roddy, covertly pointing to a man wearing a houndstooth jacket over a white shirt.

"An agent came to see me this morning," said Hannah.

"How did it go?" asked Randy.

Hannah gave details and watched with interest the contrast in the facial expressions of her two friends. Randy was amused, but Roddy had turned pale and red by turns.

"You botched it," he said, with barely concealed contempt and anger.

"What did I do wrong?"

"You should've taken the fifth, like I did."

"Fifth? I don't know what that means," she said. "A fifth of whiskey?"

Randy tried to explain, but Roddy interrupted him with outbursts.

"Did they promise you citizenship for testifying against your friend?" he asked her at one point.

"Don't rile her, buddy," said Randy. "She didn't know the drill, that's all."

"She should've kept her mouth shut," said Roddy, "instead of betraying her pals."

Hannah got up and ran out of the pub. Randy followed her and caught up with her.

"Don't mind what he says, Hannah," he said. "He'll feel bad tomorrow and apologize to you. I know him."

"I'm tired, Randy. I will get a taxi to take me home."

"Let me take you home," he pleaded.

She was adamant in her refusal, and he got her a taxi that was cruising by.

The next morning she asked Tad for the name of a lawyer.

"What do you need a lawyer for? Did you have a car accident?"

She explained the situation to him and watched his face lengthen.

"You should've kept quiet," he said. "Now they're going to ask you who else you saw that day at the Roosevelt Hotel. You've got all of us in trouble."

His words stunned her, as though he had thrown a punch at her jaw.

"I'm sorry, Tad," she protested. "I do need a lawyer to limit the damage."

"Let me call a couple of guys I know and ask them if they would take you on as a client. They may not."

He turned out to be right on both counts. The lawyers didn't want to represent her, and Hildebrand and an associate showed up at her house the next morning. They were very pleasant and relaxed as they asked her for the names of people at the Roosevelt Hotel fundraiser and also of Randy's friends. To exert subtle pressure on her, they casually brought up the name of a German refugee who had refused to cooperate with them and was now facing deportation. Hannah got the message and felt sick as she gave a few names and saw the agents checking them off a list.

She felt she had betrayed her friends and stayed home for a few days, ignoring telephone calls. Images of her brother haunted her, her refusal to help him after being warned by the Gestapo. She lived in dread of the subpoenas from the HUAC and the subsequent public interrogation by the HUAC prosecutors. I've got to take a stand, she thought. I'm not going to appear before the HUAC, even if it means deportation. I would go back to Germany and ask permission from my uncle to live on a farm he owned in Thuringia as a paying tenant and set up a studio there.

She loved California, but she hated Californians, for they were no different from Germans in coming up with conspiracy theories. She loved Americans, but she hated their paranoia about Russia and the communists. Why are they so afraid of Russia? she wanted to ask someone. Why are they so terrified of communists? I've known some who were really nice people, she thought, like my stepfather, Paul. Cooped up inside her house, refusing to meet any of her friends, her mind swinging like a pendulum from one extreme to the other, she felt confused and disoriented, unable to make up her mind.

As had happened before several times in her life, someone came to her rescue and made the decision that she wasn't able to make by herself. A bulky mail from Eric Grossman forced her to stop vacillating and take immediate action. Her uncle had passed away two weeks ago, Eric wrote, and he had died intestate. He enclosed a letter from her uncle's lawyer, Rechtsanwalt Lukas Hackmann, stating that Hannah Müller was the only living relative of Werner von Thyssen and as such was entitled to his estate, and her presence was immediately required in Nuremberg to settle important matters, including the payment of certain taxes. Eric, thoughtful as ever, had included a military pass that would enable her to travel by plane from Los Angeles to Nuremberg.

The next day she visited the army center in downtown Los Angeles, and they quickly arranged a flight to New York and from there to Berlin directly.

"Our office at the Berlin airport will help you with a local flight to Nuremberg," a woman in a sergeant's uniform told her with a smile.

"They have now flights from Berlin to Nuremberg?" asked Hannah.

"Only for army personnel," said Sergeant Williams. "We built military airports six month ago in most cities within our zone."

She had a week before the flight to settle her affairs.

She visited her landlady and paid her the rent for the month. She wrote to Agent Hildebrand, explaining that she had to be away in Germany for a few weeks to take care of matters associated with her uncle's death and attached a copy of the letter from Rechtsanwalt Lukas Hackmann as documentary proof.

She spent one evening with Randy and Roddy and another with Bruno and Tad, assuring them she would not testify before the HUAC.

"Does that mean you won't be coming back?" they asked her.

"Of course I'll be back," she said, even though she wasn't sure what she was going to do. "Santa Monica is where I want to spend the rest of my life."

Somewhat to her surprise, the US immigration office chose that week to call her for the obligatory interview prior to the granting of citizenship. Tad coached her on the questions they would ask about the Bill of Rights and the Constitution, including its amendments, and she was sworn in as a citizen a few hours before her flight.

I'm an American citizen now, she thought ironically—as she raised her hand and took the oath—even though I will never be or can be an American, for I'll always be an exile from Bauhaus.

But the new green passport with gold letters felt good in her hands, a talisman of sorts against future troubles.

PART 5

ARYAN DYSTOPIA

[Are] Germany's intellectual leaders guilty of complicity in the crimes against humanity for which Germany's top politicians and generals have been brought to trial? It seems only one answer is possible...With the political and military leaders, they prepared, instituted, and blessed the program of vilification, disenfranchisement, dispossession, expatriation, imprisonment, deportation, enslavement, torture, and murder.

—Max Weinreich, *Hitler's Professors*

TWENTY-SEVEN

GARDENS WITHOUT WALLS

B oth legs of the flight were crowded with soldiers, and she was in
one of the middle seats, with uniformed men talking across her
or over her head or smoking Lucky Strikes, whose smell she detested.
She closed her eyes and tried to sleep, but each time she dropped off,
she would be woken up by the clang of the food trolley carrying its array of Coke bottles and urns containing coffee or hot chocolate or by
someone who wanted to get to the aisle so that he could go to the toilet
or talk with one of his buddies in a different seat.

After nearly ten hours, the Douglas C-47 landed on the runway
at the Tempelhof airport. Hannah, tired and sleepy as she was, was
jolted from her lassitude by the German signs and the German speech
that greeted her eyes and ears. Here I am in my own country, and
I don't feel good about it, she thought. She deliberately suppressed
her memories of Berlin and, carrying her suitcase, walked around until she found a young man in uniform with five chevron stripes—she
wasn't sure if he was a sergeant or someone of higher rank—sitting
behind a desk marked "Airport Control."

"Can I get on a flight to Nuremberg from here?" she asked him,
hoping the answer would be no, and she could take a plane to somewhere else—Lisbon, London, or Lanzarote—it didn't matter where.

He quickly checked her papers, made a telephone call, and said, "A plane to Nuremberg is leaving in a few minutes from the other end of the airfield. Colonel Grossman has booked a flight for you. Corporal Kostowski will take you there."

Corporal Kostowski turned out to be a huge young man, with the neck and shoulders of a bull. He lifted her suitcase as though it were a makeup kit and walked with long strides across the length of the building and the well-kept grounds of the airfield until they came to a small plane with the USAF sign painted on its body and wings. Another corporal checked her papers and helped her up a nearly vertical steel ladder, while Kostowski put her suitcase in the luggage compartment, waved to her, and left.

There were ten seats on the plane and half a dozen passengers— a mixture of civilians and soldiers, who seemed to be part of a visiting delegation. They sat together in adjoining rows in the back, and Hannah was able to get a window seat, with nobody next to her.

The day was bright, and Hannah had an excellent view of the western zone of Berlin as the plane circled around to gain speed. She noticed that the rubble had been removed from the streets. What did they do with it? Did they dump it in lakes, or did they burn it? Hannah, looking down from above, couldn't believe that this was the new Berlin: gardens without walls, dried-out swimming pools, and churches without steeples—where once great buildings had stood, only jagged stones remained, like stumps of rotten teeth in a cavernous mouth. But trams and buses were running, and people were sitting in parks as in the old days, and she waved to them as the plane, which was going west, abruptly turned south. They flew over the Elbe River and the Harz Mountains, over farms and fields and small towns, and then she saw her beloved Rhine—actually its tributary Main, she corrected herself—gleaming beneath her, before reaching Nuremberg.

A group of men in suits were standing on the airfield to greet the delegation, and Hannah noticed with surprise that they were all

Germans, smiling and shaking hands. What had happened to defraternization and denazification? Was it no longer in force, or was it not applicable to bankers? She sensed that a big change had taken place and was eager to meet Eric and get the latest from him.

A striking-looking brunette made her way through the small crowd, stood before her, and asked her if she was Hannah Müller.

"Hi, I'm Naomi Bressler, Eric's fiancée," she said, putting out her hand. "Eric asked me to come and meet you because he's busy with the Einsatzgruppen trial."

She asked a porter, obviously a German POW, to take Hannah's luggage to her car waiting at the airport.

"Eric has booked a room for you at the Grand Hotel, and I'm going to drive you there," she said.

"Grand Hotel? I thought Germans weren't allowed in there."

Naomi was amused by her answer. "That was in the old days when we weren't allowed to fraternize with the Germans. There has been a sea change in our attitude since then. Germans are not considered as enemies anymore."

"I see."

"Want to hear who our new enemies are?" she asked mischievously.

"In the United States, it's the Russians."

Naomi laughed, and Hannah liked her laughter. "Here also. We've been told to be nice to the Germans because we want them to be our allies against the Russians."

As Naomi drove expertly through the streets of Nuremberg, Hannah noticed the absence of debris and wreckage that had been most prominent in her recollection of the city. The old town, her favorite spot, was gone, and in its place was a flattened-out land that looked like a grid crisscrossed by untidy paths that once had been streets.

"They used the rubble to make an artificial hill," said Naomi, on seeing Hannah's look of surprise. "The hill is at the old Nazi Party rallying ground, and its name is Silberbuck. They ran a special train called the Rubble Express to collect the debris from the old city and deposit it at the rallying ground."

"Nuremberg has changed a lot since I've been away," said Hannah.

"They're planning to rebuild the city like it was before. Our government is helping Germany financially through the Marshall Plan. The old Nazi bankers are all back in high positions. Some of them were on the plane you came in on."

"I didn't know any of this," said Hannah. "The California papers aren't big on German news. These days all they talk about is the Red Scare."

"I know. We get newspapers from home. They don't report what's going on over here because they want to quietly bring Germany back into the Western fold. You know, they've called off the denazification program. They're also dropping charges against many SS and army officers. In fact, the CIA and the FBI are hiring these guys by the dozens. Eric is very unhappy about that."

"I can understand why he would be upset."

They drove by several new US Army buildings, and Hannah realized that the US occupation was more visible now than it had been before her departure from the city. There were dozens of bars, diners, movie theaters, and clubs, and Hannah thought for a moment she was back in downtown Los Angeles. GIs were everywhere, walking with German girls, with arms around their waists.

Naomi slowed down the car as they approached the Grand Hotel. She stopped at the curb, and a uniformed porter—another POW, obviously—took Hannah's luggage and walked behind them as they entered the lobby. The last time she had been there, the hotel had rows of canvas containers holding drinking water brought in by trucks from Switzerland, since the local water supply had been contaminated by poisonous debris and decaying corpses resulting from the bombing. The containers were no longer there, but the long bar was lined with loud-voiced Americans, as before.

Naomi checked her in, and Hannah went with her upstairs to the second floor, the porter following them.

Her room was nice, with a large bed and a bathroom and two wardrobes. The porter checked out the hot and cold water, and Hannah gave him a dollar for a tip. He pocketed the money, turned on his heel, and walked out of the room, banging the door shut.

"Some of these guys have just been transferred by the Russians," Naomi said. "They're angry they can get only menial jobs. They hate Americans, being good Nazis."

She pulled back the drapes covering a large window and looked outside.

"Not much of a view, but you can see what's still left standing in Nuremberg," she said.

Hannah smiled. She liked this young woman with her sense of irony and her free and easy way of speaking.

"It must be awful for you, living in this environment," said Hannah.

"I am thinking of going back to New York," she replied. "I've been staying here only because of Eric. I think the time has come to say 'Good-bye, Nuremberg.'"

Hannah stared at her, not knowing how to respond. "You said you were his fiancée," she ventured.

"I could've used other words to describe our relationship," she said. "I could've said I was his mistress, his paramour, or his sexual partner. I wanted to elevate myself by saying I'm his fiancée, even though marriage isn't in the cards."

"I'm sorry to hear that," said Hannah. "The two of you would have made an excellent couple, in my opinion."

"He's still obsessed with you, Hannah. I hope you don't mind my frankness. I know all about you from reading a diary that he keeps. He doesn't know I've read it. I know you don't want him, but he wants you."

"I thought he had gotten over his infatuation," said Hannah.

She felt tired, exhausted from travel, weary of the conflict that seemed to pursue her like the Greek Furies wherever she went. She sat down in a chair and closed her eyes. I shouldn't have come here, she thought.

Naomi came over to her and put her hand on her shoulder.

"Don't feel bad," she said. "You aren't responsible for Eric. He sees something in you that he doesn't find in other women, including me. I'm not going to mope over it. I'm seeing another guy. His dad owns a publishing company in New York. They are going to publish my book."

She's so open, thought Hannah, and so determined to get ahead—a study in contrast against someone like me.

"You're a strong young woman," she said. "I like your attitude."

"I'm not as strong as you think," Naomi replied. "But I've to fend for myself. Anyway, the reason I picked you up today was to meet you and to see what you looked like. Now I understand why Eric has a crush on you. He has described you to a T in his diaries."

"Would you like to sit down, Naomi?" asked Hannah, embarrassed. "Shall I get you something to drink?"

"No, Hannah. I've to go now to meet my new boyfriend," she said. "The lawyer Lukas Hackmann will come up here tomorrow at ten in the morning. Eric will wrap up his brief by tomorrow afternoon and is planning to visit you after that. If you feel up to it, the three of us, or the four of us, can go for dinner tomorrow night."

She kissed Hannah on the cheek and left, closing the door after her.

Hannah took off her clothes, plopped into bed, and fell into a deep sleep. When she woke up, it was morning, and it took a while for her to get used to the new surroundings. It took a bit longer to quell the demons that had sprung up inside her mind, but with a great effort, she finally got out of her bed and turned on the water in her bath. Everything seemed to be working, to her surprise: the lights didn't flicker, the towels were freshly laundered, and hot and cold water, instead of coming in brownish drips, gushed out of the faucets with the translucence and urgency of mountain streams.

She took a leisurely bath, scrubbed her nails, washed her hair, and, feeling a lot better, got dressed and called room service to send up some toast and coffee and fruit. Soon a young German waitress appeared with a trolley and laid the breakfast table. The coffee smelled as good as in the old days, and Hannah bit into an apple that reminded her of those from the Rhineland she used to snack on when she was a little girl.

"How are things in Nuremberg?" Hannah asked the girl.

"Life is getting better here," she said. "But I'm planning to go to America after marrying my boyfriend. He's a sergeant in the US Army."

"Where in America are you going to?"

"Miami, where his parents live," she said. "Have you ever been there?"

"No, but I've heard it's nice."

"My boyfriend is going to work in his father's hardware store."

"Good luck to both of you!"

"All my friends are leaving for America. To Kansas, to Alabama, to Oklahoma—to all these places with strange names. I'll have to make new friends, start a new life."

I've done it many times, thought Hannah—building a new life isn't that hard. "You'll like it there," she said. "America is a friendly place."

The girl beamed, placed the empty tray on the trolley, and left, closing the door without banging. She's a nice girl, thought Hannah as she sat on her bed, drinking her coffee slowly. She turned on the radio and listened to a discussion by three high-level clergymen—a Catholic priest, an Evangelical bishop, and a Protestant dean—voicing support for the abandonment of the denazification policy by the Americans.

"Extremists from the left wing were behind the denazification," said Theophil Wurm, the bishop of the Evangelical Church of Württemberg, the loudest and the most unrelenting opponent of the denazification policy. "They wanted to incarcerate or execute the highly educated, the most capable of Germans, and by thus destroying the elite, they hoped to implement their Bolshevik agenda."

No regrets from the guardians of the German conscience about the war and the millions who died because of it, thought Hannah. All they want is for the past to be interred so that their support for Hitler and the Third Reich will be forgotten.

She turned off the radio and walked listlessly in the room, hating all Germans, including herself.

Why am I here, back in Nuremburg? she wondered. She thought of going back to Santa Monica so that she could walk on the beach and be soothed by the waves lapping on the shore, but then she remembered the endless rant from the press and the radio stations there on the Red Menace. She sang and danced to the tune of fee-fi-fo-fum:

The Reds they're coming
The Reds are a menace
The Reds rape women like me;
The Reds don't like Hitler
The Reds adore Stalin
The Reds want to drink the blood of Americans.

She laughed hysterically, but her mood changed after her outburst, and she plopped down on the bed, wondering if there was any place on planet earth where she could live without tension, a Utopia where she could be near the sea, holding the hand of a man she really liked. The memory of Daniel came to her, and along with it a pang of desire for his comforting, masculine presence. I've never heard from him, she thought. I was only a tryout, a casual encounter in the path he has charted out for himself. Nevertheless, she kept fantasizing about the two of them on an island in the Aegean Sea, idling in a boat or lying in the sun, with the blue sea around them. Daniel then metamorphosed into Clyfford Still, who was lecturing her that art was a process rather than a preconceived vision, and he had stretched out his arms toward her, wanting her to be his—and his alone.

The phone interrupted her reverie, and the receptionist from downstairs announced that a Herr Hackmann wanted to see her.

"Send him up," she said and hurriedly tidied up her bed.

He was a tall, slender man, about the same age as herself, with brushed-back thick blond hair tinged with gray and icy-blue eyes—the model Nazi whom one saw in propaganda newsreels, giving the stiff-armed salute and saying, "Heil Hitler." But he had changed with the times, she realized, as he bowed from the waist and smiled at her.

After introducing himself and going through the usual opening conversational exchanges, he quickly got down to the business at hand.

"Your uncle, Werner von Thyssen, was a very rich man," he said. "He didn't leave a will, based on my advice. Frankly, I didn't want him to list his assets, which is required in a will for a man of his wealth. He has bank accounts in Switzerland, Spain, and several Latin American countries. He has valuable paintings and first editions of rare books in bank vaults. My own assessment is his estate is worth nearly ten million Swiss francs, which is equivalent to two to three million US dollars. About thirty percent will have to go for death duties, and the remaining money is yours."

Hannah couldn't conceal her surprise.

"My uncle never told me any of this," she said.

"He wasn't allowed to talk about it when the Third Reich was in power," he said. "After the war ended, the Americans confiscated his funds. Now, after his death, they've released it."

"Ulrike should have the money, since she was regarded as his wife by all of us, even though they weren't legally married."

"I haven't brought you up to date on the current situation regarding your uncle's household," he said. "Ulrike's husband, who was with the police battalion fighting on the eastern front, was repatriated by the Russians in a prisoner exchange. He has been reappointed police chief in Ansbach, under the new policies of the American government, and Ulrike is now living with him. It's best that you do not bring up her relationship with your uncle. It will wreck her marriage."

"Who took care of my uncle in his last days?"

"Ulrike hired a trained nurse and a manservant to look after him. Your uncle was well cared for, I can assure you. I visited him a couple of times, and everything seemed in order."

"Frieda should have been there to help, in Ulrike's absence," said Hannah.

"Frieda left for Argentina before that," he said. "Her husband is doing very well there, in the munitions-import business. He wanted her to leave Germany for good, and she did what he asked her to do, like a good German wife."

"Who then is doing the housekeeping for the Americans?" asked Hannah.

"Oh, they're not living in that house anymore," said Herr Hackmann. "The US Army stopped billeting soldiers in German houses and moved them into barracks. This happened about three months ago. The house is empty. And it's yours."

"What shall I do with it? I don't want to live in Nuremberg," said Hannah.

"You can sell it after you decide what to do with your uncle's personal property," said Herr Hackmann. "That reminds me—your uncle also wants you to go through his papers and decide what should be kept and what should be burned."

Hannah was bewildered by this turn in the conversation.

"What papers?" she asked. "You mean his old letters?"

"In addition to letters, there are his diaries and his notes for his biography."

"I'm not capable of passing judgment on them," said Hannah. "I don't understand why he wants me to go through his papers."

"He has a left a note for you on his desk. When you read it, you will understand his reasons. In the meantime, we've to take care of a few other things."

He wanted her to sign several legal documents, including one that retained him as her attorney and investment adviser.

"We will invest the money in rebuilding Germany, Hannah, and in five years it will quadruple because of the postwar boom."

He didn't want her to sell the house for the same reason. He suggested she should live there for a while—he would hire a housekeeper, a maid, and a handyman who would also work as a gardener.

She'd forgotten the way men spoke to women in Germany, using the authoritative tone of the paterfamilias. This guy's coming on strong—at least that's what Roddy would say, she thought, for nobody spoke to women like that in California.

But, aside from his arrogance, she was impressed by his thoroughness and meticulousness and decided to appoint him as her agent in handling the complex issues arising out of her uncle's demise.

"I'll drive you to the house now so that you can look it over and decide when you want to move in," he said, after the signing ceremony was over.

The lawn was unkempt, and a front window was broken, but the lights worked, there was running water, and the phones were operational. Hannah and the lawyer went upstairs to check the rooms where the Americans had been living, and except for some litter and empty beer and Coke bottles, the place looked tidy enough.

"The staff that we will be hiring can clean all this up," said Hackmann.

"When will they start?" asked Hannah.

"Tomorrow, if it's OK with you."

"It's fine with me," said Hannah. "I'll move in the day after tomorrow."

"Do you need a car?"

"Yes. And a bicycle."

"I'll take care of all that," said Hackmann.

Hannah felt she was living in a dream world, a fairy tale in which she was transformed from a scullery maid to a princess by the touch of a magic wand. It wasn't that long ago that she had lived in this very same house as a poor relation whose presence was tolerated because of ties of blood. Now she was being treated like a lady of the manse whose slightest wish would be carried out by people like the man standing next to her.

I'm not happy in this role, she thought. Nevertheless, she decided to play along, laughing at herself when she told Hackmann she wanted a red Mercedes for her car. He nodded and suggested she hire a chauffeur also—but she drew the line at that.

When the lawyer drove her back to the hotel, she found Eric waiting for her in the lobby. He rose from his chair, came forward to greet her with open arms, and folded her in his embrace. His colonel's uniform rubbed uncomfortably against her face, but Hannah didn't pull back.

He plied her with questions about her life in California and became very agitated when she told him about the subpoena she would get from the HUAC to appear as a witness.

"We've had Red Scares before," he said. "My mother used to tell me of the Red Scare after the Soviet Revolution of 1917, when labor unions were on the rise in the US. And in the early thirties, there were Nazi marches and rallies ending up with street fights against communists and socialists. I thought it was all over and done with, but the tide is rising again, from what you're telling me."

"No matter where I go, I get into trouble," said Hannah. "And now it's going to start all over again, here in Nuremberg."

"I don't understand what you're saying," he said. "Why do you think you would be getting into trouble?"

She gave him details of her conversation with Hackmann and her fears that her uncle might have amassed his fortune through illegal means.

"He may have," said Eric, "but neither the US nor the Brits will take any action. All the industrialists and financiers who have been arrested on charges of using slave labor or building gas chambers have been released. In fact, the chief banker for the Nazis, Hermann Abs, is going to be a key figure in the rebuilding of Germany."

He spoke without bitterness, but Hannah could sense the strain he was under.

"How did it turn out this way, Eric?" she asked him. "Before I left, everyone was keen on punishing the Nazis and their supporters. Nobody wanted to socialize with Germans or even to be polite to them."

"The German industrialists and clergy have been complaining to the Congress that the original US prosecutors, most of them Jews, were out to destroy Germany by harshly punishing the people who have the brains and ability to lead the country. The tide has turned, Hannah. The Germans, including old Nazis, are our friends in our fight against the Russians. Our government says we need them on our side for the Cold War."

"Cold War?"

"It's a term used by George Orwell to describe the continual tension between two countries having different political ideologies. Everyone here is using it to describe the rivalry for world domination between us and the Soviets."

"And you're saying the US wants Germans to be on its side?"

"That's what we've been told by our congressmen and by our military leaders. In fact, neither the US nor the Brits—and I should add the Russians to the list—are keen on prosecuting Nazis. They want to leave it to the German judiciary or to the Polish tribunals. Of the three thousand members of the Einsatzgruppen, we are prosecuting only twenty-five, and that too only because we have documentary proof of the killings authorized by them. My job here will be done after this trial is over, because there won't be any more trials."

"What will you do then? Go back to the States?"

"I guess so. I need a quiet place to finish my book. I don't know if I will do it here or in New York. What about you?"

"I don't know, Eric. I don't know what I'll do next. For the next few weeks, I'll be going through my uncle's papers. I'll also get the details of his financial assets. After that, I really don't know what I'm going to do."

They looked at each other for a while, he wondering whether he should make any move toward reestablishing their sexual relationship and she hoping it would be possible to regain the friendship that had existed between them before their intimacy had ruined it.

"I want to clear the tension between us," she finally said. "I would like you to be my best friend, Eric. I would like you to come and see me in my new house and talk to me, like we used to in the old days."

He hesitated for a moment and then smiled—it was his old smile, radiant and reassuring.

"I'll be glad to," he said. "I'm going to Berlin tomorrow to meet with the Russians about some legal points. The Einsatzgruppen killings were done in their territory, and we're trying to get legal jurisdiction for the US Army to bring over witnesses. It's a contentious and complicated issue, and I'm taking an associate, an expert on international law, with me. I'll be back in a couple of weeks."

"Naomi was talking of having dinner with us tomorrow. I guess it isn't going to happen."

"No, I've to leave early tomorrow. I'll call Naomi and tell her that."

His manner was slightly evasive, and Hannah had the feeling that he was leaving because he didn't want to have dinner with her and Naomi, with the latter's boyfriend thrown in as a "maybe."

TWENTY-EIGHT

LIEBLINGSONKEL

Hannah moved into her house the next day and met the household staff. The housekeeper and the maid—a mother and daughter team—were Germans from Ukraine, brought in as part of Himmler's program to resettle Teutonic people scattered over Eastern Europe. Both spoke German with a strange accent and weren't well received by the locals, who wanted them to be sent back to Ukraine. Their eyes lit up when Hannah spoke to them in Russian.

"How did Frau Müller learn to speak such excellent Russian?" asked Alicia, the mother.

"I've had a lot of dealings with Russians," Hannah replied.

Alicia turned out to be a wonderful cook, and when she learned that Hannah liked Russian food, she came up with superb creations of chicken Kiev and beef stroganoff, supplemented by stacks of thin blinis or fluffy *pampushkis*. Through Herr Gotz, the handyman, a decorated World War I veteran and a strong Nazi sympathizer, she got the supplies she needed for her culinary creations through the black market. When Hannah learned about it, she felt that she had to take a stand but had second thoughts about getting into a confrontation with Gotz, who, no doubt, would complain to Hackmann.

She didn't want to offend Hackmann, for she had bank accounts in half a dozen countries, and if it weren't for him, she would be lost in the maze of currency fluctuation, market projections, tax regulations, and such topics that he was fond of bringing up at their daily meetings.

She was still in a daze, not quite sure that she wasn't living in a dream in a big house with servants who paid deference to her and a man who took care of her financial affairs and made her feel important. Most of her life had been a struggle for existence—for the daily bread, for the cast-off clothes sold in secondhand shops, for a handout here and there from a patron of the arts—and now she felt her past was unreal, floating like a haze beyond the palpable boundaries of her estate. At times she felt she was like a blind woman restored to sight and dazzled by the light around her, but quite often, it was the other way around, and she felt she was a woman suddenly gone blind and no longer able to sense the world as it used to appear before her—and, characteristically, she wasn't sure which was the true metaphor that described her predicament.

Her life quickly fell into a pattern. She woke up at nine—two hours later than her usual time—read the newspapers available now in Nuremberg in both German and English, rode her bike for ninety minutes, bathed, and got dressed for the daily visit of Hackmann or Eric, who would drop in for lunch. In the afternoon, she spent time with the handyman, discussing the layout of the garden and the flowers and trees to be planted. This was followed by a chat with Alicia, who invariably brought up episodes from her life in Kiev: the hatred experienced by her and other ethnic Germans from the locals after the invasion by Germany, the Jews being taken away in truckloads and lined up near ravines before slaughter, the visits by SS racial experts to establish her German ethnicity, and finally, the long train ride to Upper Silesia with her daughter to receive citizenship in the fatherland.

Alicia was a good narrator, with an eye for drama.

"My husband was standing in the garden, digging cabbages," she said, her round blue eyes resembling those of a doll, "and I heard a shot. I ran outside, and he was on the ground, his tunic soaked in blood."

"Who shot him?"

"The Russian partisans," she said. "They shot him in the back, the cowards."

Her husband obviously was one of those who had welcomed and collaborated with the German soldiers, thought Hannah. As though reading her mind, Alicia blinked her baby-round eyes and then wiped tears with her apron.

"He wouldn't pay heed to me," she said. "I told him not to be an informer. I don't like Jews, but I don't believe in killing them, I said. He wouldn't listen to me and showed the SS where the Jews lived. 'The Germans are going to win the war,' he said, 'and we've to side with them.' Men are so stubborn."

Hannah studied the woman, approximately the same age as herself, with her smooth blond hair and heavy breasts and hips. She too was a victim of the upheaval of hatred, the lava that had spewed from Germany and spread all over Europe. What was she really like? Hannah wondered. She sounded like every other woman in Germany, blaming the men for their misfortunes and ambiguous about their feelings toward Jews. It was hard to believe that she had tried to hold her husband back while he went out on missions with the Einsatzgruppen to hunt for Jews and pack them into trucks. But denial was the norm for Germans; it was their technique for survival. The Third Reich was history, and nobody wanted to admit they had been part of it.

Hannah, on the other hand, was haunted by memories of Emil and Johann, even though she had tried to push them into the recesses of her brain. Did Emil plead not guilty, like the men in the courtroom at Nuremberg? Did he hide under the protective shield of Hitler's orders? And what did Johann do when the guards kicked him or knocked him down with a rifle butt? Did he whimper? Did he beg for mercy? "I don't want to think about them," she said to herself. "I want to move on. This country is full of *ghosts*."

She didn't mean to use the word "ghost" in a literal sense, even though that morning, around three, when she had woken up feeling thirsty and gone downstairs to get a glass of water, she had seen her uncle sitting at the kitchen table. She hadn't been frightened because he was smiling as in the old days, looking dapper in his brown Tyrolean jacket. She didn't think of him as a ghost, but in her half-awakened state, she thought she had been transported by a time machine into the past. She took a step toward him, but the apparition vanished, and she remembered a line she had to write down a hundred times as a punishment in her student days:

Steh, Blendwerk!
Wenn du fähig bist, einen vernehmlichen Ton von dir zu geben,
so rede mit mir.

It was from the German version of *Hamlet*, a translation of the words spoken by Bernardo or Horatio on seeing the ghost walk by them.

What she had seen was an illusion, a creation of her mind, she reasoned. "I don't believe in ghosts. I am a twentieth-century woman; I don't believe in life after death or any such nonsensical stuff."

But last morning, she had seen the apparition again standing against her doorway when she was woken up by a gust of wind blowing her window wide open. It seemed to her he was staring at her in a mute sign of reproof, as in the old days when, as a ten-year-old, she would displease him by making too much noise or eating too many chocolates.

She remembered with a jolt his request to go through his papers and burn what she considered was inappropriate or without any intrinsic worth. I must do what he wants, she thought, or he will haunt me forever.

She went to his study, sat in his chair behind his elegant ebony desk, and glanced at a pile of papers weighted down by a pyramid-shaped glass paperweight showing a different picture of the Führer on each of its four sides. I'll keep the paperweight for posterity, she thought, as she tore open an envelope addressed to her in his handwriting.

"*Meine liebe Nichte,*" it began, in his beautiful script, written with his heavy Mont Blanc pen.

Things do not end the way we plan, especially in regard to our own lives. There are those who live from moment to moment and others, like me, who have a mission, or at least think they have one. You fight for it all your life, and when you lose, you go into a state of shock from which you can never recover.

Under this table, if you take off the rug, you will find a door to the downstairs cellar, which used to be the wine cellar when I bought the house from the Jews in 1938. Our clever engineers have made it into an easily accessible sanctum for me, with all the modern-day amenities. One of the parquet tiles on the floor will light up when you click the button on the black box I'm leaving in the right-hand bottom drawer. You can pull up that tile, and it will reveal the knob of a door that you can push open. You will see a steel staircase that will lead you to my sanctum.

I was hoping to write my book, *The Life of an Aryan,* and publish it after the war had been won, and the Third Reich was on its way to a thousand-year reign. My papers are neatly arranged, and perhaps some ghostwriter can write the book for me. Or perhaps the papers should be consigned to the flames and the ashes put in a trash can. I leave it to you to decide.

Good-bye, dear child.

Dein Lieblingsonkel

She followed his instructions and went down a narrow winding staircase to a room whose lights were automatically turned on by the lifting of the tile. In the middle of the room, there was a large desk with a reading lamp and a straight-backed chair with a red velvet cushion. Hannah sat in the chair and let her eyes wander over the bookshelves that lined the walls on both sides of the room, containing hundreds of tomes on philosophy and history in German, French, and English. Next to them were a dozen filing cabinets, a shelf containing stationery supplies and a portable typewriter, and several tall wooden racks stacked with papers. Air from the outside came through two vents attached to pumps that were running on electricity, and the hum of the motors had a soothing, almost soporific, effect.

This is like Aladdin's cave, Hannah thought as her eyes took in the exquisite blue-and-violet Persian carpet on the floor and the medieval tapestries with images of unicorns and centaurs on the wall before her. She wondered where he got them from, for the carpet and tapestries were similar to those seen in the antique galleries owned by wealthy Jews in Berlin in the prewar days.

She didn't have a clue as to what she should do with her uncle's papers and walked around the room trying to find a starting point. The racks, with dozens of pigeonholes containing alphabetically arranged mail, seemed worth exploring, and she took a handful of papers from a slot marked with the letter *J.*

Seating herself on the carpet, Hannah started reading them. The papers dealt with his correspondence with public figures on the Jewish question. This was around the year 1890, and Hannah was surprised that Germans were debating the Jewish question half a century ago, long before the birth of the Third Reich. Her uncle had written to congratulate a polemicist named Hermann Ahlwardt on his pamphlet on the Judenfrage, which had proposed a final solution of the Jewish problem through quarantine or annihilation.

Berlin

December 1, 1890

Herr Ahlwardt,

Many of my friends and associates view you as a crank, but I think of you as a prophet in the wilderness, obsessed with visions of an Aryan utopia. Your words are not those of a mad man who should be locked up, for they are the result of hours of deliberation and analysis that lead to the inevitable QED of your argument. As to your critics, I would say this to them: "What is your solution to the Jewish problem other than what Herr Ahlwardt has suggested? Do you have a better plan, a more logical solution?"

I'm a student at the Berlin University, and the great philosopher, Eugen Dühring, who came here to speak, thinks that the Jewish question has metamorphosed into an *Existenzfrage* for the Jews in Germany. You are not alone in thinking annihilation is the only alternative for the realization of an Aryan culture and the perpetuation of an Aryan stock free from pollution. Lots of people in Germany and Austria share your views. In conclusion, I would like to say that I would like to meet with you and shake your hand.

Yours, etc.

Werner von Thyssen

Her uncle had been twenty years old then. Adolf Hitler must have been a toddler at that time, and some Germans were already proposing the quarantining and annihilation of Jews!

TWENTY-NINE

LESSONS FOR AN ARYAN ON THE "JEWISH PROBLEM"

S hocked and stunned by what she had read, Hannah wanted to know more about how her uncle had come by these opinions.

I must start at the beginning and not in the middle, she thought. I must make excerpts, take notes about what I read, and type them up so that I can show them to someone who can advise me on what to do with these papers.

She searched the racks to see if he kept a *tagebuch*, like many German boys did, and found a stack of them, beginning from the year 1880, when he was nine years old, and ending in 1945. The early tagebuchs were slender, with a leather cover closed by a button clasp, unlike the bulky, clothbound books he used later.

Hannah read the first few volumes, written between the ages of nine and fifteen, dealing with his attempts at striking a balance between his impulses and his parent's wishes.

"I like Rosa a lot," began his first entry. "I like her brown curly hair and dark shining eyes. All the other kids I know—and the grownups too—have straight blond hair and pale-blue eyes. Rosa and I are planning to run away from home when we are sixteen" (Tagebuch 1880).

This was followed by a sketch of Rosa, using pencils of varying blackness for shading her eyebrows, thick tresses, and large, dark eyes. It's a good drawing, for a boy of his age, Hannah thought, and now I know where my talent comes from.

Werner found Rosa in tears one day, on her way to school.

"I asked her what was the matter, and she wouldn't say anything at first. She then said that last night mobs thronged the Scheunenviertel area where most Berlin Jews live and burned and looted their homes. Her aunt who lived there was killed by smoke and flames. How horrible such a death is! When I went home, I told my mother about Rosa's aunt. She wasn't affected by the news. She only said, 'You should know the Jews bring trouble wherever they go! You should stop being friends with Rosa'" (Tagebuch 1882).

He paid no heed to his mother's words and walked with Rosa to school every day. But, at the end of the term, Rosa told him that her family was moving to Berne. On Werner's asking her for the reason for the move, Rosa blurted out, "There is no anti-Semitism in Switzerland, unlike in Germany." He asked his father for the meaning of anti-Semitism, but instead of giving a straight answer, his father gave him a popular pamphlet by Wilhelm Marr and told him to read it to gain a proper understanding of the subject.

"I'm only a kid," Werner wrote, "but I can understand what Wilhelm Marr is saying. He says the Jews have corrupted and destroyed the German soul, and Germany will never achieve the glory that it deserves. I now know why people hate Jews. I hate them too" (Tagebuch 1882).

His father was a member of the League of Anti-Semites founded by Marr and took Werner to lectures given by the league. Werner, in several entries, expressed his gratitude to his father and to the speakers at the league for making him aware of the nature of the evil confronting the nation.

One day a team of doctors and school inspectors visited Werner's school to determine its percentage of Aryan students.

"They measured my skull," he wrote, "the length and width of my face, forehead, and nose, and, at the end of their visit, I was chosen as the model Aryan boy of the school. My mother, on hearing the news, baked a sachertorte for me. My papa gave me a folding knife with its handle made of antlers and promised to take me to meet Wilhelm Marr at the First International Anti-Semitic Congress in Dresden" (Tagebuch 1882).

The next several entries revealed his anticipatory excitement in meeting the "great Wilhelm Marr," but after hearing him speak at the conference, Werner lost interest in him.

"Marr is an old man," he wrote. "He is very pessimistic about the future of Germany. He thinks that the anti-Semitic movement in Germany will soon collapse, and Jews will take over German government and mongrelize German culture. I cried after listening to him but was cheered up when a young man, Theodor Fritsch, refuted him, point by point. Anti-Semitism is failing because there is no unity among the anti-Semites, he said. They break up into factions and form splinter parties that bicker and brawl among themselves. The only way to succeed against the Jews is to form a united front, and Fritsch is going to dedicate his life to that end" (Tagebuch 1882).

Fritsch became his new hero, and Werner started up a correspondence with him.

"It's impossible to accept Jews as human beings," Fritsch wrote to him. "Try as I might, I cannot find any human traits in them. Their mission, as far as I can tell, is to keep down the Aryan folk through usury and collusive financial practices. The looming question is, are we going to let them get away with this, or are we going to surgically remove them as one would remove a cancer from the human body?"

Fritsch also sent him some preliminary notes for his *Handbook on the Jewish Question.* A few days later, after studying the notes, Werner copied down in his diary the commandments regarding Aryan purity given by Fritsch:

1. Thou shalt keep thy blood pure.
2. Consider it a crime to sully the noble Aryan race by mixing it with the Jewish race.
3. Thou shalt avoid all contact with the Jew.
4. Thou shalt keep the Jew away from thy family, especially thy daughters, lest they suffer loss of purity. (Tagebuch 1883)

Werner had kissed Rosa Hilbert a few times and had touched her body, at her prompting.

"Never again," he wrote, "shall I pollute myself by contact with a Jewish girl. I made a mistake, and after thinking about it, I have concluded that it was a wrong action on my part."

He had lengthy discussions with his father, a court official at Kaiser Wilhelm's Berlin Palace and a tutor to one of the princes, on what it meant to be an Aryan. His father told him about Germania and its tribes, as described by Tacitus, and the Teutonic Knights of yore who had conquered and civilized vast territories in the Baltic area and Poland. Werner was greatly impressed, and several of his tagebuch entries dealt with biographies of the Teutonic Knights and their missions in Lithuania, Baltic Prussia, and Poland. One of his entries read, "Bismarck says he can Germanize Poland in three years. What is he waiting for?"

His father took him to a lecture given by the historian Heinrich von Treitschke, and Werner was mesmerized by Treitschke's call for a strong Germany—unhindered by Jewish machinations in politics—that would rule over Poland, the Baltic States, and parts of Russia. He was given a collected edition of Treitschke's works as a present by his father, and Werner wrote in his diary:

Treitschke made me proud to be a German. I shall forever remember his admonitions:

1. Beyond our eastern borders teem millions of Polish Jews who are smuggled into our country as peddlers

and tailors, and whose progeny, within the course of a generation, will subvert our system and our values by gaining control over newspapers and rigging our financial markets. Jews are treacherous speculators whose sole aim is to destroy the fabric of German life.

2. Say it with one voice: "The Jews are our misfortune!" (Tagebuch 1884).

Werner had grown close to his father, calling him his best friend and guide and praising him for providing an understanding of the Jewish question confronting an Aryan. Occasionally he wrote about his mother, but it was mostly in relation to the cakes and tarts that she made or to the frequent gifts of cash that she gave him. Of his sister Käthe, he said even less, other than to make pithy comments such as "very beautiful but fluffy-brained" or "I wish I had a brother whom I could teach things instead of a sister who spends too much time with her dolls."

A year later, he switched allegiance from his father to his science teacher, Herr Baldur Weber, who lectured his class on the scientific basis of racial superiority in the light of Darwin's theories of natural selection. Weber gave Werner a copy of Arthur de Gobineau's *Essai sur l'inégalité des races humaines*, which convinced him of the superiority of the Aryan over all other races. At the urging of Weber, Werner studied racial theories, especially works that advanced polygenesis—that is, the creation of races as different species, as opposed to monogenesis—and became a firm believer in racial hygiene. He read in the newspapers that many schools were including racial theory in their curriculum and became ecstatic about it.

"Now kids can learn the difference between the two major races in Germany, the Jew and the Aryan," he wrote. "One dark and swarthy, intent on accumulating wealth regardless of the damage done to others, and the other fair skinned, blue eyed, excelling in war, but also endowed with artistic and philosophical genius. I'm convinced that we were created as separate species, and every Aryan child should be made aware of it" (Tagebuch 1885).

Weber introduced him to Alfred Ploetz, a biologist, eugenicist, and an expert on *Rassenhygiene*, and Werner started an extensive correspondence with him on restoring the health of the German nation by euthanization of the malformed, the insane, and the racially impure and the sterilization of Jewish race polluters.

"I am proud of being an Aryan," he wrote. "With the help of my parents, I've constructed a family tree that goes up to four generations. There is no mixing with Jews, Slavs, or other inferior races in my lineage" (Tagebuch 1885).

Herr Weber was an ardent supporter of Otto Böckel, a charismatic, anti-Semitic politician who roused up crowds in beerhalls with fiery speeches and held rallies at night where his supporters marched carrying flaming torches.

"Herr Weber took me and four of my classmates to Hesse to hear Herr Böckel address the crowds," Werner wrote. "My friends and I had never seen anything like this before. Herr Böckel appeared on a white horse, young and handsome, a true leader, and the crowd roared when he promised to drive the Jewish rabble out of Germany. On our way back, my friends and I debated with Herr Weber whether Germany would have the good fortune to see a man of Herr Böckel's vision and charisma to be its leader" (Tagebuch 1885).

Hannah didn't want to read anymore Tagebuchs: she had had enough of Herr Weber and Herr Böckel, and all she wanted to do was to escape into the open air. I'll continue this work tomorrow, she thought, and wended her way up the spiraling staircase.

The gardener wanted to discuss the layout of the garden, and she had to spend more than an hour with him, even though she wasn't in the mood for it. After that she had to talk to an interior decorator, a shy, willowy young man sent by Lukas Hackmann, about hanging new drapes in the living room.

From the samples he showed her, she picked a light-blue linen.

"I would recommend the pale-orange silk," said the young man hesitantly, his eyes fixed on the floor.

Hannah was amused by his remark. "Why do you recommend that?" she asked him.

"It's feminine while the blue linen is masculine," he said. "I was picturing this room with white walls, a white table, and yellow roses or tulips in a white vase, and I was thinking the curtains would complement the colors."

I'm the woman, but he's the more feminine of the two, thought Hannah. Shall I tell him I like the blue linen because it reminds me of the sea seen from Santa Monica on a bright day? But seeing him as he stood there, forlorn and hapless, she didn't have the heart to contradict him.

"Go ahead with the pale-orange silk," she said. "I don't know if I want to live in this house anyway."

"It's such a beautiful house," he said.

"There are ghosts here, and I can't wait to get out of Nuremberg," she responded and walked toward the staircase, amused by the shocked expression on his face.

She had made plans to go to a movie with Eric that evening, and it was with a feeling of malaise that she drove to the theater. Where to live the rest of her life was the question that popped up in her mind, in spite of her efforts to tamp it down. The movie, *A Gentleman's Agreement*, which was about the subtle but pervasive anti-Semitism in the United States, didn't help to lift her mood as she sat next to Eric in the small, crowded theater.

"Why are they producing movies like this now?" she asked Eric as they were eating burgers and drinking beer at an American pub a block away from the theater. "Everyone was telling me that Hollywood was going to concentrate on the problems encountered by the returning servicemen."

"I heard one of the guys, a movie buff, say that the producer Daryl Zanuck was denied membership at the Los Angeles Club because they mistakenly thought he was a Jew, and that motivated him to make this film. Sam Goldwyn and other Hollywood big wheels tried to dissuade him, pleading with him that it would cause trouble, which it did. The HUAC called up some of the actors for questioning and put them in the Hollywood blacklist."

He speaks without rancor, she thought. He takes everything in stride.

"The Jews I worked with in California never complained about anti-Semitism," she said. "All the powerful people, the studio moguls, the art gallery owners—they were all Jewish. Does it matter if they weren't welcomed in country clubs? The real discrimination, I thought, was toward blacks."

"I agree, Hannah," he said. "After I'm done with my mission here, I will go back and do all I can to fight that."

"Why do people hate each other because of race? The Nazis used to say 'Das Raz ist alles.' There was only one race worth preserving, according to them. But that notion is so stupid. So many good things come from every race."

"I agree, Hannah. After nearly three years of studying mass slaughter based on race, I still don't know why race hatred exists. In my own country, they used to discriminate against the Irish, the Italians, and the Chinese, and before that, the American Indian, whom they decimated, and the Negroes, especially after the Civil War. And the Jews were always viewed with suspicion and contempt, even by writers who should have known better, men of the caliber of Hemingway, Fitzgerald, Pound, and Eliot. I had to study them in college, and I used to feel sick after reading some of their lines."

"If only the schools wouldn't teach these books," said Hannah.

"We can't ban all the classics from the New Testament downward, including Chaucer, Shakespeare, and Dickens. It's out of the question.

And it isn't necessary, in my opinion. People quickly learn to live like outsiders, like me, and make the best of the situation they're in."

Outsiders: that is what he and I are, she thought, and that's why we seek each other's company. He has succeeded in explaining why we—not only me and him but others I had loved, ranging from Kandinsky to Randy—are forever cast in the role of onlookers watching the eternal violence around us: the perpetually occurring image of SA men breaking shop windows and beating up Jews in Potsdamer Strasse rose in her mind—I watched them do it, unable to prevent it, and at that moment all that I had learned and believed about art seemed irrelevant, for art does not provide any weapon against brutality: Picasso's Guernica didn't help the Republicans win the Spanish Civil War.

She listened to Eric halfheartedly as he moved to other topics, pretending to take an interest in his dealings with the defense lawyers in the Einsatzgruppen trial.

"Don't you feel well, Hannah?" he asked, sensitive as ever to her moods. "Maybe we should call it a night."

She agreed and, dropping Eric on the way, drove home.

She slept fitfully, and in the early hours of the morning, climbing down the spiral staircase, went to her uncle's sanctum.

THIRTY

QUEST FOR THE FÜHRER

The next tagebuch showed a changed handwriting from the scrawl of a schoolboy to the traditional German masculine script, with its slants and flourishes. Werner had turned sixteen and joined the völkisch movement at the urging of Herr Weber. They had been to a völkisch camp in the countryside during summer, and Werner was enthralled by the experience.

"We wake up at sunrise," he wrote, "and pay obeisance to the Sun God, the source of energy and power. We bond with each other by taking blood oaths of allegiance. We swim, we take long walks, we cook healthy communal meals, and at night we light bonfires and sing old German songs.

"I learned that the Aryans come from the northern forests of India, and they flourish when they're close to Mother Nature. Their original gods, before Christianity became the religion of Germany, were the gods of thunder and rain, fire, wind, and water. Standing together in a circle, we yelled that Christianity was no longer our religion and that the gods and goddesses of Valhalla should replace the crucified Christian God of meekness, who was an invention of a Pharisee named Saul and his followers. In the morning, on waking up, I felt much refreshed, as though a rock had been lifted off my chest. 'I'm no longer a Christian, hear ye Teutonic gods!' I shouted" (Tagebuch 1886).

Werner had become very close with a boy of his own age, Alexander von Neurath, also from Berlin. They visited each other in their respective homes and were treated like family members. Alexander had a sister, Elisabeth, and Werner fell in love with her.

"She is my ideal of German womanhood," he wrote. "Even her name causes romantic vibrations in my heart because it reminds me of the heroine with the same name in *Tannhäuser*, Wagner's embodiment of sacred love. My fondest hope is that she will wait for me to finish college. What a doubly blessed event it would be if Alex marries Käthe at the same time I marry Elisabeth! Our pure Aryan strain will then continue for another generation." (Tagebuch 1888).

I hope love will cure him of his anti-Semitism and make him a new man, Hannah thought, as she meandered through pages describing Werner's longing for union with his adored one, a chiaroscuro of alternating hope and despair interspersed with excerpts from famous German love poems—*Du bist mein, ich bin dein* and *Ich denke dein, wenn mir der Sonne schimmer Vom Meere strahlt*—but the next tagebuch came as a disappointment to her.

Werner, in his first year at Berlin University, lost no time in joining an ultraconservative student bund, the *Verein Deutscher Studenten*. He went to a speech by the philosopher Eugen Dühring at one of the bund's seminars, and the old hateful notions raised their ugly heads again.

"Dühring is frail, and his eyesight is bad," he wrote. "He used to be a docent at the Berlin University but had clashed with the higher-ups and was dismissed. He is full of anger against his enemies, and it erupts out of him like a volcano. I like his ideas, though. He's against religion and characterizes the Jewish race as a 'parasitical' one that ravages the host society and ultimately destroys it. The only solution to the Jewish problem, he affirms, is *annihilation* rather than assimilation. A man after my own heart!" (Tagebuch 1890).

Like most of his fellow students, he took fencing lessons and got his dueling scars on the left side of his face. He learned to sing drinking songs and caroused with his friends, but one day, after waking up with a severe hangover, he made a resolution to stay away from drinking parties. He paid attention to his studies from then on and became active in participating in the discussion groups of the student bunds. He presented a paper to the student debating club on the disproportionately high number of Jewish students in Berlin University and its likely impact in the coming decades on German culture and society. The student newspaper printed excerpts from it, which were read by no less a personage than Heinrich von Treitschke, a professor of history at his university. Treitschke invited him to one of his soirees, and a bond was established between the two immediately.

"He's my idol," wrote Werner, after a lengthy conversation with the great man. "He doesn't have an easy life. He's losing his hearing, his wife suffers from mental illness, and he has physical ailments that cause him a lot of pain. Treitschke is a fighter, and anyone can see it's a victory of mind over matter. His beloved Germany comes before everything else, pushing aside his personal misfortunes. 'The state takes precedence over the individual,' he tells me, '*l'homme c'est rien, l'etat c'est tout.*' I had never thought of the state that way before, but his words converted me: I'm nothing; the Reich is all!" (Tagebuch 1890).

"Herr Treitschke tells me," wrote Werner, after another lengthy conversation with the sage, "that the notion of mankind living in peace for eternity is an illusion fostered by Christianity. A quick war of annihilation, a blitzkrieg, is more humane than a long-drawn-out state of domination and subjugation, which breeds discontent and social violence. We were talking about war with our enemies—France, England, and Russia—but we both knew it could be applied to the situation at home regarding Jews, our internal enemy. If he is right—he usually is, everyone says so—how do we plan an annihilation of this magnitude? My mind boggles at the immensity of such an enterprise."

"Treitschke cries when he talks about the German soul," he wrote in another entry, "the depth and vastness of human thought that came out of Germany, the transcendent philosophy that soars over the materialistic ratiocinations of a Voltaire or a Hume. 'Can you imagine a Europe without Germany?' he asks. 'In the natural order of things, Germany should rule over the entire middle Europe, from the River Rhone to the Black Sea, since she is the most powerful, the most organized, and the most developed among the nations of Europe. A bloody, quick war over the Slavic race is preferable to the alternative of elevating them to our level of civilization. The Slavs are a coarse, primitive people, incapable of law and order, and they will never be like us'" (Tagebuch 1891).

Treitschke suggested that Werner should work for a doctorate in history under his supervision.

"I was thrilled by his words," wrote Werner, "but I realized, after a period of reflection, that I didn't want to be a historian. Being a historian means delving into the past and poring over old manuscripts and documents, somewhat akin to what an archaeologist does when he digs a site with a view to unearthing shards of pottery or a few bricks belonging to an amphitheater. I don't want to go backward in time; I want to look forward. What I want to do is to study political philosophy and write a book that would become a manifesto for twentieth-century German politics. Can I do it? Am I being too ambitious? I don't know, but I'll give it a try" (Tagebuch 1894).

Treitschke encouraged him to follow his inclinations and recommended him to his colleague Max Lenz. Werner attended a series of lectures given by Professor Lenz on the evolution of German political thought from the days of enlightenment and liberalism as evinced in the writings of Goethe and Schiller and its subsequent rejection by thinkers like Paul de Lagarde and Julius Langbehn. After much deliberation, Werner decided to write his thesis on Paul de Lagarde.

"I feel Lagarde's speaking with my voice," he wrote. "He's a Berliner of my father's generation. His views are the result of keen-eyed observation and deep analysis. He proves the case for a conspiracy by what he calls the Alliance Israelite, the International Brotherhood of Jews, to dominate Germany and then the world. His solution is logical, even though it may appear brutal. 'No compromise is possible with these usurious vermin,' he writes. 'One doesn't negotiate with trichinae and bacilli, but one exterminates them quickly and thoroughly to avoid reinfestation.' Lagarde has no use for liberal democracy, which he says is advocated primarily by Jews so that they can work the system to benefit them. Lagarde wants a Führer—a man who is so beloved and admired by the Volk that he can bend them to his will—to lead the country, to make the country great again, and take over eastern European lands to give Germany lebensraum" (Tagebuch 1894).

The title of Werner's doctoral thesis was "The Führer as Germany's Savior: The Prophetic Vision of Paul de Lagarde," and it was published by a firm that specialized in conservative books. Treitschke wrote a blurb praising the "brilliant young author," as did Theodor Fritsch, with whom Werner was in regular correspondence.

The title was prophetic, thought Hannah, after she skimmed through the book, which was in Werner's library: at the end of the nineteenth century, my uncle was talking about the arrival of a Führer, the extermination of Jews, and the acquisition of lebensraum, all of which came to pass fifty years later.

She also read a few pages from the works of Lagarde and Langbehn, well-thumbed and marked-up copies owned by her uncle, and was struck by the pent-up anguish in their voices. They really cared for Germany, she thought. They were convinced Germany was dying and needed a cure. She, on the other hand, had felt, under the influence of Bauhaus, that patriotism was inherently evil since it inevitably led nations to war; in fact, even in her early years at Schwabing, where the talk in cafés was about matriarchal rule based on the doctrine of Mutterrecht, the Prussian vision for Germany, as presented by Lagarde and Langbehn, was considered an abomination. Maybe I'm not a German but a Schwabinger, she mused, as she put her uncle's books in place and went up the winding staircase to sit in her garden in the lingering twilight.

I'm not going to read my uncle's tagebuchs anymore, she thought, when she woke up the next morning. What do I care about the views of Lagarde, Langbehn, Treitschke, or Werner von Thyssen? But driven by some force she couldn't understand or resist—it's the fascination of evil, the mesmerizing eye of the snake, she thought—she went back to the hidden cellar with a mug of coffee in her hand.

The opening entry of the next tagebuch, however, surprised her.

"Treitschke has recommended me for a Lektor's position at the University of Munich, with possibilities for rapid promotion. He also suggested I should enter the married state like a good Prussian and start an Aryan family. I thanked him for his kindness and assured him I would follow his advice. I intend to propose to Elisabeth as soon as I'm given a position in Munich" (Tagebuch 1895).

The University of Munich offered him a lectureship, with a good salary and free housing, and he proposed marriage to Elisabeth. The tagebuchs for the next few months were full of details of his trips to and from Munich, sandwiched with preparations for their wedding. He was initially wary of the Müncheners because Treitschke had warned him, "They aren't like us Prussians; the Bavarians have no sense of discipline and no aptitude for intellectual effort." But Treitschke's friend, the professor who hired him, soon put him at his ease: Herr Walter Kerner, from Vienna, was a great admirer of Treitschke, Lagarde, and Langbehn, and he introduced Werner to other staff members with conservative views and helped him to settle down in his new environment. He and Elisabeth furnished their new home, which had a music room for her with a grand piano and a library for him. He wrote lyrically about the early-morning rays of the sun falling on her chestnut hair as she parted open the drapes in their bedroom or her walking like a wood nymph in their garden amid the trees and flowerbeds, while robins and sparrows flew around her keeping her company. The two young marrieds spent hours together in the parks and gardens of Munich, went to plays and operas, and joined the revelers during the Oktoberfest. Elisabeth soon became pregnant, and Werner, in his meticulous way, recorded changes in her weight, moods, and eating habits, especially her craving for chocolate-covered marzipan. They designated a room upstairs as the nursery and furnished it with stuffed animals and dolls. They ordered a cradle and a bassinet with three wheels and a hood after a lot of discussion as to whether a three- or four-wheeled carriage would be better for the baby.

His sister Käthe came to live with them during the Christmas season, as also Elisabeth's brother, Alexander, on vacation from his job as a mining engineer in South Africa.

"They are two very beautiful people," wrote Werner. "He is tall and broad shouldered, the personification of the Aryan man, and she—slender, with golden curls and large blue eyes that sparkle with vitality—is the Nordic maiden one finds in the fairy tales of Andersen and Grimm. They seem to be fond of each other, and it's my dearest wish that Alexander would ask my sister to be his wife during his stay here. Yesterday, as we two men sipped brandy and watched the two women playing "Licht und Liebe"—Elisabeth on the piano, and Käthe singing so beautifully—it dawned on me that domesticity could indeed be blissful" (Tagebuch 1896).

The expected proposal to Käthe did not take place. Alexander got a telegram from his employer in Johannesburg asking him to return forthwith to excavate a newly discovered chromite site, and he left in a hurry.

Three weeks later, Werner got a shock.

"Elisabeth told me that Käthe is pregnant with Alexander's child. My first thought was about my father, who is planning to present Käthe at the court of Kaiser Wilhelm. This news will upset him. The obvious thing to do is to make Alexander aware of the situation so that he can take an honorable course of action. I sent him a telegram asking him to come home immediately. And later, after learning from Elisabeth that Käthe and Alexander have been lovers for years, I reprimanded my sister for her moral laxity. It was the first time I had spoken harsh words to her. It hurt her pride, and she left my house. A day later I learned from Elisabeth that Käthe is working as a singer in a cabaret in Schwabing and living in a rented room nearby" (Tagebuch 1896).

A telegram from the South African mining company notified him that Alexander and a dozen others had been killed in a mining explosion. "We suspect sabotage, led by a native subversive group called the Black Hand," it stated. Werner, true to form, made inquiries about the Black Hand and learned from a colleague that it was led by a man with the Jewish name of Mandelbaum. The next several pages in his diary were filled with anti-Semitic outbursts.

His wife, distraught over her brother's death, suffered a miscarriage.

"On returning home from work," he wrote, "I saw her lying in her bed, covered with blood, unconscious. Congealed lumps of plasma and red stains were everywhere" (Tagebuch 1897).

She was in the hospital for several days, with severe abdominal pains and cramps and intermittent fever. Upon her return, she suffered from moodiness and lethargy.

"I'm besieged from all sides," he wrote. "My wife walks around like a wraith, ignoring me. My sister is not responding to my attempts to bring her back into the family fold. I've offered to send her to a home for unwed mothers in Switzerland, with the understanding that Elisabeth and I would go there and adopt the baby immediately after its birth. Käthe doesn't like the idea. She says she will bring up the baby on her own. My parents haven't been told, since all hell will break loose if I tell them that Käthe is a cabaret singer. Knowing the old man, he would disinherit Käthe, and that is not what I want" (Tagebuch 1897).

The paternal eruption did not take place because his father died of a heart attack after being discharged ignominiously from the court by the mercurial Kaiser Wilhelm II.

"First, Treitschke is gone—and now my father," Werner wrote. "These are two men who made me realize what it means to be an

Aryan, to be a Prussian. With heritage comes responsibility, and now I've to don the *toga virilis*, so to speak, and fight for what they had taught me. But before I do that, I've to take care of pressing family matters" (Tagebuch 1897).

For the next several months, he was busy taking care of his mother, wife, and sister. His mother soon died of a stroke, and his wife, sent to a sanatorium in Switzerland, returned home a semi-invalid. She became pregnant but miscarried again and died of hemorrhage. Werner was inconsolable, and Käthe came and lived with him for a while, bringing her baby (Hooray! That's me, thought Hannah) with her. Werner became quite attached to the baby, and after Käthe went back to her own home, he visited her frequently, often taking the baby out for an airing in the crowded streets of Schwabing.

He couldn't get over the death of his wife and spent his free nights in beerhalls seeking the company of Munich barmaids well known for their irresistible appeal to lonely men. He was not promiscuous by nature, yet he went home night after night with the buxom Helgas, Hildas, and Heddas—available, compliant, and eager to please.

"I don't even know their last names," he wrote. "I go home with them in a haze of alcohol and leave them, guilty and hungover, furtively leaving cash on a table. I'm not temperamentally suited for whoring, and I need a woman to love" (Tagebuch 1900).

He was invited to parties given by his fellow professors and met several unattached women but didn't find any of them interesting until a friend introduced him to a recently widowed Munich socialite named Gudrun Engelhardt. She was rich, her late husband, a banker from Nuremberg, having bequeathed to her his vast holdings in the entire Bavarian region. She was two years Werner's senior, and after a brief courtship, they got married.

"She doesn't invoke in me the romantic feelings that Elisabeth did," Werner wrote. "Gudrun is cold, almost frigid, in the sexual side of marriage, and I attribute this to her religious upbringing. But she's very considerate and tries her best to be loving and affectionate. There's a deep friendship between us, a mental closeness that I've never experienced with Elisabeth. On my first visit to Gudrun's house, I saw a bust of Treitschke on the mantelpiece in her living room and a copy of Houston Chamberlain's *Die Grundlagen des neunzehnten Jahrhunderts* on the coffee table. It immediately established an intellectual affinity between us, which quickly grew into an unbreakable bond. She dreams like I do about a glorious Germany, a Germany that would be a *Weltmacht,* free from the turmoil caused by parliamentary democracy advocated by the treacherous Jewish elements in our society" (Tagebuch 1902).

He moved into her palatial home in Munich after their marriage and quickly transformed himself into a society host. He met rich and powerful people having the same political views as Gudrun and himself, and this spurred him on to be more active in promoting his right-wing ideas. He joined a number of societies, of which the Pan-German League was the one that took up most of his time and energy. He quickly bonded with its chairman, Heinrich Class, another Treitschke student and adherent, and the two of them worked together to sign up several top military officers and business magnates as the league's members or supporters.

The next several tagebuchs were filled with accounts of his efforts to make the public aware of the need for what he called a "defensive war" against Germany's enemies—Russia, France, and Britain—who, according to him, were erecting roadblocks to Germany's growth and prosperity. He wrote articles in conservative newspapers, spoke at gatherings organized by the Pan-German League and others, and he converted hordes of students to his way of thinking by harping on the enemies faced by Germany from within and without. He was on friendly terms with many military men and cabinet members, not to mention philosophers and historians from all over Germany, and he pressed them to send petitions to the Reichstag to pass a resolution in favor of a defensive war, since the choice that Germany faced was between war or decline leading to collapse.

He was euphoric when war broke out in August 1914 and "Die Wacht am Rhein" was played on the streets of Munich all day. He immediately offered his services to the army, even though he was in his forties, and was assigned to the propaganda section, with the rank of a colonel.

"I'm on my way to Berlin," he had said to Hannah, after receiving the appointment. "I'm hoping they would send me to Paris so that I can take photographs of the fall of France. I will be back in six weeks and bring you French perfume and chocolates."

But none of his predictions came true. France didn't fall in six weeks, Belgium didn't capitulate as postulated in the Schlieffen Plan drawn up by Werner's friend General von Moltke who lost his job as a result. Werner was called back to Berlin to write subversive propaganda against the enemies—Russia, Britain, and France—and to reassure the German public that victory was in sight despite setbacks.

"I've a damnable job," he wrote. "I know that we are not winning, but I've to pretend that victory is imminent. The Schlieffen Plan has failed, and General von Moltke could not come up with a backup plan. The fact of the matter is that they underestimated the capabilities of the enemies. General Ludendorff is now claiming that he is going to launch an attack that's bound to devastate the enemy and bring the war to an end. I, for one, don't believe him. Seeing malnourished people everywhere, especially children deprived of milk, I'm tempted to play the whistleblower and bring the war to an end. What prevents me is the specter of socialists and Bolsheviks—need I say they are organized and masterminded by the Jews, who, according to my friends and colleagues, would be running the country at the end of the war? Already Vladimir Lenin has named Karl Liebknecht as his point man in Germany, and he is expected to set up Germany for a Marxist revolution. I've to do my best to see that this doesn't happen by turning out counterpropaganda to prevent our returning soldiers from going over to the Bolsheviks" (Tagebuch 1918).

Munich was indeed a hotbed of revolution and counterrevolution. Werner's old hero, Theodor Fritsch, was active in bringing unity among the anti-Semites and formed two new parties, the *Reichshammerbund* and the *Germanenorden*. Werner joined both and also worked with the Pan-German League to set up a special front to deal with the "Jewish menace." His anti-Semitic zeal undiminished, he signed up with a new organization called the Fatherland Party set up by Admiral Tirpitz and other conservatives to lay the blame for Germany's defeat in the war on the "stab in the back" by the left, which was now synonymous with Jewish subversion; and he wrote articles in conservative newspapers, prophesying the birth of a Third Reich and comparing Germany to the phoenix that rises from its ashes after each death. His friend and publisher, Julius Lehmann, asked him to write a book based on the articles, and Werner came up with his *Foundations for a Third Reich*, which brought him national fame.

Hannah found the book on one of the shelves and skimmed through its pages. It was written in lucid prose, avoiding the obscurantist style of Oswald Spengler's *Decline of the West*, which was also on the bestseller list at that time. The book was divided into six parts titled "Reich," "Führer," "Lebensraum," "War," "Racial Biology," and "Propaganda." It reads like a manifesto for the Nazis, thought Hannah, even though it had been written nearly fifteen years before the birth of the Nazi Party. It had won praise from many quarters, and there were laudatory letters from people all around the world, including the likes of Mussolini, Henry Ford, and the Prince of Wales. And the Thule Society, an ultranationalist secret society metamorphosed from Theodor Fritsch's Germanenorden, gave a special dinner in his honor in Munich, at the posh Four Seasons Hotel.

"I joined the Thule Society at the urging of the publisher Jules Lehmann," Werner wrote. "We had to do something to prevent the takeover of the Bavarian government by the Jews. Munich has changed drastically in the past few months, and the Jews are openly predicting a Bolshevik revolution. As Bavaria goes, so goes the rest of Germany! We are not going to allow Bavaria to be a cradle for socialist revolutionaries and are going to start a counterrevolution. We have white brigades made up of Freikorps, and the other side has red brigades made up of discontented workers spurred on by Jews. We will win this fight, but we have to get the workers and the demobbed soldiers on our side. At Munich University, my colleagues Karl Haushofer and Alexander von Müller are training selected veterans as secret counterintelligence agents to fight the impending danger facing Germany from socialists and Bolsheviks. My fellow Thule member, Gottfried Feder, is giving them a course on economics, stressing the evils of the capitalist economy and the international banking system, both controlled by Jews. All three pleaded with me, since I was a nationally recognized expert in that area, to give lectures to the counterintelligence agents on the Jewish menace, with its many disguises, facing native Germans, and I agreed to their request, even though I'm very busy right now.

"The war between the Aryan and the Jew is not over. As of now, we're locked in mortal combat. Germany needs a knight errant to slay the Jewish dragon, someone like Benito Mussolini, to stand tall and wear the mantle of leadership" (Tagebuch 1919).

Werner never changed his views throughout his life, Hannah thought. His basic themes were a Germany free of Jews (the code word for them being an "internal enemy"), a blitzkrieg against the external enemies—France, Russia, and possibly England—and the acquisition of lebensraum by the occupying of Poland and Ukraine: the three nerve centers of the political brain of the German conservative male.

THIRTY-ONE

ARRIVAL OF DER FÜHRER

"Munich is not the best place to search for a future leader. We've dozens of conservative parties—the four largest being the German National Conservative Party, the Fatherland Party, the *Stahlhelm*, and the Pan-German Association—but they don't agree on anything other than the need to make Germany *Judenfrei* by forced deportation or extermination of Jews and all mischlinge. In the dozens of beer hall meetings I've been to in the past few months, every speech ends with shouts of 'Death to the Jews.' There's no discussion at all about organizing ourselves as a Reich, a nation that would survive the threat of Bolshevism from within and invasion by our enemies from without" (Tagebuch 1920).

He was quick to pay attention to a new arrival on the political scene, a Dr. Otto Dickel, a charismatic orator with his own pan-Germanic and Völkisch party, and strong views on the political regeneration of Germany. Werner joined his party and gave a friendly review of Dickel's book *Resurgence of the West.*

"His views are very similar to mine and I'm thinking of throwing my support fully behind him. He is a very good speaker, he is an intellectual, and his love of Germany is so deep that I'm prepared stand before him and say, 'I choose you as my Führer'" (Tagebuch 1920).

But one evening, after having dinner with Dietrich Eckart, publisher of the arch conservative journal *Auf Gut Deutsch* and a fellow Thule member, Werner accepted Eckart's invitation to go to a beer hall to hear another "crowd-stirring orator" and accompanied him to the Hofbräuhaus, where some sixty people were assembled, with beer mugs in hand, presumably to hear the usual threats hurled at those who "stabbed us in the back" and diatribes against Jews.

"I knew who Eckart's protégé was as soon as I saw him," Werner wrote. "He was the best of the sixteen counterintelligence agents trained at Munich University by von Müller, Haushofer, Feder, and myself at the request of Captain Karl Mayr of the Bavarian Army. It was Mayr who had asked him to speak at beerhalls so that that he would get a chance to display his oratorical skills to the right-wing Müncheners who frequented such places and alert them to the link between the Bolsheviks and the Jews.

"Adolf Hitler is a lanky, awkward man, about thirty, in an ill-fitting suit, and needing a haircut, no different from the hundreds of returned soldiers wandering in the streets of Munich: down-at-the-heel war heroes—some with Iron Crosses—now turned into panhandlers or peddlers selling pencils and shoelaces. Nothing about him struck me as a leader. Quite the contrary. He spoke with a guttural Viennese accent and appeared ill at ease in addressing the boisterous, bawdy beer drinkers who are as likely to hit you with a beer stein as buy you a drink.

"I was ready to leave the beerhall when something happened that pulled me down to my seat. Hitler's voice, until then a monotone, went up several decibels as he spoke about the shame, the humiliation he had experienced as a soldier in the frontline upon hearing that Germany had lost the war and the estrangement he felt when he returned to Munich after demobilization, finding the city an alien place, run over by Jews who made no pretense of hiding their allegiance to the Bolsheviks. He spoke of the pitiful plight of Germany, its downfall from a mighty Reich to a destitute nation saddled with debt and taken over by usurers and black marketeers. 'Who is to blame for all of this?'

he screamed. 'Who should hang?' His whole body changed at that instant, his eyes blazed, his voice rose and fell like the waves of the sea, and the audience—including a couple of misty-eyed barmaids—became one with him, crying with him, laughing with him, raging with him against the Jews, our eternal enemy, until they became exhausted, as though they had run a marathon with him.

"'What do you think of him?' Eckart asked me.

"'He's a rough diamond and needs polishing, before he can shine. He's an empty man, a discharged corporal, with very little schooling, incapable of rational thinking or strategy formulation.'

"'Hitler is an intuitive person. He's not an intellectual but a man of action,' Eckart replied, after some deliberation. 'What impresses me is that he's a man with a mission, unlike the other beerhall orators. He's convinced he's the only man who can save Germany.'

"I laughed. 'Don't get carried away,' I said. 'This man has no leadership qualities.'

"'You underestimate him. Near the end of the war, he was blinded by mustard gas for several days. All around him in the hospital, he heard talk of our imminent defeat from fellow soldiers. This made him so angry that he would curse their cowardice and lack of patriotism. The psychiatrist who worked in that ward, a Dr. Foster, heard one of his rants and went over to him. He diagnosed his case as hysterical blindness and cured him by hypnotizing him into believing that the fatherland needed him to fight its enemies, both external and internal. After a few sessions, Hitler regained his sight and along with it, a sense of mission to save Germany from enemies and traitors and restore it to greatness.'

"'You believe this nonsense?'

"'It isn't nonsense. Dr. Foster is a pioneer in hypnosis therapy. According to my medical friends, he implants seeds of motivation in the minds of patients to enable them to overcome their disabilities. If a patient is afraid to go back to the front, he would cure him by convincing him that he had to prove to his comrades he isn't a coward and regain his self-esteem. In Hitler's case, he was eager to get back to the front, and the doctor urged him to regain his sight so that he could do great things for the fatherland. I really believe that Dr. Foster created the Hitler we see now.'

"Seeing the expression of skepticism on my face, Eckart paused for a few seconds before continuing, 'I'm going to work with Hitler because, out of the dozens of rabble-rousers and demagogues who can be found in our beerhalls, he's the one most likely to succeed. He has faith in himself, which is what a true leader needs. We intellectuals who write books can never accomplish change without a determined personality like Hitler'" (Tagebuch 1920).

"Eckart was true to his word. He changed Hitler's appearance from that of a shabbily dressed agitator to that of a political leader with national aspirations. He took him to his tailor and bought him a couple of well-fitting suits and then to his dentist to fix Hitler's bad teeth. He spent hours correcting his grammar and improving his prose style. He polished his table manners and took him to parties given by the social set of Munich. And he sent him to a mentalist, Erik Jan Hanussen, who gave Hitler lessons in elocution and crowd-control techniques using mass-hypnosis techniques known only to a few.

"More importantly, Eckart gave Hitler an understanding of the machinations of International Jewry in keeping down the German Volk, especially in the rural areas, through usury and collusive action. Eckart's pamphlet *A Dialog between Adolf Hitler and Myself on Bolshevism from Moses to Marx* shows how he convinced Hitler that Bolshevism was not about a class struggle as represented by Karl Marx but the culmination of a diabolical plot by Jews to gain control over nations by planting the seeds of their internal destruction.

"Alfred Rosenberg—an émigré from the Baltic region, a self-styled philosopher, and a Thule member—reinforced what Eckart had taught Hitler by giving him a tutorial on the *Protocols of the Elders of Zion*, which Rosenberg had recently translated from Russian to German. The Protocols document the minutes of a meeting of Jewish leaders gathered to formulate a plan for the subversion and domination of the nations of the world by manipulating the global economy and controlling the news media. Rosenberg, a genuine believer in the authenticity of the Protocols, pointed out to Hitler that the Jewish plan was already working: Germany was now a *Judenrepublik* for all practical purposes, Russia and Hungary were under the control of Bolshevists, and America's Jewish bankers were reducing Germany to dire economic straits with their monetary policies. At a signal from the Jewish leaders of the Weimar Republic, the Russians would gobble up Poland and then invade Germany, fulfilling the prophecy of the Protocols. The only way to prevent this from happening is to cripple the power of Jews in Germany, build up its military strength, and invade Poland and Russia before they strike us. From a world-historical perspective, another war was inevitable, and even though it would be fought between nations, the real war would be between the races—the Aryan and the Jew.

"The need to invade Poland, and then Russia, was also stressed by Karl Haushofer and his erstwhile student and admirer Rudolf Hess in their meetings with Hitler. Boundaries seen on the map were meaningless, they said, because they do not represent the physical requirements of nations or their ethnic makeup. Hence, there was a geopolitical justification for Germany to annex those countries whose resources were vital for her survival or whose populations contained a significant proportion of ethnic Germans" (Tagebuch 1922).

Dietrich Eckart died of a heart attack a year later, and Werner went to his funeral at Berchtesgaden to give an oration.

"Each time I sit in the lounge of the Thule, I miss Eckart's presence," he wrote in his tagebuch. "His urbane, sophisticated style and his witty conversation set him apart from the other members. I knew of his drug addiction—we all have our foibles—and I can't help thinking how much he would have achieved if he had taken the cure offered by Swiss doctors. I miss crossing swords with him, intellectually speaking, and I still have scars left similar to the dueling marks on my face.

"Eckart created Hitler, with some help from other Munich intellectuals, and Eckart was the only one who could control Hitler. I remember him saying once to me, 'Hitler is malleable and will do what we tell him to do. He will be the puppet, and we will be the ventriloquists. We will remake the Third Reich in accordance with our vision and our plan.'

"Now that he's gone, Hitler has become a law unto himself. The conviction that he is the only one who can lead Germany out of its present deplorable state has grown to enormous proportions inside his psyche. Oratory is his one unmatched gift, and he has used it effectively, supplementing it with the pageantry that Germans love—the parades, the rallies, the songs, and above all the lengthy, winding, emotionally exhausting speeches, at the end of which Rudolf Hess would say, 'Hitler is Germany, Germany is Hitler, Hitler is our Führer.' All this adulation has gone to Hitler's head, and he refers to himself in the third person as Der Führer.

"The others I talk to, von Müller, Karl Haushofer and Alfred Rosenberg, have tacitly accepted Hitler as the Führer. Haushofer is not an original thinker, even though he pretends to be. He is prolix with words, and after listening to him, one is left with a feeling of being lost in the words and missing the point he's making. Rosenberg is worse. He is writing a book with the title *The Myth of the Twentieth Century* and says it will be the sequel to Chamberlain's *Foundations of the Nineteenth Century*. It's like a cat comparing itself to a lion—at least that's my feeling after reading the first few chapters he showed me. Rosenberg states as a fact that Aryans came from the mythical Atlantis, and I nearly threw the book out my library window when I read that sentence.

"Hitler thinks that Haushofer and Rosenberg are geniuses—he prefers their loose talk to my rigorous analysis. I sometimes feel I shouldn't have joined his party and should have allied myself with Otto Dickel's conservative movement. It was under pressure from my fellow professors at Munich University, and also some Thule members, especially Eckart, that I joined Hitler's *Nationalsozialistische*

Deutsche Arbeiterpartei, commonly known as the Nazi Party. 'Hitler wants you to join the party because Mussolini has said you're the foremost fascist philosopher in Europe,' Eckert told me. I've cast my die, and I've to take what comes. The only ones that I feel comfortable among the Nazis are Rudolf Hess and some of the younger intellectuals of the party—Philipp Bouhler, Hans Frank, and Gregor Strasser—whom I try to cultivate whenever I visit the party headquarters in Schellingstrasse. The ones that scare me are thugs like Julius Streicher and Heinrich Himmler—two favorites of Hitler, two unattractive, uncouth, unpleasant men who feed his ego.

"Munich is a scene of strife and turmoil, with power shifting from the right to the left and from the left to the right. Every party has its own gang of street fighters, and brawls are an everyday occurrence. Hitler has his own bunch of storm troopers (called the SA), and he's in constant trouble with the police. Criminal cases have been filed against him by his political opponents for inciting physical assault against them. It doesn't seem to faze him. Egged on by his advisors, he led a march, reminiscent of Mussolini's March to Rome, to seize power from the Bavarian government of Prime Minister Kahr. The newspapers called it the Beerhall Putsch. Hitler was arrested, put on trial, and sent to prison in Landsberg, a hundred miles away from Munich. The trial brought him a lot of publicity, and he became a national figure. Can he lead? Should he be the leader of Germany? These questions worry me, and I feel depressed about Germany's political future" (Tagebuch 1923).

Urged by his fellow intellectuals, Werner worked assiduously to persuade the various conservative parties to cast their lot with Hitler. He won over the bastions of the Prussian right wing—General Ludendorff, Admiral von Tirpitz, Theodor Fritsch—and also made new converts such as Alfred Hugenberg, one of the richest businessmen in Germany, and leader of the *Deutschnationale Volkspartei,* known by its acronym, DNVP, which had grown to be the largest far-right party in Germany. And, at the *Herrenklub,* of which he was a member, he convinced the elite that Hitler was the only leader who had the energy and the passion to achieve the vision of Führerprinzip, which is at the core of the German conservative credo. He gave lectures to the German Student Union comparing Hitler to Frederick the Great and Bismarck, the founders and builders of the earlier Reichs, and told them that Hitler was the only leader who could elevate their downtrodden country into a mighty Judenfrei Third Reich that would dominate Europe. He was greeted with rounds of applause, and his picture appeared in the front page of the student union's newspaper.

One of Werner's students, Kerstin Krämer, "a red rose from Saxony," as he called her, fell in love with him, and they exchanged wonderful, passionate love letters. They were the best part of his writing, thought Hannah, full of warmth, love, and passion.

"Within months after Hitler became chancellor, Germany underwent a transformation," wrote Werner. "Every German of Aryan descent now wants to be a Nazi and willingly performs the *Hitlergruß*, the raised-arm salute. Every lawn, including mine, displays a 'Jews not welcome' sign, and every household, including mine, has a framed photo of the Führer in its living room.

"At my university, the students no longer respect the professors and behave in the worst way possible. They mercilessly torment Jewish professors and students. The German Student Union organized a huge book-burning party to protest against the criticism leveled at Hitler by the news media in Britain and America. They asked a librarian, Wolfgang Hermann, to make a list of 'un-German' books that should be burned, and he came up with a list that included some of my favorite novelists, such as Heinrich Mann, D. H. Lawrence, H. G. Wells, and Fyodor Dostoevsky. As a student was burning these books, I asked him whether he had read any of these novelists, and his answer was, 'No, and I don't want to read them.' It was with great sorrow that I parted with a large part of my library to the arsonists who came to my home to collect the 'blacklisted' books.

"Now I am told by the German Student Union that I should skip Goethe, Schiller, and if possible, the entire enlightenment period of

Germany while teaching political history and lay stress on the Teutonic Knights, Frederick the Great, and other heroes approved by the Nazi Party. This initiative, as in the case of the book burning, came from a group of third-year students, rabid Nazis, all of them.

"What's my county coming to? Acting on their own, bands of SA thugs, most of them recruited recently from the pool of young unemployed laborers, beat up shopkeepers and rob them, not only in Munich, but all over the country. '*Deutschland, Erwache!*' they chant as they swagger by the university gate, doing the goose-step. People are acting on their own, making rules of their own. Many professions—medicine, law, and teaching—are expelling Jews from their accredited societies. A colleague tells me that in some states Jews are forbidden to use public facilities, and Yiddish is not allowed to be spoken in public places. Some of the gauleiters have been pleading with Hitler to take measures to stop actions by individuals and pass national legislation against Jews. What form will that take? Above all, what will the answer to the eternal Judenfrage look like? Hitler has passed laws to boycott Jewish businesses, and Joseph Goebbels has organized a national boycott of Jewish shops and department stores, with chanting SA men holding placards preventing customers from entering the stores. The Jews are scared; one can see it in their faces. 'We are Germans,' they say. 'We've been here for generations.' The Gestapo, has been already established by Hitler, and they've imprisoned Jews from Poland and Russia who have entered here without immigration papers. Arrests, boycotts—will these lead to chaos? I want answers, and so far I haven't gotten them" (Tagebuch 1933).

"Is this the Third Reich I wrote about? Is Hitler the Führer conceived by Lagarde, Treitschke, or myself, for that matter? Is this the Führer that the great German visionaries hoped for? Hitler is out for himself, even though he talks a good game. He'll kill his best friend if that will advance his career. The question arises, if I don't like him, why am I supporting him? The answer is that the other conservative leaders do not have his charisma or popular support. The sad truth is if it were not for Hitler, we would have Jewish politicians deciding the fate of our fatherland, and my stomach turns at the thought of a Marxist Germany headed by a Mandelbaum or a Shapiro.

"I expressed my concerns to my friends Hans Frank, an eminent jurist, Hans Lammers, head of the Reich Chancellery, and Alfred Rosenberg after a party meeting. I was dismayed by the idolatry they displayed toward Hitler: he was like a god in their eyes. They told me over and over Hitler was going to transform Germany from its current feeble state into a Third Reich, as envisioned by me in my book—make it into a mighty superpower that would be the envy and the terror of the world. And, within a few years, they assured me, Germany will be Judenfrei. Everything we had dreamed of now seemed achievable— the Pan-German unity envisioned by Heinrich Class, the conquest of Poland, and perhaps Russia, to achieve the lebensraum hoped for by so many of our political philosophers, and the racial purity that is the ideal of the völkisch movement.

"Hitler is now the Führer, whether I like it or not. He's more like an actor playing a role than a genuine political leader who is concerned with the interests of the German Volk. Perhaps I should say he's like a robot programmed by Dr. Foster or Erik Jan Hanussen, ready to go on its predetermined mission of achieving total control, regardless of con-sequences. He still thinks in simple terms and believes that complex issues can be resolved by breaking them down into elementary con-cepts, which probably explains his success with the crowds. But can we afford to have a statesman whose mental equipment is limited to a few catchphrases pertaining to the superiority of the Nordic race, the con-spiracy of the Jews to subjugate them, and the Darwinian inevitability of the survival of the fittest? Hitler is shrewd and an expert at manipu-lating situations so that he comes out a winner. But animal cunning is no substitute for long-range planning and solidifying incremental gains. I fear for my beloved Germany, in spite of all the drumbeating and triumphal marches that I see every day" (Tagebuch 1934).

I like him when he talks this way, Hannah thought. Unfortunately, there's another side to him when he turns from Dr. Jekyll to Mr. Hyde.

Werner was in Nuremberg when the racial laws were passed by the Third Reich, and he was telling his friends that the new laws were too lenient toward the Jews. If he had his way, he would abort any fetus born out of racial misalliance and would sterilize the perpetrators of such offenses. He would not let Jews attend schools and colleges, nor would he allow them to live next door to Aryans in apartment houses. His colleagues were in complete agreement with his sentiments and celebrated their camaraderie by drowning themselves in Nuremberg beer served in the rock-hewn taverns underneath the streets.

After the annexation of Austria and the wrenching away of Sudetenland from Czechoslovakia, Werner's mood was buoyant, and he was full of praise for Hitler.

"Our Führer is a genius," he wrote. "He not only made Germany into a Reich but convinced Britain and France that it wasn't in their interests to counter his Pan-German policy. Now, if we can somehow gain territory from Poland and Ukraine, our lebensraum problem will be solved. From what Lammers and Rosenberg tell me, the Führer, who is only forty-six, is afraid he would die early and wants to establish a Judenfrei Third Reich incorporating the western parts of Poland and some areas of Ukraine as soon as possible."

Werner was soon caught up in the war frenzy that culminated in the invasion of Poland. The blitzkrieg worked perfectly, and Poland, devastated by the bombings of the Luftwaffe and the incessant pounding by the German artillery, surrendered in eighteen days. Werner and his wife celebrated the event by throwing a party for five hundred guests in Munich.

THIRTY-TWO

A FAUSTIAN BARGAIN

T he Fuehrer had made Alfred Rosenberg head of the cultural and educational affairs of the Third Reich, and Werner received an invitation to dine with him at the Four Seasons in Berlin.

"To ingratiate myself with Rosenberg who is in charge of funding academic institutions, I had written a good review of his *Myth of the Twentieth Century* in a philosophical journal. Rosenberg had been putting pressure on me and my friend Alfred Baeumler to do this for a while, and despite our serious reservations about the quality of the book, both of us gave in. What does it say about us, the finest of German minds? Anyway, Rosenberg was very pleased with my review and was thanking me profusely, almost to the point of embarrassment, before offering a quid pro quo.

"'The Führer thinks the Italians have done a better job of making fascism an integral part of their higher educational system than we in Germany have been able to do,' he began. 'He has asked me to give guidance to our universities to mold the minds of young Germans so that they think like Aryans, without any of the moral hang-ups induced by Christianity. I want you to take the leadership in that area since you're the foremost philosopher in the Third Reich. The Führer is appreciative of the fact that you joined the party when it started, unlike some of the other intellectuals who had waited until we were in power to join our movement.'

"I knew exactly what Rosenberg—or the Führer—was asking me to do: make our universities into brainwashing centers, give no room for honest, intellectual debate that is an essential ingredient for development of young minds, and weed out those who do not conform; the academy should create automatons who would obey Hitler and no one else.

"There was an implicit threat behind Rosenberg's offer, the threat of banishment from the academy, vilification, imprisonment for Hannah, to name the obvious ones. Coward that I am, I agreed to what he was saying and expressed gratitude for choosing me to be the caretaker of young Nazi minds. I made a Faustian bargain" (Tagebuch 1934).

Werner talked to his fellow professors at Munich University, Alexander von Müller and Karl Haushofer, on the need to revise the curriculum to make the students aware of the moral and political concepts at work in what Rosenberg called the New Germany.

"We've to be careful, because there will be auditors from the Nazi Party in the class," Werner told them. "Make sure a Hitler photo hangs right on the wall behind you, and begin and end the class with a 'Heil Hitler.'"

The three discussed the courses to be offered by the university and, after some debate, agreed on a syllabus. The first-year students would be taught that the precepts given in the Bible, including the Ten Commandments, are non-Aryan, and the Bible had been written by Jews to corrupt the innate warlike mentality of the Aryan. They should then be given an introduction to ancient German history using texts like Tacitus's *Germania* and Treitschke's essay on the Teutonic Knights' conquest of east Europe, and this should be followed by a history of the völkisch and Wandervogel movements.

The concept of Führerprinzip should then be introduced as an integral part of German political thinking of the past and reformulated as the political tenet of the future, not only for Germany but for all nations of Europe, using selections from the works on fascism by Giovanni Gentile, Filippo Marinetti, and other European philosophers. The second year should cover a variety of reading material, including the works of Houston Chamberlain, Eugen Dühring, Wagner, Fritsch, Lagarde, and Langbehn. The next two years would be spent in deep analysis of the pressing questions—Judenfrage, lebensraum, racial hygiene and eugenics—and readings of Nietzsche and modern Nazi philosophers such as Werner von Thyssen, Karl Haushofer, and Alfred Baeumler. Special lectures should be given on themes such as "The Jew as the Enemy," "The Führer as the Savior of the Aryan people," and "The need for unquestioned obedience to the orders of the Führer," using the Führer's *Mein Kampf* and Alfred Rosenberg's *The Myth of the Twentieth Century* as supplementary reading.

The three men, in agreement so far, got into a heated argument over what to do with Jewish names in the bibliographies of doctoral theses done under their supervision. Haushofer was for omitting such names from the bibliography, but Werner and von Müller did not like the idea because it ran contrary to the academic traditions of the university.

"Solving the Judenfrage isn't easy," said von Müller. "What do we do with these people? They're everywhere, and their roots run deep in the academia."

"We will list the Jewish names in a separate bibliography," suggested Werner, and the other two agreed.

The indefatigable Rosenberg called again, asking Werner to meet him in a safe house in Berlin.

"Goebbels and Himmler are setting up thinktanks to enable them to provide the best advice to meet the goals set by the Führer.

The people they picked to head the thinktanks aren't first rate minds. To give you an instance, Himmler has picked Konrad Meyer, a professor of agriculture, to head the institute for Germany's space expansion vis a vis the lebensraum. What I want you to do is to come up with a list of thinktanks that will be funded by me, and the staffing of the same by the best minds in Germany."

Werner and his colleagues then proceeded to contact philosophers, historians, and scholars on the creation of new think tanks suggested by Rosenberg, and after some discussions, agreed to establish new institutes on racial science, Nazi law, Nazi political theory, history of the New Germany, lebensraum, and the Jewish question, staffed by their old students with ideological beliefs and credentials similar to theirs.

Hannah, out of curiosity, went through the folders containing newspaper articles and press releases issued by the eminent men with whom Werner and his colleagues had corresponded. All of them—Martin Heidegger, Alfred Baeumler, Carl Schmidt, and Hans Naumann—seemed to be of one mind with Hitler, as though they were his psychological clones. Some of them sported the Hitler moustache, wearing it like a badge to show their racist and anti-Semitic credentials. Others, like Ernest Krieck, a vehement denouncer of Einstein and his "Jewish physics," joined the SS or the SA to prove that they would fight for the Nazi cause.

From what Hannah was able to gather, none of the newly founded institutes were doing original research; instead, they reworked old themes, slanting them toward the views found in Hitler's *Mein Kampf* or Rosenberg's *Myth of the Twentieth Century*.

The Institute of Racial Science published articles that applied Darwin's theory of natural selection to the racial struggle between Aryans and Jews, concluding that the latter were doomed for extinction since they were the inferior race—an assertion that was made without any scientific basis and contrary to empirical evidence. The lebensraum scholars posited that the whole of Central Europe belonged to the Aryan race, and the current non-Aryan inhabitants of countries surrounding Germany should be conquered, enslaved, and deprived of the choicest part of their lands to make way for the expansion of Germanic people. And the Judenfrage scholars argued that extirpation, and even extinction, of the Jews were justifiable actions. The path from *Auslese* (racial selection) to *Ausmerze* (racial extinction) was repeated ad nauseam by these savants, who presented their work in attractive pamphlets, often with a plea to Werner to include them in Munich University's curriculum.

His higher-up friends—Hans Frank, Alfred Rosenberg, Hans Lammers, and others—asked him to evaluate the various plans for the conquered eastern territories that were being proposed to them by think tanks that had sprung up all over Germany and to make recommendations. Some of the best philosophers in the Reich had turned out treatises giving legal, moral, or existential justification of the wisdom of the Führer in invading Poland and offering visions for the new German Reich based on master-race theories. Hannah was surprised by the echoing and reechoing of views held by Hitler in the articles that had been sent to Werner: the savants, without exception, said that Poles were of inferior intelligence and should be trained to work as laborers under German landholders in the newly conquered territories, and the Jews were a bacterial infestation that should be isolated immediately and removed from the German body politic by excision (i.e., deportation) or cauterization (i.e., annihilation).

"What am I to make of all these proposals?" wrote Werner, in a Dr. Jekyll moment. "I feel as helpless as a man without oars in a boat that is being carried by a river into an abyss. Every one of my friends now wants to be more of a Nazi than Hitler—my beloved student Walter Frank, head of the institute for New Germany, wants to kill off all Jews in Europe, and so do my brilliant fellow philosophers Peter Seraphim and Theodor Schieder, jettisoning their objectivity for the sake of conformity. To be fair, they have to prove their Nazi credentials to hold on to their professorships, just like in my case. Besides, how do I know what they really feel? We're afraid to speak our minds, even to close friends."

But soon Mr. Hyde took over. Two of Werner's ex-students—Max Huncke and Kurt Brockelmann, both with doctorates in philosophy—worked as planners for the SD and the SS. In spite of his dislike for their bosses Heydrich and Himmler, Werner was very close to Max and Kurt, and they frequently were guests at his house parties.

"I never thought the Führerprinzip implied the control of power by the secret police," wrote Werner. "But from what Max and Kurt are telling me, both national and international policies regarding aliens and Jews are going to be made and implemented by Himmler and Heydrich—I should say Heydrich and Himmler—since the former is the stronger personality of the two and wants to be the next Führer. Hitler gives orders directly to Heydrich, bypassing Himmler. Heydrich is now in charge of killing 'enemies of the state,' the code word for Jews, and he is training the Einsatzgruppen—well-educated and personable men, some of them my best students—to do the job quietly and efficiently.

"Himmler, in the meantime, is toying with the idea of depopulating Europe by the annihilation of millions of Jews and Slavs and re-populating it with ethnic Germans who would be resettled in the best agricultural zones of Europe to take up life as Aryan farmers, in line with his basic völkisch principles.

"Max and Kurt asked me to make peace with Himmler and Heydrich. They pressured me to prepare our undergraduates for killing enemies of the state, which includes women and children, without compunction. 'We don't want moral scruples in our young men,' they said. 'Rosenberg is namby-pamby in his thinking. You should cooperate with us, instead of him.'

"I said I would do what they wanted, not being sure which way the wind was blowing. I wanted to know what the Führer was thinking, and set up a lunch meeting with Reich Chancellor Hans Lammers at the

Horcher restaurant in Berlin. The Führer, he said, wants the newly acquired Polish districts of East Prussia and Wartheland to be German in appearance and culture within four to five years. He hasn't chosen Heydrich and Himmler over Rosenberg. The Führer gives orders on the spur of the moment and modifies them if one of his underlings complains to him. He tells Arthur Greiser, who is the new governor of Wartheland, that he has a free hand to do what he wants in cleaning up and Aryanizing his territory. Then Goering goes to him with a plea to spare the highly skilled Jewish artisans who are indispensable for production of armaments. The Führer agrees to that too. Next Himmler comes along with a request to be given authority to resolve the Jewish question in all areas under Germany's control and also to move millions of ethnic Germans from the conquered territories into Wartheland, and Hitler gives him the green light. Rosenberg then approaches him with administrative plans for an extended Reich including vast areas of eastern Europe, and the Führer tells him he's on the right track.

"Lammers is an intelligent man and very shrewd. Of course, he would say nothing against Hitler, but it isn't difficult to read in between the lines. Hitler agrees when a favorite comes up with some scheme, most of them off-the-cuff proposals rather than well-thought-out plans. When two underlings come into conflict, both parties go to Hitler, who acts as the mediator. This is how the Third Reich is being run, not as a modern state but as a fiefdom with stewards competing against each other and treading on each other's toes. Lammers was also hinting that to be on the safe side of the Führer, one has to continually praise him, like Himmler and Rosenberg do." (Tagebuch 1940).

Anxious to be on the safe side of the Führer, Werner decided to compile a collection of essays in book form with the title *Hitler's Weltanschauung*, to be presented to the Führer on the occasion of the victory celebration at the end of the Second World War, which

Werner hoped would be achieved within a year. Twenty eminent men were chosen to write chapters in the book, and Alfred Baeumler was the editor. Special arrangements were made with printers regarding the quality of the leather binding, the typography, and the embossing of the swastika with fourteen-carat gold. Werner had been assigned to write the last chapter, named "Der Führer als Nietzsche's Übermensch."

Hannah went through the manuscript of that chapter and was surprised to find that Nietzsche, in his later years, held views identical to those of the Nazis.

"Men have no God-given right for life, liberty, or happiness, according to Nietzsche," Werner had written. "And a weaker race will always be subjugated by a race of superior men who have the necessary strength, will, and desire to conquer them. Nietzsche prophesizes the coming of an elite who would rule the world and become the 'Lords of the Earth.' These strong men, the masters, are monsters filled with joy when they return from a fearful succession of murder, arson, rape, and torture, with the same contentment in their souls as if they had indulged in some students' romp...when a man is capable of commanding, when he is by nature a master, when he is violent in act and gesture, of what importance are laws and treaties to him? To judge morality properly, it must be placed against two concepts borrowed from zoology: the law of the jungle and the emergence of the strongest as the leader of the pack.

"Nietzsche wrote from a crisis of frustration generated by the mediocrity he saw around him. He despised the Germans, and toward the end, the great philosopher wrote about a superman who would rule Germany and lead the herd. Maybe he had the gift of prophecy and portrayed the future, which is our present, and we will acclaim with one voice, 'Our Führer is Nietzsche's superman.'"

Werner was rewarded lavishly by the Reich. His money was managed by the Nazi bankers of Munich, on the recommendation of Rosenberg, and after the absorption of assets of Jewish banks by

German financial institutions, he, along with some of his associates, became very wealthy. He was also given a gold Nazi badge, the *Goldenes Parteiabzeichen,* and a letter of commendation for being "our foremost advocate of the Führer state."

Thirty-Three

The New Teutonic Knights

Rosenberg asked Werner to meet him at one of their safe houses in Munich to discuss "certain secret matters."

"'Werner, the Führer is likely to appoint me as head of our eastern territories,' Rosenberg said. 'Nothing is official yet, but I would like a first-hand account of what's going on there. Poland has been divided into three zones, two of which, East Prussia and Wartheland, both on the western part of Poland, are to be repopulated by ethnic Germans brought over from Germany and various conquered parts of Europe. The third zone, called the General Government, with Hans Frank as its governor, is to be the dumping ground for Poles, Gypsies, and other inferior races. The ultimate fate of the Polish and German Jews is yet to be decided, but they will initially be transported to the General Government from other parts of the Reich; after Germany had won the war, they will be sent to Madagascar, or some other inhospitable territory as yet unspecified, to fend for themselves.'

"Rosenberg then asked me to go on a fact-finding trip to Poland and to convey my impressions in the form of an unofficial report. A plane and a secretary were put at my disposal. I have a fear of flying and tried hard to conceal it from the secretary, a middle-aged, prim-faced super-Nazi, whom I suspect of being an informer for Himmler.

"My first stop was at Krakow, to visit my friend Hans Frank, who now lives in a palace. Opulence is the word to describe his life, for I've never seen such an abundance of beautiful glass and silver utensils, tapestries, and carved antique furniture, all confiscated from wealthy Jews. His wife, Brigitte, rides in an open Mercedes and buys watches, jewelry, and fur coats at cheap prices from Jews in the Warsaw ghetto who are starving for food and are willing to barter personal belongings they had hidden from the guards. She showed me her collection of rings, bracelets, necklaces, and Breguet and Longines timepieces. I quickly learned that the couple hate each other and are staying together because the Führer wouldn't allow them to divorce.

"Frank is a mercurial personality, alternately warm and cold. One evening, after dinner, when we were drinking old cognac from cut-glass stemware, he opened up to me. He hates his wife—he wants to get rid of her, would pay for someone to kill her. Goebbels and his henchmen covet his powers and are spreading rumors about him that have reached the Führer's ears. Bormann and Himmler are plotting to replace him with the hardliner Arthur Greiser. And he doesn't know what he should do about the Jews who are being dumped daily into his territory by Himmler and the ambitious governors of neighboring gaus. When he accepted the position, he thought his job was to civilize the Poles and bring them to the level of Germans like the Teutonic Knights of yore, but he now finds out that Poles are to be decivilized—in plain words, they are to be trained as servants for Germans and their children taught only the rudiments of writing and arithmetic necessary to eke out an existence as hewers of wood and drawers of water. There's an unending demand for young Polish women to work as maids, governesses, and sweepers, for a lot of the old Nazi guard think that Poland is a labor pool to get unpaid workers for their wives and children. And above all, there is the looming question of what to do with the Jews who now live in the ghettos in Warsaw and other cities in the Central Government under insanitary conditions that provide a breeding ground for typhus and other epidemic diseases. The Führer had an initial plan for sending them to the northeast part of Poland, between the rivers Vistula and Bug, but now nobody talks about it. He, Hans Frank, wants to starve them to death, just like Stalin wiped out six million peasants in Ukraine in 1933. The Jewish problem, originally a German issue, has metamorphosed into a huge European crisis, with every agency promoting its own solution. The German Foreign Office wants to settle the Jews in Madagascar after we win the war; Goering wants to keep the Jewish artisans to boost war production; and Heydrich, entrusted with the final solution of the Jewish problem, wants to kill all Jews right away and is deploying his Einsatzgruppen to do just that, despite Frank's opposition, while his boss, Himmler, wants to dump more and more Jews in Frank's territory to make room for the new Aryan settlers brought over to other parts of Poland.

"'I've nothing against the Jews except that they should vanish from Poland, actually from Europe,' he said, in conclusion.

"He then burst into tears and, after a few moments of weeping, wiped his eyes and offered to play Beethoven's *Moonlight Sonata* before turning in for the night. He took me to his music room, which has a fine collection of pianos, violins, and cellos expropriated from rich Jewish families. He played the Beethoven piece beautifully, and I wondered about the two sides of him as I sat there listening" (Tagebuch 1941).

Werner then wended his way by car to the western districts of Poland, which were now part of the Greater Reich.

"The Polish Jews, with their yellow badges, are very different from their German counterparts," he wrote, after visiting Lodz, now called Litzmannstadt in honor of the German General Karl Litzmann of World War I fame. "They look more Asian, they have no dignity, they cringe before every German, and they smile ingratiatingly, showing broken teeth. They are prohibited from making contact with us, but they sneak around the police and pester us. I've seen them kissing the hands of German soldiers who are revolted by such servility, and they react by punching or kicking them. It's hard to think of these subhumans as our enemies, for they are like pests, a nuisance and a burden. I hate ghettos, and I want to get away as fast as possible.

"I'm surprised at the number of German tourists visiting the ghettos. Most of them are relatives of the Wehrmacht and SS soldiers, sleek pot-bellied men and buxom wide-bottomed women wearing Hitler pins, watching the emaciated Jews behind barbed wire fences going about their daily business—lighting fires to cook their meals or bringing water from nearby pumps. I passed by one group staring in fascination at the corpses of Jews, stacked up neatly, waiting for burial. 'We don't need these useless eaters,' said one man, laughing. 'We need food for our boys who are fighting for our country. These people are better off dead anyway.' There was a general nodding of heads, and I moved on" (Tagebuch 1941).

He stayed at the mansion of Governor Arthur Greiser and was treated as an honored guest.

"Greiser wants to make Wartheland into a model gau," wrote Werner. "In five years, according to him, this place will look like a prosperous German district, filled with blond, blue-eyed people chosen from the ethnic Germans in Poland and neighboring countries. Hitler has given him carte blanche to do what he thinks best in regard to the Jewish question.

"'The ghetto is my brainchild,' he says. 'I want the credit for being the first one to create a ghetto for Jews in the modern age. I had to evict the Jews from their homes, seize their assets, put them in crowded quarters, and make them do slave labor on skimpy rations. To achieve the Fuhrer's vision, one has to be ruthless.'

"Greiser adores Himmler and believes wholeheartedly in the *Generalplan Ost* that has been promulgated by him. That plan has been the amalgam of numerous lebensraum and ethnic resettlement proposals put out by think tanks set up under the direction of Alexander Karl von Müller, myself, and other intellectuals. But an agricultural economist by the name of Konrad Meyer, who built model villages and towns as envisaged in the plan, organized an exhibition that was

attended by Himmler and Heydrich, and from then on, the plan became known as Konrad Meyer's plan. Himmler hired him as an expert,
and the plan was circulated within Nazi circles as having Himmler's
approval. According to the Generalplan Ost, not only Poland and
Ukraine but many other middle European states, such as Lithuania,
Latvia, Estonia, Czechoslovakia, and Belorussia, would be absorbed
into the expanded Third Reich. The German element, varying from
15 to 30 percent of the population in each of these states, would be
assimilated as Reichsburgers (i.e., citizens of the Reich), and the rest,
with the exception of Jews, would be given the status of colonial subjects, whose function was to serve the Germans.

"'We've to decide soon what to do with the Jews,' Greiser says.
'There are three million of them in Poland, and we can't keep them
in ghettos forever. One of my assistants, Rolf-Heinz Höppner, has suggested that the most humane way of getting rid of them is by closing
the ghettos and killing them. I know the technology exists for doing
that, but it hasn't been put into practice.'

"Greiser is confident that Hitler would win the war and he himself
would rise to a high position in the Nazi hierarchy. The way he strut-
ted around reminded me of Goering, whom he was probably trying to
emulate. A lady I was speaking to at dinner told me of his son's death
in a car crash a few months ago and how badly it had affected him. I
was surprised to hear that, because there was no hint in his behavior to
conclude that he had suffered a personal tragedy. He is easily the most
arrogant and the haughtiest Nazi I have known" (Tagebuch 1941).

Werner's next visit was to Albert Forster, governor of West Prussia,
a jovial comrade from old times.

"We had a few drinks together at a beerhall," wrote Werner.
"Forster is the polar opposite of Greiser. He hates Himmler, Heydrich,
and Eichmann. He says someone who looks as ugly as Himmler has no
right to decide who is an Aryan and who is not. Foster was asked by his
bosses to select Poles of Aryan blood who could stay in his district and
to deport the others to Hans Frank's territory. He kept all the Poles

who looked like ordinary Germans within his territory, and Himmler was furious at him for not following the guidelines of his racial expert to select only the blond, blue-eyed ones. 'Half of the people in Saxony or Bavaria are dark haired,' Forster said. 'I don't understand this craze for blondness by Himmler. The SS men here steal blond babies from Poles to raise them as Germans, and I think it's wrong. Himmler thinks that color of hair denotes a person's intelligence. The Führer has brown hair, but Himmler forgets that in his obsessiveness to breed the master race. Himmler is also sending the wrong kind of Germans to settle down in Poland as farmers because these folks know nothing about farming. Himmler is fixated on the idea that every true German is a son of the soil, deriving strength from the nature all around him. These were the notions that were promoted by the völkisch and Wandervogel movements. Himmler wants to implement them in the new German Reich. We live in very foolish times, Werner. As Schiller said, even the gods fight in vain against stupidity.'

"All in all, it was a relief to talk to Foster, and we reminisced about the old days in Munich when we dreamt of a utopia, a Germany without Jews. He has no great love toward the Jewish race but would rather deport them than kill them or keep them in ghettos like Greiser does. 'This is like catching a tiger by its tail. What do we do with these people? We can't wave a wand and make them vanish into thin air. We never thought things would end in such a mess,' he said. I agreed with him" (Tagebuch 1941).

On his return, Werner wrote his report to Rosenberg, pointing out that the situation in Poland was unstable: the gauleiters and governors he had spoken to wanted to get rich, and the easiest way for them to do so was to seize the assets of Jews and put the Jews in ghettos without any concrete plans regarding the fate of the ghettos; furthermore, each governor followed his own agenda, getting approval directly from the Führer for whatever strategy he was using and colluding with Himmler or Goering in order not to be isolated from the two centers of power within the Reich.

Rosenberg, however, didn't want to spend time on the report when Werner went to see him a week later. He was in a celebratory mood because the Führer had told him that he is going to invade Russia.

"Seeing the expression of shock on my face," wrote Werner, "Rosenberg tells me that the war would be over in less than six months, and we would be masters of the entire European continent. We can then move the Jews from ghettos to Siberia and take possession of the choicest of Russian lands. The army hadn't raised any objections, as they had done before we went to war with Poland. The success of the blitzkrieg has convinced them that Russia too will fall. Now all the generals are counting on becoming governors, acquiring wealth and power like Hans Frank and Arthur Greiser.

"'Why now?' I ask him. 'Why go to war with Russia since we've signed a pact with them?'

"'I've been advising him to go to war with Russia for years,' Rosenberg said, with a smug look on his face. 'Russia is not really a country but a collection of disparate races and nationalities who are eager to break off and declare individual statehoods. They will fight with us if we support their nationalistic ambitions. My gut feeling is that the war will be over soon, and after we defeat the Bolsheviks, we can negotiate a peace treaty with Britain, under which we will keep all the conquered territory. That's roughly the Führer's plan.'

"I brought up Napoleon's failed attempt, but Rosenberg dismissed it as irrelevant because the French army had moved too slowly and was destroyed by the Russian winter. He pointed out that the Russians had sued for peace in World War I and had surrendered large areas of territory. The same thing is going to happen again, he said, because Stalin has no military experience and will surrender quickly or be ousted by his own army, who will then make peace with us.

"'Overall, I'm very hopeful of the outcome on the eastern front,' he said. 'In strict confidence, I would like you to know that the Führer has appointed me as the plenipotentiary of our eastern Reich. I would like you to come with me and set up new universities and institutes over there that would be needed to train our new leaders of the world.'

"It was in a mood of elation I returned from the meeting. It was possible that Hitler would prevail again, and the dreams of Treitschke, Lagarde, and Langbehn would finally come true! The Third Reich would become the largest empire in the world, and all the European Jews would be moved to their own space in an inhospitable part of Russia. All my dreams would then be realized, and I would be able to stand tall and proud as an Aryan and hold my head high" (Tagebuch 1941).

THIRTY-FOUR

THE JEWISH PROBLEM RESOLVED

A high-level conference on suggestions to handle the problems presented by Jews in the Reich's newly conquered territories was hosted by the Frankfort Institute for Research into the Jewish Question, and Werner, along with his elite philosopher friends, was invited to present his thoughts on the subject.

"I was the last speaker, since I was the oldest," Werner wrote, "and it came as a surprise to me to hear the others unanimously proclaim that we are going to win the forthcoming war with Russia and the time is ripe to solve the Jewish problem, once and for all, not only for Germany but for Europe as a whole.

"Alfred Rosenberg opened the conference by saying, 'Germany's Jewish problem has now metamorphosed into the European Jewish problem, and it will be solved for Germany, for the German Reich, and for Europe only when the last Jew has left the European continent.' My jaw dropped when I heard this. How's this going to be possible? I wondered. There are some seven million Jews in Poland and Russia alone, not to speak of Hungary and the Baltic states. How do we make them disappear?

"As though reading my mind, my friend Professor Peter Heinz Seraphim gave a masterly presentation on the difficulties associated with solving the Jewish problem at the European level. We can't go on creating ghettos, he said, because they're unsanitary—as evidenced by frequent breakouts of typhus and dysentery—and present insurmountable problems in creating clean, healthy Aryan cities in the east. Talk of deportation of Jews to Siberia or some other remote region is meaningless because Europe is overcrowded, and no area can be found to accommodate seven million people. The expense of transportation to Madagascar or some other place in Africa will be prohibitive. Seraphim didn't offer any solution, but the next speaker, my friend and head of the Institute for Racial Policy, Professor Walter Gross, wearing a Nazi uniform, said bluntly that the final hour of the European Jew has arrived and there was no turning back from total annihilation.

"My own contribution to the conference was of a personal nature. I spoke about my dream from childhood on to live in a Germany without a single Jew inside it. Now it appears close to realization, I said, and we can hope for the emergence of a unified Europe without a single Jew in it, a great Reich devoid of black markets, currency manipulation, hoarding of capital, impoverishment of peasants, or internecine wars. There's no gainsaying it's a difficult task, and we've to evaluate all the options available to us—from deportation to annihilation—in a calm, detached manner and decide what's in the best interests of Europe. Ghettos are no solution, and the most effective way of clearing the population inside them is through rapid annihilation. Humanity and empathy should be set aside to give priority to expedience in achieving a solution so vital to Europe's welfare.

"Rosenberg gave a concluding speech in Hitler's style, saying that Europe will be in a state of turmoil until the bacilli of Jewry is eradicated, and once that is done, there will be peace among all nations, with Aryans ruling the world.

"Max Hunke and Kurt Brockelmann were also there as observers from the SS. They were probably spying on Rosenberg, at the behest of Heydrich or Himmler. This shows that one has to be careful in speaking, even at a conference like this. I had dinner with them, and they told me that Heydrich and Himmler have decided not to create ghettos in the Soviet Union, unlike in Poland, but to send Einsatzgruppen units in the wake of the Wehrmacht to kill all Jews in each conquered territory. They also thanked me profusely for the new batch of students trained by me and my colleagues who excelled in carrying out Himmler's orders in the Einsatzgruppen units, unswayed by moral scruples or humane sentiments. I didn't feel proud of myself. I've joined the barbarians, and barbarism has won the day" (Tagebuch 1941).

When Werner got home, he got a call from one of Himmler's underlings that his great love, Kerstin Krämer, who had been working at the Nazi Party Office in Munich as a publicity officer, had been put into a detention camp because the Gestapo had discovered that one of her grandparents was Jewish.

"I can do nothing about her," Werner wrote sadly. "With Hess taking off to Britain on his mad mission to end the war, I have no one to go to for help. Poor devil! Hitler had given him a nice title, that of deputy Führer, but Hess's primary function seemed to be making introductory remarks at gatherings preliminary to the Führer's speeches. He had helped me and Professor Haushofer get protection from the Gestapo for our relatives—in my case, my beloved niece, and in Haushofer's case, his wife, who is Jewish. Hess is an introvert—perhaps I should call him a mystic—the only decent man among the Streichers, Goerings, Himmlers, and Bormanns who surround the Führer. Now Bormann will control access to Hitler, and this means Himmler, who is close to Bormann, will be able to push his proposals for the Aryanization of Europe by enslaving Slavs and decimating Jews. This is what I hear from Haushofer and others. The Third Reich has become a police state now, run by the RSHA, using Stalin's NKVD as the model. Himmler is cut from the same cloth as Stalin's police chief Beria, a fanatic who would think nothing of murdering millions of people in the name of an ideology. This isn't the Third Reich I had dreamed of all my life.

"The SS man who broke the news about Kerstin to me was gloating when he was talking to me. They will hold my relationship with Kerstin against me, I'm sure. I've to be more watchful than ever.

I've been paying underground art dealers in Berlin and Munich to keep Hannah alive by giving her odd jobs, but now I've to find other ways of helping her. (I had no inkling that my foxy uncle was the one who saved me from starvation, thought Hannah). I can send her some of the jewelry belonging to my wife anonymously, but she may recognize them. What else can I do, with the SS intelligence keeping watch on me? Himmler doesn't want me associating with Rosenberg, and this is his warning shot. I don't want to end up as a dead body in a Munich park with a hole in my head" (Tagebuch 1941).

Werner became very depressed and started taking medication for anxiety and sleeplessness. He tried to seek solace in the arms of another woman he had been carrying on with, Frau Frieda Schürmann, head of the Nazi Women's Organization in Munich, but found out, to his frustration and humiliation, that he was impotent.

Demoralized, he sat at home and compulsively collected newspaper cuttings about Operation Barbarossa—the largest ever invasion in the history of mankind, with four million troops traversing a two-thousand-mile boundary. Three thousand Russian aircraft were destroyed as a result of a blitzkrieg, and the Luftwaffe reigned supreme over Russian skies. The German panzer tanks made short work of the Soviet armored vehicles, and the damage inflicted on the Russian army was so great that most Germans thought the war would be over within weeks. The next two months weren't so good, with heavy rains and mud slowing down the German attack, giving the Russian army a chance to regroup. Hitler and the army brass didn't see eye to eye on how to conduct the offensive. The generals wanted to drive on to Moscow, but Hitler was intent on splitting the attack two ways—driving to the south to seize the Caucasian oil wells and, at the same time, marching to Leningrad in the north. The dispute between them ended by Hitler bypassing the commanding officers and giving direct orders to their underlings to accomplish his goals. He made it clear to the generals that they had no say in the conduct of war from that point onward, and he was directing the war, taking on the role of the commander in chief. The German Army in the south defeated the Russians badly, taking half a million prisoners, and advanced to Moscow and crushed the Russians at Vyazma, capturing some seven hundred thousand prisoners. Unfortunately, the weather turned against the Germans, and they were mired in knee-deep mud, with broken supply links. Winter began to take its dreadful toll on the troops, inflicting very high casualties. Operation Barbarossa fizzled out, and the German Army retreated.

"Are we winning or losing?" wrote Werner. "To me, it looks like the blitzkrieg will not work against a country like Russia. Why don't we retreat from Russia and fight on the western front? But I'm rambling, since I'm no military man. My concern is about the deaths of a large number of ex-students from Munich University. During the past several months, the three of us—Haushofer, von Müller, and myself—have been visiting bereaved parents. It isn't an easy job. The fathers, being German, keep a stiff upper lip, but the women keep on asking if this is going to be like the First World War, with no end in sight. 'The Führer told us that we are going to conquer the Russians in a few months, but that isn't happening,' they say. 'We don't want more of our kids to die in Russia.' Heart-wrenching as these scenes are, the letters we get from our students are even worse. Three months ago, I got a letter from Gunter Andersen, who used to be my graduate assistant. He was drafted by the SS and sent to Kiev. He tells me the SS and Wehrmacht rounded up fifty thousand or so Jews in Kiev, marched them into a ravine called Babi Yar, and shot all of them, placing the dead in layers, like sardines. Andersen was responsible for twenty deaths, including those of four small kids. He had to do what his commander told him to do since he was a soldier, but he was sick for several days and is now thinking of deserting the army. 'I studied philosophy under you, and you, echoing Treitschke, told us that a man was part of the state and had no existence apart from the state. Why didn't you instead teach us to rebel? Why didn't you teach us to nurture human values? Why didn't you teach us that that the individual should make his own decisions instead of letting the state make decisions for him?'

"That letter disturbed me more than anything else, and I went to see Rosenberg in Berlin, at the Herrenklub, to find out what was really going on behind the scenes in Russia. He told me that Heydrich is deploying four detachments of Einsatzgruppen to kill partisans in Russia, and all Jews in the Soviet Union were included in the 'partisan' category.

"'But this wasn't your plan,' I told him. 'You wanted to encourage Ukraine and other states to break away from Russia and bring down the Bolshevik government as a collaborative effort.'

"'I did propose that plan,' he said. 'But Heydrich and Himmler convinced the Führer that we wouldn't be able to keep the territories we gained unless we exterminate all partisans, which category includes all Jews.'

"'Didn't anyone object to killing women and children?' I asked.

"His reply was that the Führer had decided we are engaged in a racial war with the Jews, and it was necessary to kill them regardless of sex or age.

"'What else can we do with them?' he asked, irritably. 'We cannot put them in ghettos and continue feeding them, and we can't deport them because there is no place we can send them to. Don't forget they are Bolsheviks and consequently our enemies. If we don't eliminate them, they will constitute a fifth column, an ever-present enemy in our midst.'

"I saw that he was getting upset, and to smooth out the situation, I told him that there was logic in what he was saying, and I could see that the Jewish problem in the Greater Reich called for extermination—there was no other way out. But I expressed my concern about the psychological impact of murdering unarmed civilians on young soldiers such as my student Andersen, who had deserted the SS and was captured and court-martialed.

"'This is a problem that has come up again and again,' said Rosenberg. 'Even Himmler is concerned with the effects on his SS men of killing Jews by shooting. He is trying to come up with a more sophisticated approach for extermination, by using lethal assembly-line methods for liquidating the two million Jews in the General Government area controlled by Hans Frank. He has given orders to build death factories in Belzec and Treblinka. I also understand that Arthur Greiser, with the Führer's approval, is in the process of building the world's first human-extermination factory at Chelmno. Let's hope it proves to be a success.'

"Whether Hitler wins or loses the war, it looks like Europe would be Judenfrei. We toasted to that" (Tagebuch 1941).

Werner got a letter from Kerstin asking him to save her, and he devoted several pages of his diary on the situation he was in. He felt that he was being spied upon by the students in his class, by Max and Kurt, and by the Gestapo.

"There's nothing I can do to save my sweetheart," he wrote, becoming Dr. Jekyll. "I keep on thinking of Rosa, my first love. Kerstin evokes the same intensity of love that I experienced six decades ago. There's nothing as tragic as the love of an Aryan man toward a Jewish woman, and there's nothing I can do to save Kerstin from her doom" (Tagebuch 1941).

That mood didn't last very long, and he soon turned into Mr. Hyde. He gave dozens of interviews to magazines with names like *Die Judenfrage, Judentum und Recht,* and *Der Weltkampf* from institutes headed by his friends. He wrote several learned papers defending the attacks on Russia and the "extinction" of the Jewish race as necessary from a world-historical—God, how much I hate that word, the favorite of every German thinker, thought Hannah—perspective.

He accepted an invitation from Philipp Bouhler—chief of the chancellery of the Führer and specifically responsible for killing methods using lethal gas—to visit the death factories established by Himmler all over Poland.

"The four of us—Bouhler, an aide of his who is a gassing expert, a colleague of mine from the Munich University, and myself—went to visit Treblinka and Auschwitz in a special military plane. The facilities were clean and very efficient, managed by a few SS men and a squad of *sondercommandos*. The entire facility seemed like a marvel of German engineering, and the technician accompanying us explained in simple terms the mechanics of the killing rooms and the crematoria. In a scene reminiscent of a modern version of Dante's *Inferno*, I witnessed a line of new arrivals, weeping, howling, and screaming, being led to their inevitable end by merciless guides who divested them of their belongings, sheared them like sheep in springtime, stripped them, and forced them into the lethal chamber. A batch of five hundred, half of them women and children, were liquidated in one session, and we watched them, impervious to pleadings and imprecations that we heard. It was a job that had to be done, and compassion had to be counterbalanced by the folly in treating a mortal enemy with kindness. From what I learned from my friends, the people who pushed the United States to go to war with Germany are Jews like Henry Morgenthau, and the Führer is right in calling world Jewry our mortal enemy. The Führer had promised that world Jewry would be exterminated after declaring war on the United States, and his promise is being carried out in this camp. We have to win this war, and it's a war of annihilation" (Tagebuch 1942).

The next few entries in his tagebuch dealt with his wife's sudden illness—he thought it was due to cancer of the blood cells and was angry at the contrary opinions given to him by specialists—and her sudden death. This was followed by, to him, a more devastating tragedy—the defeat of the German Army at Stalingrad, with the capture of 350,000 German soldiers, which set off protests and riots all over Germany. In Munich, there were posters and graffiti mocking the Führer, and two young students were caught distributing anti-Hitler flyers at the university campus by a janitor who was in the SA. An investigation followed, and it turned out that a brilliant colleague of Werner at the university, Kurt Huber, with the reputation of being a maverick, had written the leaflet. He and the two students were executed by guillotine. Werner, Haushofer, and von Müller, as members of the investigation committee, witnessed the executions. The beheadings took place at the Stadelheim prison, and Werner was sickened by the sight of their heads rolling on the platform, alive for a few seconds with rapidly blinking eyes and twitching nostrils, after severance by the mighty blades.

"This is barbarism, and the civilized German in me revolts at the idea of killing our own children with this horrible instrument," wrote Werner. "There was no need to kill them; they could have been kept in jail for a few years. The gathered people were cheering for Hitler, and I swallowed my bile while I too shouted 'Heil Hitler.'

"'I couldn't help them, because I would be ruined if I helped them,' said Haushofer, in a whisper.

"'I'm in the same boat as you,' I whispered back. 'I couldn't help them, either'" (Tagebuch 1943).

His mood became darker after this incident. Even the sight of the Munich Jews who had been rounded up and put in a temporary camp, waiting to be shipped east, did not cheer him as he passed by them on his way to work. The country was now in the throes of the "total war" declared by the Führer. Bread and potatoes were rationed, and ordinary people had to stand in line for hours to get the essential supplies for day-to-day living. There was no more news of victories in battle, as the war, expanded in scope, was being fought in several fronts, with British and American forces digging in for a protracted fight.

Bombs were raining on Munich, causing much damage and destruction. The Luftwaffe was powerless against the enemy planes as they appeared in broad daylight and dropped tons of incendiary bombs on rich and poor neighborhoods alike. It was a common occurrence to see sheets of flame sweeping across streets, followed by deafening explosions.

Despite the bombing, the Führer wanted to celebrate the twentieth anniversary of the Beerhall Putsch, at the Lowenbraukeller in Munich. Werner was there, wearing his gold Nazi badge on his dinner jacket.

"The Old Guard was there in the Banquet Hall," he wrote, "looking coarser and heavier. The Führer, gray haired and old looking, with a tremor in his hand that he was trying unsuccessfully to control, spoke of the necessity of total war against our well-known enemies—the East, the West, and the ubiquitous International Jewish Conspiracy. He would win in the end, he said; not only that, he was going to wipe out the entire Jewish race in Europe. He ruled out any negotiated peace settlement with the enemy, as at the end of the First World War, and he warned that anyone, abroad or at home, who doubted the ability of Germany to win the war would be in for an unpleasant surprise. There were deafening cheers and shouts of 'Heil Hitler' from the assembled personages, but I felt alone and isolated, even though I was in their midst, dutifully clapping my vein-swollen old hands. Hitler has Parkinson's disease, I learned from his physician, Dr. Brandt. The fear that all of us Nazis have is that he may become incapacitated and one of the watchdogs around him—Himmler, Bormann, or Goebbels—would become the dictator of Germany, which is an unbearable thought" (Tagebuch 1943).

Rosenberg, seated at the high table with Hitler, Himmler, Goering, and other leaders, spoke to him, after the banquet, about the necessity of holding an international conference on the danger to the rest of the world from Jews who lived in areas not controlled by the Greater German Reich.

"Rosenberg wants me to chair the conference and come up with a list of invitees from the various institutes and universities of Europe," wrote Werner. "He wants it to be a landmark conference where our views are made clear to European intellectuals and political leaders. We have control over most of Europe now, he says, and hence we have an obligation to present a coherent view of our position on the Jewish question.

"I was confused by his request because the need for such a conference wasn't clear to me.

"'Haven't we solved the Jewish problem in Europe?' I asked him.

"'Pretty much,' he replied, 'except for a few pockets in Hungary. We have liquidated six million, from what I understand from Himmler. But ten million remain in our planet, and they are still a powerful enemy. We know they're putting pressure on Britain and

America to create a Zionist state in Palestine, which means the Jews will rise to power again with renewed strength. We're going to invite the Grand Mufti of Jerusalem, Amin al-Husseini, to this conference and hear his views on having a Jewish state in their midst. I've to get the Führer's approval, but I don't think he will withhold it'" (Tagebuch 1943).

Werner got in touch with his various academic friends inside Germany, most of whom were in favor of such a project and were anxious to be invited to the conference. The foreign intellectuals he wrote to were noncommittal, raising doubts about their safety in the context of the devastating air raids on Germany.

A few weeks later, Rosenberg invited him to the Reich Chancellery to discuss the project.

"The Führer has given his approval," wrote Werner. "He wants Rosenberg to coordinate with Goebbels, Hans Frank, and Himmler before he sends out invitations. Hans Frank wants to hold the conference in Krakow, in an old castle there. The tentative date is set at July 25, 1944.

"'The Führer hopes to roll back the attack from the West by June and believes we may very well be in Britain during the first week of July,' Rosenberg said. 'All in all, I would say July 25 is a realistic date, and Krakow is an ideal site. At the end of the conference, we expect all the foreign participants to be signatories to an agreement for the complete extermination of Jewry from Europe.'

"Why was he doing this? I wondered. The broadcasts from foreign radio stations that I listen to in the privacy of my bedroom tell me that we're losing the war on all fronts, and the Third Reich is on its last legs. Obviously, he knows it too, but doesn't want to admit it.

"It seems to me that we are actors in a tragic play, playing our parts until the curtain comes down" (Tagebuch 1944).

Werner received more than a hundred papers, the bulk of them submitted by German savants, on the evils perpetrated by Jews in every country in the world. There was nothing about the contemporary situation in these papers, no word about the ghettos, Einsatzgruppen, or the death factories in Poland.

Werner reviewed the papers with his coterie—von Müller, Baeumler, and Walter Gross—and selected sixty of them, giving preference to the few French, Baltic, and Italian authors. He and von Müller spent several weary hours with the contentious representatives from the offices of Goebbels, Himmler, and Rosenberg in planning the conference. An agreement was reached to set up an exhibition on the theme of "Role of the Jew in Contemporaneous Politics" to please Dr. Goebbels, but objections were raised to showing his propaganda movies, *The Eternal Jew* and *Dr. Suss* because some feared they were only caricatures that did not portray correctly the menace of the Jewish race. They then spent hours debating on the race of the prostitutes who were going to be installed in a house within walking distance from the exhibition hall; originally, they were to include Poles and Russians, but at the insistence of Himmler's representatives, it was decided that the women should all be Aryan. Goebbels's representatives wanted the invited guests to be taken on a tour of the death factories, but the idea was rebuffed by the Himmler faction. "We are in the process of dismantling ghettos and death factories," they said. "We have liquidated several and hope to raze the remaining ones in the next few months. Himmler doesn't want to leave any evidence of the final solution. The Führer agrees with him." A tit for tat followed when the proposal by the Himmler faction to show the model villages built by Konrad Meyer as a visual aid in understanding the Generalplan Ost was rebuffed by the rest of the attendees as being inappropriate for the occasion.

They couldn't even reach agreement on the concert to be played on the opening night of the conference. Goebbels's representative wanted the Berlin Philharmonic, with its conductor Wilhelm Furtwangler, to give performances of Beethoven and Mozart, but other members thought the Führer would prefer the Vienna Philharmonic playing *Tristan und Isolde* under Karl Böhm, and a decision was postponed until the next meeting, set four weeks later.

The best-laid plans of mice and men can go awry, and that happened here also. An assassination attempt against Hitler was made by a Wehrmacht officer, Count Claus von Stauffenberg, who carried a time bomb in his briefcase into the makeshift briefing room of Hitler's military headquarters in the east and left it there, as close to Hitler as he could manage. The explosion caused a lot of damage, but Hitler somehow survived, although badly shaken up. He gave a midnight broadcast to the nation to assure the German people he was alive and well, and Werner listened to it.

"He's really a robot, repeating the same words he used twenty years ago," wrote Werner. "He says the assassination attempt was a stab in the back, an act of betrayal, and he is going to deal with the perpetrators with the utmost severity. The fact that he escaped from the attack unscathed proves that he is the man endowed with the historical mission to defeat the enemies from the East and the West and to lead Germany to victory. I am torn between two states of mind—grieving because he's still alive and relieved because he's still alive and his boorish henchmen haven't taken control over Germany" (Tagebuch 1944).

The next day Werner got a call from the Propaganda Ministry telling him that the International Conference on Jews had been postponed indefinitely for reasons of national security.

"I don't care about the postponement of the conference," wrote Werner. "I am in a state of shock after hearing that Professor Haushofer's son, Albrecht, has been arrested as one of the conspirators in Stauffenberg's plot to kill Hitler and is likely to be put to death for treason. I went to see Haushofer and found him stoical. When I offered a few words of condolence, he brushed me off by saying, 'My son has betrayed his country and the German people and deserves no sympathy from me.' Of such stuff are we Germans made! I'm in the same boat as he, anyway. My niece is a traitor to her country, and my nephew is a Jew who has been sent to a camp to die. I've tried to save Hannah from the camp all these years, but the situation has changed because of the rise of Himmler" (Tagebuch 1944).

Werner tried to get in touch with Alfred Rosenberg, but he was somewhere in Poland, and the phone lines had either been cut or were out of order. He drove to Berlin to see if he could speak to someone at the Reich Chancellery and found that many of his old friends had been transferred to new positions. But he met Hans Lammers, and the two of them went, in the middle of a bomb-attack warning, for lunch at a nearby restaurant frequented by the Nazi elite.

"Lammers talked to me in the confines of a private room at the restaurant where the walls are soundproofed and there are no hidden microphones," he wrote. "The Führer is not doing well physically or mentally. His hair has turned white, his hands shake worse than before, and his left eardrum has been shattered by the bomb explosion. Bormann, Himmler, and Goebbels are literally running the country. Goebbels is now responsible for conducting the total war, Bormann has control over whom Hitler can see, and Himmler, in addition to all his other duties, is a general in charge of the reserve army. Lammers doesn't have access to the Führer anymore, and he's bitter about it. 'How can I, the head of the Reich Chancellery, function if I can't talk to my Führer?' he asked me, with sadness. The Führer is in a prison of his making, and Goebbels is making key decisions on every matter ranging from war production to the induction of older males in the Volkssturm, the national guard that is going to put up the last-ditch fight. Himmler, while acting as the most loyal of the Führer's subordinates, is looking to protect his own turf in the eastern part of the Reich. He has entered into peace negotiations with the West, hoping that they would let him rule over the conquered territories in Poland and Czechoslovakia. His henchmen are digging up the graves of murdered Jews and burning the corpses, to destroy evidence of the Einsatzgruppen killings. They are also going to ship the ovens and gas chambers in the death factories back to Germany. It's like wiping a slate clean, and the world can't raise a mass-murder charge in the absence of victims' bodies or ovens and crematoria. Himmler is hoping to be the next Führer, whether we win or lose the war. We all know by now that losing the war is the most likely outcome and must prepare for our defeat" (Tagebuch 1944).

THIRTY-FIVE

GÖTTERDÄMMERUNG

"I'm saddened by the devastation of Munich, the ruins that stand everywhere like symbols of defeat," wrote Werner. "Even the zoo at Hellabrunn was not spared, and my favorite giraffe, the one whom I used to call Frederick the Great because he was taller than the rest, was killed.

"Gone is the Germany of my youth: the classical architecture I used to feast my eyes on is now an eyesore and a heartache, a Venus de Milo with arms cut off. It is not only Munich, but a lot of our great cites—Hamburg, Berlin, Dresden, Cologne, Hanover, and Dusseldorf—are wreckages, mutilated remnants of their former vibrant selves. Hitler came to power twelve years ago, and this is his legacy—not to speak of the millions of carcasses that are buried or burned all over Europe. He carried out, in principle, a program suggested by us—I mean Eckart, Müller, Haushofer, Rosenberg, and myself. Germany should be Judenfrei, we said, and he achieved that. Germany should have lebensraum, we said, and he achieved that also. But we didn't tell him to go to war on two fronts. We didn't tell him that we wanted a Judenfrei Europe. If he had negotiated with Britain in 1939 and offered peace in exchange of western territories of Poland, we wouldn't be in this unenviable situation. He surrounded himself with evil men hungry for power like Goebbels, Bormann, and Himmler and, in the end, destroyed himself and Germany" (Tagebuch 1944).

The incessant bombing unnerved him, and he decided to move to his house in Nuremberg, which had spacious cellars. He got help from his students to move his books and papers and spent the next few weeks arranging them and setting up a work environment for himself.

"Yesterday I came back to Munich. I wanted to resign my professorship and tie up loose ends. I met with Karl Haushofer and Alexander von Müller, men who are in the same situation as myself.

"'The Yanks are coming from the south, the French from the west, the Brits from the north, and the Russians from the east,' Haushofer said. 'I was in Berlin the other day and learned that the senior SS officers are busy getting false passports and establishing fake identities. They're planning to migrate to South America. The Führer is not a well man. In fact, he's a physical wreck, out of touch with reality and unable to function. His old associates, Goering and Himmler, want to step into his shoes, and the Führer runs around shrieking, "Shoot the traitors!" He wants to pursue a scorched-earth policy inside Germany and has asked the Wehrmacht to blow up buildings and factories that are still standing. The people I spoke to sarcastically call it Operation Nero. The Wehrmacht wouldn't comply with his orders, and Bormann, directed by the Führer, is asking the gauleiters to demolish plants and buildings in each gau. That's not going to happen, either. As far as the Führer is concerned, it's a fight unto death—his death and Germany's death.'

"'What will happen to us after the war is lost?' von Müller asked. 'We indoctrinated Hitler, and we trained thousands of students to be his henchmen. In return, we received grants and honorariums from Rosenberg and Hess and invested them with the Deutsche Bank in very profitable takeovers of Jewish companies and Jewish real estate. When the facts are known, the new rulers of Germany are going to come after us.'

"'I think you're being unduly harsh on us,' I said. 'Hitler got most of his ideas in regard to the Jews from Dietrich Eckart and Alfred Rosenberg. More than anyone else, Rosenberg convinced Hitler of an international Jewish conspiracy against the Aryan folk. You and I know there's no such conspiracy. Hitler was also influenced by another fanatic, Heinrich Himmler, in the matter of exterminating Jews from every country in Europe and resettling Germans all over the continent as the master race. I agree with you that we established think tanks, provided intellectual impetus for the Führer state, and trained thousands of future Nazis who would do the bidding of Hitler. Maybe they will arrest us, but we can always say we were doing what the state expected us to do.'

"'Saying we were only obeying the orders won't work,' von Müller said. 'Hitler has been the logical outcome of our lives' work. We made him, we set him up on his pedestal, we made plans or assisted in making them regarding the invasion of Poland and Russia, we proposed and justified the Endlösung, and now we can't seek refuge in denial or evasion, for there's a paper trail we left behind us. It's better to take it on the chin, like our friend Baeumler, and get arrested and put in jail.'

"'I don't want to be arrested and put in jail,' said Haushofer. 'I'll do what Brutus and Cato the Younger did.'

"'Shall we make a suicide pact?' asked von Müller. 'I've cyanide pills I can share with you.'

"We debated for a while on the pros and cons of such a pact and finally decided to go our own separate ways" (Tagebuch 1945).

A bomb hit Werner's house in Munich that night, damaging his attic, bedroom, study, and garden.

"What did my poor daisies and carnations do to deserve this fate?" he wrote. "I can't live in this house, with gaping holes and broken beams. I'll resign from the university and move to Nuremberg for good."

His tagebuchs, from then on, contained data about the advancement of the enemy, details of bombing in various German cities, and his blood pressure readings, which ranged from high to very high. On hearing about the Führer's death, he wrote, "Siegfried is dead, and it is Götterdämmerung. Hitler's last wish had been granted. Germany is destroyed. I can't even go for a walk because of the debris choking up the streets of Nuremberg. We survive by eating eggs laid by Ulrike's hens."

The Americans had taken over Bavaria, and a Captain Stan Lieberman showed up at his doorstep one day.

"The ultimate humiliation for an Aryan," he wrote, "is to be forced to be subservient to a Jew. Here he was—kinky haired and brown eyed, with a full red mouth and a swarthy skin—asking me about my philosophic and journalistic publications. 'Did you write this?' he asked me, holding a copy of my book *Foundations of the Third Reich*. I admitted to the authorship of the book. He brought out a set of articles I had written in the early thirties on lebensraum, the Führerprinzep, and the pros and cons of solving the Jewish problem through extermination.

"'You were an architect of Hitler's policies,' he said.

"'Many German philosophers, living and dead, had expressed similar views. There are dozens of people in every university or research institute in Germany who had written books and papers that justify or even glorify the policies executed by the Third Reich,' I replied.

"'You trained killers in your classes, removing the last vestiges of moral impulses and human values from them. You turned young men into killer robots.'

"'We wanted a new German nation and had to train its future leaders.'

"The Jew looked at me with concealed distaste. 'You're worse than the fiends at the extermination centers who practice every kind of cruelty on the inmates. You are a scholar, a well-educated man. You should know better.'

"'Sometimes a man has to steel himself to do things for his country and play the role of the hangman if necessary.'

"'I don't want to bandy words with you. I would like you to come with me to our office so that we can interrogate you properly,' he said.

"'What if I refuse?' I asked.

"'I'll have to handcuff you and take you with me,' he said.

"I went with him to his office, and there were four of them who threw a spate of questions at me. Was I a Nazi? Did I know Hitler, Himmler, Goering, Lammers, or Rosenberg? Did I know of the operation of extermination camps? Did I visit any of them? Did I enjoy seeing Jews killed? Would I tell them what von Müller did and what Haushofer did or Baeumler did?

"I felt old and tired and confused. I don't remember what I told them. I felt weak at the knees and collapsed, and they took me to the hospital" (Tagebuch 1945).

There were a few blank pages after that, followed by a scrawl: "*Und so macht das Gewissen uns alle zu Memmen.*" That was the last entry in his tagebuch, the line from Hamlet, "Thus conscience does make cowards of us all." Was he contemplating suicide, the German way out, like many of his comrades? Did he have cyanide pills? Or did he resolve to stick it out until the new rulers decided to hang him? Hannah, wondering why he didn't write more about his interrogation, concluded that Werner was suppressing important information. I'll ask Eric to get me a copy of the transcript of the interview, she thought, before turning off the lights in the basement and going to sleep.

The next day, Hannah was in a depressed mood as she rode her bicycle along her usual route. Never having known a father, her uncle had taken his place in her mind. She knew he had supported the Nazis, but she thought it was like some of her friends on the left idolizing Stalin, as a symbol for a new world order. Now, after reading his papers, she felt polluted because of the evil in him, which she was sure had somehow been transmitted to her through the affinities of blood and kinship.

What should she do with his papers? She wasn't sure they had any intrinsic worth, except to psychologists who wanted to study the mind of a Nazi, and even in that case, there were more compelling narratives, such as the autobiographical writings of Hans Frank and Rudolf Höss, which were readily available as Nuremberg trial documents.

She had been chosen by her uncle to make decisions that he should have made himself, and she didn't like her role as judge or executor. She had no one to turn to for independent assessment, other than Eric, who probably was as good a judge as anyone else in these matters. But she was ashamed to show him the papers, with its diatribes against Jews and calls for their extermination. Besides, she was not sure if he would have the time to go over the voluminous material in the underground rooms in her uncle's house. She really didn't want to bother Eric, but as she passed by a newly built phone booth—all glass and chrome—near his house, she got off her bicycle and gave him a call.

He picked up on the first ring.

"Eric, I've finished reading my uncle's papers," she said. "I need to talk to you. It's important."

"Sure, Hannah. I'll be in court all day. Drop in anytime, and I'll come over and talk to you."

Two hours later, she was in the courtroom at the Palace of Justice, where the Einsatzgruppen trials were in progress. She had gone there reluctantly because she did not want to hear any more testimonies about their activities in eastern Europe.

She sat in the gallery for four hours and watched the trial. They were all there—Ohlendorf, Shulz, Braune, Blume, and a dozen other good Germans responsible for the murder of two million Jews in Russia and Baltic states. They stood there defiantly, upright, proud Aryans in their forties and fifties, as their lawyers argued for their acquittal.

"The defendants were only obeying orders from Hitler, orally communicated to them by Himmler or his authorized deputies," said one attorney. "They were following the Führerprinzip."

"They were killing Jews because the Führer had decided that the real war was against Jews, and they were our enemies," argued another.

A cloud of questions rose up in Hannah's mind. These were highly educated men, some with PhDs, students of her uncle or one of his numerous cronies. Education seemed to have robbed them of any moral will of their own, deprived them of internal censors to judge their actions. They thought of themselves as public executioners, not to be blamed but commended for carrying out their duties. Her uncle and people like him, with their highbrow talk of Nietzsche and his Übermensch, had subtly molded their minds by telling them that the blond beast of prey should have no regrets in killing or starving to death women and babies or old and sick Jews. This led to the question: who had molded her uncle's mind? His father, his teachers, and later on, his associates. They in turn, had been corrupted by their forefathers, on and on, each generation tainted by its ancestors during the inexorable process of German history.

The men standing before her had stoic, impassive faces even as the charges—mass murder, cruel and inhuman treatment of prisoners of war and unarmed civilians, wanton and willful destruction of property—were read to them, and every one of them responded "Not guilty" as though they were robots who didn't understand they had committed heinous crimes. Why did they not say they were guilty and should be punished? Or was it un-Deutsch to show contrition, to display signs of humanity?

"These guys are out-and-out liars," said Eric to her as they were having drinks at a nearby café. "It was obvious to our interrogators that they were not telling the truth about obeying their Führer's orders because of the discrepancies found in their testimonies as to when and by whom the order was conveyed to them. My belief is that they were told to act on their own in regard to killing Jews, and they thought they could win favor by killing as many as possible. But I can't prove it, and I wouldn't be surprised if a lot of these guys got away scot-free."

"You don't seem upset about it," she said.

"I'm past being upset, Hannah. According to some of my associates, nearly two million Germans were directly involved in the killing of Jews: a million SS, thousands of police and Wehrmacht soldiers, and tens of thousands of civilians working on the railways or as contractors and auxiliaries. We can't arrest them all. The murder of the Jews was a collaborative effort, and the more I delve into it, the more I'm convinced that the trials we're holding are meaningless. I was at the doctors' trial, when twenty-four top-ranked physicians were in the dock, and only two were condemned to death. I wondered why the nurses, technicians, medical suppliers, and orderlies who worked with these doctors for several months were allowed to go free. They knew what was going on and tacitly went along with it. The trial was a showcase to let the world get a picture of the evil Nazis. The evil went deeper than the men on trial, right into the heart of Germany."

She, observing his face and gestures, became concerned about him.

"It isn't good for you to stay in Germany any longer, Eric," she said, placing her hand over his arm. "Why don't you go back to America? I know there are problems there too, but here you're surrounded by ex-Nazis and anti-Semites. Contact with them will corrode your inner self. It may even destroy you."

"I'm going to stay here until I find answers to all my questions," he replied, after thinking about what she said. "For nearly two years, I've been reading every document I could lay hands on, and I've learned a lot. Yet there are many questions that plague me. How did Hitler rise to power? There is a hidden organization that helped him become the Führer, and I would like to know who that was. Who set him up, fully knowing his anti-Semitic agenda? The mass murder of the Jews started in Russia, simultaneous with the invasion of Russia. Why did they want to kill the Russian Jews first instead of the Polish Jews who were already in the ghettos? Why did they want to build death factories in Poland and not in Russia? Why did they want to kill all the European Jews by sending them to the extermination centers in Poland? I've no answer but only a lot of questions."

The same questions, over and over again, Hannah thought. I should give him my notes right now and ask him to comb through my uncle's papers. She opened her mouth to speak, but he seemed intent on continuing his monologue, and there was no way of stopping him.

"I worked so hard in putting this case together," he said. "It makes me mad that very few will be given the punishment they deserve. I tried to push the case for genocide against Ohlendorf and other Einsatzgruppen leaders, but I couldn't do much with it. To prove a case of genocide, there must be some document showing a plan for genocide. We couldn't find any such document, and so we charged them with crimes against humanity. Their defense is that in a war, you've to kill your enemies, whether they are soldiers or partisans. They thought they were going to win the war and wanted to prove they were good Nazis, with prospects of wealth and power as future rulers of the Third Reich. The Polish trials, which I've studied in detail, were much better conducted. The guy responsible for the creation of the Warsaw Ghetto, mass executions, and the razing of Warsaw, Ludwig Fischer, was tried in Poland and executed based on oral and documentary evidence. The Poles weren't buying any of this nonsense about obeying orders from above or killing in self-defense. We're dealing with very evil people, Hannah, and we don't seem to realize that."

Seeing his tortured face, she wanted to take him in her arms as though he were her son. "Let the past be buried, there's no need to excavate it, looking for artifacts," she wanted to tell him, but she knew it would be of no use. She clasped his hand, and they sat there without saying anything for a while.

"If what you're saying is true, the premises of the Nuremberg trial are wrong," she ventured. "The indictments in that trial were based on a conspiracy by the top Nazi officials to commit aggression and crimes against humanity."

"Hitler provided the impetus and stirred up the latent anti-Semitism in the German psyche, but the torture and killing of the Jews were planned, arranged, and carried out by others, millions of others, I should say."

"That's what my uncle's diaries show. I would like you to read them."

"I would certainly read them, Hannah. Before I do that, I've to find out if we have any data on your uncle in our files."

"I've put together a set of notes as I was reading his papers. I brought it with me. After reading them, if you're still interested, give me a ring."

He took the notes from her and put them in his briefcase without looking at them.

"I'm exhausted from lack of sleep," he said. "I came last night from Berlin, in a noisy train full of GIs, after two weeks of trying to persuade the Russians to collaborate with us on the trial. They wouldn't say yes or no. But I got the distinct feeling they don't approve of our holding trials right now. We will proceed on our own, without their help."

"Get some sleep, Eric. I'll drive you home," she said.

"No, Hannah. I've to talk to my boss about a couple of things and have dinner with him afterward. I'll look over the notes you gave me when I've some free time."

He's busy with his own problems, thought Hannah, and it isn't right to burden him with mine—I should've left him alone. As she drove home, she felt frustrated that there was no one else she could get help from before making a decision.

She didn't hear from him for several days and began to think he wasn't interested in reading her uncle's papers. One morning, in a moment of exasperation, she toyed with the idea of burning the whole lot and was thinking of the most effective way of doing it: in small batches or in a huge bonfire? She preferred the second option, a sort of delayed reprisal for the book burnings of 1933 by the incineration of a hard-core Nazi's books and papers.

I've to get out of Nuremberg, I can't live here for another day, she thought; I've to go someplace where I won't be reminded of my past. Where? She thought of going south, to Switzerland—to Geneva, with its parks and lake, and the Jura Mountains on the horizon. She had been there with her mother on vacation when she was fourteen years old, and the city always had a special place in her mind. The hotel where they had stayed had a large revolving bookcase in its lounge, filled with atlases, guidebooks, and Swiss history books, but she couldn't think of its name or its location. If I could see a map of Geneva, it will all come back to me, she thought. She rose to go to her uncle's sanctum and look among his atlases when she saw a car coming into her driveway, and a few seconds later, Eric was walking toward her.

"I read your notes this morning," he said, excitement and eagerness written all over him. "This is exactly what I am looking for—an account of the rise and fall of Hitler and the Third Reich, giving an explanation of why and how events unfolded, presenting a coherent structure to the anti-Semitic tradition that led inevitably to the Holocaust. It's so different from what I have now—a set of testimonies and memos that may be used as evidence but do not give the whole picture. I came to ask your permission to look at your uncle's papers."

"Your timing is right. I was planning to burn them this afternoon."

"Don't do that, Hannah," he said in a shocked voice. "These papers are too valuable to be burned."

"They show his ugly side, and I don't want that to be his legacy."

"Let me at least look at them and study them. We will talk about burning them after I've finished with them."

His eyes shone like those of a fanatic while he spoke, and Hannah realized he was never going to give up his pursuit of his elusive target, the how and why of the final solution. She wasn't sure whether she should admire him for his persistence or feel sorry toward him for his obsession. Sensing his eagerness, she took him downstairs and followed him as he moved from aisle to aisle, picking papers and scanning them, like a dog following a scent. After a while, she got tired of watching him and started a search among her uncle's maps and guidebooks for material pertaining to Geneva, but she couldn't find anything that was of use to her.

Leaving Eric, she went upstairs and, after telling the house-keeper to make lunch for him, drove her car downtown to see if there were any interesting movies shown by the theaters near the old town. She finally settled for *The Postman Always Rings Twice* and was quickly drawn into the tale of passion and intrigue that took place at the Twin Oaks diner between the sultry blonde—the owner's wife—and the good-looking drifter, the two of them hatching a plot to kill the middle-aged owner.

"Good escape," she said to herself as she stepped into the dreary street after the show. "Even though it lasted only for an hour and a half—it was a reprieve from the horrors of Nuremberg."

Eric was still in the basement, and she went downstairs to see what he was doing.

"Your notes are excellent, Hannah," he said. "I had a good look at Werner's books and papers. I also did some checking on him. The three of them—Alfred Haushofer, Karl Alexander von Müller, and your uncle—had been classified as high-level Nazis and interrogated by the US prior to the Nuremberg trials. Müller lost his professorship and was banned from teaching, and Haushofer committed suicide. Our doctors didn't think your uncle would be able to stand trial because of his bad heart. The prosecutors made a deal with him—he should reveal the names of his current students, ex-students, and fellow employees at Munich University who were active Nazis and be under house arrest in Nuremberg, with the US Army occupying the top floors of his house and keeping an eye on his movements to make sure that he didn't disappear, like a lot of his friends did. Your uncle collaborated."

Hannah was shocked.

"My uncle would never be an informer," she stammered.

Eric was silent for a while, feeling sorry for his friend's discomfiture.

"A lot of his colleagues followed the same path, Hannah," he said gently. "There were a few holdouts, but most of them didn't want to be put on trial. So they either collaborated with us or committed suicide. Your uncle at least left all his papers intact, unlike most of his colleagues. Those documents would be of immense value to posterity in understanding the Third Reich, especially the final solution."

"My uncle says that the SS and the governors of the expanded Reich were the prime movers of the final solution."

"He is very convincing, very credible. His diaries show that throughout his entire life span, there had been an ongoing debate among the German people over the Judenfrage and a clamor for a Germany that was Judenfrei, which gained momentum and led to the Endlösung. There was an inevitability to it. It was the result of the will of a large segment of the German people—not only the Nazi Party members, the SS, the SA and the police but countless middle-class men and women including bureaucrats, railway workers, doctors, nurses, teachers, and college professors. Heydrich initiated the Einsatzgruppen killings, Übelhör started ghettoization, Rolf-Heinz Höppner of the SS proposed that the most humane way of solving the Jewish problem was by closing the ghettos and killing the Jews, Greiser built the first gas chamber and started the mass killings, and Himmler, with help from technocrats, perfected the death factories in Poland so that he could empty out the Jews in Europe and populate the continent with the Nordics. Hitler gave his consent to all these activities and fanned the flames with his rhetoric. That was how it happened. As to why it happened, modern German anti-Semitism started shortly after Napoleon liberated Jews from the ghettos and gave them equal rights. They became a problem and a burden because they competed aggressively in every area of German life. The Third Reich confiscated their assets and put them back in the ghettos. The money thus obtained flowed back to the Germans, including your uncle. It was also used to finance the German rearmament and military expansion and, finally, to kill the Jews."

"What shall I do with my uncle's papers? Do you want to keep them?"

"I want to study them for a while. They can be used as evidence in future trials, though my interest is in their historical value. It will take me about four weeks before I can give an answer to your question."

"I don't want to live in Nuremberg anymore, Eric," she said, near tears. "I'm so unhappy here—in this house, in this city, in this country. I'm thinking of going to Geneva. You can work in my house as long as you want."

"Does this mean you won't be coming back?"

"I don't know, Eric. All I know is that I want to get rid of these papers and also the money I inherited from my uncle. I want to give that money to a good charity. Can you help me in that respect?"

She could see that he was taken aback by her words. "I need some time to digest all this," he said. "Where are you staying in Geneva?"

"I was there with my mother when I was fourteen. I would like to stay in the same hotel, but I don't remember its name."

"My friends tell me the Hotel du Rhone is pretty good," he said. "Call me when you're in a more settled frame of mind, and I'll help you in doing whatever you want."

"It's hard to start all over again at my age," she said. "I'll be forty-seven in a few months. Many women my age are holding grandbabies in their arms and cooing to them, while I..."

She couldn't control her tears, while he watched her, hesitating about whether or not he should put his arms around her. He decided against it and handed her his handkerchief. She wiped her eyes and looked at him gratefully. He took her hand and told her he would ask his secretary to make reservations for her flight to Geneva and book her a room at the hotel.

PART 6

ABSCHIED, EUROPA

Philip was puzzled, and he asked himself what rule of life was there...why people acted in one way rather than in another. They acted according to their emotions, but their emotions might be good or bad; it seemed just a chance whether they led to triumph or disaster. Life seemed an inextricable confusion. Men hurried hither and thither, urged by forces they knew not; and the purpose of it all escaped them.

—Somerset Maugham, *Of Human Bondage*

THIRTY-SIX

GENEVA

In Geneva, the street signs were in French—Hannah had forgotten that they spoke French and was surprised to see every street name prefixed with "Rue" or "Boulevard," and everyone gesturing like the French, even the immigrants who had arrived recently from the east, west, and from the south, as a result of the upheavals caused by the north.

The city looked tidy and prosperous, like the Munich of her girlhood. She breathed the clean, autumnal air, free of death, debris, and the lingering smell of bomb explosions—and it occurred to her that this was the first city she had been in that had not participated in the Second World War.

The hotel that had been booked for her was in the Old Town, what they called the *Vieille Ville*. It was a luxury hotel, and Hannah, who wasn't yet used to wealthy living, felt out of place amid the wealthy bankers' wives in fur coats and jewelry reclining in velvet sofas in the lounge and drinking chocolate.

The staff was nice to her and made her feel very welcome.

"Madame is here for the skiing?" asked a young busboy with curly black hair and the brown liquid eyes of a spaniel, as he took her bags up to her room.

She had forgotten about the mountains—Mont Blanc and Mont Salève—where she had gone skiing with her mother some thirty odd years ago.

"No, I'm here to see friends of mine," she said.

She saw him looking at her speculatively as he moved about the room, drawing the drapes to let her see the views and folding up the bedspread. No, not again, she thought, no more May-December stuff for me.

"It's been nice weather here," he said. "No rain, and not cold at all. In Riga, it snows or rains all the time."

"You're from Riga?"

"Born and raised there. Now I don't know where to go—to America, where I have an uncle, or back to Riga, where the Russians control everything."

I can't escape the ghosts of the past, she thought. I don't know why, but I feel guilty about the plight of this Jewish young man, hunted by the Nazis, dreaming of another world where he can live and breathe. I too am like him, running, running…to where?

"My name is Josef. I work during the week from eight to four. If madame wants something, please ring the front desk, and ask for me."

She gave him a tip and smiled at him—and after he left, opened her suitcase, hung up her clothes in the wardrobe, washed her hands and face, and walked down the stairs into the narrow, winding streets of the old city.

The streets were steep, making it hard for her to walk because she tended to stumble on the smooth, slippery cobblestones. She purchased a guidebook from a small bookstore and walked up Rue Etienne-Dumont toward the Place du Burg-de-Four, a placid city square with fountains and cafés and pricey, touristy stores. On a side street, she saw a tiny outdoor café, and she sat down at a table, flipping the pages of her guidebook while waiting for someone to take her order. A waiter came out after a while, and she asked for café au lait and a brioche. The guidebook mentioned Saint Peter's Cathedral and the Museum of Reformation as nearby attractions, but she didn't want to spend time indoors on such a nice day. Today I'll cruise around in the old city, she thought, and for the next few days, I'll do things at Lake Geneva, unless it rains.

She strolled for a couple of hours along the winding streets, often ending in cul-de-sacs or unexpectedly debouching into boulevards where stout, fur-clad Swiss women came out of fancy stores and waddled toward their chauffeur-driven cars, until she found herself at the entrance of the University of Geneva. She went inside and wandered amid statues of John Calvin and other reformers for a while and, feeling tired, sat on a bench and watched the students go by, singly or in batches. An ice cream vendor passed by her, and she bought a raspberry-peppermint cone, wondering why she was doing something she hadn't done for more than thirty years. The taste of the peppermint-flavored ice cream was cloying, and she got up and walked over to a trashcan—freshly painted and immaculately clean—a few yards away to dump it. Something is happening to me, she thought. I'm not used to peace, at least not this kind of peace, a clockwork order of regulated movement that deadens the brain cells and induces somnolence similar to that caused by the ticking of a metronome.

She walked some more, without aim or direction, and stopped when she saw a park, with rows of trees whose foliage displayed autumnal yellows and reds. She went inside and sat on a bench facing east and watched the setting sun's light falling on the leaves, making them appear incandescent. She was alone, except for two pigeons who waddled back and forth, searching for fallen crumbs or anything else that was edible under the benches.

When it began to grow dark, she went back to the Place du Burg-de-Four and ate a ham-and-cheese ramekin in a small café and drank a couple of glasses of Swiss white wine. I don't know how to live like a rich woman, she thought as she paid the small bill at the cash register and left a tip at the table for the young immigrant waitress who had brought her the food.

Her legs were aching from all the walking when she reached her hotel. As she was going up the staircase to her room, she noticed the spa on the second floor and went inside. A young, dark-eyed, curly-haired woman greeted her in Parisian French and introduced herself as Giselle. Another refugee from the jaws of death, Hannah thought, slipping through the net that the Nazis had spread all over France.

"My knees hurt," she said. "My calf muscles are cramped."

"We will take care of you, madame," the young woman said, cheerfully, reassuringly.

She led her to a locker room and asked her to remove her clothes and put them in a closet. She then took her to the sauna room, electrically heated, unlike the ones in Berlin or Munich, which were heated by stoves.

After fifteen minutes of relaxing warmth, doused in perspiration, Hannah stood under a shower and sprayed herself with jets of hot and cold water. She scrubbed her body with a washcloth and shampooed her hair. After drying herself, she went to the massage room, where Giselle asked her to lie on her stomach on a long table covered by a Turkish towel.

"Madame is Danish?" Giselle asked.

"Yes," said Hannah, thinking that a lie was better than the truth, which might upset the young woman.

"The Danes were good to us," she said. "I'm Jewish, and my father's relatives in Hungary and Austria were killed by the Nazis. But my mother's cousins were in Denmark, and they wrote to us that they were saved from death because the Danes ferried thousands of Jews to Sweden when they learned that the Germans were going to round them up and send them to the death camps."

All I want is a massage, Hannah thought. I don't want to hear any more stories of the Holocaust. Yet she knew it was a vain hope and realized that for the rest of her life, no matter where she went, she would hear these tales over and over.

Soon her muscles relaxed under skillful fingers that knew where to probe and press and where to knead, and she was in a comatose state when the woman slapped her gently on the back and asked her to turn over.

"Madame has a wonderful body," she heard, as though in a dream. "Slim and young looking."

She was surprised when her breasts were touched. One part of her mind resented the familiarity, but the other part was compliant, and in the end, she did not protest. Her nipples were kissed by a hungry mouth, and then the mouth moved south toward her belly, and her body convulsed, even as her restless mind analyzed the situation: a young woman was making love to her, even though she was not in love with her; the young woman was a lesbian, a displaced person, someone who would never regain her existential equilibrium but would grasp like a child anything that appealed to her senses, even though she knew such gratification would be transient.

"Tomorrow is my day off," Giselle said, putting her face close to Hannah's. "I love blondes. Maybe we can go to Lausanne for the day."

Hannah hesitated before answering her. If I had not told her I was from Denmark, I would've gone with her, she thought. I can't keep up the lie if I've to spend a whole day with her.

"I'll be leaving tomorrow, unfortunately," she said, making up a new lie to cover the older lie.

The young woman shrugged in the characteristic French manner, with shoulders raised high and head downcast.

"C'est la vie," she said, her face turning into stony immobility.

Hannah got up, feeling sad and uneasy; she went back to the locker, put on her clothes quickly, and left the spa to go to her own room.

The next day she changed hotels early in the morning.

"Take me to a hotel near the lake," she said to the cabdriver. "A nice one, but not expensive."

"I know a very good place," said the man—another Jewish refugee, from Poland or Russia from his appearance—and took her to the Hotel Normandie, a small hotel run by a French couple. The hotel had only a dozen rooms, and she was lucky to get one with a small terrace facing the lake. After unpacking her suitcase, Hannah went downstairs to the hotel's café for breakfast. She was the only customer there, and the owner's wife brought her a plate of assorted cheeses and a basket of croissants, brioche, and baguette slices, followed by a fluffy omelet with french fries, cooked by her husband. The food was tasty and the man and wife so charming that Hannah made up her mind to stay in that hotel for a couple of weeks.

Outside, it was mild and sunny, and she decided to spend the day at the lake, whose color, continually shifting from cerulean to ultramarine, fascinated her as she walked along the promenade. She sat on a bench for a while, trying to memorize the tone variations so that she could paint them at some future time when her life would be more settled. Her mind wandered back to her Santa Monica paintings, and she wondered if she should go back there and cooperate with the FBI. That's not an option, she said to herself. I cannot be an informer against my friends. Maybe I should go to San Francisco, she thought, and start a new life—try to become friends with Clyfford Still, build a new art school...I don't want to make up my mind right now, she thought, since decisions are always difficult for me, and I'll wait until I leave Geneva.

There was so much activity in the lake, with large and small craft—sailboats, paddleboats, inflatable boats, rowboats, and yachts—coming within a few feet of each other before changing course. The Jet d'Eau, a column of water that spouted to three hundred feet, was visible from where she sat, and she saw people walking on a jetty to get closer to it. Consulting her guidebook, she learned that it had been originally installed as a safety valve for a hydraulic power plant by engineers but quickly became a tourist attraction. Hannah thought it was more of a distraction than an attraction, a man-made intrusion thrusting itself like an uninvited guest to disrupt the vast blue canvas that was the lake's surface.

She rented a bicycle and rode on the streets close to the lake, fascinated by the play of light and the reflection of clouds on the water. Paint the lake, paint the lake, an inner voice whispered. A vague memory of seeing the works of two masters—Turner and Courbet—many years ago at a museum in Berlin shimmered and vanished. Both artists had painted the lake as part of a landscape, and the blues used by them had mesmerized her even then, especially Courbet's.

Soon her legs got tired, and getting off her bicycle, she took rides across the lake in ferry boats, idly watching the shifting views of Mont Blanc and the fall-colored foliage on the hills amid which well-kept chateaus nestled like Easter eggs partially hidden in grass, until it began to grow dark, and Hannah returned to her side of the lake in the lingering twilight. She found another small and cozy café and, after a meal of bread, cheese, and beer, walked back to the Hotel Normandie.

During the next few days, Hannah checked out what her guidebook called "the popular attractions" of Geneva and devised a pattern of activity that suited her mood. On rainy days, she would visit the watch collection at the Patek Philippe Museum, fascinated by the evolution in design and mechanical intricacy of the timepieces over the span of several decades; but after a couple of hours, she would get restless and escape to a nearby *cinéma théâtre* to watch the English, French, or German movies that were being shown, taking in two or three films until her mind was stultified by the images of beautiful men and women defying the laws of reality and living in a world where plots and counterplots were controlled by coincidence, and love overcame all obstacles to provide the happy ending that life seldom provided. On sunny days, in a livelier frame of mind, she would bicycle across the Pont du

Mont Blanc spanning the Rhone and visit the Jardin Anglais, strolling down its various tree-lined paths and admiring the colors of the autumn leaves or sitting on a bench under a shady tree at one of the several well-kept parks in that area, reading a mystery novel or watching people—the lovers, the loners, and the misfits—who passed by her.

It was during one of her visits to the Parc Des Bastions that Hannah realized that she was getting bored with Geneva. She was walking past the Reformation Wall, which showed statues of John Calvin, John Knox, Oliver Cromwell and other leaders of the Reformation—their faces showing expressions of grim righteousness and disapproval of moral lapses—and she thought they were all hypocrites, scaring people with visions of hell to make them into believers of a road map to heaven, the secret of which was only known to them. Living in Geneva seemed like being in a time capsule amid the Patek Philippe watch collections, an abundance of cheese, ice cream, chocolates, and fondues, and the harmless diversions of bicycling and sailing prevalent among the Swiss burghers when they were not paying homage to the eternal verities of Calvinism. I'll become brain dead if I stay here any longer, she thought.

She walked over the bridge to the other side of the lake and got on a bus that took her over to the Avenue de France and from there toward the Palais des Nations, all the while thinking of her next move. Should she go to Corsica or to Cypress? Or to Peru and Chile? By chance, her eyes fell on a big tourism poster that advertised Australia and New Zealand next to a travel agency office, and she got off the bus when it stopped a few yards away from it. New Zealand, with its glaciers and sunken mountains, its volcanic plateaus and vast lakes, and above all the Pacific Ocean surrounding it, had captured her imagination, and she walked over to the agency to find out if she needed a visa to get there. The staff was very helpful and explained to her that no visa was necessary since she was an American citizen. They gave her the details of a tour package and provided her with a guidebook, maps, and travel schedules.

I've found a place to go to, Hannah thought, as she came out of the agency. But a moment later she caught sight of someone from her past, and she stopped in her tracks. Daniel Neumann, her lover on the banks of the Rudawa River, was coming out of the UN building, dressed in a beautiful three-piece suit and carrying a briefcase. She waved toward him, and when their eyes met, she saw surprise and then sheer joy on his face as he hurriedly walked toward her across the street, dodging traffic.

"You!" he said. "I can't believe it. I wrote to you five times to your Nuremberg address, and I never got any response. I thought I would never see you again."

"And you, what are you doing here, dressed like a banker?"

"I'm now living in Palestine, Hannah. Very soon, we Jews will have a state of our own. It will be called Israel. I'm here as an economist to meet with international bankers, and that explains why I'm dressed this way."

"Can we go someplace and have a cup of coffee?" she asked.

"Not now, Hannah. I'm on my way to meet the president of a big American bank. I would love to meet you for dinner tonight."

Hannah accepted his invitation and gave him the address of her hotel.

Daniel was casually dressed in a heather-mixture tweed suit and brown wool knit tie when he showed up at her hotel that evening. Hannah, who was talking to the owner's wife at the front desk, embraced him and introduced him to her as *mon cher ami*. Daniel spoke French well, albeit with a slight accent, and satisfied the woman's curiosity by telling her that he was on a "diplomatic mission at the United Nations."

As they were leaving, the woman wished them a nice evening and gave Hannah a key to the side entrance to the hotel.

"We close the front door at ten, and you have to come in through the side entrance," she said, with a wink and a smile.

They crossed the Mont Blanc Bridge and, walking through the winding streets of the Old Town, reached a tiny restaurant called *La Vieille Russe*. It was charming and romantic inside the place, with a fireplace and red candles on tables. Hannah looked at Daniel and smiled, grateful for taking her to this small, cozy place instead of some posh restaurant with a snotty maître d', stuck-up hostess, and condescending waiters.

"You choose for me, Daniel," she said, as they were looking at the menus.

He ordered white wine, blinis, borscht, and scallops wrapped in bacon for her and a striped bass for himself.

"I rarely eat meat these days," he said.

"Me too," she said.

He told her that his friendship with David Ben Gurion was the primary reason for his moving to Palestine, and the work he was doing in Geneva was critical in establishing the economic foundations of the new state of Israel. She, in turn, told him about her stay in Santa Monica and her return to Nuremberg after her uncle's death.

"My uncle left me a very large sum of money," she said. "He was a Nazi, a close friend of Alfred Rosenberg, Rudolph Hess, and the like. He was an intellectual, a professor at Munich University who trained Hitler when he came out of the army and later coached hundreds, or even thousands, of his students to become good Nazis. He, along with other intellectuals, came up with plans for the decimation of Jews and enslavement of Poles. I don't want his money, which came from the stolen assets of Jews in Germany and Austria. My problem is I don't know who to give it to. Also, I'm at a loss as to what to do with his papers that deal with his Nazi past and his evil Aryan beliefs."

He thought for a few moments, his eyes probingly deeply into hers. "I can sense your unease in being put in this situation, Hannah," he said. "You can give the money to relief agencies that resettle Jewish refugees pouring into Palestine. They are perpetually short of money, and it's only poetic justice to give back to the Jews the money taken from them. And as for the papers, there will be libraries set up in Israel that deal with the Holocaust, and I can arrange for their transfer."

Relief swept over her, as though a great burden had been lifted from her shoulders. His advice is very practical, she thought, and I'm going to follow it.

Daniel studied her face for a few seconds. "You loved your uncle very much, didn't you?" he asked.

"I did," she said. "He was one of the few people who really cared for me. I was his precious little girl, his princess. He was more like a father to me than an uncle. And when I went through his papers, I got sick. He apparently had another personality, quite different from that of the gentle, kind man I knew. He was a party to the evil that was going on around him, in fact he was one of its architects, yet I always thought of him as a scholar, more devoted to Germany's past than to the present."

She paused for a few seconds and wiped her eyes with the napkin.

"I don't want to talk about him anymore," she said. "I'm glad that you're here, offering me these suggestions. I need your help in following them through."

He smiled, reached out for her hand across the table, and held it. They sat in silence for a while, sipping their wine, while the waiters moved chairs and tables to make room for a Russian soprano who sang arias from Tchaikovsky's *Queen of Spades* and *Eugene Onegin*. It was a good performance and was followed by a Russian bass singing from *Boris Godunov*. Hannah mechanically translated his Russian words into English. "My heart is heavy / A primeval fear—dark and foreboding / Grips my being..."

It's exactly the way I feel, she thought.

By the time they came out of the restaurant, it was past midnight, and the streets were lit up by a full moon on a cloudless sky.

"Let's walk home," said Hannah.

They spent a few minutes at the Pont Mont Blanc watching the reflection of the moon on the Rhone River, each involuntarily reaching out for the other's hand.

The front door of the hotel was closed, and Hannah gave Daniel the key to the side door.

"You can stay with me, if you would like to," she said.

"I was waiting for you to ask," he said.

They crept upstairs, not wanting to disturb anyone, undressed, and got into bed.

When Hannah woke up the next morning, she found Daniel reading the brochures on New Zealand that she had placed on the mantelpiece the previous evening. When he had finished, he put the material back and stared at her speculatively.

"Good morning," she said, smiling and waving her hand.

"Are you planning to go to New Zealand, Hannah?" he asked her.

"Just before I met you, I picked up those brochures from a travel agency," she replied. "I have no idea what New Zealand is like, but I don't want to stay in Germany, and I don't want to go back to the United States."

He was in deep thought for several seconds, as though he was struggling with an idea that had just risen in his mind.

"Why don't you come with me to Palestine?" he asked, hesitantly, tentatively. "I mean, as my wife."

Stunned by the proposal, she lay back on the bed as though knocked out by an invisible opponent. She didn't know anything about Palestine, and her brain buzzed with questions and riddles. Did Christ live there? Did the Crusaders fight wars there? Was it the land of olives and archaeological wonders? Was it a desert, or was it near the sea? Would she have to live with Jewish women and men who spoke only Hebrew? Did the Arabs who live there hate the Jews? Above all, was there art and culture, painters whom she could talk to in French, Russian, English, or German?

"Will I fit in there?" she asked, her face flushed and uncomfortably warm. "I mean, I'm a German, niece of a dyed-in-the-wool Nazi. They

486

won't believe me when I tell them all that I had to endure during those thirteen years of hell."

"They won't taunt you or ostracize you, Hannah. They're smart, cultured people. Besides, there are quite a few German women there, the wives of Jewish émigrés who had left the Third Reich in the early thirties, and they lead productive, well-adjusted lives. There are so many things you can do there—teach art, teach European languages, or just paint. The light is very different there, and you can paint the Negev Desert or the Sea of Galilee or the rocky landscapes that you find everywhere. Besides, after the State of Israel is formally created, I would have completed my assignment for Ben Gurion, and I would be free to go with you wherever you wish to go."

His last words removed all doubts from her mind. He really cares for me, she thought.

"Come here, my darling," she invited him impulsively. "Come here and kiss me."

They got married that afternoon at a Swiss Registry Office, with Monsieur and Madame DuMarchier—the owner of the hotel and his wife—as witnesses. The four of them went afterward to Madame's favorite restaurant, the Auberge du Poisson Blanc on the right bank of the River Rhone, where they dined on pâté, champagne and caviar, filleted perch from the lake, and filet mignon.

The next morning they went to an international law firm known to Daniel and drafted documents transferring Werner's assets to a Jewish agency that specialized in resettling Jewish refugees from Europe. Werner's papers were donated to the Holocaust Archives, an agency that had offices in Germany, Austria, and Russia and was planning to move to Israel after the state's formation.

After the deeds were signed, Hannah called her Nuremberg attorney from the conference room of the law firm. Herr Hackmann was disturbed and angry upon hearing what Hannah had to say.

"It isn't right what you're doing," he barked. "Your uncle wouldn't have liked it all. After all, it's his estate. I can understand your giving away the money to charity, but there are people in Germany who need it more than the Jews. Your husband must have persuaded you to do that, but as a German I must ask you to reconsider your decision."

When Hannah told him that there was not going to be any reconsideration, he cursed her for being a traitor and hung up.

Her next call was to Eric Grossman, who picked up at the first ring.

"Hannah, I'm so glad you called," he said. "I must have left four messages for you at the Hotel du Rhone, even though they told me you had left without a forwarding address."

"You sound so excited, Eric."

"I'm excited because I found what I was really looking for—the master plan that Justice Jackson was talking about in the Nuremberg trial—in a stack of publications that you didn't look into. It is the final version of the Generalplan Ost. Your uncle talks about it in his diary, and you have mentioned it in your notes, but you didn't search for the plan itself, which was buried in a stack of reports. My prosecutorial instinct made me do that, and I'm glad I took the trouble. The final version of the plan was officially adopted by the Third Reich, and Himmler was in charge of its implementation. Its circulation list was limited to a few high-level individuals and they were asked to destroy their copies shortly before the war was lost. I don't know how your uncle got a copy, probably from Max Huncke or Kurt Brockelmann—both of whom, by the way, are in hiding. The plan describes in detail, along with a companion paper called the General Settlement Plan, the decimation, enslavement, and resettlement of the entire population of Europe. The planners wanted to restructure Europe as a Teutonic continent by liquidating one hundred percent of the Jews, eighty percent of the Poles, sixty-four percent of the Ukrainians, and so on, adding up to thirty million people. After the Jews, the next in line for liquidation were the Poles. There were so many research institutes involved in the planning process that I lost count after a while. I never thought that professors could plan mass murder and look upon it like a chess game, but that's what happened here. They were the brains behind the genocide, providing the tables, the statistics, and the logistics of population transfers and extinctions. Himmler implemented their plan, with Hitler giving his approval."

Hannah was moved by his eagerness and fervor. The poor boy, she thought. He has found what he's been looking for—the treasure hunt is over.

"So there was a master plan after all?" said Hannah. "I'm glad you found it."

"I double-checked with some of the top SS guys who are now in jail, and they told me they knew of the plan and were orally instructed to use it as the blueprint for the future. I should thank you for leading me to it. When are you returning here, Hannah? I would like you to read the finished chapters of my book."

"Eric, I won't be returning to Nuremberg," she said. "I married Daniel Neumann, the professor we met in Poland some months ago. I'm going with him to Palestine."

"You're joking," he said, in disbelief, but his innate decency quickly asserted itself, and he congratulated her on her choice.

"I wish I had been at your wedding, Hannah," he said. "I would have liked to give you away or be Daniel's best man or something. Please stay in touch with me, because your friendship means so much to me."

The conversation went along these lines for a few minutes before it was terminated with assurances of mutual friendship and promises to keep in touch with each other.

Hannah then got up and went over to Daniel, who was patiently standing at the door.

"What's the next step, my love?" she asked.

"A car is waiting downstairs. We're going to the airport and take the plane to Cairo. And from there, to Palestine."

As they went downstairs and onto the street, Hannah wondered what her new world would be like. Would it be riven with hatred and rancor, like the one she was leaving behind, or would it be a utopia? She remembered the last lines from *Paradise Lost* that Patrick O'Farrell had read to them in his English class:

The World was all before them, where to choose
Their place of rest, and Providence their guide:
They hand in hand with wandering steps and slow,
Through Eden took their solitary way.

I'm looking forward to being in Palestine, my new abode, thought Hannah, as she sat inside the car, where I'll begin my life anew.

But when they reached the airport, she saw that a BOAC flight to Australia was ready to leave in thirty minutes and impulsively changed her mind.

"I'm going to New Zealand, Daniel," she said. "I love you, but I can't face any more Jewish refugees. They will never accept me for what I really am, and I, on the other hand, will carry my burden of being a German with me. All those memories will flood my brain—the Jews huddled in street corners in Berlin waiting to be sent east, those horrid radio broadcasts and newsreels, and my poor brother asking for my help—"

She broke off because she didn't want to cry and make a spectacle of herself. Sensing her state of mind, he put his arm around her.

"Why New Zealand?" he asked, a few seconds later.

"I want to forget I'm a German, which means I want to live in a place where I won't run into escaped Nazis or Jewish refugees. I like the mountains and the lakes and the ocean around New Zealand, and I think I can heal myself there."

He looked at her, his eyes probing hers. He could see the anguish in them, her deep pain. He took her hand and held it for a few seconds. "I understand how you feel," he said, after a pause. "The only

490

thing I can say to you is that I'll join you, as soon as my task is finished. And if you don't want me to, that will be fine too."

"Don't say that, Daniel," said Hannah. "I want you to come to me when you're done."

They hugged each other and kissed lingeringly—and then separated, each hurrying to a different ticket counter. As she was buying the ticket, she mumbled to herself, "My life is a film noir: it doesn't deserve a happy ending. I don't know if I'll ever see him again."

"The plane will take off in fifteen minutes," said the girl at the counter.

Hannah walked toward the gates, suddenly aware of all that she was leaving behind—Daniel, Eric, Germany, and Europe. She hesitated for a moment before taking the final step of going to a new country and starting her life all over again. I'm giving up continuity and cohesion, she thought, but the next moment she mocked herself, thinking that the blueprint of her life, if there was one, never seemed anything other than fragmented and haphazardly put back together.

GLOSSARY OF FOREIGN PHRASES

Altstadt. Old city.

Anschluss. The union of Austria with Germany, achieved through forced annexation by Adolf Hitler in 1938.

Bahnhof. Railway station.

Bund Deutscher Mädel. The League of German Girls, the girls' wing of the Hitler Youth.

Christbaumgeback. Pastry ornaments hung on the Christmas tree and eaten by children.

Christkindl. Baby Jesus.

Churchkhela. A Russian sweet made from nuts strung up and dipped in a paste of grape juice and flour.

der Held des Landes. Hero of the land.

Deutschbund. A right-wing organization.

Deutschland, Erwache. "Germany, wake up."

Die Grundlagen des neunzehnten Jahrhunderts. *The Foundations of the Nineteenth Century,* a book by Houston Stewart Chamberlain that glorifies the role of Aryans in human history.

Diese Schandtaten Eure Schuld. Roughly, "These shameful deeds are your fault."

Dringender Appell für die Einheit. The "Urgent Call for Unity," signed by many scientists and artists to voice their concerns about Hitler and the Nazi Party before the German federal election in July 1932.

Endlösung der Judenfrage. Final solution of the Jewish question.

Festung. A stronghold, a fortress.

Fragebogen. Questionnaire.

Frauenkirche. Church of Our Lady.

Frauenschaft. The women's wing of the Nazi Party.

Freikorps. Right-wing paramilitary organizations in Germany after World War I.

Führerbefehl. Führer's order.

Führerprinzip. Leader Principle, under which the Führer had ultimate authority, was answerable to no one else, and orders were passed down hierarchically and executed with unconditional obedience.

gau. A district.

gauleiter. The head of a gau.

Generalplan Ost. A plan to alter the population genetics of Eastern Europe by resettling Germans in Poland, Ukraine, and other rich and fertile areas and subjugating or exterminating the native population.

Glühwein. German mulled wine.

Hauptfeldwebel. A sergeant.

Hejnał mariacki. A five-note Polish tune.

Hitlerjugend. Hitler Youth.

Hitlergruß. The Nazi salute, performed by extending the right arm with hand held straight.

Hofbräuhaus. An informal restaurant cum brewery.

Horilka. Ukrainian version of vodka.

Judenfrage. The Jewish question.

Konditorei. A café serving pastries, cakes, and coffee.

Kristallnacht. Literally, "Crystal Night"; refers to the broken glass as a result of the Nazi attack on Jewish businesses in 1938.

lebensraum. Living space.

MauNazi. Someone who was forced by circumstances to become a Nazi.

mischlinge. Children of mixed race.

Mutterrecht. Mother's right; that is, matriarchy as a form of social structure.

Nachtkrapp. A mythical German ogre who abducted children and then tore them limb from limb.

nicht schuldig. Not guilty.

Niedersächsische Tageszeitung. Lower Saxony daily newspaper.

Nikolaustag. Saint Nicholas Day, celebrated in Germany on December 6.

Oberschütze. Private first class.

Obersturmbannführer. Equivalent of a lieutenant colonel.

Ordnungspolizei. The uniformed police.

panzerfaust. A World War II antitank weapon, relatively unsophisticated, weighing around fifteen pounds, for use by a soldier.

Rassenhygiene. Racial hygiene.

Rathaus. Official office, like a mayor's.

Ratskeller. A bar or restaurant located in a basement.

Reichsburger. Citizen of the Reich.

schuldig. Guilty.

Silvester. What Germans call New Year's Eve.

Sipo. The security police.

sonderkommandos. Jewish prisoners at German camps who buried or burned the dead Jews.

Standartenführer. In the SS, the equivalent of a colonel.

tagebuch. Day book, a diary.

Tannenbaum. Fir tree.

Übermensch. Superman.

Umschlagplatz. Collection point.

un-Deutsch. Un-German.

vae victis. Woe to the conquered.

Verein Deutscher Studenten. Association of German Students.

Vernichtung. Annihilation, destruction.

Viktualienmarkt. Food market.

völkisch. Pertaining to the folk, ethnic.

Völkischer Beobachter. Roughly, *People's Observer*, a daily newspaper published by the Nazi Party from its inception until its demise.

Volkssturm. Local militia.

Voyna kaput. Russian for "The war is over."

Wehrmacht. The unified armed forces of Germany from 1935 to 1945, comprising the army, navy, and air force.

Weltanschauung. Worldview, a philosophy toward life.

Weltmacht. World power.

Werwolves. German underground resistance movement, sponsored by Nazis, especially Goebbels.

ABOUT THE AUTHOR

J ay Prasad has written plays, screenplays, and novels. He lives in New York City and loves outdoor sports, going to the theater, watching films, and reading.

CPSIA information can be obtained
at www.ICGtesting.com
Printed in the USA
LVHW080000210519
618553LV00031B/1109/P

9 781542 679428